CANDLELIGHT BRIDGE

A NOVEL

CARA LOPEZ LEE

FLOWERSONG PRESS

PRAISE FOR
CANDLELIGHT BRIDGE

"Cara Lopez Lee is a talented and audacious author. And *Candlelight Bridge* is a wonderful book, a book to savor and revisit."
—Luis Alberto Urrea, author of *Good Night, Irene* and *The Hummingbird's Daughter*

"Sweeping yet intimate, *Candlelight Bridge* traces the epic journey of Candelaria and Yankee across China, Mexico and the borderlands of America. With these defiant and determined characters, Cara Lopez Lee powerfully portrays the costs of survival. Deeply moving."
—Vanessa Hua, author of *Forbidden City*

"*Candlelight Bridge* is a novel of tremendous heart. Cara Lopez Lee delivers a well-researched, moving, grand adventure of hope and sacrifice and of what it means to create and define the true meaning of home."
—Kali Fajardo-Anstine, bestselling author of *Woman of Light* and *Sabrina & Corina*

"*Candlelight Bridge* unflinchingly illustrates the sacrifices required to make a home in an unwelcoming place. With vivid prose, Cara Lopez Lee brings to life the story of two immigrants from opposite sides of the world who form an unlikely and surprising partnership. This is a gripping tale of resilience, redemption, and survival. I highly recommend it."
—Tiffany Quay Tyson, author of *The Past Is Never*

"*Candlelight Bridge* poignantly portrays the journeys of Candelaria Rivera and Yankee Wong, fleeing violence and revolutions and heading toward each other in a new world. Impeccably researched, this heartfelt story offers no stereotypes, no cliches—only interconnected stories of life's struggles and resilience."
—Eleanor Parker Sapia, multi-award-winning author of *A Decent Woman, A Novel* and *Tight Knots, Loose Threads, Poetry*

"In *Candlelight Bridge*, Cara Lopez Lee masterfully weaves together two compelling perspectives to explore geographical and emotional borderlands. Elegantly told, dazzling in its verisimilitude, and fascinating in its cultural complexity, this gorgeous novel shows just how far we are willing to go in our quest for home."
—Erika Krouse, author of *Tell Me Everything: The Story of a Private Investigation*

"Happy families are all alike; every unhappy family is unhappy in its own way." While the family at the center of Cara Lopez Lee's beautiful, luminous historical saga *Candlelight Bridge* experiences as much joy as sorrow, Tolstoy's principle still applies: you have never met a family like them. At the same time, this is as American a story as there is: two immigrants from different cultures escaping dangers and demons in their own lands, coming to the US to create better lives in a country that barely tolerates them. Highly recommended!"
—Lisa Brackmann, NYT best-selling author of *Rock Paper Tiger* and *Black Swan Rising*

"If Maxine Hong Kingston and Luis Alberto Urrea were to come together to write a masterpiece, I imagine it would read much like Cara Lopez Lee's brilliant novel, *Candlelight Bridge*. Set amid the Mexican Revolution and the ramifications of the Chinese Exclusion Act in the U.S., her characters form an unlikely union in El Paso, Texas. At once heartrending and deeply human, this is a story you won't forget."
—Susan Blumberg-Kason, author of *Bernardine's Shanghai Saloon* and *Good Chinese Wife*

"From the very first sentence, readers are pulled into an epic, beautifully written, rich, and vivid story that leaves us breathless, hopeful, and excited for the sequel. This untold immigrant story is nothing short of amazing!"
—J.D. Mason, national bestselling author of *The Real Mrs. Price* and *One Day I Saw A Black King*

"This timely gem shines as does Candelaria herself, a born fighter if ever there was one. Set against the turbulent backdrop of the Mexican Revolution, the Riveras—an impoverished family escaping the long reach of war—head for what they hope is a better life in America. The story follows the oldest daughter, Candelaria, in an unexpected and sweeping saga that stretches from Mexico to China and into America. Settling in the wild west town of El Paso on the cusp of Prohibition forces Candelaria and her family to make dangerous and difficult decisions. *Candlelight Bridge* delivers a profoundly moving story of one strong and determined woman. Highly Recommended!"
—Randi Samuelson-Brown, author of *Market Street Madam* and *On the Fringes*

FlowerSong Press/Candlelight Bridge
Printed in the United States of America

Cover design by Carlos Fidel Espinoza and Cara Lopez Lee

Candlelight Bridge is a work of fiction. The names, characters, places, and events in this book are all either products of the author's imagination or used fictitiously. Any resemblance to actual persons, living or dead, is entirely coincidental and not intended by the author.

ISBN 978-1-963245-07-3 Print Edition

For my sister, keeper of our stories

AUTHOR'S NOTE

I cherish the power of language, and the unique communication between writers and readers. With that in mind, I'd like to share a few details about my language choices in this novel, particularly with regard to: writing in English to convey the culture of characters who speak and think in other languages, using words from those other languages to convey a sense of these characters' cultures, and engaging in occasional odd usage or syntax to represent the challenges of cross-cultural communication. I made these choices to honor the different cultures that cross paths in this story and to create a richer multicultural experience for those I hope will read it.

I've written *Candlelight Bridge* in English because it's my mother tongue, the primary language with which I meet the world, and the language in which my paternal grandmother told me the family stories that inspired this novel. However, I've included a few words here and there in Spanish, my second language, which my grandma, father, extended family, and many people I grew up with spoke either to me or in my presence throughout my life. I did this because it reflects the way I hear many of my grandma's stories in my head, and this novel is my homage to those stories. I hope this choice helps convey to readers some of the feeling of my Mexican roots and Mexican American culture, with which I strive to maintain my own connection.

My family has a complicated relationship with our Chinese roots, but I honor my Chinese ancestry with pride. So, I've also added words and phrases from China, though it was tough to choose a dialect for this purpose. It was with trepidation and deliberation that I chose Cantonese. Much of this fictional story takes place in Toisan (a.k.a. Taishan), China or among Overseas Chinese people in America, at a time when most such people would have spoken Toisanese. Toisanese is a separate language from a distinct culture. However, it shares many words and sounds in common with Cantonese, and for many reasons Cantonese became the alternative that best allowed me to serve the overarching story and, hopefully, most of my readers.

When I started this project, it was beyond difficult for me to find professional teachers and translators of Toisanese. It was also a challenge to find Cantonese teachers and translators, but much more doable. Leaning on these experts gave me more certainty of accurate language usage.

What's more, much of this novel's sequel will take place in Guangzhou (a.k.a. Canton), where Cantonese has historically been a primary language, and in Hong Kong, where it continues to be a primary language. Many of my relatives who inspired both this book and its sequel lived in those places and therefore spoke Cantonese. So, since Cantonese is a more historically and geographically correct choice for the sequel, it made sense to me to use Cantonese as the default Chinese language for both books, to maintain consistency.

Another consideration—which might only interest language nerds—is that there is no standard Romanization system to represent Toisanese sounds in an English language text, but there are a few such systems for Cantonese. I chose to represent Cantonese words, and a few Toisanese names, by relying largely on the Jyutping system. In situations where Jyutping strays far enough from English phonetics to create possible confusion, I combined it with American English phonetic representations, so English language readers might more easily read and approximate the pronunciation of the Cantonese words. Since Cantonese and Toisanese share much in common, I hope this helps readers imagine the sounds they might have heard if they'd been able to eavesdrop on the fictional characters in this book.

This novel includes a few sections in which immigrants speak broken English, which I've kept as brief and subtle as I could. I don't wish to convey that immigrants in their situation might have been less than intelligent people with serious things to communicate. I've experienced the challenge of speaking and learning a second and a third language, which has increased my empathy for others who do so. This motivated me to shine a brighter light on that aspect of immigration. I also wanted to explore how two people who each speak a different non-English language as their mother tongue, yet both live in America, might find English their only option to communicate, and how full of pitfalls that might be. Since my family and I have encountered related issues, I'd feel remiss if I didn't address these ideas in a story inspired by family history.

Researching and writing *Candlelight Bridge* has increased my awe of the American experiment we call the Melting Pot and deepened my gratitude to those who reach across cultural divides to attempt understanding. Whatever my language choices in these pages, I hope to illuminate the beautiful possibilities of words to build bridges. In my dreams, these bridges lead to a place where we recognize our shared humanity, and we all cross with ease, sharing the view as we walk along a river of peace.

PART ONE
THE CROSSING

1. Pilgrims

Christmas Eve, 1910 – Chihuahua, Mexico

Her heavy braids bounced up into cold blue sky and dusty feet pounded down into warm red earth as she darted out from between the adobe houses to splash through the trickling acequia. She ran round the pueblo of Mata Flores as if this weren't the last day of her childhood: Christmas Eve, 1910, when she was twelve, back when Papá still called her Candelita, his little light in the dark.

The squish of mud between her toes made her laugh till she was too breathless to keep up with Juliana, her dearest friend in the world, fastest of all the girls, wild, strong, and fleet-footed as a pronghorn. Juliana's long ponytail always impossible to catch.

Candelita's feet were strong but her legs too short to run fast. Her shy brown eyes saw everything, but her tiny wolfberry mouth was made for quiet. Yet she never envied Juliana's bossiness or talent for escape, never minded following or struggling to keep up. She was only sorry she wasn't allowed to tell Juliana that next day she would run someplace her friend couldn't follow. It felt wrong, keeping a secret from Juliana, keeper of all her secrets.

Candelita left muddy footprints as she ran. She always went barefoot, so her soles were always deep red with Chihuahuan desert clay. *Caliche*. Her big brother, Miguel, taught her the word for it. She hated the way Miguel, a restless boy of sharp angles and outraged eyes, always added,

"Didn't you *know*?" as if he was smarter than her—just because she had only finished sixth grade while he'd made it through eighth.

He got away with so much conceit, got away with everything, because he was a boy.

Maybe that's why, when Juliana's brother, Angel, threw the raggedy ball to Miguel, Candelita snatched it in midair before he could catch it. Why she rolled with Miguel in the caliche till it painted them both red, head to toe. Why she passed the ball to Juliana, who would never surrender. Why she and her friend now led their brothers on a breathless chase.

Served those pendejos right for saying, "Girls can't play ball!"

"Ball" was a generous word for the knotted rags the boys had taken to tossing and kicking around the plaza, closest thing they had to a ball in the days leading to the revolución. Their brothers used to throw around an old baseball. An americano had given it to Juliana's father, foreman of the ranch where Candelita's father used to be a cowboy. Nobody had seen that ball since the leva, when the military swept through Chihuahua's villages to steal anything that wasn't hidden: rubber, metal, guns, chickens. Boys. Both armies had descended on Mata Flores to conscript soldiers for their cause.

First came the rebels, without uniforms. The Ramirez twins next door were among the many boys who had volunteered, left their mother lying before her door, grabbing fistfuls of dirt and crying into her palms as if hoping to make enough mud to shape into two new sons.

President Díaz' federales followed, wearing dusty blue uniforms and hats like upside-down buckets. The few boys left in the pueblo had run to hide in the hills, but Guillermo Sanchez was slow. A soldier tackled him, hit Guillermo in the head with a gun and dragged him away crying. His mother never cried, though, just walked into her hut like she didn't hear.

That's when Papá decided home was no longer safe. He and Mamá explained this to Candelita and Miguel a few nights ago, around the glow of the hearth-fire, the only light in their one-room casita. Her younger brother and sister spent that night with cousins. She could barely see her parents' faces in the smoky dimness. Maybe they'd planned it that way.

Like most people in Mata Flores, her parents were mestizos, but Mamá was darker, with limbs, body, and face all straight and firm as tree trunks, while Papá was paler, a man slender, quick, and shy as a coyote. Her father once told her his light skin came from a long line of Spanish caballeros, men with horsemanship in their blood. Maybe he would've spoken of it more if not for the horse that had thrown him and stepped on his back, ending his cowboy story. Mamá often boasted her darkness came from her ancestors: the wandering Suma and bold Apache (great horsemen in their own right), people who worshipped the red earth that guided their steps.

Candelita listened in silent shock as they explained their decision, but Miguel was quick to argue as always. He moaned that if they went to America, he'd never finish school. She envied his rage at every injustice, a feeling she wasn't allowed to express, especially over losing something nobody expected her to have: an education.

"You say a wise man plans for the future, Papá," Miguel said. "Maybe a brave man also *fights* for the future."

"How can a man live with honor in the future, son, if he must kill to get there?"

"Maybe that man's not afraid of killing but dying," Miguel said. "Maybe he's a coward."

"Show your father some respect!" Mamá's voice sliced through theirs like a machete. "He's fighting to keep our family safe."

"From the federales?" Candelita asked.

"Federales, Maderistas, Rurales, Villistas—no importa," Mamá said. "Bullets don't care which side we're on. Death doesn't care which side we're on. This revolution will change nothing for people like us."

She worried if she argued, Mamá would scold her to behave like a lady, but the scarier prospect of leaving home made it hard to keep her mouth shut. "Mamá, didn't the rancheros steal the land from us—I mean, from all the campesinos? Isn't Pancho Villa fighting to get it back?"

"Ay, mija, who do you think is paying for this revolution?" Mamá said. "Just different rancheros. When this is over, you think they'll give us campesinos the land they win? They'll keep it as their payment for freeing us. You'll see."

That explanation only confused her more, but she asked no more questions. Maria Rivera's standards for obedient daughters were high, and a single challenge to authority was all Candelita dared. Once her parents made up their mind about anything, there was no changing it. If only Miguel would learn that lesson, life in the Rivera household might be peaceful.

But, for a boy who was supposed to be so smart, Miguel could act so stupid. "You can't make me go! I won't abandon our people. I'll join the rebels myself."

"If you're eager to die, maldito, keep pushing me," Papá said.

"I thought killing was beneath you," Miguel said.

Papá raised an open hand. He did that sometimes, but never swung it, at any of them. The threat was always enough. Miguel fell silent. The hand lowered. Miguel ran outside.

"Get back here!" Mamá twitched as if to bolt after him.

Papá laid a hand on her arm. "Let him go. Don't worry. He won't go far." He winked at Candelita like he always did when a family upheaval troubled her. Like the time they lost her little brother Lalo at the market or the night baby Graciela had a fever so high she almost died.

She winked back at her father, but the exchange gave her no comfort. She knew Eduardo Rivera was the most honorable father in the pueblo and would never lie. But might he be wrong? Might he believe all would be well when that was impossible?

Right or wrong, the six of them would sneak away in the waiting hours between Christmas Eve and Christmas morning, when soldiers were least likely to be on the move, when the village would be sleeping off the feast of the ninth night of Las Posadas. Till then, they must act like it was any other Christmas, so nobody would suspect they were leaving. They must tell no one, not even her little brother and sister, too young to trust with secrets.

Not that eight-year-old Lalo cared where they lived or whether he ever went to school. With his wild green eyes and talent for making people laugh like crazy, Lalo never seemed to notice the dirt underfoot or to conjure any dreams in his head.

As for three-year-old Graciela, the baby of La Familia Rivera, she would never remember the red desert sunset or the slap of bare feet on hard red caliche. Unlike the rest of them, Graciela wouldn't have to work at forgetting.

Candelita found it easy to keep secrets, except from Juliana, closer to her than her own sister (who could barely speak after all). With Juliana, silence felt like betrayal. Still, Candelita did what she always did: obeyed. Maybe that was the real reason she stole the muddy "ball" and threw it to Juliana: if they were running they couldn't talk, and she wouldn't have to lie.

Juliana's ponytail wagged ahead. The boys closed in. Candelita fell behind in the dry grass that scratched her legs. The pueblo shrank as the shoulders of the Sierra Madre rose ahead and behind, a mother who never let her children out of sight. Crackling gold desert opened before her, making her feel exposed. Nowhere to hide. A stabbing sensation struck like a knife in her side. She halted, doubled over, and cried out, "¡Espérame, Juliana! I can't run anymore!"

Juliana stopped, let the boys take the ball, and trotted back to her. They walked home hand in hand as the sun sank behind the mountains, a dying fire at the end of the world. It seemed too much to hope she might share such friendship with an American girl. Who knew how long it might be before she returned to Mexico? She might never see Juliana again.

Tears rose in her chest. Fearing a flood, she blurted, "I have to get ready for Las Posadas or my mother will kill me!"

"Me too," Juliana said. "Let's race! Whoever gets to the procession first, wins."

Off they ran in opposite directions.

"¡Ay! Hold still, mija!" Mamá said.

Candelita stopped bobbing from foot to foot, though she shivered in the draft that snuck past the door—the hearth's orange coals heated little more than the backs of her legs. Her mother brushed her thunderclouds of hair while Candelita studied her reflection in the splotchy mirror on the wall, trying to decide if she looked more like Mamá or Papá: tree or coyote, Suma or Spaniard, earth or air. Her image flickered, refusing to answer.

Mamá tied a red ribbon round her head, "to keep that wild mane out of your pretty eyes!"

"Don't be vain," Candelita said.

"What're you talking about? They're your eyes, not mine."

"Papá says I have *your* eyes: 'Big, dark, and twinkling like God's universe.'"

Mamá smacked her shoulder. "Don't be vain!" They both laughed. Then Mamá waved her hands. "Hurry and put on your skirt!"

Candelita had left the skirt for last to avoid swinging the hem into the hearth while she got ready. Even in the light of dying embers, the generous cotton tiers glowed bright gold. Her blouse was undyed, which made the skirt stand out more, a swirl of flame. How had Mamá made time for this magic, between cooking, tending her garden, feeding chickens, and packing? Candelita threw her arms around her mother's neck and gave her a noisy kiss.

Her mother hugged back so hard it knocked the breath from her, said, "All right! ¡Basta!" and pushed her away. Mamá confused her—back-and-forth, hot-and-cold—but that was her way of love. She flung open the door to the rest of the Riveras fidgeting in the courtyard.

Candelita swept outside, plucked up her skirt, and twirled till its generous folds fanned open. "Look what Mamá made me, Papá!"

He shielded his eyes. "It's like looking into the sun: too bright for mortal men!"

Mamá clapped. "¡Ándale! Don't hold up the procession!" Then, "Wait-wait-wait, I forgot!" She ran inside and returned with an armful of candles. Each child took a votive, poked through a cardboard circle cut from old oatmeal boxes. Mamá lit them with a taper, one by one.

Miguel thrust his candle at her first, impatient to go. He was dressed as Joseph and would lead the mule carrying sixteen-year-old Anna, this year's Blessed Virgin. Everybody knew Anna had hoped for Guillermo, who she was sweet on. If only the leva hadn't taken him. It was hard to imagine any girl being sweet on Miguel, much less a girl two years older. There were few boys left in the pueblo older than him, and none would join the procession, for fear the military might use the event to conscript them. Mamá had begged to keep Miguel home, until Papá said, "It's the boy's last night. Let him go. It'll look like we have nothing to hide."

Miguel rushed off while Candelita waited for her two younger siblings, who she was expected to keep an eye on. Lalo slipped past her, grinning, and ran to catch up to his brother. He tripped on the hem of his shepherd costume, popped up with lit candle held high, and ran on.

"Careful, mijo!" Mamá shouted. "Don't set anything on fire!"

Graciela, an angel with crooked wings and falling halo, stared at her candle's flame so intently that Candelita grabbed her free hand to prevent her blindly walking into someone.

Papá laughed and scooped her up. "Go on, Candelita. We'll take this little devil."

She skipped to the gate, where a reluctance to leave overcame her. She turned, just in time to catch Papá kissing Mamá by the wavering light of Graciela's votive, the trio framed by the crooked red door—Graciela called it the mouth of their casita. *Home.* Candelita's heart gave a hiccup of apprehension. So she waved. That was a mistake.

"Want to go with my sister!" Graciela shouted and struggled out of Papá's arms.

She tottered to Candelita, who sighed and tugged her hand. "¡Venga! Let's run!"

Graciela tried, but her wobbly legs couldn't keep up.

Candelita shrugged, gave up, and walked her the rest of the way.

The procession was small this year: only two dozen youngsters, since a dozen boys were hiding or gone. She deposited Graciela up front with the angels and shepherds, then ran to the rear to find Juliana among the jóvenes without costumes—too old to play angels and shepherds, too young to play Mary and Joseph. To her surprise, Juliana wore a gold skirt just like hers.

"I win!" Juliana announced her triumph at arriving first.

"Yes, yes, of course," she said. "But did you know we'd be twins?"

Juliana nodded. "My mother can't keep a secret like I can. Our mothers went together to the mercado, and the seller offered your mother a special price if she bought more fabric, so they split it. But look, your ruffle's ruby and mine's turquoise—" She stopped. "¡Ay, no! Are you crying? Did you want to be more different?"

"No! I love it. Like looking in a mirror, only better. I'm just happy."

Juliana looked skeptical.

Candelita craned her neck for a look at this year's virgin atop the burro. She'd hoped one day to play La Virgen Maria, to wear a flowing white dress and crown of flowers. Even Juliana, who despised girlish nonsense, wanted her to win the part.

"You're perfect for it since you're already a saint."

"Not according to my mother," Candelita said.

"She doesn't know you like I do."

That might be true. Though Mamá loved her, she showed almost no softness, like a tortoise in a shell. How well did they actually know each other?

Padre Eladio stepped up into the plaza's gazebo and held up his hands to quiet the chatter. He warned everyone to watch their candles and not walk too close together.

Juliana remarked loudly, "We don't want anyone's hair catching fire again!"

Everyone laughed. Mean Felicia rolled her eyes. Candelita elbowed Juliana.

Last year, Juliana's brother, Angel, had stood behind Candelita and burned her hair. Convinced he'd done it on purpose, she'd punched him in the belly. The only reason Mamá didn't punish her unladylike behavior was because she had to cut the singed mane, while Juliana held her hand and they all wept. Angel's apology made it hard to stay mad. His voice cracked with such regret she believed his excuse: "I only wanted a closer look because your hair's so pretty. It still is, even short." He'd been sweet to her since: helped her carry firewood, bought her a notebook "to write your songs," even asked her and Juliana to play ball, to Miguel's dismay.

Then, last Sunday, as the pueblo's boys and girls circled the plaza for the evening paseo, he stepped before her, bowed, and presented her with a bouquet of purple salvia. She accepted the flowers, took his arm, and turned with him to stroll clockwise around the gazebo. This left Juliana to walk counterclockwise alone, till Mean Felicia ran to catch up with her. Candelita tried not to be jealous. Juliana would need a new friend when she was gone. Still, she hated to be forgotten. Juliana gave her a comforting smile as they passed. She wasn't replaced yet.

She would always treasure that moment with her hand tucked in the warm crook of Angel's elbow, despite how nervous she felt, especially with her parents watching. It caused a disagreement between them later that night, when they thought the children asleep.

"She's too young to walk with boys," her father grumbled.

"Don't you see, viejo? She won't be here to walk with Angel when she's old enough."

Candelita held her breath, waiting for Papá to say they'd be back by then. But he didn't.

It felt as if she'd been holding her breath ever since.

Now Juliana looked over her shoulder and elbowed Candelita, prompting her to look too. Angel pushed through to a spot right behind her, like last year. Juliana wagged a finger at him, "Cuídado con tu candelita," a play on the fact that this was both Candelita's name and another word for the votives they carried. Angel smiled at Candelita. Warmth spread through her at the sight of his straight white teeth, but she looked away.

The children began to sing, the procession surged forward, and Candelita clasped Juliana's hand so they wouldn't get separated. This was the ninth night of their pilgrimage, snaking between houses, singing at one doorway after another:

In the name of heaven, I request lodging from you
Because my beloved wife cannot walk anymore.

"How can the Blessed Virgin get tired if the burro does all the walking?" Juliana said.

"Maybe only her rear-end gets tired," Candelita said.

Juliana rolled her eyes. "You're too nice, always making excuses for everyone."

At each house, adult singers turned Mary and Joseph away:

This is not an inn. Keep moving.
I cannot open up for you, lest you turn out to be a thief.

Candelita and Juliana sang well, even better in unison. It was her friend's only talent that struck her as feminine, mouth a perfect circle of sound. Juliana caught her staring, opened wide, and mimicked a manly baritone. Candelita topped her volume. Juliana sang louder.

Angel leaned forward. "Keep that up and nobody'll let us in."

Juliana said, "If sleeping outside was good enough for Jesus, it's good enough for me."

A snort escaped Candelita. "Juliana, you're so bad."

Every year was the same: Juliana misbehaved, the youngest kids sang off-key, and the pilgrims were turned away at every door but one. That night's party was at Juliana and Angel's, where a piñata swung from the laurel tree, and the adult "innkeepers" sang from the courtyard:

Come in travelers!
I didn't recognize you.

"A likely story," Candelita muttered.

Juliana gaped in reply—her highest compliment.

Juliana's house had two bedrooms in addition to the main room, making it the biggest in Mata Flores. Even so, it grew crowded as people wandered in to fill up on food and ponche and to warm up. Hard to say which was worse, the body heat steaming the house or the dry chill outside. At least it gave the adults something new to complain about besides rumors of war—a topic at once dull and terrifying.

Youngsters lined up in front of Juliana's mother to receive their cochinitos. Candelita snuck one of the pig-shaped cookies into the hidden pocket her mother had sewn into her skirt, hoping to carry a piece of Christmas with her on her real-life pilgrimage to America.

She and Juliana exchanged looks when they saw how few food tables were set up. Still, there were plenty of tamales and beans, and the piñata was full of candies for the little ones. Meals had shrunk at the Rivera house too. Mostly it affected her parents, who she knew often pretended to be full so Lalo and Graciela could eat without worry. Her mouth had watered all the day before, helping the women smear masa into each corn husk, plop the pork-and-red-chile filling in the center, then roll up each bundle and tie it with a corn husk bow, like a gift.

It wouldn't be Christmas without tamales.

Mamá assured her El Paso Mexicans ate tamales too, but how did she *know* if she'd never been? Miguel had learned at school that Americans ate modern foods like peanut-butter-and-jelly and pizza, which sounded interesting, but also hot dogs, which were made of discarded animal parts and sounded disgusting.

"Don't you know what chorizo is made of, tonta?" he'd said.

"Don't call me tonta, baboso!" she'd replied.

Miguel was impossible.

Now, to her dismay, he was leading Angel toward her. Much as she liked him, tonight she wanted Juliana to herself. She grabbed her tamale plate with one hand, Juliana's hand with the other, and pulled her through the crowded courtyard and out the gate.

Angel caught up to them on the path. "Where are you sneaking off to?"

"A secret place for girls only."

"Don't be mean, Candelita," he accused mildly. "Sit with your brother and me."

Miguel hung back, scowling to make it clear this wasn't his idea.

Her plans for the night didn't include boys, but Angel's hurt look made her feel guilty. With a nervous glance at the others, she darted forward to peck his cheek. He jerked in surprise, and she caught his mouth by mistake. Flustered, she hurried off, but not before seeing him touch his lips in wonder. She prayed nobody would tell. Mamá would spank her bare nalgas if she knew. The sensation the kiss sent through her was worth it. Tiny stars sparked under her skin.

Juliana followed her to the empty courtyard of Candelita's house. Careful not to tip their plates, they slid down to sit against the wall in the shadows.

Juliana gave her a teasing push. "What's gotten into you? I don't know whether you broke my brother's heart or made him believe in Christmas miracles."

She pushed back. "Forget him. There'll be plenty of time for men when we grow up. Pues, you and I always exchange gifts on Christmas Eve. Or did you forget?"

"No, I didn't forget, greedy." Juliana held up a bolsita, dangling from her wrist by a drawstring. The little purse bulged roundly with whatever was inside.

"First let's eat our tamales while they're hot."

Their stomachs gurgled agreement. They made short work of it, though she swallowed around a lump in her throat. Juliana, who rarely shut up even with her mouth full, ate in silence.

The moment they finished, Juliana said, "Before we do gifts…"—she took Candelita's hands and peered into her eyes—"tell me the truth: are you dying?"

Candelita drew in her chin, taken aback. "What makes you ask?"

"You keep staring at me. Are you running away with the rebels to become a soldadera?"

"Are you crazy? Can you imagine me shooting a gun?"

"No. But the way you punched Angel last year, who knows?"

They both snorted laughter.

That was the moment she felt sure she must tell her secret. Only a bad friend would leave without saying goodbye. Even if she returned, the lie would hang between them. But Mamá had warned her anyone she told might be in danger. And if Juliana let it slip, it could endanger Papá, Miguel, her whole family. Both sides of the coming war would consider them traitors.

So she said, "I'm only sad it's our last Navidad as children. Next year we'll be thirteen."

"We'll still have three years before we're old enough to marry. Then you'll marry Angel and we'll be sisters forever."

"We're already sisters," she said.

Juliana held up her fat little purse and lowered it into Candelita's cupped palms. Its hard weight told her what was inside. The boys had moaned over its loss for weeks. She tugged open the cloth to reveal the American baseball, yellowed with age, smudged red with dirt.

She ran a thumb over its red stitches, mystified. "You hid it all this time?"

"I knew if we played with it, the boys would take it back."

"So why give it to me now?"

"You know why." Juliana placed her hand over the ball, tucking it within their mutual grasp. "They say baseball is America's pastime."

She knew? How? Did Miguel tell Angel? She didn't ask any of her many questions. Even if Juliana knew, the less said the better. She only replied, "Maybe someday we'll both play," and reverently returned the ball to the purse. Then she jumped to her feet and said, "Your turn!"

She scurried into the house and emerged with her vihuela, Papá's tiny old mariachi guitar, which he'd given her because she played better than him. She stopped short at the sight of Juliana's stunned face, looked down at the compact gleaming wood curves with the mother-of-pearl sunburst rosette, and shook her head. "No, greedy, I'm not giving you my vihuela."

Juliana's face relaxed. "That's a relief. I'd have to learn to play. What then?"

"I wrote you a song." She waited for a joke.

Instead, Juliana clasped her knees and leaned forward, eyes intent.

Candelita sat cross-legged in the dirt, skirt splayed like a flower, guitar in her lap. She plucked a soft melody, the acequia in spring, its pulse and splash. Then she sang:

El corazón está hecho de risa. Así es como aumenta.
El agua está hecha de deseo. Se queda en casa mientras se va.

The heart is made of laughter. This is the way it grows.
The water is made of longing. It stays home even as it goes.

The last note drifted into the night. Juliana pulled Candelita's hand to her heart. "I'll never tell a soul, but I know you're going. Don't worry, you know the way home."

In years to come, she would forget Juliana's beloved face, but the music would remain: of bare feet slapping the earth, water laughing in the desert, secrets hidden in the hearts of girls. It was the sound of Mata Flores, the song of her first friend, the sorrow of an unspoken goodbye.

2. Gold Mountain Men

1910 – Toisan County and Hong Kong, China

Wong Yan Chi was supposed to look out for bandits, standing midnight duty in the fifth-floor gallery of the diu lau, Bok Nan's village watchtower. Instead, he looked down, lowered the wet bamboo ladder through the trapdoor, and knelt on the cold, damp stone floor—glad he wore the gift his brother sent from America for his twentieth birthday, thick blue denim pants invented by a man named Levi. He peered into the dark abyss, waiting for his bride-to-be to climb up and meet him.

Yan Chi usually enjoyed guard duty, preferring his own company to that of others. Most people talked too much. Typically, his only companion on these long nights was the tower's small stone Kei Lun, standing watch with him from atop the tile roof overhead. Part dragon, part deer, part horse, and part ox, the legendary Kei Lun served as a protector of good men and scourge to evil men. His fiancée, Mei Yin, always said Yan Chi reminded her of Kei Lun.

"Because I'm one of a kind?" he always asked.

"Because you're a strange monster made of mismatched parts with an oversized head. Except your tail is short." She pointed at his braided queue—his hair never quite as long as most men's—and laughed. At sixteen, she laughed loud as a man, making it difficult to meet in secret.

He didn't care. Yan Chi's voice boomed like a cannon, and his laugh startled people. It amused him to be betrothed to the only girl whose volume came close. She'd always played rougher than his girl cousins, most now living in the House of Waiting Brides. In that cottage at the center of Bok Nan, the village's marriageable girls fourteen and older waited for a match, chaperoned by aunties with no sense of humor. Mei Yin lived in such a house in nearby Git Ngon. Waiting brides covered their giggles with a shy hand. But in the secret moments he and Mei Yin stole by night, under the banyan tree at the village crossroads, her thunderous laugh lit a flame in his heart, filling it like a sky lantern, a rice paper balloon floating toward heaven.

He marveled at his good fortune of being matched with her, even as he shook his head at the clumsy sound of her unbound feet clomping up the tower stairs. Lucky his parents couldn't afford to pay the matchmaker enough to search beyond the eleven villages of Gong Hau district, lucky the old woman chose his bride from nearby Git Ngon Village, lucky she declared the stars in favor of his best friend's sister—the only two companions he'd trusted since childhood.

Mei Yin had refused to meet him in the tower before. But they would marry in two days, and he'd convinced her this was no time at all when they were to be joined for eternity.

Her pale hand waved through the trapdoor, and she gasped when he grabbed it to haul her up. She stumbled into him, tumbled him backwards, and landed on top. They shook with silent giggles, giddy with the thrill of doing what the elders forbid. Standing watch in the towers was a job for men, and no respectable girl in all Toisan would spend time alone with a man. But Yan Chi only pretended to care about rules.

Mei Yin's suppressed giggles turned to snorts till her hand flew to her mouth, stifling the sound. She rose to her feet with unexpected grace, like water poured upwards. He watched from the floor as she leaned delicate elbows on the parapet, rested her soft cheek on one tiny fist, and tilted her face to the milky night sky. He stared at her in a way he never could when their many relatives hovered near, both the Wong and Ma clans preventing them from drawing close to each other. The Silver River of stars spilled through a break in the clouds to glimmer in her black eyes, as if the starlight came from her.

The clouds lowered their veil again, and she murmured in disappointment, "You said we'd look at constellations, that you'd show me the Cowherd and Weaver Girl."

He jumped up and slouched next to her, close enough to feel the warmth of her arms, but tilted his face to the sky to evade her gaze. "I'm sorry. Last night was clear. I didn't expect clouds to roll in so fast."

"What shall we do instead?" She turned to him, and he leaned in, anticipating her plump, watery mouth against his. But she turned her head aside. "Let's not interfere with what heaven has planned. We'll be married soon enough. That's when our lips are destined to meet."

"You know I don't believe in superstitious nonsense," he said.

"Maybe I do believe. And what if someone sees us? At the House of Waiting Brides, all the girls spy on each other."

"At the House of Waiting Grooms, no one cares. Though I see why you'd worry, since all the unmarried girls of Gong Hau are in love with me, so they might get jealous and turn on you."

"Pht!" She pressed her fingertips into his shoulder and pushed him away. "I'm only worried about my father. Tonight I return to his house one last time, and I must be able to look him in the eye."

Despite her words, the hint of breasts under her tunic rose and fell in quick bursts that told him, if he tried to steal the kiss, she'd let him. But it was true: if anyone found out, it could harm her reputation, now joined to his. A groan escaped him as he relented. He would wait. By tradition, he wasn't even permitted to see her face before the wedding, but in a farming district like Gong Hau it wasn't always possible to hide bride from groom, and for that he was grateful.

A deep rasping cough cut through the night.

Mei Yin gasped.

He pulled her to the floor, both of them crouching behind the gallery wall.

"Bandits?" she hissed. He really must teach her how to whisper.

He pressed a finger to her lips but shook his head. No bandit had ever struck his village. Still, he instinctively reached for his rifle. It wasn't leaning against the wall next to him as he'd thought. Dismayed, he looked around till he spied its silhouette in the far corner. How could he be so careless? If that was a coughing bandit, whatever happened next would be Yan Chi's fault.

He turned, still squatting, and poked his head over the wall. Saw a tiny glowing red spot. Gave an explosive exhale. "It's just Uncle Fu Ying stepping out to smoke his early morning cigarette. He does that when Auntie's snoring wakes him."

She didn't laugh. "I should go before anyone else wakes."

He nodded. She was right. The cloudy night had fooled him. Dawn was coming.

He led her back to the ladder and helped her down. His hand lingered at the racing pulse of her wrist, the sweat of her tiny palm, the tremble of her slender fingers.

"Soon we'll watch stars together any night we wish," he whispered.

"Only if you promise better weather." A trick of light escaped the clouds to give him a last glimpse of her eyes, sparkling with hushed laughter as she descended into the dark.

He watched from the gallery as she slipped past the fishpond to stop at the low stone altar beyond. She lit a bundle of joss sticks, stuck them in the incense burner, and lowered her head in prayer to Tou Dei Gung. To all appearances, a girl so devoted to her future in-laws that she'd woken before dawn to ask *Grandpa Earth* to give them protection, prosperity, and plentiful rice.

Yan Chi knew quiet grace didn't come naturally to Mei Yin, that she tamed her wild nature into the gentle yet unbreakable creature their world required. She'd make a good wife. But a wife who also loved him: that was a gift brighter than the Silver River of stars.

The night after Mei Yin's visit, Yan Chi paced the tower gallery alone as fog buried Bok Nan in a thick white shroud. How would he ever see bandits coming in all this mist?

Before his grandfather's generation, the villages hadn't needed watchtowers. In those days, Bok Nan depended on its layout for protection: forty soot-colored brick homes huddled between a manmade fishpond, a cluster of hills, a tree-grove, and a chessboard of rice paddies. There was once nothing to steal, not from poor families who had more mouths than their rice could feed. Then many of Toisan County's young men left for America, the land they called Gold Mountain, to chase the Gold Rush, to build railroads, to sell and serve and save. They sent home fortunes or rumors of fortunes, and Gold Mountain Dollars attracted outlaws. Many claimed to be revolutionaries against the Ching Empire—some even were—but most were common tou fei: bandits, marauders, kidnappers.

From his perch, it was usually possible to see strangers approach long before they arrived, giving villagers time to gather valuables and hide inside the tower. But now the Ching Ming holiday approached, sent its annual mist crawling down hillsides, creeping through rice paddies, concealing both the known and unknown. "It always rains at Ching Ming": that's what elders said about the tomb-sweeping festival, with wise nods, as if spring drizzle were fate.

Yan Chi put no faith in destiny. At any moment, unexpected events could engulf a man in fog, make him lose all sense of direction, leave him with nothing but cleverness or luck to determine where he'd land. Such was the dark direction of his thoughts when, well past midnight, a soundless rumble drummed his chest. Something was coming.

He lifted his old Sharps rifle to the groove in his shoulder, pressed cheek to stock, and squinted through the sight. Saw nothing. He lowered the rifle to chest-level and paced some more, counting footsteps till he lost track. The rifle grew heavy, but its weight comforted him. It was a work of art, the one happy thing that came of his baby brother's birth.

That bad-luck boy had arrived the hungry year of the Jiawu war, the year Yan Chi turned four. Like most in Toisan County, the Wongs had counted on rice from overseas to supplement their meagre crop, until the Japanese began sinking shipments bound for China. Yan Chi was too young then to understand war, only knew it made his belly burn and his baby brother cry, a grating sound more like a baby goat than a human. Yet that puny bleat had terrible power: it made Mama choose the baby over him.

When Yan Chi frowned into his empty bowl and begged, "More rice!" she hissed, "Stop whining!" Yet she never scolded that toothless hole of want for whining day and night. She fed *him* milk from her breast. Yan Chi's gut gurgled at the sight, and he reached for her other breast. Her slap stunned him, handprint hot and stinging on his cheek. "Do you want to lose face, stealing milk from your brother's mouth? You're a big boy and must learn to sacrifice."

Her third son died anyway. Little Yan Chi didn't understand the many gestures of grief: all those downturned mouths, watery eyes, hands patting his mother's arm. The neighbors stared at him and whispered loudly as if they wanted him to know how shocked they were at his satisfied smile. How could he help his joy at becoming Mama's baby boy again? He pressed his face to her warm breast, plump nipple pulsing against his eye through her tunic, his reward for being strong enough not to die.

Of course, his parents would never praise him the way they did their first son, his big brother, his hero: Tsi Chaum. At the start of the Jiawu War, Tsi Chaum had sailed to Gold Mountain, having sold his first year's wages in advance for a chance to make his fortune and save his family. He and two partners had opened a Chinese grocery in San Francisco. He still sent most of his profits home, to help Mama buy food and Baba save for a bigger house.

Tsi Chaum's good fortune came too late for their dead brother but not too late for Yan Chi. His elder brother sometimes sent him gifts—coins, windup toys, seashells—but the greatest was the one he delivered in person for Yan Chi's thirteenth birthday. The 1874 Sharps rifle had .50 caliber black-powder cartridges, a polished walnut stock, and swirling waves engraved in its shiny blue steel—except for the 30-inch barrel, naked of decoration. Tsi Chaum stood in the tower gallery and bestowed the American rifle on him like some ancestral offering. Yan Chi slid admiring fingers down its gleaming length while his brother touted its wonders:

"It can hit a moving target at a thousand feet. It's the kind cowboys once used to kill bison."

"What's a bison?"

Tsi Chaum laughed. "Don't they teach you anything in school? Americans call them buffalo, but they're bigger than water buffalo."

Yan Chi felt ashamed when his elder brother laughed at his questions yet was too curious to stop asking them. "Why did they kill buffalo?"

"They're not farm animals. They're wild—or used to be. Hunters killed them for fur. They look like this." He pointed out the rifle's receiver, where tiny gold-inlay animals with hunchbacks charged amid curling blue-steel waves. "In real life, they're enormous. Millions once ran free across America."

Yan Chi rubbed a wondering thumb over the golden beasts, whose heads and horns reminded him of the mystical Kei Lun. He'd never seen a million of anything. "Have you seen one?"

More laughter. "No. I live in San Francisco, a big city. Anyway, most of them are gone."

From then on, bison herds had stampeded though his mind, till his head felt heavy with them. Tsi Chaum had saved their parents, but maybe Yan Chi could still do something big.

Sometimes he wished bandits would just come already so he could shoot his rifle at a living target instead of old tree stumps. Not that he'd admit such a thing. What kind of man wished for violence over peace? He told himself he'd be proud to defend his home, that's all. He was eager to be a hero, not to kill or die. He was bored, not stupid.

So it was that, on the last dawn before his wedding, he stood in the tower clutching his rifle with dread and desire as sunrise pierced the fog to reveal what was coming: not a bandit, but his only friend, his bride's only brother, Bing Sam, limping down the gossip path between houses, a gap so narrow no neighbor's secret could survive it. Yan Chi could smell the bad news rising toward him, like the stench of low tide riding a wind from the sea.

His friend, Bing Sam, had sailed home from America to attend Yan Chi's wedding. Bing Sam's father—who Yan Chi thought of as Old Mr. Ma, though he was only forty—came with him, to throw a lavish betrothal celebration in the Ma Family village of Git Ngon. Not only to mark the union of Ma and Wong clans, but also to show off the Ma family's American wealth.

People from all eleven Gong Hau villages attended, eager to spy Old Mr. Ma's new Western-style mansion: a three-story showpiece of Greek columns, English pediments, and Italian glass, where bas-relief fish swam across stone walls and hand-painted birds flew across Chinese tiles. Feasts thrown by Gold Mountain Men were legend: roast suckling pigs, geese, dim sum, egg tarts, bottomless rice. Elders circled round to sing off-key muk yu songs of forgotten times, interrupted by shouts of "Gon bui!" as men in their prime, and even a few bold wives, gulped shots of baak zau. Many partygoers lingered to play cards, tell stories, and laugh till sunup, when they slumped where they sat and gave in to snoring slumber.

After that, the Wong and Ma in-laws spent days parading between their villages with gifts: boxes and baskets of porcelain, tea, spices, oranges, jewelry, and silk bedding hand-embroidered by Mei Yin. Both families competed to outdo each other with American luxuries: rare plants, wood furnishings, and gold coins. The winner was clear: everyone for miles talked about Old Mr. Ma bringing "half of Gold Mountain" home with him.

Now all that gossip was returning to exact a price, in the shape of his stumbling friend. Bing Sam neared the tower, arm pressed to stomach, tunic splashed red, face a lopsided mask. Yan Chi knew he should rush down to help, but he wanted nothing to do with the pain lurching toward him. He ducked behind the parapet, willing Bing Sam to take his bad news elsewhere. His desire to be a hero vanished. He still wished to marry Bing Sam's sister, but not enough to die for the privilege.

"Yan Chi!" Bing Sam's voice floated up to him, low, gurgling, liquid. "Yan Chi!" he repeated, startling a flock of birds into blank sky, wings loud in the quiet. "Wong Yan Chi!" he shouted.

Bing Sam was usually one who gave up easily, but this time he refused to relent. Yan Chi climbed down the ladder, recalling Mei Yin's soft hand as he'd pulled her up the night before. He took his time descending the dark stairs to step into pale daybreak, where Mei Yin's snorting laughter echoed in the sobs of her brother doubled over before him.

Bing Sam looked up, revealing an inflamed eye ringed in black, purple, and green. Blood dripped from his swollen nose. Yan Chi closed his eyes against those revolting signs of weakness and waited to hear what he'd already guessed: during the night, outlaws had snuck into Git Ngon to kidnap the Gold Mountain men whose riches were the talk of the county.

At first, Bing Sam's mouth worked without sound. Then he released his story between clenched teeth, one word at a time, as if afraid to set them loose all at once. His auntie had been visiting the outhouse, so she wasn't taken, but the kidnappers dragged the rest of them— Bing Sam, his father, and sister—to a shallow cave in the hills.

Impatient to get the worst over with, Yan Chi interrupted, "Did they hurt anyone?" He avoided naming the thing they both knew most bandits did to women.

Bing Sam shook his head. "Both my sister and father were…untouched when I left."

"How did *you* escape?" He wanted to shout: How could you desert the one thing I love?!

"I didn't escape," Bing Sam said. "They demanded a ransom of five thousand Gold Mountain dollars and sent me to retrieve it. I have five days, or they'll kill Baba and Mei Yin."

Yan Chi clenched his fists, resisting the urge to strangle him. "Then why did you waste time coming here? Five days is barely enough time to get to Hong Kong and back."

"That's what I came to tell you: our account at the wui gun is empty. Rumors always have more gold than men do. We saved many American dollars, it's true, but most of it went to my father's new house…and Mei Yin's dowry."

Yan Chi understood his friend was reminding him of the debt he owed his future in-laws. He didn't resent this. It was a fact of life: to marry was to accept obligations. "Of course, my father will give what he can, but he too spent his savings on the wedding." He pictured the white pearl skin and black silk hair of Mei Yin, lone woman in a cave full of men, and regretted that the price of her life was already spent on a wedding that might never happen.

He tried to think what his elder brother would say. He clenched his jaw. "Here's what you'll do: you'll convince the wui gun to *lend* you the ransom. You're a member after all, and isn't this what the wui gun is for, community support of our men overseas?"

Bing Sam nodded rapidly. "Of course, of course. But won't you come with me? It's a lot of money, and I fear they'll say no. People never say no to you."

Yan Chi shook his head in humble denial, though the compliment secretly pleased him. "I don't know about that. But if you think it'll help, I'll go with you."

Bing Sam's shoulders sagged with relief.

Yan Chi grabbed his arm and dragged him toward the pond.

Bing Sam flinched. "Aiya! That hurts. What're you doing?"

"You can't go to Hong Kong and ask for money looking like a beggar. We must clean you up."

Bing Sam relented, let Yan Chi push him to his knees at the water's edge, and gazed up with unwavering trust. Here was Yan Chi's chance to be a hero. He might rescue Mei Yin yet.

He shoved his future brother-in-law's ruined face underwater, and an unsettling thrill shot through him at this momentary power. Not that Yan Chi intended to drown his friend. But he was tempted to hold him under just long enough to sample the terror Mei Yin must have felt when her only brother left her behind.

3. The Rattle

Christmas Day, 1910 – Chihuahua, Mexico

One soldier dragged Candelita from the house by her long braid, then another kicked her in the ribs as she lay in the dirt. She tried to scream but instead opened her eyes to the splotchy dark of early morning, gasping for air, blood pumping fear into her ears. She felt another kick and knew what had woken her: her little sister whining and pedaling her feet, caught in her own nightmare. If Graciela woke, she was sure to declare, "Want a song!" expecting Candelita to soothe her with the lullaby about barefoot angels. The thought irritated her. Her mouth felt empty of songs.

Irritation gave way to guilt. Poor baby had no idea that today they'd leave home forever. She clasped one churning foot and rocked it. "Sh-sh-sh. It's just a bad dream, mija."

Bad dreams or not, real soldiers would return soon enough. Even once her family left Mata Flores, they could run into soldiers anywhere. What good would singing do then?

She usually loved the final hours of night, starlight drifting through the only window, the smells of clay floor and hearth ash, Mamá's sighs and Papá's snorts across the room. She felt safe nestled amid her siblings on the big mattress, one arm curved over baby Graciela's doughy flesh. She was used to Lalo's stinky frijole farts, and she didn't even mind Miguel's crusty toes near her face (though he once kicked so hard her nose bled).

This time, though, the dark hush before dawn gave her a new sensation: both lonely and expectant. Poised between the comfort of home and the coming journey into the unknown, she sensed possibilities that might be hers alone. Such ownership was hard to come by in a family of six, and scared as she was, she savored her solitude as she tiptoed from the casita's relative warmth out to the chilly courtyard.

She hauled the water bucket up from the well and rinsed her face, spluttering at the freezing shock, then tilted her head back to find the night's final star: Venus, goddess of love and beauty. A solitary star, unlike the 46 stars on Our Lady of Guadalupe's blue rebozo. Venus belonged to her alone.

She re-entered the house with a shiver, re-braiding her hair by feel. Mamá was kneeling before the hearth, blowing the faint orange light of wood coals into flame. As always, her mother greeted the morning in silence, yet the family answered her unspoken call, rising one by one.

Till now they'd always moved in rhythm with sun, season, and each other. Now they spun too fast, bumping into each other, stirring the hearth's flames into confusion as they packed.

There must've been important decisions about what to take, but later she'd only recall those that gained significance because they called up memories of the desert: Mamá's bone-handled butcher knife, Miguel's silver whistle from the Grito de Dolores festival, Papá's jingling spurs from his days as a vaquero, Graciela's faceless cornhusk doll, Candelita's vihuela. Mamá told Lalo to leave his rusty old lucky horseshoe behind. He dropped it with a clang and shrugged at the family chorus of "Sssh!"

That's when she understood, they were never coming back.

"Keep moving, Candelita!" Mamá scolded.

"But I packed last night."

"Don't talk back!"

She clenched her jaw but did as she was told, refolding the only extra clothes she was bringing: her Christmas skirt and blouse. Already hopelessly wrinkled. "¡Tch!"

"Where we going, Candelita?" Graciela demanded, cranky over being woken at "night."

Candelita turned a helpless look to her mother, who nodded. No need to keep the secret from the little ones anymore. They'd be gone before the village woke.

So she spoke the words aloud for the first time, "We're going to America."

"Where's that?" Graciela asked.

"North."

"Where's north?"

Candelita pointed up.

"Heaven?"

Candelita laughed. "Not exactly."

"Why are we going?"

"We can't be here when the soldiers come back."

"Why?" Clearly no answer would shut up this frustrated little apestosa staring up at her, arms crossed, forehead a question mark.

How could she explain that war was coming, that men were needed to do the killing and dying, that Papá didn't want to be one of them? Instead, she sniffed the air, gave a sly smile, and asked her own question, "Smell that?"

"What?"

"Mamá's champurrado!"

Graciela hopped with joy, legs still kicking as Candelita picked up the little stinker and set her down in a corner. Mamá lifted a bubbling pot from one of the hearthstones encircling the fire, poured the champurrado into mugs, and handed them around. They gathered cross-legged round the hearth in the gloom, deeply inhaling the steam of corn masa and chocolate as if to memorize it.

"Who'll come for you, Papá, the good soldiers or the bad?" Lalo's voice startled the quiet.

"Not so loud, mijo," Papá murmured. "Most soldiers are neither good nor bad. They just want to feed their families. Some want to eat now. Others want to eat in the years to come. And when people get hungry, they all can be dangerous."

"Pues, aren't you too old for the army, Papá?" Lalo said.

"Don't be a tonto," Candelita said. "Thirty-one's not old."

Papá cupped a hand atop her head. "If this war really gets going, they'll need every man they can get." He looked at Miguel and gulped air as if to say more.

Mamá cut him off, "¡Basta! You're scaring the baby."

Candelita turned worried eyes to Graciela.

But her baby sister jutted out a pointy chin and said, "I'm not scared!" What a relief to realize this was true. Her sister was too young to understand words like *war* or *die*.

As for Candelita, it wasn't the dying that scared her but the leaving. She wanted to feel excited about traveling to a new place, making new friends, starting a new life. Yet those were only ideas. Home was real.

They all took a last look around the single smoky room of the half-empty casita. Mamá pinched her nose, squeezing the inner corners of her eyes. She reached down to pat Graciela's face and said not to worry, she was only sorry she had to leave her largest pots behind. Candelita looked at the plump iron bellies hung on the wall, and her stomach gurgled at the thought of eating Mamá's cocido, sucking fat from the beef bones, slurping cumin-rich soup from the corncob she always left for last.

She swallowed the memory and said, "The poor house will be lone-ly without us."

Lalo, who seemed excited by this sudden upheaval in their lives, gave a crooked grin. "The mice and cucarachas will keep it company."

"And the spiders." Miguel sent his fingers crawling up Graciela's arm.

"Nooo!" Graciela tightened her grip on Candelita's neck.

Candelita slapped his hand, but he only laughed. Why must Miguel always make things harder?

Papá stood at the closed door, finger to his lips, reminding them to keep quiet. Then he opened the door and beckoned them into the grey chill of the courtyard. Mamá emerged last, clutching the doorknob till he gently pried her fingers loose. She reached up to cup his cheeks in her palms. He did the same in return, and they pressed their foreheads together. They did this sometimes, as if to transfer their secrets to each other without revealing them to anyone else.

Mamá gave Papá a firm nod. He gave her a firm kiss. Then he eased the door shut and led them out of the courtyard, single file: Mamá, Miguel, Lalo, and then Candelita bringing up the rear with Graciela in her arms. They shuffled out of the pueblo in silence.

The Rivera family had sold their burro months ago, so they carried everything.

Papá bore a mochila of firewood on his shoulders, a machete at his belt, and something hidden in his waistband which he kept tucking and re-tucking. Nobody asked what it was.

Mamá shouldered a pack full of cooking gear with long spoons sticking out the top, and alternated slinging a basket of clothes and blankets from one arm to the other.

A strap across Miguel's forehead balanced the sack of food on his back: beans, potatoes, chiles, dried beef machaca. Over his shoulder hung a satchel, boasting the only two books he hadn't sold to help pay for their supplies: *Don Quixote de la Mancha*, which he'd gotten at school—stolen was more like it, though only she knew that part—and a Spanish translation of *Call of the Wild*, which Papá had given him as a gift when his teacher recommended him for preparatory school.

How jealous she'd been.

Miguel always promised to let her read his books once he was done, but he never seemed to finish. "You wouldn't understand them anyway," he always said. She'd resorted to sneaking them from his satchel while he was off with friends. *Don Quixote* wasn't bad, though she felt impatient with the idea that men, even old ones, could do whatever they wanted: go on adventures or fight battles, even silly ones. She sympathized more with Buck, the brave dog in *Call of the Wild*, who ended up on a journey he had no say in.

Lalo carried whatever didn't fit elsewhere: Candelita's vihuela strapped to his back and a bag of two live chickens swinging from his fist, angry little heads poking through two holes near the bottom. Like Jack London's Buck, the hens began this journey under protest, though after an initial squawking struggle in which many feathers flew away, they fell into stunned silence.

She carried only Graciela. Her parents acted like this was the easy job. But it seemed to her Graciela was as much a burden as any other—more, if you considered her squirming.

Graciela clutched only her cornhusk doll, which weighed next to nothing. Still, she acted dissatisfied with her lazy place in the caravan. Candelita often carried her to and from church, the market, and most fiestas. Sometimes Graciela faked sleep for the privilege. But on this day, she wanted her mother, though Mamá's arms were too full to hold her.

They weren't quite out of the village, when Graciela took to whining, kicking, and trying to wriggle from Candelita's grasp. "¡Quiero Mamá!"

Candelita squeezed her tighter, looked around the sleeping village in alarm, and whispered, "Shhh! You have to stay with me, mamis!"

The endearment seemed to make Graciela madder. "I want Mamá!"

"¡Cállate!" Miguel hissed. "You want the rurales to arrest us?"

Graciela's eyes grew round as an owl's, and she burst into tears.

Candelita kicked at Miguel. "Nice work."

He dodged her foot and held up his hands. "¡Cálmate, señorita, cálmate!"

"Don't worry, mamis," Candelita said. "No one will arrest us." It would take her years to realize it wasn't the word "arrest" that scared Graciela, only the easy rage of their big brother.

Graciela hiccuped back to sleep, cheek bouncing against her shoulder with the rhythmic comfort-and-pain, comfort-and-pain of skin on bone.

The sky was a purple bruise sparkling with tears. Venus was gone. Candelita refused to look back, but it was no use. She would never stop seeing it: the only home she'd ever known, squinting after them, its red mouth twisted shut in confusion as they left it behind.

Home must have become dangerous indeed if leaving it for this enormous silence was their sole option. They left behind all signs of villages, ranches, or churches, of humans, cattle, or horses, headed deeper into the desert than Candelita had ever been.

She had no idea the world was so wide. The flush of dawn awoke the distant mountains, which spread their wings to rise from the edge of a flat valley spread with squat bushes, unruly cactus, and stray rocks. The only sounds: the pad of bare feet and flap of Papá's loose boot sole. Creosote bushes marched alongside, spaced perfectly as a parade. Mamá said those bushes were called gobernadoras, because they ruled the desert—she said the leaves were good for curing foot fungus. The winter sun was small and cool, yet her thirst grew as dust salted her mouth.

"When do we get to Rica?" Graciela asked.

"Los Estados Unidos de A-me-rica," Lalo corrected her.

Graciela shook her head at the ridiculously complicated name.

"Are you kidding?" Miguel said. "America is far."

"Not too far, mija," Candelita said. "El Paso is next to Juárez, and *that's* here in México."

"It might take weeks," Papá said in his distracted way.

Mamá gave him a hard look, opened her mouth, slammed it shut. She turned a grim stare into the shimmering desert. Papá was usually so quiet that nobody discouraged him from talking when he chose. But she understood Mamá's irritation. To walk for weeks? Impossible.

"Wait and see, Graciela," Lalo blurted. "You'll love America! It's full of magic!"

"Magic?"

"You dream it, they have it: bathtubs of hot water if you're cold, boxes of ice if you're hot, cities sparkling with lights when it's dark. And to take you there? Trains that go on forever."

"México has all that too!" Miguel said. "We're just too poor to afford it."

"Trains?" Graciela said.

Candelita made chugging noises. "Chuka-chuka-chuka-chuka…"

"Woo-woo!" Lalo hooted.

"¡Cállate!" Mamá said. "Listen!"

A high-pitched rattle cracked the silence. Candelita glanced sideways and saw a fat snake the color of dead leaves coiled between two rocks, nose pointed at her, tail vibrating a warning.

She froze.

"What?" Graciela's voice startled her so much she almost threw her at the snake in anger.

"Keep walking, Candelita," Mamá said. "No-no, don't run! Just walk naturally."

She tried not to cry as she struggled to remember how she normally walked. Papá circled behind the serpent, tossing her a wink before he crept up on it, forked stick in one hand, machete in the other, and struck fast: trapped the head with the fork, chopped it off in one stroke, and leapt back. The headless beast's tail rattled on, and her heart clenched in horror.

Papá said, "Don't worry. He's dead. He just doesn't know it yet."

It seemed nothing frightened Papá, despite his quiet ways and Miguel's accusations of cowardice. But was fearlessness enough? Papá used to break wild horses at the rancho, animals possessed by demons till he roped them tight, ran them dizzy, and cast them into the dust. But his courage hadn't stopped one wild bronco from stomping his back and breaking *him*, ending his job—and any hope Papá might pay for Candelita to finish school. Now he'd killed a snake, but that wouldn't prevent the next one from killing him. Then what would happen to them all?

Mamá dropped her pack, rummaged inside, and pulled out her bone-handled knife. She whipped the snake's length against the ground to stop its writhing, gutted the entrails, and cast them aside. Her movements had a ruthlessness, a certainty Candelita admired but felt sure she would never know. Mamá pointed the knife at her, presenting the bloody tip like a priest presenting the blood of Christ. "You'll help me butcher this beast for dinner."

Candelita had carved many a fresh kill before—chickens, pigs, rabbits—but this felt different, slicing up a snake that almost sank poisonous fangs into her moments ago. Not that she was still scared. Not at all. She enjoyed cutting this monster to bits.

Lalo smirked, "Can I give Graciela the rattle before you chop that up too?"

She hacked it off and tossed it to him. He showed Graciela how to shake it, dancing around her like a brujo casting a spell, making them all laugh. Graciela couldn't get enough of the chattering sound. Even after they resumed walking, this time with Graciela riding her back, she didn't stop shaking it till Candelita clutched her hand to halt the maddening rattle.

The quiet was no better. That and the repetitive scenery sent her into a trance, until she saw her friend just ahead in the rippling warmth of midday: Juliana, skipping through the trickling acequia of Mata Flores. Candelita followed till she heard footsteps behind, looked back, and saw soldiers giving chase. She tried to lose them, fled into a vast earthen maze that rose before her, frantically choosing turn after turn. Left or right? Right or left? Desperate to find the red door that led home. But each turn only led to another till she was lost.

The dream dissolved, and a terrifying reality dawned on her, the thing her parents wouldn't say: they might never find a way out of this desert.

4. Bandits

1910 – Toisan County, China

They trudged muddy hills, muddy fields, and muddy footpaths to reach Toisan City, every step slower as Yan Chi's boots thickened with clay, until the earth swallowed his foot, jolting him to a halt. He tugged at his ankle with increasing fury till the boot released him with a slurp, flinging him to the wet ground. "Puk gaai!" he swore. He jumped to his feet, shook yet more mud from his already travel-stained suit, and rescued his tumbled fedora—more gifts from his brother in San Francisco. Now he saw why Bing Sam insisted on wearing his old farmer's tunic despite the serious financial nature of their journey.

"Watch out, you're splattering me!" Bing Sam said.

"Your family's running out of time, and you're scared of a little mud?"

"You're the one who told me I'll never get a loan if I go to Hong Kong covered in filth."

"Lou yau, that was a lifetime ago," Yan Chi said, though it had only been an hour. "If we don't hurry, we'll never make the kidnappers' deadline." He shoved muddy foot back into muddy boot and sloshed ahead.

It took three hours to reach the chattering marketplace of Toisan. Touts vied for attention, hawking fresh fish, fried dumplings, cheap umbrellas. He waved them all away. At the train station, he shoved to the front of the ticket line, raising complaints in their wake.

"What're *you* looking at?" Yan Chi snarled as he pushed past.

"M hou yi si! M hou yi si!" Bing Sam apologized.

Yan Chi scowled at him. Who cared what these strangers thought?

They caught a train to the port city of Gong Mun, where many soldiers patrolled the crowds amid murmurs of revolution. There, they boarded an overpopulated steamboat that floated so low in the river it threatened to sink.

By nightfall, Yan Chi could no longer tell whether he sat aboard a moving ferry or on a crowded bench heading nowhere. Beyond the banks of the Pearl River, a ball of fire hung suspended in the dark, a farmer burning his field for planting. It called to mind the fireworks from the engagement celebration less than two weeks before. With each explosion, Mei Yin flashed into view only to disappear again, as if she was receding from him even then. They'd both snuck away from the party to watch the show from his own village's quiet pond, just the two of them. The still water formed a perfect mirror for the shattering night sky.

"Your father must be doing well, to afford such a spectacle," he said.

"Or that's what he wants everyone to think." A crackle like gunshots burst nearby, and she threw herself against him, "Aiya!" Just as quickly, she withdrew her arms from around his neck and reestablished a respectable distance between them, but not before he caught the scent of her skin: cinnamon, sandalwood, and rain.

Then he turned toward the more overpowering smell of gunpowder and laughed at the sight of two small boys emerging from a cloud of smoke to run off between the houses.

She tipped her head and wiggled a finger in her ear. "Those firecrackers shout louder than my auntie when she drinks."

"The noise is the best part," he said. "And firecrackers scare away evil spirits."

She narrowed her eyes. "You don't believe in spirits."

"True. Men make their own luck."

Still, the idea of unseen forces excited him. He often doubted he was a man of earth, instead saw himself as a creature of wind who longed to be carried away. But, if he sailed to a faraway land like America, he couldn't bring her. She would become a grass widow, like so many who grew old waiting for husbands to return. Such women were the envy of wives whose husbands scolded, slapped, or blew their noses into their hands. But he wasn't like those men.

He shuddered now at the thought of a filthy outlaw sniffing the subtle spices of Mei Yin's skin, while he sat stuck on this damned ferry bench, wiped his sleeping friend's drool from his sleeve, and endured the open-mouthed stench of too many snoring travelers.

So, because Mei Yin believed in spirits, even though he didn't, he closed his eyes and prayed, "Tou Dei Gung, if you do watch over Gong Hau, please keep my bride safe and I promise I'll never leave her or the land of my ancestors."

Even as he mouthed that prayer, his heart beat in eager rhythm with the steamer's engine. He'd seen Hong Kong as a boy and couldn't help feeling excited to see it again. He considered what it might be like to keep going from there, to board an ocean liner and never return.

Yan Chi swayed like a sleepwalker as he descended from the quiet rocking of the steamboat into the bellowing hurry of a Hong Kong morning. He felt woozy after two sleepless nights, but Mei Yin pulled him by the arm through the elbowing crowd. Except it was not Mei Yin, still captive in Toisan, but her brother who clutched his arm. At first, Yan Chi thought his friend held on for fear of getting lost, but Bing Sam often visited Hong Kong. Could it be Bing Sam worried about *him*? Yan Chi shook off his doting friend. He could take care of himself.

They hurried through the smells of fish and sea, the cries of lychee-sellers, wonton-vendors, and men hawking cheap passage across the

Pacific. Wood signs dangled overhead like city fruit, advertising tailors, jewelers, teahouses, and hope. Victoria Harbor beckoned, blue as tomorrow, the border of Yan Chi's dreams. Sampans, sails, and steamships slipped between Kowloon and Hong Kong Island. The long deep moan of a passenger ship's horn quickened his blood like strong tea.

They turned down a steamy alley to a narrow building with green-tiled awning, where a black sign announced in gold characters their arrival at Ning Yang Wui Gun, the benevolent association of Toisanese men in America. Ning Yang was one of several wui gun that brokered services for Overseas Chinese: emigration papers, jobs, lodging, financial transactions. They stepped into a crowded roomful of young men poised on the balls of impatient feet, waiting to flee to uncrowded, un-hungry, unlimited new lands. He and Bing Sam shoved to the front of the queue and shouted down the protests of the others to explain their plight to a clerk. Upon the word "kidnapped," outrage faded to murmurs, as strangers found entertainment in a fate more uncertain than theirs.

The clerk led them behind the counter to a tiny office, where he leaned in and whispered to a middle-aged man in a British waistcoat, who sat behind a desk that filled the room: the lending officer. There was no place else to sit and barely room to stand.

Yan Chi bowed to the lending officer and opened his mouth to plead his friend's case.

But before he could speak, the man popped to his feet, took Bing Sam's hand, and pumped it like a well handle. "How can we be of service, Mr. Ma?"

Yan Chi gaped at Bing Sam, who stood tall as he reported with stoic brevity the kidnapping of his father and sister, explained that most of the family savings went to his sister's wedding, but promised that he and his father would soon return to America to repay the ransom with future wages. Yan Chi leaned against the wall to study this new Bing Sam, so in command that he wondered why he'd come along. Then

Bing Sam gestured to him and said, "My oldest friend was supposed to marry my sister today. He's counting on me to save her. I can't let him down."

It struck him then: he wasn't here to take control but to elicit sympathy. Though he was offended, he was also impressed at Bing Sam's unexpected cleverness. So Yan Chi played his role to the hilt, wringing his damp fedora and offering up a desolate gaze.

The lender appeared unmoved, and for a second Yan Chi worried. But the man approved the loan and completed the paperwork with surprising speed, as if ransom payouts were routine. Bing Sam sighed as he signed documents to sell more years of his life. Then the lender turned his chair around and bent down to open a safe behind him.

"Don't worry," Yan Chi whispered to his friend. "You'll make the money back and more." He thumped Bing Sam's shoulder in reassurance but let his hand slide away when Bing Sam turned a stony face on him, a story written there that he couldn't read.

Whenever Yan Chi asked him about America, Bing Sam spoke of mansions, motorcars, single farms as big as all Gong Hau's communal fields, and mountains five times the size of any in Toisan. He never spoke of his work, except vague references to his partnership in a shop where white men paid good money for fine suits. Perhaps he thought Yan Chi wouldn't understand American business. Yan Chi never asked him to explain. He didn't want to lose face.

The lender cleared his desk and laid out the money, several long strands of silver *man* coins, threaded on strings through the holes in their centers.

Yan Chi addressed the man for the first time, voice booming off the close walls, "But the kidnappers named their price in Gold Mountain dollars."

With an odd glance at Bing Sam, the man said, "Trust me, they'll want Chinese coins. American dollars would draw attention."

Yan Chi clamped his mouth shut, face burning, dangling from the edge of a world he didn't understand. He felt betrayed by his friend, who'd put him in this humbling situation. Bing Sam wound the coins inside a long tea-stained strip of cotton cloth, which he wrapped around his waist under his tunic.

Neither of them spoke during the walk back to the harbor.

On board the return ferry to Gong Mun, he imagined himself riding to Mei Yin's rescue astride an avenging Kei Lun. But by the time they boarded the train to Toisan, the smoke trailing from its stack seemed to him the last breath of a dying dragon. He examined his reflection in the lamp-lit window, disgusted by what he saw: a cloddish farmer trapped in a shrinking life.

He closed his eyes against that sight, only to see Mei Yin's reflection in the pond, the night of the fireworks. Bursts of red, green, and white set the water alight. But what most struck him was her face so close to his, both glowing pale in the dark, as if sun and moon floated side by side in a watery sky. Waiting for an eclipse, their one chance to meet again. The train whistle startled him, waking him to an unbearable question: What if they never did?

Bearded banyan trees flung their limbs wide in surrender, as if to prepare Yan Chi and Bing Sam for the worst on their long walk through the night in Toisan's countryside. Yan Chi swung the old Sharps rifle in time with his determined strides, ignoring the broken blisters where his boots rubbed his heels raw. The glow of dawn behind the hills goaded him, telling him they were too late. He pushed past Bing Sam with an animal growl, sure his friend was slowing him down. Bing Sam picked up his pace without complaint.

Yan Chi shifted the rifle into various positions as he walked, rehearsing his demand that the bandits hand over his bride. Braced the weapon against his shoulder: a ready warrior. Slung it across his chest: a trained marksman. Leaned on it like a walking stick: a casual killer. The rifle sank into mud. He yanked it free, cursed the wasted seconds, and pressed on.

Still his friend said nothing. Bing Sam used to act so simple, which made him easy to get along with, yet America seemed to have sharpened him. Yan Chi wasn't sure he liked the change, but he was glad they'd spent enough years together to sense each other's moods.

Then Bing Sam spoke for the first time in hours, startling him. "There it is!"

Yan Chi squinted against the rising sun and searched for the mouth of the shallow cave Bing Sam had described. All he saw was a fold in a hill thick with tousled greenery. Then he spotted an almost invisible gap in a towering stand of bamboo, where four figures emerged. Upon seeing them, all the courage he'd summoned for this moment scattered in confusion. His rifle dangled from his hand like an afterthought.

The bandits didn't look as he'd expected. He was a man of imagination who read when he could—not uncommon in Toisan thanks to the wealth Gold Mountain Men sent home for schools and libraries—and he'd pictured tall, muscular, well-armed men in old-fashioned armor, like warriors from traditional lore. These were stick-bone, threadbare boys.

The leader was perhaps Yan Chi's age, twenty, though his thousand-mile stare made him appear ageless. His hair was cut in the short style of the West, and he wore the navy-blue uniform of Sun Yat-sen's soldiers though it was disheveled and dirty. The other three appeared younger. They wore the loose cotton shirts of poor farmers, stank as if they hadn't bathed in weeks, and looked more bewildered than menacing. Two of them aimed battered rifles at him and Bing Sam.

The third strode right up to Yan Chi and reached out to take his rifle.

Yan Chi stepped back, swung the rifle to his shoulder, and aimed at the boy, who didn't back off. The other two cocked their weapons. He hesitated, silently cursing the idiot lump of rice that was his friend, for failing to bring so much as a kitchen knife to back him up. He let the boy take the rifle, though his eyes followed the red walnut stock and blue steel barrel of his brother's treasured gift. Bing Sam had warned him to leave it at home and, damn him, he was right.

"Who are you?" the leader asked. His diction sounded educated, his tone reasonable—though his eyes remained hard.

"Yan Chi is my future brother-in-law," Bing Sam replied. "He helped get the ransom."

"Then we're glad to see him." The leader smiled and his insufferable grin revealed a gap where his right front tooth should've been. Yan Chi imagined punching out the left one, but the soldier's amused eyes said he was ready for that.

So Yan Chi remained motionless. He'd be no use to Mei Yin if he struck without advantage.

"Where's my money?" the leader asked.

"Where's my family?" Bing Sam's voice rang with unfamiliar rage. Had he always carried this hidden flame?

The leader flapped a casual hand to beckon someone from the shadowy curve that was the cave's narrow entrance. Bing Sam's father stumbled forward, blinking into the dim morning, and fell to his knees. Mr. Ma's face looked like a rotted plum: purple, mashed, leaking red juice. Bing Sam rushed forward to help him up.

Yan Chi remained rooted to the spot, eyes fixed on the cave entrance, waiting for Mei Yin. No one else emerged. He held his breath, listening for her too-heavy footfalls, her too-deep voice. The breeze set bamboo creaking, the only sound. His throat clenched around her name. He didn't say it, dreading to receive no reply.

Bing Sam's eyes shrank to pebbles. "Where's my sister?"

"I've given you your father without asking anything in return. It's your turn."

Bing Sam lifted his shirt with steady hands and unwound the cloth bundle from his belt.

One of the subordinates snatched it and handed it to the leader. He set the bundle on the ground, untied it, and counted the silver coins inside, sliding them along their strings like beads on a necklace. He nodded. It was all here.

"Now give me my sister."

The leader gave Bing Sam a look of regret and tipped his head at one of the boys.

The boy headed not toward the cave but to a nearby bush. He emerged carrying what looked like a pale melon tangled in weeds and set it on the ground before Bing Sam. It didn't roll so much as tilt onto one perfect ear. Bing Sam stumbled back in horror, fell to his knees, and threw up.

Yan Chi held his ground, staring in astonishment at the streamers of arteries, tendons, and bone that dangled from the place where Mei Yin's slender neck once leaned toward him from eager shoulders. He struggled to feel something in the face of this impossible vision. But though he loved Mei Yin completely, this was not the complete Mei Yin.

He knelt and ran a finger down one white cheek, traced a muddy trail till it split into another, and another. Tear-stained map of a vanished world. Where was her body, which had always vibrated with movement even when she sat still, like a pond that looked lifeless at first yet teemed with fish and frogs, birds and dragonflies? He cradled her head in his lap, brushed a hair from her face, touching her more intimately than he ever had when she lived. Her eyes remained black as midnight but empty of stars. He would never sample the taste of rain on her lips or citrus on her tongue. That wasn't the greatest loss.

Never again would he hear her uncontrolled laugh, the kind of laugh only the unsorrowed can know. That absence of sound made him question whether he'd imagined her life. As if she'd always been dead and he only now realized it.

"I *am* sorry." The leader's voice was heavy with sincerity, and this was the deepest cut of all. Yan Chi would never forgive this outlaw for daring to feel remorse. He wanted his hatred to feel pure, uncomplicated by understanding. Yet the leader continued with his worthless words, "I didn't order her death. One of my men recently lost his wife and child, and he was lonely. I thought he only wanted female company. I didn't realize his loss had driven him mad. I did reprimand him." He paused. "At least Mr. Ma has only lost a daughter, not a son."

Yan Chi refused to respond. Others had angered him in life. He'd fought some of them in his youth. But never before had he felt this: wishing he'd brought a machete to cut away pieces of a man, slowly, so he could listen to his agony. Not the man who'd killed her, but *this* arrogant young cock, who'd led these lost boys on a false and ignoble quest.

Yan Chi dared no such thing. He and Bing Sam were outnumbered, and they knew no martial arts. He wanted revenge but saw no purpose to sacrificing his life for a girl already dead. He'd trekked far to become a hero only to discover himself less than a coward, a man whose choices made no difference. The only thing he could do for Mei Yin was refuse to acknowledge her killers. He silently closed her eyes and waited for them to leave.

Out of the corner of his eye, he caught a last glimpse of the leader, who held up the sack of money and declared to no one in particular, "Death to the Ching Emperor!" He muttered his next words so quietly they were hard to hear, "We will return the land to the people." Then he walked away. His comrades followed, a half-dozen scared, hungry boys with nowhere to go.

The American buffalo rifle went with them. Yan Chi ignored it, looked only at what was left of his bride, silenced forever by a Gold Mountain dream.

5. Barefoot Angels

Christmas Night, 1910 – Chihuahua, Mexico

Candelita lagged under Graciela's sleepy weight, far behind the rest of the family, until the vision jolted her to a halt, even before Papá raised his hand to signal *stop*. The giant maze she'd dreamed during their long walk now rose from the desert to face the six Riveras. This time it was real. Fat adobe walls zigzagged in lazy directions, a labyrinth bigger than the entire village of Mata Flores. The eroding caliche flushed red in the sunset, as if the structure were a living, warm-blooded thing. It stood tall in the middle but melted into the earth at the edges. No roof enclosed it, open to the sky so she could see the walls dividing it into dozens of rooms. Like a fortress— or heaven. Didn't Padre Eladio say Jesus promised many rooms in His Father's house?

"What's that?" she asked Papá.

"The güeros call it *Las Casas Grandes*," he replied. "But the Aztecs call it *Paquimé*. It was once a great city, back when the ancient ones ruled."

"What ancient ones?" Lalo asked.

"Nobody knows," Papá said.

"They say it's haunted by ghosts," Miguel said.

Graciela turned to Lalo with a concerned look. "Ghosts?"

He shrugged and pushed out his lower lip, not daring to question his big brother.

Miguel leaned down to Graciela's ear. "Like La Llorona, but hundreds of them."

"Nonsense," Candelita said. "Stop teasing."

"The ancient spirits are nothing like La Llorona," Mamá said, "but not nonsense either."

"Or at least they're useful nonsense," Papá said. "Since so many people believe those ghost stories, they avoid this place at night. We'll be safe camping here."

Mamá gave him a skeptical look. "What if bandidos decide the same?"

"Criminals as clever as me wandering the desert on Christmas Day? ¡Claro que no!"

Candelita was so tired of walking, it inclined her to believe Papá. Even if ghosts did haunt Casas Grandes, dead spirits sounded safer than live bandits. And she was glad of any excuse to set down Graciela, who ran toward a nearby cluster of cottonwoods, alder, and willow, to answer the chuckling call of a small river amid the trees.

"Candelita!" Mamá snapped.

"I know, I know," she sighed. "Don't let her fall in."

She trotted after Graciela—feet aching so bad they felt inside out—and caught her before she could scramble into the water. Candelita eyed the river with mistrust. It looked shallow yet seemed in an unusual rush considering this was the dry season. She slung her sister over her shoulder and hauled her back to the family. They were making camp under a cottonwood so top-heavy it bent over till its crown touched the ground, as if it were praying.

She plopped Graciela and her cornhusk doll under the tree-arch and pointed. "Stay here."

Graciela demanded, "Play with me!"

"After I carried you all day, gordita? Are you kidding?"

"No, I'm not kidding." Graciela turned irritable whenever anyone called her chubby—or teased her at all. Since she was the baby, this meant she got irritated a lot.

Candelita threw herself down in the tree's slender shade as if daring anyone to make her do anything. Which her mother did before she could close her eyes, setting her to skewer the meat from the rattlesnake they'd butchered that morning.

Papá put the boys to work building a lean-to at the hunchback cottonwood's base, using a tarp, three branches, and rope. Mostly they pretended to sword fight with the branches. Miguel was winning—swinging, thrusting, and striking too hard as usual, though Lalo would let his big brother beat him bruised and bloody before he'd ever stop giggling or admit he was hurt.

"Laugh at *me*, will you?" Miguel thrust his branch into Lalo's belly with such force he fell backward with a huff, the wind knocked out of him.

Papá strode up, ripped Miguel's branch from his hand, and held it over his head, shaking with rage. "Does it ever occur to you that you and your brother are on the same side? Do you ever consider teaching *him* how to win?" He tossed the branch back to Miguel and lowered his voice. "If you really want to play at being a hero, finish this shelter before dark."

Miguel lowered his eyes. "Yes, Papá." He gave Lalo a hand up off the ground.

Odd. Her brothers always fought and their father never interfered before. He stalked off to gather wood, muttering to himself. Mamá's mouth twitched as if she had much to say, but she remained silent as she wandered around camp gathering rocks in her skirt.

Papá returned with kindling, then large branches, and made a small pyramid of wood, which Mamá surrounded with her rocks to create a hearth. Graciela followed, pushing each rock into her notion of a perfect circle. Papá nudged her aside, "Stay out of the way," and set the kindling ablaze with a match. Mamá set gorditas on the flame-licked stones, heating the little pouches of cornmeal and meat, which weren't as plump as their name suggested.

Graciela prodded one gordita with a finger.

Mamá swatted her hand. "¡Cuídate, mija, it's hot!"

Graciela gave up trying to help and switched to scolding her doll: "Stay out of the way… Careful, it's hot… I don't care if it's pretty!"

Candelita smiled. The flames *were* pretty, especially as the sun dropped low to kiss Casas Grandes goodnight. But she caught Mamá looking from the fire to the ruins to Papá with a distressed frown, as if she feared the fire, or the ghosts. In reply, he stopped stacking firewood, said he needed to make pipi, and wandered into the trees.

Candelita was turning away to give him privacy when a glint of sun on metal caught her eye. She was stunned to see him pull a pistola from under his shirt. He peered into the chamber, head bowed, lips moving, as if praying over the bullets like rosary beads. He'd long owned the revolver, but she'd never seen him shoot it. She'd only seen it once before, when he instructed them all never to touch it. Then he'd put it on a high shelf to gather dust. Did he expect to use it in the desert? Why run from the federal leva, or reject joining the rebels, if he still must fight?

He caught her staring and shook his head. A warning: don't tell the others. She turned away and pretended to see nothing. It made her feel grown up, sharing a secret with her father.

At dusk, La Familia Rivera sat around the fire to eat, but before Candelita took one bite, a low drumming throbbed across the skin of the desert. They exchanged alarmed looks and crouched as if to run. It was the sound of boots as at least two dozen federal soldiers marched toward the ancient fortress of Casas Grandes. Not ghosts. Men.

Mamá hissed, "The fire, viejo!" She leapt to her feet, ready to kick dirt on the blaze.

Papá jumped up to stop her. "No, vieja! They've already seen the fire. If we put it out now, we'll only draw attention. Best to go about our evening, like it's nothing, like we belong."

"They're only after real fighters," Miguel said, "not a sorry bunch like us."

Candelita scowled at this insult till he smiled at the little ones. Was he trying to protect them?

"Exactly, mijo," Papá said. He and Mamá eased back into their places around the fire.

Candelita's heart thumped in time with the boots marching into the labyrinth, but she followed Papá's lead and settled on her haunches, pretending there was nothing to fear.

Soon the soldiers' tall shadows climbed Casas Grandes' walls in the light of scattered campfires, while her family's shadows skipped across the cottonwood arch as they ate. She'd known hunger before, but this deep hole in her stomach felt new. She wanted to make each bite last, but restraint was impossible. She bolted her chorizo gordita, spicy-sweet as home, and barely chewed her snake meat, wild and smoky as the desert. Despite the unexpected mix of flavors, Graciela's head bobbed with pleasure, reminding Candelita of a roadrunner.

An eerie howl split the night air.

"¡Ay, La Llorona!" Graciela dropped her gordita.

Mamá rescued it from the dirt, dusted it off, and handed it back. "Don't worry, that's not La Llorona. It's a pack of coyotes. Shall I tell you a story about a coyote?"

Graciela nodded.

Mamá scooped the girl onto her lap, and the others leaned forward to watch firelight rearrange her features into a visitor who only appeared at night, a witch or angel: The Storyteller. No one told stories like Mamá, whose voice could make the real world disappear.

"One full-moon night, much like this one, a rabbit hopped down to the river for a drink of water. Señor Conejo began to sip, when who do you think snuck out from behind a tree?"

"El Coyote!" Graciela sang.

"Riiiiight. Pues, as you know, Coyote is clever and likes to play tricks, so you might worry about Conejo. But this night the moon was so bright Coyote's reflection in the water gave him away. Conejo started to hop off, but Coyote leapt in front of him and blocked his path.

"Coyote said, 'No use trying to get away. In one pounce, I'll catch you and eat you.'

"Then Conejo said, 'Wouldn't you rather eat the delicious cheese?'

"'Where?'

"'There!' Conejo pointed his paw at a yellow ball floating in the river's black water.

"Coyote admitted, 'Cheese is my favorite.'

"'Mine, too!' Conejo replied."

"Mine, too!" interrupted Papá.

"Who's telling this story, viejo?" Mamá scolded.

Papá clapped a hand over his mouth in mock apology. He'd broken the Riveras' first commandment: Thou shalt not interrupt the story.

"Hmph," Mamá snorted. "So, Conejo said, 'The problem is I can't swim. I tell you what: if you get the cheese, I'll go home to get beans and tortillas. Then together we'll eat a feast!'

"Coyote agreed, 'That does sound delicious.'

"Then he leapt into the river, swam to the cheese, and snapped his jaws around it. But all he got was a mouthful of water! He bit into the wheel of cheese again and again, spluttering and nearly drowning in the effort. No matter how hard he tried, he couldn't catch it…"

"Coyote gave up and swam to shore, so angry at his failure that he couldn't wait to gobble the rabbit. But Conejo was gone. Coyote gazed sadly at the cheese in the water, until he realized: that was no cheese. It was only a reflection—"

"—of the mooooon," Lalo intoned as if this were a profound revelation.

"¡Exactamente!" Mamá grinned—nobody minded Lalo's interruptions because he never stole the stage. "When he realized Conejo's trick, Coyote looked up at the real moon and let out his frustration in a great long howl."

Papá looked up at the moon, pursed his lips, and cut loose a piercing coyote cry so real it prickled Candelita's skin. Mamá shot a nervous glance at the army outpost and gave him a stern look, but he shrugged her off. For the first time, it occurred to Candelita that maybe Papá was neither a coward nor a hero, simply a man who didn't like being told what to do.

"Pobrecito Coyote," Graciela said.

"It's either poor coyote or poor rabbit," Papá said.

"Unless you want to give him your gordita." Miguel reached for Graciela's last bite.

"No!" She stuffed it into her already full mouth, cheeks puffed out.

They all broke into laughter.

Lalo stepped from the firelight into the shadows and returned with Candelita's vihuela. He handed her the little guitar, his chin cast downward and eyes cast upward in a wheedling plea.

"Tonight?" she asked Papá, with an uncertain glance toward the nearby ruins.

"Especially tonight."

At that moment, she would've followed him anywhere. "What should I sing?"

"The barefoot angels!" Graciela declared in a voice that would not be denied.

Candelita closed her eyes to the silhouettes dancing on the walls of Casas Grandes, plucked her vihuela, and sang to her family as if they were the only people in the world.

A la puerta del cielo venden zapatos
Para los angelitos que andan descalzos.
Duérmete, niño, Duérmete, niño,
Duérmete, niño, arru, arru.

At the gate of heaven little shoes they are selling.
For the little barefooted angels there dwelling.
Slumber my baby, slumber my baby,
Slumber my baby, arru, arru.

The whole family joined in. Then she heard it: the faint refrain of many young male voices singing along. The Riveras exchanged disbelieving looks and turned toward the glow of Casas Grandes. When the family stopped singing, so did the unexpected chorus.

She sang another song, but the soldiers' voices did not return.

Papá nodded at her in approval. "Your lullaby was so sweet it soothed them to sleep."

She blinked back tears before Miguel could see them and tease her for crying.

Papá clapped once and announced they should sleep too because they must cross the river come morning. This news startled Candelita, who was no strong swimmer. "Don't worry, mija, you won't have to swim." He ran a rough hand through her hair, but it only increased her uneasiness.

They slept on rugged ground, sharing three blankets between them: one for the boys, one for the girls, one for Mamá and Papá. She pressed her palm against the cool earth. "Please keep us safe as we cross," she muttered, unsure to whom she prayed. God? The Desert? The River? A low hum rose from the ground, as if the earth answered with its own lullaby.

She sat up with a start. They'd forgotten to sing Christmas songs! Today was their last Christmas in Mexico, and now it was over. She reached into her skirt pocket, feeling for the cookie she'd hidden there just last night in Mata Flores, but nothing was left of it except crumbs.

"What is it?" her mother murmured.

"Merry Christmas, Mamá."

"Feliz Navidad, Candelita."

Though the water didn't look deep and the river wasn't all that wide, Papá said, "We're taking no chances." He handed one end of a rope to Miguel, then pulled the length across the river, wading through a current that rushed between his knees. On the other side, he tied his end to a small cottonwood, then returned, hand gliding along the taut rope. He carried Graciela across first. They swayed and jerked through the uneven course, but it looked easy enough.

He returned to guide the rest of them.

The river was sneaky. Candelita clutched the rope with both hands, but slick stones tripped her feet and the strong current sucked at her thighs, trying to pull her down. Her skirt was hiked between her legs and tucked at her waist, but swirling water yanked it loose till it billowed and wrapped around her, slowing her progress. She stumbled, and a whine escaped her. She emerged on the far side, skirt clinging to shaking legs, and turned to anxiously watch the others.

Mamá and Miguel crossed in no time, even with their heavy bags, as if they did this every day.

Lalo came second to last, Papá close behind, holding the rope taut round his waist. Her vihuela bounced against Lalo's back. Maybe she should've carried it. But he gripped the rope with one hand, held up the bag of chickens with the other, and grinned as he called to everyone on the bank, "This is easy!"

Then he tripped.

He still clung to the rope single-handed but landed face-down in the water. He had no leverage to push up because his free hand held the chickens high. His head went under. Candelita held her breath. Papá grabbed the hens, freeing Lalo's other hand. He pushed up, spluttering, and rose toward the trees that leaned over the bank. He laughed in victory. Then the strap that held the vihuela to his back snagged on a branch and ripped. The guitar fell with a splash.

Lalo let go the rope to reach for the vihuela. Candelita leaned forward and sent a silent plea to the river: Please, let him grab it. But it was already drifting away like a small, badly made boat. He poised himself to swim after it. Mamá gasped. Papá seized a fistful of shirt and ordered, "Grab the rope, Lalo!" He obeyed, and they finished crossing, soaked but safe.

"¡Tonto! Why did you let go?" Mamá shook him, then threw her arms around him.

He pulled away. "I'm fine. But the vihuela, it's gone!" He sank onto the bank, clasped both hands behind his head, and hid his face between his knees. "I'm sorry, Candelita."

She stared downriver to a bend where the vihuela dipped from sight. Pressed both hands to her mouth, but not to pray. The desert, the river, God: they might watch, listen, even sing, but she decided they didn't answer prayers. Her family would live or die by their own efforts.

6. It Always Rains

The Day Before Ching Ming, 1911 –
Toisan County, China

The day before the Ching Ming Festival, a year after his bride's death, Yan Chi rose early to walk through his village, hoping to avoid people. Because Mei Yin died before the wedding, he still lived in the House of Waiting Grooms, but he walked to his father's house for breakfast each morning. Drizzle again entombed the eleven villages. Here in Bok Nan, pine smoke from cooking fires clawed the mist like ghostly fingers as women in every house began their long day preparing feasts for the ancestors. *Ching Ming* was a festival of opposites: it meant *Clear Bright* yet brought only clouds; it was a time to plant for spring's rebirth yet also to feed the dead.

Mei Yin once stalked his heart, but now memories of her life, or even her grim death, prompted little feeling in him. He didn't romanticize the past. Yet, since her death, the covert glances of his cousins told him that his stoicism made others uneasy. They seemed to see it as stoniness of heart rather than acceptance of reality.

These days the only memory that brought tears to his eyes was his last encounter with Hong Kong's salt sea air. He yearned to return to Victoria Harbor and set sail across The Peaceful Ocean bound for The Beautiful Country, *America*. There, he imagined riding a train through the Wild West, in search of the bison carved into his lost American rifle, legendary creatures even his brother had never seen, cousins to the Kei Lun. But even with Mei Yin gone, his parents expected him to stay home and work the farm. And now that she'd been gone a year, they also expected him to accept a new bride to work with him.

He approached his father's house, where his mother wailed a muk yu song that burst through her open kitchen door, mixed with sounds of pounding, chopping, and sizzling. Her cooking songs were always chaotic, scattered with her moody interpretations of their family story:

The willow branch, hung bright and green,
awaits death at the door.
Though I am bent and dried with age,
young men come home once more.

It was enough to make him consider turning back. He sighed and ducked under the young willow branch hung over the door to welcome Grandpa's spirit, only to recoil when he saw a disembodied head floating in a veil of smoke. His first thought was, Mei Yin? But her half-remembered voice chided him, You don't believe in ghosts, remember? His eyes adjusted to the dimness, revealing it was only Mama's square head poised over a steaming wok as she stirred hot water, rice, and bits of pork to make their morning juk. Once a famed beauty, in the years since his baby brother's death, a permanent frown split her forehead, lines spread from there like cracked mud, and gray hairs sprang from the stern bun at her neck. Her song wasn't wrong.

"What're you staring at?" she accused.

"The prettiest mama in all Gong Hau." He offered a dimpled smile.

She snorted. "And you're the blindest son. Come here." She took his cheeks between her hands, peered into his eyes, then gave a mournful shake of her head as if it hurt to look at him.

"I know you're happy to see me," he said, though he wasn't so sure. "You can't fool me."

"Hmph, anyone can fool you." She waved a hand as if to erase her words and start over. "I'm only sad to see you alone. I'll be happier once the matchmaker finds your new bride."

Unexpected rage flushed through him. "Maybe the matchmaker is letting my first bride finish her journey to the afterlife before replacing her."

"Hush! How dare you talk to me this way? As if I'm responsible for her death."

"No, I'm responsible, Mama. I should've run straight to the cave to save her, not wasted time going to Hong Kong for the money."

She turned to punish her garlic cloves with brusque little chops. "Nobody thinks that."

"Everybody thinks that. They whisper, 'He left with a rifle but came back with a head.'"

She turned back to him, jaw clenched, tears in her eyes. "Let them dare say it to me!"

"To the fiercest mother in Gong Hau? Nobody would dare." He clapped a hand over her shoulder, uncomfortable staying angry with her.

She covered his hand with hers, patted it, and flung it away. Then she turned to the largest bowl on her crowded counter and stirred its contents with a wooden spoon, declaring an end to the subject. He refused to be dismissed, leaning over her to inhale the smells of childhood: red bean curd, five-spice powder, soy, oyster sauce, and honey, folded with fat bites of barbecued pork. All to create the filling for his favorite steamed buns: cha siu baau. He knew better than to compliment her cooking—she'd scold him for making the ancestors jealous.

Instead, he said, "You work too hard, Mama!"

"You're not helping, lazy! Move-move-move! You're in my way."

He stepped left just as she tried to slip past him in that direction. Then he dodged right, only to cut her off again.

She grabbed his arms and dragged him to the table. "Sit-sit-sit." Then she set out the steaming teapot and two cups for morning cha.

"What about Baba?"

"The second one's for him," she said, then shouted at the ceiling, "if he ever gets out of bed! I have too much to do." With that she scurried out of the house.

She hadn't always been so moody. When he was small, he'd wrap his arms and legs around her leg and cry, "Don't go!" She'd walk away with him riding atop her foot, pretending not to notice him till she swung him up into her arms and they both burst into giggles. Each year made her harder to charm.

This time, he was glad she left. It would be easier to convince Baba to put off this betrothal business. He wanted not a new bride but a new life.

The moment Mama left, a creak announced Baba sneaking down the ladder from the loft. Yan Chi used to sleep up there near his parents till he turned fourteen and moved to the House of Waiting Grooms. Nobody slept in the newer downstairs bedroom, which they'd partitioned off for his parents to live in so Yan Chi and Mei Yin could take the loft. Now his father stepped before the door of the unused room and winked, one eye disappearing in a tree-knot of wrinkles.

Yan Chi laughed. "Hoping to escape the Ching Ming storm, Baba?"

"Your mama stirs up the kind of storm no mortal man can outrun."

"So you hide like a mouse?"

Baba shook his head. "Have you seen what she does to mice?" He pointed to a gouge in the floor.

Yan Chi chuckled. "You think we'll finish planting rice today?" He poured the tea.

Baba sat down, took a long sip, and said, "I don't see why not. There's not much left to do—and I'm not as old as I look. When you're my age, you'll be lucky to have half my stamina."

"Maybe I won't arrive at your age by the same road."

Baba set down his cup and wiped a wet tea leaf from the rim. "What road then? You know we can't afford to send another paper son to America."

This threw Yan Chi. He hadn't expected his scheme to be dismissed before he ever proposed it. "Why not?" he blurted. "My brother sends home plenty of money."

"True. But buying the name of an American son is expensive, especially at your age, already twenty-one. And when I'm gone, *someone* must take my place, to care for our ancestors and their land." Baba spoke not in anger but as one who instructs a beloved yet errant child.

"Nei hai ngaam ge," Yan Chi conceded the point though inside he still bristled.

His father reached out and rubbed his arm, and this fleeting approval calmed him.

Baba let go his arm the moment Mama bustled inside, clutching to her chest a dripping silver carp from the pond. "It always rains at Ching Ming," she chuckled, shaking drops from her glistening hair. Yan Chi laughed obediently though he didn't find the saying funny anymore. She gutted the carp and dumped it into a pot of boiling water, but it made a reflexive leap to the floor. Stupid ghost fish didn't know it was dead. She bent, grasped head and tail, forced her captive back in the pot, and slammed the lid, leaning on it till the stove stopped rattling. She turned to the men with a triumphant grin. Mama was only half his size, but she still frightened him.

She scurried to ladle juk into their bowls, then resumed cooking for the dead. Yan Chi and Baba slurped their rice porridge as fast as possible. When Mama bent over the wok stove to hurl more wood into the fire, Baba saw his chance. He slipped out the door unnoticed. But Yan Chi couldn't resist sneaking a boiled egg from the counter.

"Aiya! That's for the ancestors! You want bad luck? Out-out-out!" Mama grabbed the dried willow branch she'd cut to sweep the family tombs and used it to sweep him out the door.

He ran to catch up to Baba. Together, they headed to the rice paddies and hitched the ancient ox to the plow. Baba insisted on doing the plowing himself, and Yan Chi didn't argue, though the sight made him itch with irritation: Baba's chest curved inward and the ox's back swayed downward as the plodding pair strained to push the single-blade plow through heavy mud.

Yan Chi snatched up a tray of rice seedlings and stepped into the next paddy. Lowered a seedling through ankle-deep water, pushed it into mud, and stepped forward to push in another. For him, Ching Ming conjured neither reverence for the dead nor the promise of new life, merely another year burying his youth and unearthing disappointment.

Stoop, push, step. Stoop, push, step.

7. Horse Thieves

1910 – Chihuahua, Mexico

This time, Candelita's mother refused to hand her a knife. She insisted on battling the prickly pear cactus alone. "No sense both of us tearing our skin," Mamá said, though she still tried to teach her how to harvest nopales without getting scratched: raising her knife in one rag-covered fist, gripping a thorny pad in the other, severing it at the joint. But Candelita's attention fixed on the nearby hut where Papá and a one-armed man sat atop sacks of grain murmuring urgently.

The one-armed man was her father's primo, letting them stay the night with him here in the outskirts of Corralitos in the Sierra Madre foothills. He'd lost his left arm in a cave-in at the silver mine up the canyon, a mine called Candelaria, like her. He gestured as he talked, and his stump twitched with the same nervous rhythm as his uninjured arm. It looked like a twist of chorizo. She couldn't recall his name, only Lalo's nickname for him: Primo Chorizito. She'd scolded Lalo, but Primo Chorizito overheard and clapped the boy's back with a hearty laugh.

Whatever Papá was saying now had the opposite effect. Why was Primo frowning so hard? If only Mamá would stop talking so she could hear them.

She gave up on both parents and followed a splashing sound to its source: the cool green throat of the arroyo beyond the hut, where Lalo and Graciela were stalking frogs. In a shallow pool between twisted oaks, Lalo crouched, still and silent. His hands shot out and trapped one. He stared into its bulging eyes till it squirmed free, then wagged a finger after it, "We'll meet again, Señor Rana!" Graciela chased the escapee, sending more frogs hopping. Lalo clapped a palm to his forehead. "You're scaring them away!" He gave up, laughing, and splashed with her. Candelita hiked her skirt to join the hunt just as a loud clatter rolled down the canyon.

She looked up to see Miguel sprinting toward them through the canyon's stream, waving his arms, shouting, "Someone's coming!"

This is it, she thought, not knowing what *it* might be, only that it terrified her. She picked up Graciela, Miguel picked up Lalo, and they ducked into the brush. They held their breath, peering between branches. A mud-spattered Appaloosa and rider flew round a bend in the stream, hooves kicking up spray. The horse charged toward the hut at the canyon's mouth, where her father and Primo Chorizito leapt to their feet.

The breathless young rider pulled to a stop and, between gasps, shouted from astride the horse, "Papá…a journalist named Guerrero… and a band of rebels…stole the train from Juárez."

The rider's excitement suggested this was good news. But the way Papá chewed his cheek and Primo twitched his chorizo arm, she knew the news worried them.

"How many, mijo?" Primo asked the rider, apparently his son.

The son shook his head. "Maybe a dozen, maybe a hundred. They're at the mine."

"Then they'll be here in a couple of hours!"

"No. They're dynamiting the bridges so the federales can't follow. That's how I beat them here. But they could arrive by nightfall."

His father told him to alert the town, and he galloped away.

Mamá walked toward them, dragging her bag of freshly scraped nopales like an afterthought. Only then did Miguel lead the children out of the bushes. All four siblings stared at Mamá, waiting. Back home, she would've told them what to do. Here, she looked to Papá. His gaze brushed the top of each child's head. "We're leaving."

Primo offered food and ammunition. Papá accepted the food but refused the bullets. "You'll need those. As for us, we'll either make it to Ascensión or we won't." Primo then drew a map in the dirt with a stick. Papá hunkered down to watch.

Lalo tried to join them, but Mamá shepherded him and the other children toward the shack. "¡Apúrate! Get your things."

Miguel hung back. "I'm staying to fight." He turned to Papá and raised a fist in the air. "¡Viva la revolución! Better to die in battle like a man than hide in the desert like a mouse."

Papá charged at him, but Mamá was faster. She stepped between them and slapped Miguel so hard he staggered. She pressed her palm to her mouth, eyes brimming and voice shaking as she said, "*We* are your people!" She had spanked them all before, but neither she nor Papá ever hit any of them in the face, till now.

Miguel's chin jutted higher, cheek crimson with her handprint, but he said nothing.

Papá rested a hand on his shoulder. "Mijo, I'm not against this fight. But as men, we protect our family first, or the rest means nothing. Do as your mother says."

Miguel shook him off and slouched into the hut. Candelita followed. It was dim inside, sun filtered through one dusty window, but she still saw the movement he tried to hide, swiping both palms across his eyes. He lugged two bags out front and called her and Lalo to join him.

"You two carry these—"

"You're leaving?!" Lalo's voice rang with dismay.

"No. You'll carry these, so I can carry Graciela." He locked eyes with Candelita.

She wanted to protest. Her parents only ever asked her to watch the little ones. Miguel was too rough, picked on them, acted like he didn't even like them. *She* carried Graciela for three days, not him. But his eyes were determined. She knew why. She nodded.

He crouched and held his arms out to Graciela.

She threw her doll at him and clung to Candelita's waist. "No! Want my sister!"

"Mamis, we have to run far. You're too heavy for me!" She poked Graciela's middle.

Graciela sucked her tummy away from the offending finger, her face stricken.

Miguel picked up the doll and held it out to her.

She turned her question-mark frown on Lalo.

He nodded. "Miguel is the strongest, Gracielita. He'll take good care of you."

Her eyes still on Lalo, she accepted the doll from Miguel, climbed onto his back, and wrapped her arms round his neck. He wrapped his hands round her ankles.

"Don't let go!" Candelita and Lalo said in unison—her warning Miguel, him warning Graciela.

Within minutes, burdens reshuffled, the Riveras trotted back into the desert, Candelita at the rear, eyes on Graciela.

A sudden thunder in the silence sent a hot sting of anxiety through her. She looked overhead but saw neither lightning nor clouds. Her father looked over his shoulder, and she followed his gaze to the shrinking town of Corralitos, where tiny people scurried like grains of sand stirred by wind. A column of smoke rose between the hills. "Guerrero must have blown the last bridge," Papá said. "We should hurry. Someone might notice us and get curious."

She and Lalo struggled to keep up with Miguel, who didn't slow despite Graciela's weight. The siblings formed a ragged line, wheezing in chorus. Each breath knifed her gut. The sun went down in flames, which burned away to dusk. If she fell in the dark, would they see her, or run on without noticing?

A drawn-out inhuman wail stopped them all in their tracks.

"What's that?" Graciela asked.

"The train," Miguel said.

The train didn't make the playful noise she and Lalo had mimicked their first day in the desert. It howled like a beast. As if this were a signal, she sank to her knees, pressed her forehead to the earth, and clutched the invisible stab wound in her side.

"Viejo, the children can't run anymore, and neither can I," Mamá said.

"I'll carry you, mija." She looked up to see Papá kneeling before her, his face so crumpled with concern, she felt guilty for giving up.

"No hay problema." She pressed down on his shoulders to push herself onto her feet.

The family slowed to a walk. If it was for her sake, they never said and she never asked.

A short time later she heard popping, like young wood in a cookfire. They all turned again to stare at Corralitos, no more than a distant ember trembling in the dusk.

"What's that?" Graciela asked again.

"Guns," Papá said.

Miguel and Lalo used to chase through Mata Flores pretending to shoot at each other, made noises like clearing their throats until one or the other clutched his chest, fell, and groaned. This didn't sound like that. Between gunshots, distant shouts skimmed the night air. Impossible to tell at this distance if they were raised in celebration, anger, or dismay. Maybe all three. A single shriek pierced through it all, only to be cut short. Woman? Man? Primo Chorizito?

The family staggered on until the next sound closed in: galloping hooves. She expected to see Primo's son on his freckled Appaloosa. But this horse was red as clay except for a white blaze on his forehead.

His saddle sat empty. He flew past, eyes crazed, whites showing. She'd never seen anything so beautiful. Despite his obvious distress, he ran with purpose, as if he knew where to go. Papá gave a long, low whistle as the beast vanished into the indigo twilight.

Papá followed the horse's tracks, which led to a crooked line of trees huddled over the secret desire of the desert: water. The low, black river winked in the moonlight as if to say, I knew you'd be back. Hard to believe this was the same river that tried to drown Lalo two days ago. Thirsty roots now tamed its progress. There stood the horse, scratching his salt-stained neck against one wide-hipped tree. He snorted a gentle warning as they approached.

The Riveras skidded past him and scrambled down the steep bank, clutching willow scrub and each other, till they stumbled to a halt at the water's edge. The moment Miguel set Graciela down, she knelt in the mud, put her face in the cold water, and gulped.

Papá snatched her up. "Not so fast, mija. You'll throw up."

"I'm thirsty!"

"Trust me."

Trust Papá. That sounded so easy. He'd always taken care of them, provided a warm, safe home and enough to eat. Sometimes he yelled when they picked on each other or acted careless, but neither his words nor his hands were ever cruel. Except now he'd abandoned their home. What if next he was forced to join the war and abandon *them*? Mamá was strong, but how could they make a home without Papá? That's when it struck her: if he left, then the eldest son would become head of the family. Could they trust Miguel?

For now at least, Papá remained with them. So, for now, she put her faith in him. Though she'd never been thirstier, she drank the water in tiny sips as he instructed.

She dipped her feet in the river with a sharp intake of breath. Though her feet were callused from a lifetime spent barefoot, the soles now stung with torn and bloody blisters. Two long strips fluttered before her eyes—her mother dangling two cloth bandages. Candelita assumed Mamá would bind the wounds. Instead, she said, "You know what to do." True: Mamá had taught her all she knew. She bit back tears, accepted the bandages, and wrapped her own feet.

Miguel leaned back to watch. "At least you didn't have to carry Graciela, the little fatso."

"I'm not fat!" Graciela said, then threw up in the river. So, Papá was right about drinking fast.

"Pobrecita!" Candelita helped her rinse thin vomit from her face.

She and Lalo led Graciela up the slope to join their parents.

Miguel remained alone at the bottom, lying against the bank, head resting on clasped hands, staring up at the half-moon.

Atop the bank, the rest flung themselves amid rocks and roots, too exhausted to set up camp. Mamá handed out machaca, still in jerky form. Candelita could barely chew. Graciela leaned against her, jaw working till it went slack and gave way to snores. Mamá tossed a blanket over them.

Candelita couldn't sleep, staring into the desert's thousand directions, sure it hid a thousand eyes. A silhouette crept toward the horse and his tree. She feared it was a ladrón come to steal their things. Then she heard Papá murmur. He rested a palm against the animal's neck, eased the harness into his other hand, and used a rope to tie it to the tree. The beast snorted but didn't resist. The horse trusts him, she thought. Papá patted his flank. "Que sueñes con los angelitos," he said in the same sweet voice he used when tucking his children into bed.

She wished she were the horse, who seemed sure not only of Papá but also of himself. If she were alone in the desert, she'd never survive. She shivered and watched her breath rise.

A red glow pressed against Candelita's eyelids as she tried to identify a crackling sound. More gunfire? No. She inhaled and relaxed, grinning at the smells of grease and green: nopalitos and eggs frying in a pan. She wondered how much longer they'd have eggs. Mamá had left the hens with Primo Chorizito in exchange for food easier to run with.

Her parents whispered while Papá cooked. She pretended to sleep so she could listen.

"No!" Mamá hissed. "What if the owner comes looking for it?"

"No one's coming for him, vieja. His owner's dead."

"How do you know?"

"Blood. But not the *horse's* blood. ¿Me entiendes?"

"Maybe the rider was only injured."

"Trust me. I rinsed more than just blood off that horse."

What else had the dead rider left behind? Guts? She shuddered. Whatever it was, she hoped Mamá let them keep the horse. She pictured galloping across the desert, her knees hugging his flanks, his courage flowing into her. Together, they could face anything.

"How will we feed it?" Mamá asked.

"We'll stay near the river, where there's water and grass. I'll buy feed in Ascensión."

"With what? Your good looks?"

"My spurs."

"You'd sell your spurs to feed a horse but not to feed your children? You always refused before."

"I needed the spurs before, so el jefe could see my value shining astride his best and know me as a cowboy of quality. And our children never missed a meal."

"Maybe you've noticed times are harder?"

"You don't understand. He can carry supplies. He can carry the children. Who knows when I'll find work in El Paso? But we can sell this horse."

"It's a good idea, Mamá," Miguel said.

"No one asked you," Papá said.

"But I'm defending you!"

"Listen to your father."

Why couldn't Miguel learn it never paid to take sides between their parents?

Now that he'd broken the morning, she sat up, then looked down and giggled. The others turned and laughed with her. Graciela had flipped in her sleep: head now at Candelita's feet, rear poking up in the air. Candelita stepped over her and rummaged through the bags for gourds. "I'll get water." She was always the one to change the subject when things grew tense.

After breakfast, Papá introduced the children to the horse, who he'd named Feo. The horse was anything but ugly, but this was how nicknames worked in Mata Flores: skinny kids became Fatso, tall kids Tiny, handsome kids Feo.

"Mucho gusto, Feo," she said. His ears flicked forward as if eager for her secrets, and she stroked the white flame between his eyes.

"Not there," Papá said. "Not till he knows you better. He's blind there."

She jerked her hand away.

Then he lifted Graciela to pet the horse. She beat his neck with the same casual violence she used to spank her doll. "Good Feo!"

The horse nodded and nickered, apparently used to harsh treatment.

"Graciela, Lalo," their father said, "would you like to ride Feo to Juárez?"

Lalo rocked onto his toes and gave one stirrup an eager tug. "Can we?"

"Graciela hits him and *she* gets to ride?" Candelita's hand flew to her mouth, too late.

Papá shook his head. Not angry—disappointed. They were running for their lives, so of course the smallest should ride. Even so, it felt unfair. She used to think growing up would mean doing more of what she wanted, but it seemed adults were just the people who survived childhood. With that thought came understanding: her parents' argument over the horse was about their children's survival. She looked into one of the horse's big brown eyes, and the word came to her as if Feo had spoken it: *sacrifice*. Ashamed, she hung her head.

Papá and Miguel proved Feo's worth by balancing the family's entire supplies in two bundles secured across his flanks. She held his bridle while they worked. "Feo, I wish I was brave like you." She petted his neck till her hand brushed something crusted there, then scratched at it till a white, buttery substance came away on her fingertips. She stared. What was it?

Miguel whispered in her ear, "Brains."

"Liar!" Still, she wiped her fingers on her skirt in disgust. Then she touched her own head, marveling. Was it possible all her thoughts, and all the ideas Papá taught her—trust, honor, sacrifice—could come from contents so soft?

Papá lifted the little ones into the saddle, took the reins, and clucked at Feo, who let the man lead him. The walk went faster with Feo carrying their burdens. They followed the flats along the Río Casas Grandes, though the river meandered like a drunk with no idea where to go.

For days they looked over their shoulders, for fear they'd be followed—even her sister, because whatever Candelita did, Graciela copied. Maybe that's why they failed to spot what was right in front of them until it was too late to hide from the arrow of dust kicked up by someone's approach. Whoever it was surely saw them too; the Riveras kicked up their own cloud.

Papá held up a hand, signaling the family to stop, and squinted into the distance.

Miguel blurted, "It's a wagon!"

"Don't shout." Papá yanked off his hat and raked a hand through his hair.

The wagon headed straight for them, till they saw first the mule pulling it, then the driver. Papá warned them not to assume he was alone. "More men might be hiding under the canvas."

Once they were in shouting distance, the driver waved his cowboy hat. "¡Buenos días!" His baritone scattered the quiet like a burst of unfamiliar music.

"¡Buenas!" Papá's wave looked casual, but Mamá's eyes looked startled, and the children gawked as the sun's late-morning glare revealed the face of this strangest of strangers.

She'd never seen anyone like him. In addition to his cowboy hat, he wore a cowboy shirt and Levi's. That wasn't the unusual part. Papá used to dress like that. Sometimes he still did. What made the teamster unique was he appeared to be neither mestizo nor güero European nor Tarahumara—nor from any local tribe. His eyes squinted more than could be explained by the sun. To her, his nose seemed small, his face round, skin amber. Not ugly, just unexpected. His age, impossible to guess.

"Whoa!" The driver pulled his mule to a halt and leapt down with ease. "Benito Chung at your service." He smiled but kept his mouth shut firm as a gate as he held out a hand to Papá.

Papá matched his smile and shook his hand without hesitation, as if he'd made this decision during the wagon's approach. "Eduardo Rivera. May I present my wife, Maria?"

"Señora." The stranger removed his hat and bowed, looking somewhere near her feet.

Mamá nodded, but with the same wary stare she'd given the rattlesnake. The man didn't act threatening, but between the desert and the war it must be safer to treat everything as a threat.

"These are my children." Papá's gesture embraced his whole unblinking brood.

"Muchachos." The man's smile opened to reveal perfect white teeth. City teeth. Then his eyes landed on Feo and he frowned. Still, he said, "What luck to have such a beautiful family."

"Gracias, Señor Chung, though perhaps less lucky in such troubled times." Papá's eyes shifted between Feo and the stranger, who stared at the horse. The man looked angry, but why?

"I'd like to predict you won't meet trouble," he said, "unless you meet my friend, Señor Morales of Corralitos." He circled Feo, who still carried the little ones. Papá's eyes followed him. The caginess of the two men called to mind Rabbit and Coyote, but which was which? The stranger clapped Feo's flank, and this gesture of familiarity irritated her. To her, Feo was already family. "Morales owns a horse just like this one. If you run into him, your luck might change."

Papá picked his next words like individual notes plucked on a guitar. "We won't be crossing paths with Feo's previous owner. He was killed when the rebels arrived in Corralitos."

The stranger looked alarmed. "Rebels? In Corralitos?"

"Yes!" Miguel balled his hands into fists at his sides. "And they'll keep coming, so you should go back to where you came from before they kill you!"

Papá raised and lowered his arm like a meat cleaver. "¡Basta!" he told Miguel though his eyes remained on the stranger. "Forgive my son. We've walked a long way and we're all tired."

"No hay problema." The man chuckled at Miguel the way folks do at babies, though he looked her brother up and down as if he might yet prove dangerous: a baby scorpion maybe. "So, young man, you think I'll be safer if I go back to Juárez? That's where I came from."

Miguel clenched his jaw. "Sorry, señor, I thought you were Chinese."

Chinese! That was why he looked like that! But why did it make Miguel mad?

"I haven't lived in China for years," he told Miguel. "Mexico is my home. My wife is Mexican. My daughter is Mexican." He turned back to Papá. "So, rebels took Corralitos?"

Papá nodded. "Last night. We left before they came, but we heard the gunfire. Most of it sounded like celebration, but not all of it. Not everyone wants change, Señor Chung."

"Por favor, call me Benito."

Papá dipped his chin politely. "We've seen no one since then, until you…Benito."

What was left of Benito's smile fell apart. "This is bad news. I carry supplies for Chinese miners in the canyon. Villa hates the Chinese. This past week Villistas killed at least a dozen throughout Chihuahua. If rebels hit the mine, I'll be short a few customers. Only a man with a death-wish would deliver these supplies now." He removed his hat, slapped it against his thigh. "Who am I kidding? None of Mexico is safe, for me or my family. America doesn't want us either, now they've finished their railroads. What will I do?"

Papá placed a hand on his arm. "Is there any way we can help?"

Benito looked as if he'd just woken. "Forgive me. These are my problems, not yours. There's nothing for me to do but return to Juárez."

Graciela blurted, "We're going to Juárez! Come with us!"

"¡Cállate!" Miguel said. He cut a look at their father, who scratched his chin. "Papá, no! He'll put us in danger."

"Your son's not wrong," Benito said. "I'm Chinese, an accused thief of Mexican jobs."

Papá raised his hands as if surrendering to the air. "*We* might put *you* in danger. My family boasts two able men crossing a desert that's thirsty for war. We could attract attention."

Benito relaxed into an unguarded smile. "We're even then." He snapped his fingers as if he'd thought of something. "Maybe you need supplies?"

Mamá picked at her chapped lips. "We're sorry, we can't afford to pay."

"Good company has its own value." He shook the mule's reins. "El Presidente is a faithful friend, but he falls asleep during my stories. Let me repay your company with a meal or two."

"Do you have cheese? The Riveras like cheese." Lalo's grin was charming as ever, though Candelita knew he spoke from hunger.

"Sorry, no cheese. I have salty fish and dried plums…and plenty of rice."

Mamá crinkled her nose at Lalo. "The Riveras like rice too."

With that, they agreed to share the journey.

Papá handed her and her sister up to Benito on the buckboard. She studied his face as he sang strange words to his sleepy mule, coaxing El Presidente to turn the wagon. She decided he didn't look odd after all, almost Apache, except for the nose. He didn't seem like a thief. He had a wife and daughter. Did thieves have families? Her family had taken a horse. Were they thieves? The rebels who took Corralitos, were they?

Maybe war made thieves of everyone.

She looked down at Papá, leading the horse that now carried Mamá and Lalo. Candelita no longer felt disappointed about not riding Feo. She was more interested in the mystery of this man from a faraway land. Let Miguel scowl.

Still, what if Miguel was right? Even if Benito's intentions were good, might he get them killed simply by becoming their friend?

8. Feeding the Dead

Ching Ming Day, 1911 – Toisan County, China

Thanks to Yan Chi's brother in America, 1911 marked the first Ching Ming their father could afford a suckling pig to feed the ancestors. Yan Chi and Cousin Ning Kang lifted the palanquin that carried the piglet: a rosy-cheeked jester splayed on barbecued belly, crispy ears festooned in red ribbon, eyes seared into permanent sleep. Ning Kang held the front poles, Yan Chi the rear—knees bent to keep the pig from sliding into his shorter cousin. He saw no dignity in this procession: three dozen Wong men and boys waddling out of the village, feet caked with mud, clothes dripping, eyes blinking into a blinding rain.

Uncle Fu Ying brandished his black umbrella as if he saw himself a warrior with a sword, though at eighty he could barely hold it aloft. Other elders carried umbrellas too, hanging overhead like judgmental frowns, useless against rain that attacked from all directions. Married men carried baskets of food their wives made: roast goose, barbecued pork buns, sweet green rice balls with red bean paste. Unmarried men carried candles, incense, firecrackers—paper-wrapped against the damp. Elders swung bottles of baak zau to toast the dead.

Women stood in doorways to watch the men pass, though they all avoided eye contact with Yan Chi. Ning Kang turned to grin at his mother and skidded in the mud, sending the pig sliding forward. The tittering Zhu Zhu sisters darted out to push it back into place—any excuse to skip alongside the parade.

"Man Zhu, Ling Zhu, get back here!" their mama scolded. "Girls aren't allowed."

Back they ran.

The village faded from view as the men passed under a bower of lychee trees hunched with the weight of round red fruit. On they carried the feast to the far rice paddies. How the dead must envy us, he thought, we who can still eat, drink, and make love. Except Yan Chi had never experienced the pleasure of physical love because his waiting bride had died waiting. How I envy the dead, he thought.

The farther they got from the village, the more unruly the march. Young boys dared each other to poke the piglet without getting caught. Older boys pretended to be ghosts, tapping each other when their backs were turned, then playing innocent when startled friends turned around. Young men passed around a bottle of American whiskey.

All the while, shuffling elders issued unnecessary orders:

"Don't drop the pig!" Uncle Fu Ying called from his place in front.

"Yes, Baba," replied Ning Kang, obedient son of the patriarch.

Yan Chi's baba, moving like a slug to ensure his elder brother kept the lead, fell back with Yan Chi. "Did you sharpen the cleaver, son?"

"Oh no, was I supposed to bring a cleaver?"

"Don't act smart. You're not too old for a beating."

"No one's beating anyone," Uncle Fu Ying snapped. "Show respect for the dead."

"And for the pig, who is also dead." Yan Chi pressed a hand to his heart, causing the palanquin to tilt and the pig to slide his way.

His father slapped the back of his head.

In this fashion, they reached the paddies. Beyond, lay fallow fields. Beyond those, the cemetery. All of it—paddies, fields, cemetery—lay divided into squares by slender dirt ridges. One by one, men stepped onto a ridge and continued single file to the graves: mounds of mud topped with gray granite headstones.

They approached Ye Ye's resting place. The evening before, Mama had swept Grandpa's burial mound and laid down magenta bougainvillea and wild pink roses, but now a single white water lily joined them, adorning the headstone. Surely Mama hadn't added it. Women didn't come here on Ching Ming Day, and it wasn't the right kind of flower for a grave.

Then he heard it: the unabashed laugh of Mei Yin.

He turned toward the sound, which came from her village's graveyard at the far end of the fields. There she stood on a low rise, apart from the men: head and body rejoined, her sky-blue tunic the only brightness in the rain, silk so wet it clung to each subtle curve. Stunned, he stopped in his tracks just as Ning Kang stepped off the ridge into their ancestral plot. Not expecting the jolt, Yan Chi released his end of the palanquin all at once, catapulting the pig over his cousin's head, straight into his grandpa's grave, snout first, crushing the flowers.

Gasps went up. One old ye ye stumbled into another, who grappled the shoulder of another, who windmilled his arms, tumbling a half-dozen old men into a pile, twitching like frogs. Three small boys pitched into a paddy, clambered out covered in mud, then wrestled each other back in with a splash. Older boys from the House of Waiting Grooms guffawed, ignoring fathers who pounded the tops of their heads to shut their mouths.

Baba and Fu Ying, brothers who never touched in public, now held each other like women and gaped at the pig that straddled their father's grave in a most perverse manner.

Yan Chi returned his attention across the field where Mei Yin stood, looking from him to the pig and back, her eyes merry, mouth open wide, wispy ghost-body shaking with belly laughs. He snorted with her, till he caught Ning Kang staring at him with reproach.

In response, he crossed his arms, struck a dignified pose, and said, "Ye Ye has been waiting to eat since last Ching Ming. His hungry ghost-stomach obviously called the pig to him."

Baba raised a hand to slap him but let it drop as he and his brother collapsed against each other in hilarity. The tangled pile of elders giggled with them.

Yan Chi and Ning Kang rescued the desecrated pig, brushed off the mud as best they could, and laid the beast on its bier at the foot of the grave. Laughter died as men presented gifts to their ancestors, offerings to make the afterlife more comfortable: mouthwatering dumplings, sweet incense, whiskey to warm old bones. Candlelight guttered in the mist.

A crackle of gunfire gave him a start. Bandits! He reached for his absent rifle, ready to fight this time, but the noise was only firecrackers. Smoke engulfed him. He let loose a coughing fit, the perfect excuse to step away from the group, so he could peer across the paddies at the Ma graveyard and steal another glimpse of Mei Yin.

She'd vanished. In her place stood her brother, waving at him. Had it been him all along? Yan Chi held up a palm in reply, signaling his friend to wait for him to come pay his respects.

The two had barely spoken since Mei Yin's death. Bing Sam had spent months helping his aunt nurse his father back to health. Yan Chi had visited at first, only to feel rising within him unfair bitterness toward his friend. Nobody blamed Bing Sam. Though Gold Mountain Men had a reputation for boldness, everyone knew Bing Sam wouldn't kill a mosquito for drinking his blood. Courage was not his nature, so the eleven villages had expected little from him.

On the other hand, of all Gong Hau's men, Yan Chi was the fastest runner, strongest fighter, and only owner of a rifle from America's Wild West. He was the one they'd counted on to be the hero, so he was the one who had failed. He knew Bing Sam never blamed him, but this only increased his guilt—until he could no longer bear the sight of his loyal friend.

He returned his gaze to Ye Ye's grave, where his father cut a boiled egg in two halves to lay at the headstone, granting Ye Ye eyeballs. One half rolled Yan Chi's way, and the yolk glared up at him: *You needn't worry about being forced to marry another bride, Grandson*, the yellow eye accused. *What family would entrust a daughter to a man so careless?*

Then Baba turned to him with his knife laid across upraised palms, and for the first time, invited him to carve. Relieved to have something to do, Yan Chi knelt before the piglet, plunged the knife in its tender back, and dug in. His mouth watered at the smell of barbecued flesh.

The elders selected the choicest slices of pork for themselves. They fed the next-best tidbits to the youngest grandsons. Waiting grooms ate last. Yan Chi tossed a chunk in his mouth and bit into a piece of grit so loud he worried he'd cracked a tooth. A cough tickled his ear.

He turned, startled to see Mei Yin at his shoulder. He longed to touch her but didn't dare. What if one touch was all it took to join the dead? He was sorry she was gone, but he wasn't ready for that.

She bowed, corner of her mouth turned up in a teasing smile, and gestured to his bowl of pork as if to ask, May I?

He held out an open palm: Be my guest.

Women never took part in this ceremony, but who could say no to a ghost? He looked at the others. Did they see her too? As usual these days, everyone avoided looking his way.

She popped a glistening morsel between her lips. Her confused expression told him she too had gotten a piece mixed with graveyard grit. Like him, she kept chewing anyway, her eyes holding his. He didn't look away, not wanting to break the spell. A speck of mud clung to her lip, and her tongue poked out to lick it, as if she didn't want to miss a single delicious bite.

The dead weren't done with him yet.

9. Sand

1911 – Chihuahua, Mexico

Candelita's family came to rely on Benito Chung's familiarity with the unmarked passage to the border. They followed two crooked lines: Río Casas Grandes flowing to the left, Sierra del Capulín rolling to the right. The desert between looked smooth, but that was a trick: the wagon was rattling her nalgas black-and-blue. She held the buckboard with one hand, Graciela with the other, ready to jump if Benito tricked her too. The Chinese merchant peered into the distance with the intensity of a hawk, hunting something beyond the horizon. But what?

Her little sister frowned up at him. She knew why: Graciela wasn't used to being ignored. Without warning, he snapped his head sideways, nose close to Graciela's, and wriggled his brows. She reared back. His eyes creased with amusement.

Candelita snickered. "That's what you get for staring, apestosa."

Graciela puffed out her chest, defiant. "I like his face."

"I like your face, too," he said.

She dimpled, sidled back to his side, and tucked a hand in the pocket of his duster.

It was Candelita's turn to frown. Graciela was too forward. Candelita adored her but worried her sister's knack for getting attention would spoil her. Still, she wished she could make friends half so easily.

A week of traveling and still America was nowhere in sight, forcing her to face the truth: she had left Juliana behind forever. For now, her only options for friendship were her siblings and Benito—who remained more stranger than friend. He caught her studying him. She looked away.

"I have a daughter only three years older than you," he said.

"Oh." She pretended indifference, though she was eager to know more.

"Her name's Marcela," he said as if she'd asked.

The name sounded like music, though she was embarrassed to say so.

Graciela was never too shy to speak. "Does she have funny eyes like you?"

Candelita elbowed her.

Graciela elbowed back. "Stop it!"

He chuckled. "Marcela's eyes have a little bit of China, a little bit of Mexico."

"What's China?"

"The home where I was born."

"You left home? Like us?"

"Sí."

"Were you scared?"

"Pues, I threw up on the ride across the ocean."

Graciela started to giggle but cut herself short. "What's ocean?"

"Like the desert, but full of water instead of dirt."

She turned an astonished face to Candelita, who verified, "It's true, although I've never seen it."

Graciela wrinkled her nose. "I don't like the desert. I miss home."

"I'll tell you a secret," Benito leaned down to her. "I get homesick, too. Not for China but Juárez. Sometimes it helps if I picture what my family's doing: right now, I can see my wife stocking shelves in our shop and my daughter writing at her school-desk."

"She goes to a preparatoria?" Candelita turned to see if anyone else heard this news, but Mamá and Lalo rode ahead on Feo, and Papá and Miguel lagged behind on foot.

"You don't go to school?" Benito asked.

"I used to." She stared ahead, hoping he wouldn't ask her to explain.

He didn't, though he glanced back at her father with a sympathetic look. "Marcela's a good student. The teacher asked her to recite her last essay in front of the school: it was about the day we took supplies to the orphanage. She sounded grown up." His gaze drifted to the horizon again. "I hope they don't stop her from attending. It's my dream to see her graduate."

For a moment, the only sound was the squeak of axles beneath them. Why would someone stop Marcela from going to school? It sounded like he could afford to pay. Candelita dreaded the twin cities at the border, Juárez and El Paso, worried both cities would reveal her as the "ignorant peasant" Miguel called her. She felt an irrational dislike of Marcela, certain she would act superior like Miguel. She envied Marcela her writing, her desk, her teacher. "Do all girls at la frontera graduate?"

"Sadly no. Not all." He poked out his lower lip.

In some ways, he reminded her of her father, who also spoke of his family with pride. Unlike Papá, once he started talking he didn't stop for a long time. She didn't mind. It saved her from having to think of anything to say.

"In my village in China," he told her, "men and women don't dance together. But in Juárez, Isabel taught me to dance hand in hand. People stared, and I thought it was because I was Chinese. No, it was because her skirt twirled when she spun. Men wanted to see her legs, and women wanted to see what the fuss was about." He leaned toward her as if to speak in confidence, but his voice boomed, "I confess, I married her so I could watch her skirt twirl anytime I wanted… It was not disappointing." He threw back his head and laughed so hard his hat almost fell off.

"Why didn't your family come?" Graciela asked.

He exchanged a look with Candelita over her sister's head, a look that said, *Nobody* should be out here. But all he said was, "My family's happier at home."

"I never go without my family." Graciela leaned her head against Candelita, who couldn't suppress an indulgent smile.

"Someday you'll make your own family. Then who knows where you'll go?" He rested a palm atop her head, cupping it like an egg.

Candelita understood then: it was his own daughter's head Benito was trying to pat, his own daughter's face he kept trying to find, staring past the horizon where war lurked, all the way to the border, where everything was about to end or begin. He talked on and on till the sun lowered toward afternoon. Then the desert did something she thought it could never do.

It changed.

The quiet sounded wrong. Juliana used to say the desert was dead as a graveyard, but Candelita had come to sense its wing-flapping and paw-scurrying, its breathing burrows and shifting earth. All those stirrings ceased. Her father approached the wagon to exchange a baffled look with Benito, who jerked El Presidente to a stop. Papá ran ahead and slipped Feo's reins from Mamá's slack hands. Everyone stilled to listen, even Graciela. Candelita wasn't sure what they expected to hear, but she felt an urgent need to pee.

Then Benito pointed to the southwestern horizon, where, by some trick, the desert was pouring upward into the sky. He exhaled a word she'd never heard before, "Puk gaai!"

"*¡Mierda!*" swore Miguel. She knew that one. *Shit.*

Papá's shout left no doubt: "Sandstorm!" He couldn't hide the horror in his eyes as an approaching wind commanded the desert floor to rise.

Benito flung the girls down from the wagon into Papá's arms. Mamá slid off Feo and lifted Lalo down. His eyes burned with excitement, as if this were the best thing to happen to them instead of the worst.

Miguel ran back and forth, yelling, "¡Apúrate! Apúrate!" though not suggesting to what they might apply this hurry.

Papá grabbed him and shook him. "Stop screaming like a girl. Time to be a man." He dragged Miguel to the wagon's rear, pausing mid-drag to point a finger at her. "Wait here!"

She stood paralyzed, clutching the little ones to her. Graciela pressed into her as if to burrow under her ribs while Lalo tried to pull free as if eager to run toward the wall of sand. Mamá reached into her pack, pulled out a bundle of bandanas, and helped the children tie them over their noses and mouths, masking them like bandits.

Miguel returned with a folded tarp and shouted to Candelita, "Follow me!"

She followed him to the riverbank, dragging the little ones, leaning into a growing wind that threatened to roll them all away with the tumbleweeds. She looked back at her parents, afraid to lose them. Mamá flung a faded red skirt—her only spare—at Feo's head like a matador. The horse fretted and reared till the skirt fell over his eyes. Then, as if blindness were a love charm, he nuzzled her and let her lead him to shelter under a clutch of cottonwoods on the bank.

Papá and Benito pulled and pushed El Presidente, to no avail. Papá broke a tree branch and whipped him. Candelita flinched. She'd never seen him hit an animal before. It worked. The mule lurched forward, pulling the wagon to the trees. They unhitched him to huddle next to Feo.

"¡Venga!" Miguel called up to her from the riverway below. "Don't just stand there!"

His words broke her trance. She and the little ones skidded downslope to the water's edge.

He handed her a corner of the windblown tarp. "Hold tight!"

She tried, but the tarp was ripped from her hands. Startled, she looked up to see Benito had grabbed her end.

"Not the riverbed!" he shouted as he tried to pull the other end away from Miguel.

Miguel yanked it back, his face as tight as his fists. "We have to stay out of the wind!"

A tug-of-war ensued. She was transfixed by the tarp, sure the wind would take it.

"Think!" Benito said. "A sandstorm can hide rain. Rain can cause floods. We need high ground."

"What do you know, foreigner?"

"I've lived in Mexico longer than you've been alive."

She looked from one to the other. Would it be wrong to side against her own brother?

Lalo made his choice: joined Benito at his end of the tarp and pulled. "Miguel, let go!"

Once Lalo chose sides, Graciela charged Miguel, slapping and pushing. "Give it to Lalo!"

Miguel locked eyes with Candelita, his rage replaced by silent pleading. For once, she felt sorry for him. But, despite Miguel's education, the grownup made more sense to her. She joined Lalo and Benito, pulling hard. Miguel's shoulders sagged and he let go.

They followed Benito and the tarp back up the bank, past her parents—who seemed to be dancing. Papá held Mamá's arm as she swung in wild circles around him. What were they doing? At a low rise in the otherwise flat terrain, Benito stopped to snap open the tarp. He instructed them to sit in a circle, tucking the edges under their rears to create a pocket of air between them and the thickening dust. Then he left them!

She blinked at the three silhouettes of her siblings.

"Don't like the dark," Graciela said.

"Is there a lamp?" Lalo asked.

"Estúpido," Miguel said, "a flame will eat the air so we can't breathe."

"Maybe I'm stupid today, but you're a cabrón every day," Lalo said.

"Hush!" Candelita said. "You're using all the air."

She pictured them all lying here come morning, eyes bulging, suffocated to death.

A corner of canvas lifted, and grit stung her eyes. Benito crawled in with rocks to hold down the cloth. Papá ducked in behind him, dragging Mamá. Moments ago, their mother had acted confident in the face of the coming storm. Now she thrashed, moaned, and yelled, "I won't be buried alive!" She clawed free, yanked open the tarp, and flung herself into the fury. Graciela darted after her. Candelita, sure the wind would toss her tiny sister into the sky, took chase.

She emerged into a world split in two: half of it naked blue sky, the other half billowing brown clouds. Mamá tilted toward the wagon, carrying Graciela. Candelita parted wind with her arms as if swimming. She understood what had driven her mother into the open: the tarp felt like a trap. Out here, despite flaying dust and flying branches, she could distinguish between dark in one direction and light in the other, could hope to escape what she could still see.

Mamá, in command again, hurled Graciela into the wagon's rear and then beckoned Candelita. Mamá stood firm, feet planted, knees bent, as if she'd stand there forever if that was how long her elder daughter needed to reach her. Candelita couldn't resist one last look over her shoulder. She'd never seen the ocean, but here was her first wave, a tidal wave of sand about to swallow them whole. It was exhilarating, and the reason she would distrust beauty ever after, because of the deadly power it could hide. She lurched into outstretched arms, Mamá launched her inside, Candelita hauled up Mamá in turn, and together they wrestled the flap shut behind them.

They were tucking themselves among crates and sacks, when the rear flap opened again to reveal Miguel. His mouth opened wide, shouting, but they couldn't hear him over the wind.

He scrambled inside and screamed in their faces, "It's not safe in here! The wind—"

"I can't go back!" Mamá said.

They were still arguing when the wagon bucked, gave a thunderous crack, tipped onto two wheels, and flung Candelita into the air, along with two questions: *Will I die?* and *How much will it hurt?* The next instant was chaos, though later she swore she could see Graciela's squeezed-shut eyelashes, the yellow fringe on Mamá's blue rebozo, the spray of blood from Miguel's nose as a can struck it. She bounced into canvas, bit her tongue, got smacked in the eye, and flopped to earth. Sticky liquid oozed down her forehead. Blood? She rubbed it away and squinted at her fingertips: not red but gold. What was it?

"Are you alive, queridas?!" Mamá pulled a stunned Graciela from a jumble of jars. Two broken ones leaked the same liquid-gold Candelita wiped from her eyes. It smelled sweet.

She licked a finger, held it up, and burst out laughing. "It's honey!"

Nobody else laughed.

A string of curses behind a barrel announced Miguel was still alive. "I told you!"

"Nobody asked you to follow us," she said.

He ducked his head out the rear flap, shouted, "¡Chingado!" and started to climb out into a flickering black-and-blue blur. Grains of sand flew inside, stinging her skin like broken glass.

She grabbed his heel to haul him back. "You'll be killed!"

He yelled in her ear, "They're going the wrong way!" Then his eyes lit with a revelation. He dug into his pocket, pulled out a flash of silver, put it to his lips, and leaned outside to blow a long, high-pitched note into the storm's roar. The whistle he'd won at the Grito de Dolores festival. He blew and blew, until a creature made of sand climbed into the felled wagon.

Lalo! Graciela threw her arms around his neck. Papá and Benito followed. A horsetail of dust swatted them all before they lashed the flap shut.

Everyone shifted to make room for each other in the tumbled, broken, shrunken space. Miguel sat as far as possible from Benito, who moved a box to make a seat for Mamá. The dim light darkened from amber to charcoal.

Mamá removed Graciela's bandana and doused it with water from her gourd. "I'm going to cover your eyes."

Graciela pushed it away. "I want to see!"

Mamá pushed back. "Soon it'll be too dark to see and angry sand will come in."

Graciela gave in and let Mamá wrap the wet bandana around her eyes, nose, and mouth. Like a mummy. Everyone followed her lead, binding their heads in darkness.

Candelita wanted to cry, but other sensations crowded out tears: her aching eye socket, skin sticky with sand and honey, suffocating cloth sucking in and out of her mouth. She couldn't hear her family, only the screeching wind. One astonishing gust sent the wagon sliding at least a foot. Arms enfolded her, and she recognized the ropy muscles were Papá's. He squeezed too tight, but she resisted the urge to squirm free, terrified a current would lasso her and toss her into the sudden night, alone. If death took her, she wanted Papá to come too—she didn't care if it was selfish.

Time stopped, but the storm didn't. It shoveled sand around them like a gravedigger. Maybe they were already dead. That would be so sad, she thought, just when she was getting excited about going to the cities at the border, where sometimes girls finished school.

10. The Kei Lun

Ching Ming Night, 1911 –Toisan County, China

Yan Chi stopped at the intersection of the village paths, before the pale outstretched arms of the banyan tree, and cocked his ear to the insect murmur of night. That's when he heard the straw shoes skitter to a halt behind him. If he didn't believe in ghosts before, now he—wondered. Mei Yin had followed him all day.

This time he didn't look back, not sure whether he hoped she'd be there or not. He looked up at the sky, but rainclouds once again hid their constellation: the Cowherd and Weaver Girl, separated by the Silver River. Her breath parted the air near his ear, whispering without words, asking him not to leave.

But it was *she* who'd left *him*! Angry, he turned to confront her.

He didn't see her this time, only smelled her. She always smelled of rain—but then it always rained at Ching Ming. He scolded the relentless mist: "Why did you return to your father's house before our wedding? Why didn't you stay in the House of Waiting Brides like other girls?"

She gave no reply. Maybe he was sleepwalking. How would he know the difference? He tried to shake himself awake. Everything looked the same. He walked on. The footsteps resumed following. Each time he stopped, they stopped. Each time he continued, so did they. His heart would have led him on in any case: to the Git Ngon graveyard, where Mei Yin lay buried in two pieces, head forever separated from her body.

Her grave was easy to find, covered in more offerings than the graves of ancestors who had achieved ripe old age. This wasn't a measure of her standing in the Ma village, he knew, but of her family's fear she might haunt them as a hungry ghost, bitter over her unlucky life. Flowers, egg yolks, tea, fruit, the ash and tallow of burnt candles and incense, laid in rows like bribes. He pushed aside a bundle of joss sticks and knelt. The mud soaked his pants and chilled his knees.

He traced a finger over her name, engraved above four words: "respectful daughter, loyal sister." Nowhere did it say, "raped fiancée, murdered bride." As far as the future would know, she'd never been his beloved. As far as the present was concerned, her death was a mercy. If she had lived, her lost maidenhood would have shamed not only her but also her family, village, and groom. He understood why people could blame their loved ones for suffering a bad fate: it frightened them less than admitting they had no control over their own lives.

Her headstone should have felt cold in the night air, but it radiated heat. "Mei Yin?" he rasped. He heard rustling and held his breath in case she answered. Then . . . nothing. He closed his eyes to pray, in his own fashion, a prayer without words, only an image: Mei Yin leaping across the Milky Way, from star to star, moving toward him. She was laughing. He heard it, not gentle as rain but shameless as thunder. He longed to touch her, to taste her, to enter her. To reclaim the wedding night the bandits stole from them. The smell of rain on her skin overwhelmed him. He opened his eyes.

That's when he saw it, crouched atop her gravestone. The Kei Lun.

He told himself it was a hallucination. Then why did he feel the heat when it opened its mouth and roared a roiling spout of fire? Why did he feel a rush of air when its thick ox tail whipped behind it? Yan Chi's ban zau shriveled at the sight of long, sharp, yellow teeth circling the beast's cavernous mouth. Its gold mane flared a warning. The night flashed with its shimmering blue dragon scales and blood-red tongue. The Kei Lun's eyes glowed like twin fires as it leapt off the gravestone toward him.

He ran away, fast as he could, and left Mei Yin behind.

He splashed through rice paddies and tripped across muddy fields, falling more than once. But he didn't slow to a walk until homes came into sight.

He'd finally done right by his lost bride, leaving her alone in the graveyard where she belonged. He understood now: by dying before she married him, she'd escaped a lonely fate. Because, much as he loved her, deep down he'd always intended to leave.

The Kei Lun was a protector of the kind-hearted, who only pursued evil men. The Kei Lun had come for him.

He turned to look back the way he'd come. Both Kei Lun and Mei Yin were gone. He was alone. Maybe that wasn't a curse, like everyone else thought. Maybe it was an open door.

He hunched over his knees to catch his breath, then looked up to see where his feet had carried him. Not back to his village but Mei Yin's village, to her father's Western style mansion, to stand before its majestic double doors perched with painted birds. Not to see her father but her brother. Bing Sam was his natural ally for what he must do next.

The time had come to talk to his friend, to remind him he had a full life ahead even if his father didn't. Old Mr. Ma still suffered headaches, ringing in one ear, and difficulty moving his left arm where the bandits tore his shoulder. Yan Chi was sorry for his misfortune, but it left an opening for him: to accompany Bing Sam to America in his father's place.

He strode up to the oversized doors, lifted one of the gold rings, and knocked. Though the house stood two fat stories tall, the right-hand door flew open in almost no time. Bing Sam stepped out of the dark house in a rumpled robe, finger to his lips, and gently shut the door behind him. Despite his crazed hair, he looked wide awake. But he remained silent and led Yan Chi to the Git Ngon village pond, so they could talk without waking anyone. Yan Chi raised a brow. "Waiting up for someone?"

"Only for sleep. It takes longer to arrive than before."

"That makes sense." For the first time since he'd cradled Mei Yin's severed head in his arms, he looked his friend in the eyes. When had they grown dull as an old man's eyes?

Bing Sam cleared his throat. "Why have you come at this hour? Is everything all right?"

"No. Nothing has been right for a year. I've become a ghost…or less than that. At Ching Ming people talk to their ghosts, but nobody in Gong Hau speaks to me since your sister died."

"Don't you think I know that? It's the same for me."

"It is?" How had he failed to notice this?

"I was at the cave too, remember?"

"But nobody blames you."

"Maybe not. But they're afraid of catching my bad luck."

Yan Chi nodded understanding. "Then I propose we give them what they want."

"Which is?"

"For us to leave the eleven villages and take our bad luck with us."

"Where will we go?"

He gave Bing Sam an astonished look. "America of course."

"You forget, we've lost everything. And the wui gun will never lend to us again. Where will we get money for our passage?"

"I've decided to take my inheritance early." He braced himself, ready for objections.

Instead, Bing Sam folded his arms and said, "I'm listening."

Yan Chi wasn't sure his plan would work, only that he must answer Gold Mountain's call. What would he do when he got there? Who cared? Anything must be better than wasting his life here, trudging muddy fields that didn't yield enough food, watching from a lonely tower for bandits who didn't return, waiting for redemption that never came.

11. In the Wagon

1911 – Chihuahua, Mexico

The wind fell to an unsettling hum, like notes on an untuned guitar. In the dark, Candelita heard coughs and groans, then a snap and hiss, followed by the smell of a burnt match. Padre Eladio said hell stank like that. She tugged her bandana from her eyes, revealing Mamá's face haloed in the glow of a lantern—which explained the lit match. Benito set the lantern on a box and turned up the flame till it smoked. Her family's faces were a shocked patchwork of dirt, surrounded by dented cans and broken bottles. She smiled. If this was hell, at least they were together.

Papá looked from Benito to Miguel, his face stern. "Miguel, apologize to Señor Chung."

Miguel looked down. "Sorry I kicked you when you wouldn't let me out of the tarp. I understand you only wanted to protect me… Señor Chung."

Benito nodded. "You only wanted to reach your mother and sisters. And you saved us."

She hadn't thought of that. If not for Miguel's stupid whistle, Papá, Benito, and Lalo might've been lost forever.

"Can we go outside?" Graciela asked.

"When the sun returns," Benito said.

Graciela set her elbows on her thighs and her cheeks on her fists. "Tell us a story!"

He chuckled, the way people always did before they knew her sister's demands were serious. Then he leaned back to study his battered audience.

They leaned toward him, musky with fear, waiting for him to deliver escape.

"Pues entonces…" Benito folded his hands between his knees and began: "One moonless night long ago, the stars shined so bright they could see each other from far across the sky. That night a girl star and boy star fell in love at first sight. Now, it was against the rules of heaven for stars to marry. How would travelers find their way at night if stars ran away, paired up, and gave birth to new stars?

"Well, word of their forbidden love reached the girl's grandma, the powerful Queen of Heaven. Furious, she flung her granddaughter's lover to earth as a shooting star."

"I've seen those!" Lalo said. "Mamá says they're God's spears. He throws them at the devil's snakes to stop them from making storms and wars."

"Your mamá is wise. And most of the time those shooting stars *are* God's spears. But this time, it was a boy star being punished by the Queen of Heaven."

"Is she the Blessed Virgin?" Graciela asked.

"It's a story," Miguel said. "It's not real."

Couldn't her family ever shut up? "What happened to the stars?" Candelita asked.

"Good question. After he fell to earth, the boy star was reborn a mortal. He became second son to a farmer and wife and forgot his old life in the sky. Meanwhile, the queen punished the girl star. She made her work at a loom day and night, weaving colorful silk into clouds."

"Like red and purple clouds at sunset," Candelita interrupted without thinking, then clapped both hands over her mouth.

"¡Exactamente!" They all stifled grins at Benito's Chinese accent.

"When the boy's parents grew old and died, he stayed with his elder brother and his brother's wife, working as a cowherd on the family farm. But the brothers fought a lot, until the older brother threw him out."

"I can imagine that," Lalo said.

Miguel bumped his shoulder. "So can I." They both laughed.

Benito smirked as if he knew all about brothers. "The elder brother refused to give the Cowherd anything except an old ox and a broken-down cart. Luckily, the Cowherd had saved enough coins to buy a tiny plot of land. The ox helped him plow it, and together they grew rice till the Cowherd could afford a herd of cows all his own."

Benito paused as the canvas rustled and snapped in the wind. Then he continued, "Time passes differently in heaven. For the Weaver Girl, only a few lonely days had gone by. Then a group of fairies decided to fly to the mortal world to bathe in Bi Lian Lake. The fairies pitied the Weaver Girl, so they begged the queen to give her a holiday. The queen, who loved her granddaughter really, decided she'd punished her enough and let her go with them.

"That same day, for the first time, much to the Cowherd's astonishment, the Ox spoke! You see, he used to be a star too, and when the Cowherd fell to earth, he'd followed to look after him. 'Master,' Ox said, 'Go to Bi Lian Lake. You'll find fairies bathing there. They'll leave their dresses on a rock. Take the red one. The fairy who owns it will be your bride.'

"The Cowherd was lonely for human company. So, trusting his faithful Ox, he walked to the lake, hid amid the trees, and waited. As Ox predicted, fairies flew down from the sky."

"What did they look like?" Candelita asked.

"They had wings in every color of the rainbow," Benito said, "with dresses to match. Once they landed, they took off the dresses, set them on a rock, and waded into the lake."

She bit back a grin. She used to swim naked with the other children of Mata Flores in the stream that fed the acequia.

"While the fairies splashed and laughed, the Cowherd snuck out from the trees, snatched the red dress, and darted back to hide. But he stepped on a branch, it snapped, and they spotted him. A man had seen them! They grabbed their dresses in a panic and flew back to heaven"—he smiled at Candelita—"rising from the lake like butterflies, till only the Weaver Girl remained.

"The Cowherd still had her dress, so she was embarrassed to get out of the water. Then they caught one another's eyes, saw the starlight there, and instantly recognized each other.

"The Cowherd's memories returned. He said, 'I'll give back your dress, if you'll be my wife.'

"The Weaver Girl cried tears of joy. 'When I saw you fall in a blaze of fire, I thought I'd never see you again. Of course I'll be your wife.' He handed her the dress, and she put it on as she rose from the water.

"'But how will we hide from the queen?' he asked.

"'She's not interested in Earth. She'll never find us here.'"

Candelita gasped, but no one else reacted. Couldn't they tell the lovers were doomed?

"Life on Earth was happy for the Cowherd and his Weaver Girl. They had a son and daughter and lived a peaceful life as humble farmers, until one day…" He took a deep breath.

"What happened?!" Graciela asked.

Benito looked at her as if he'd forgotten she was there. He hesitated, then hurried on, "As I said, time passes differently in heaven, where only a few days had gone by. When the queen's granddaughter failed to return, she sent soldiers to catch her."

"Soldiers catch boys, not girls." Graciela sounded proud to know something he didn't.

Benito turned to Mamá, his face stricken. "I'm sorry, I wasn't thinking…"

Candelita sat up, willing her mother to say, *No more, you'll scare the children.*

Instead, Mamá sat back in defeat, sending a jar rolling. Her face suggested the Rivera family story would always come down to this: as little as they had, there'd always be too much to lose. She smiled sadly, "It's a good story, Benito. Please tell us how it ends."

He tried to retrace the magical hush of the fairytale world, but it was gone. The wind hissed as he pressed on, "The Cowherd was in the fields when soldiers broke into the house, grabbed the Weaver Girl, and dragged her into the sky. They left her children behind, crying.

"'Help!' she called.

"The Cowherd looked up and saw her. He got his cart, loaded the children, and hooked up his friend the Ox. Ox ran up the sky as the Cowherd shouted, 'Weaver Girl, wait for me!'

"The children cried, 'Mama!'"

Graciela clasped her hands together as if to will a happy ending.

If they'd been sitting around the hearth at home, Candelita would've been eager to hear the ending, happy or not. Here in this wagon, she felt only dread. She wanted to cover her sister's ears, to protect her from what was coming.

"The cart drew closer. The Cowherd reached for his wife. But the queen pulled a pin from her hair and sliced the sky in two, tearing a rift between the Weaver Girl and her family. The rift filled with stars and became the great Silver River—what you call the Milky Way. The family cried out to each other from opposite shores. The river was too vast to swim across."

Mamá pulled Graciela onto her lap. Graciela tolerated this with an annoyed frown, too young to understand the story was real. Which it was, no matter what Miguel said.

"The gods pitied the family torn apart. Even the queen regretted her harshness, but she was too proud to set them free. Instead, she turned them back into stars and let them meet once a year, on the seventh day of the seventh month. That day, countless magpies fly over the Silver River, wingtip-to-wingtip, forming a bridge for the Cowherd to cross and join his Weaver Girl."

Mamá nodded. "The Silver River. Yes, I see. I'll never again look at the Milky Way without thinking of your story." She pressed a knuckle to the corner of one wet eye.

Papá pulled her to him and kissed her hair. He grinned at Benito. "Don't worry. She loves stories that make her cry."

Graciela frowned. "He sees her only one day?"

"Just one day," Benito sighed.

"Better than nothing," Lalo said, throwing open his arms in surrender.

Miguel snorted, threw himself back against a lumpy bag, and closed his eyes to nap.

Candelita stayed upright against a crate, wide awake in the guttering lamplight, listening for the wind to stop. She felt acutely aware of her family around her: a fist against her thigh, foot against her neck, head against her belly. The wagon was crowded, but she welcomed every kick, scratch, and poke. How would it feel to be separated from these people by a river for eternity?

She thought she heard wings fluttering, but it was only the sound of more sand settling on the pile heaped against the tipped-over wagon.

12. SS *Siberia*

1911 – Pacific Ocean

Yan Chi always expected to hear the splash when they dumped a body overboard. He heard nothing except the steam-engine chug of the SS *Siberia* carrying the living onward across the Pacific. *Peaceful Ocean*, that's what Americans called it too. But there are many kinds of peace.

After the first three deaths, fewer men bothered showing up on deck to pay last respects. Now, another storm was brewing, his second on this journey. So, this time he watched alone as the body flew into the dark and vanished. Some said it was disrespectful to toss the dead in the sea without shrouds, but what did it matter? Sharks would eat them either way.

Was it only last night Bing Sam died of fever? It seemed years ago. They shared no parting words, his friend too far gone before they knew it was the end. Yan Chi had held his hot, limp hand as his final breath hissed free. Three more days and they would've arrived in San Francisco together. Now he must face immigration authorities alone.

Night and day, rough seas or calm, he rehearsed the story he would tell them: *I am an American citizen. I was born in San Francisco, California in 1890.*

To make this journey, he'd become what he feared: a bandit. Whenever his brother sent money home, his father hid it in case of raiders, tucked in a tin candy-box under the ancestral altar below the stairs. Yan Chi raided the box to pay for both his passage and Bing Sam's. To his dismay, Baba's savings weren't enough to buy papers declaring him the son of a Gold Mountain Man. No matter. Tsi Chaum said the Great San Francisco Fire meant opportunity for a bold liar.

So Yan Chi prepared to be bold: *My birth certificate was lost in the Great Fire of 1906.*

He'd lost count of the bodies tossed overboard. Four weeks ago, they'd sailed from Hong Kong with 800 passengers, some 200 of them in steerage, a village of voices competing with the hissing boilers. Now the boilers sounded louder and the hold felt less crowded, maybe because seasick men didn't talk much or because passengers ate so many sacks of food—but also because at least a dozen, maybe dozens, had died. Of what? Doctors wouldn't say.

"He didn't drink enough tea," one experienced traveler said when Bing Sam fell ill. After that, Yan Chi choked down cup after cup of tea, though most of it came back up.

He'd hoped to get used to the stink of vomit and human waste, to the perpetual roll of the waves. But no. Only the rats remained eager to gnaw at sacks and crates of rancid vegetables, fruits, and grains. Two men with advanced knife-throwing skills made a sport of hunting them. Still the rats multiplied, fat and bold, while around them men grew thin.

One raindrop pelted him, then another. He hugged his shoulders toward icy ears, stared at the heaving burial ground of the sea, and pondered the strangest American word Bing Sam taught him: freedom. Nausea gripped him and he retched over the side, his first taste of freedom flavored with sea-spray and bile. The Chinese word for "freedom" was zi yau, "following the wishes of self." One paid for such pleasure. His first payment: survive the voyage. His next: lie.

My parents are merchants. They used to own a grocery and dry goods store in Chinatown.

No self-respecting Toisanese man would run from a little rain, but the rising wind lifted muscular waves that slugged the ship like a prizefighter. His gorge rose again. The rocking would decrease below decks. He careened to the hatch, climbed down the ladder into the hold, and teetered between groaning men to his own cramped bunk.

He grabbed his Western bowler hat and hung it over the air-vent. Usually, that vent relieved the hot stench of steerage, but during storms its draft left him aching cold. He crawled under the thin, wet blanket and hugged it to him, body rigid in one constant shiver. He considered unlocking his trunk to pull out his brother's old American suit-jacket, but then it might grow as mildewed as the clothes he now wore. In case he made it to America, he needed that suit to support his story.

My father's name is Wong Wing Chung and my mother's name is Fong Lai Syut. They left San Francisco before the Great Earthquake and Great Fire.

The slightest shift hurt him, all bone and brittle angles. He didn't dare guess how much weight he'd lost. He scratched, head to crotch and back again, raking open pus-oozing scabs. He had cut off his braided queue and shaved his head to get rid of the lice, though his skin crawled with the maddening certainty they lingered.

If he were going to die, he wished he could do it alone, away from this stinking, puking horde. If only he could sleep. He grabbed the spare pants from his bundle to pillow his head, but ended up pulling the legs over his ears to muffle the shameless weeping of a nearby bunkmate. Yan Chi gave him a baleful stare, until the man's red-rimmed eyes met his and he fell silent. "Never show weakness in front of other passengers," Bing Sam, of all people, had advised. "Some will steal the jacket off your back."

Most men huddled in trios and slept in shifts, guarding each other's possessions. He and Bing Sam alone had bunked without a third, because they trusted no one else. As expected, Bing Sam's father had declined to come, because he could no longer afford a second-class ticket and wasn't well enough to sail below decks. Now he'd never see his son again.

Would Yan Chi ever see his father again?

My parents went to China to visit family, and they planned to return to San Francisco. But after the Great Fire, they had nothing to return to.

The last storm had dumped a foot of water into steerage, and he'd swallowed more than his share. He considered lying on the floor this time, mouth open like a fish to welcome the flood. A fisherman once told him drowning was a peaceful way to die. He couldn't see how. The ocean was a wild beast. Maybe Kei Lun still chased him, eager to swallow him alive.

A small fire flared deeper in the hold, then another, and another. It was against the rules to light cook-fires anywhere besides galley or deck, or to cook at all during a storm. But a few men remained hungry despite this bucking beast, and they sneered at such rules. Wet wood choked the hold with smoke, wracking him with coughs till he grew desperate for air.

He staggered to his feet and stumbled up the ladder to the wave-pummeled deck. He slid several feet through slick water till he slammed into a pipe, wrapped his arms round it, and held on. The seesawing deck increased his nausea. The man who'd booked his passage on the Pacific Mail Line had bragged, "The SS *Siberia*'s grand size, superior hull construction, and bilge keels guarantee no motion sickness." He'd been seasick twenty-nine days. He never used to believe sick people who claimed they wanted to die. Now he knew it was no lie.

Not that *he* wanted to die. Did he? He had a new life to look forward to. Didn't he?

My father sent me to China for a Chinese education when I was a boy. That's why I don't speak much English. I'm returning to San Francisco to rebuild my father's dream.

What if he failed to build anything? Tsi Chaum always made their parents proud. Yan Chi only ever threatened them with shame.

Stealing their savings was the least of it. As second son, he was expected to work the land, take care of his parents in old age, and provide grandchildren. Instead, he'd not only left home but also failed to get married before doing so. Unmarried Chinese women rarely emigrated to America, except those sold as prostitutes. By going to America without leaving behind a pregnant bride, he was abandoning his duty to continue the Wong line. Till he remedied this, his name would sink deeper than the ocean.

What good was a man without his name? However far he ran, the Kei Lun would pursue him.

He closed his eyes and, just to see how it felt, let go of the pole with one hand, momentarily weightless as the deck bobbed beneath him, then caught the pole in his other hand. He did it again: grasp, release, grasp, release. A wave opened overhead, the jaws of a beast. Freezing water soaked him, salt gagged him, the Kei Lun sucked him into its maw—then let him go. He looked down and laughed at himself. All four limbs were wrapped around the pole.

So. Seemed he did not wish to die.

"Are you crazy?!" The shout sounded far away, but he opened his eyes to a Chinese face inches from his. The crewman had tied a rope round his waist, tethered to the deck like a dog.

"No!" Yan Chi shouted. "Not crazy. Just learning about freedom."

The crewman's mouth moved again, but Yan Chi heard nothing over the Kei Lun's roar. The man scowled, grabbed him around the middle, and dragged him across the deck. Yan Chi kicked and punched, once, twice, then gave up in exhaustion. The man tossed him down the hatch, where he fell into the compartment with a splash.

He rose to his feet, dripping resignation, sloshed through ankle-deep water, and slouched against a pillar. There he eavesdropped on conversations that bounced from bunk to bunk, the hum and bumble of flies trapped in a jar.

"I hear some men still pay for everything with gold."

"Where?"

"San Francisco."

"Nonsense."

"Where're you going?"

"El Paso. I'm taking the train."

"My father helped build that railroad."

"My father died building that railroad."

How many would get into America? How many get sent back? Some had bribed ship's officers for crew identification cards. Would anyone believe one ship needed so many crew? That was *their* problem. His was convincing immigration agents of his particular lie.

The Sing Fat Bazaar stands where the cable cars pass, on the corner of California Street and Grant Avenue, not far from the Shanghai Low Café.

A few young men pulled out tiny scrolls and muttered to themselves, memorizing their coaching papers. They claimed to be sons of Chinese American citizens or sons of legal immigrants with wives in China. When husbands visited grass widows back home but produced no sons, they often claimed they did anyway. If they produced one, they claimed two. They sold the names of those nonexistent sons to the highest bidders: paper sons like these.

His weepy bunkmate recited his paper story till Yan Chi knew it by heart: "We have no bamboo in my village. But a bamboo grove grows behind the hill at Jeung Bin village."

Yan Chi bought no name. Not only was it costly, it required too much memorizing: the village layout, what the family home looked like, names of cousins, grandparents, neighbors, what they looked like, what crops they grew, how many chickens they kept. His brother didn't live as a Wong in America but as the paper son of a man he'd never met. He'd memorized a fake life and regurgitated it for hours of interrogation. Telling the right story made him American.

Such a risk was not for Yan Chi. The trick to lying was to keep it simple:

I returned to China as a boy, so I'm unfamiliar with San Francisco's changes since the fire. But my brother's last letter says a new building went up near our store. He says it looks like a pagoda.

He didn't recite aloud like the others, only in his head. His inward stare must have looked like sorrow, because his weepy bunkmate waded over, handed him a bowl of rice, and walked away before he could thank him. No one else approached him all night, perhaps fearing he carried the bad luck that killed his friend. The only friend he'd ever had. He choked down a sob, lest the bunkmate return to express concern—he could only stand so much charity.

He went to his bunk for chopsticks, lifted the bowl, forced down a few grains, and swallowed. Rice lurched back up. He clenched his jaw, swallowed again, took another bite. He'd come too far to give up. That would dishonor Bing Sam, who gave his life for this voyage.

His grief-stricken friend would never have come if not for him. Bing Sam had understood his need to get away and agreed it would be best to go together. "You may be smarter than me," he'd said, "but you shouldn't meet America alone. It's indeed a Beautiful Country, but not always what it seems. You'll need a friend who knows what lies beneath."

I am an American citizen. I was born in San Francisco, California in 1890... He repeated the lie until he *remembered* America, a traveler homesick for a country he'd never seen, an imposter the Kei Lun wouldn't recognize, a stranger he himself did not know.

13. The Shout

1911 – Chihuahua, Mexico

Where were the people who lived in this town? Candelita sat tall on the buckboard, peering through thready bean vines to one side of the wagon, down malnourished corn rows to the other. Ascención's tumble of farms looked abandoned, yet she felt convinced the residents were hiding. She didn't say so, mostly to avoid waking Graciela, who never knew when to keep quiet and would surely attract attention.

Lalo, astride Feo with Mamá, was the one who spoke, "It feels like someone's watching."

"Of course someone's watching," said Miguel, walking with Papá. "We're strangers."

"Every town's like this now," Benito said, "ever since Diaz' men murdered the Serdán brothers in Puebla. For weeks, everyone's been waiting for the next shot to be fired. Last time I stopped here, people said thirty years of Diaz is enough and they're glad the revolution has come. They just don't want it to come here."

"The revolution started weeks ago?" Papá asked.

"Who knows when any war starts?" Benito said.

Mamá wrestled Feo's reins to keep him from prancing side-to-side. The horse seemed eager to turn back. "Let's not stop here, viejo."

Papá looked up at Benito on the buckboard. "You think Ascención is safe?"

Benito sniffed the air. "I don't think war's come here yet."

Candelita wondered what he was smelling for. Gunpowder? Fire? Blood?

Papá shrugged at Mamá. "We need food."

Benito shared his supplies without restraint, assuring them that, despite all he lost in the sandstorm, he had more than he needed. But he didn't try to talk Papá out of buying more. Mamá once explained to her that men preferred to stand on their own. Candelita didn't get it. She liked depending on others, though she didn't like *others* depending on *her*. She wished she could switch places with Graciela, who she was expected to protect even when she herself felt scared.

They dropped off Feo, El Presidente, and the wagon at a livery on the plaza's edge. The plaza sat empty except for two old vaqueros in cowboy hats gossiping on a bench. A bell atop an adobe church swayed in the stiff breeze, clanging a fretful tune into a cloud-whipped sky. Papá and the boys planned to head to the nearby grain-and-feed store. Meanwhile, Benito, Mamá, and the girls would visit the general store across the plaza.

First, Mamá reached into the horse's saddlebag, pulled out Papá's silver spurs, and handed them to him, her face rigid. He snatched them and stalked away, little loops and wheels chiming where they dangled from his fingers. She recalled the day she sat on a fence to watch, full of pride, as Papá trotted a horse into the ring, kicked those wheels into its flanks, and shouted, "¡Arre, arre!" coaxing the horse to a gallop. Those days were over. She wondered how much the spurs were worth. They must be valuable for Papá to look so sad.

Candelita asked Benito why he wanted to shop with the girls and not the boys. He said he hoped to sell some things at the general store, "At least, my less Chinese things." She understood why he added that. Though she loved the way his dried plums puckered her mouth—salty, sweet, and sour all at once—he'd had to coax her to try them because they were unfamiliar.

They stepped from the bright day into the dim shop—Benito, Mamá, Graciela, and her—and halted in momentary blindness. She blinked at the sight of a ghost behind the counter until her eyes adjusted to reveal he was an ordinary shopkeeper with unruly white hair.

"Buenas tardes," Mamá said.

But the shopkeeper's eyes fixed on Benito like someone staring into the barrel of a gun.

Benito doffed his hat. "How's business, amigo?"

The shopkeeper looked away. "Sorry, I can't sell to you today."

Benito tipped his head as if confused. "I came to sell, not buy."

"Either way."

Benito's smile faded. "But, Señor López, I've traded with you for years."

Señor López lifted his palms heavenward in a gesture of helplessness. "I'm sorry, my friend, but it's not safe anymore. Foreigners are unpopular with the rebels, and the rebels took Janos last night. They're likely to come to Ascensión next. If it was only me, I'd help you and tell complainers to go to the devil. But I have a family. Please, you must leave."

Benito nodded as if this made sense yet didn't move. As if he'd forgotten how.

Mamá squeezed Candelita's hand, then marched to the counter. "What if *I* sell you supplies?"

Señor López wagged his chin. "What kind of supplies?"

Mamá ignored Benito's effort to catch her eyes, keeping them on the grocer. "They're in my wagon. I need a few minutes to check my inventory, then maybe you can join me outside?"

He nodded in Benito's direction. "Bien."

Benito donned his hat, touched a finger to it, and left.

Mamá gave Candelita stern instructions: "You'll do the shopping. We need three pounds of beans, two pounds of jerky, a pound of chiles, a dozen potatoes, two dozen eggs." She pressed several pesos into her hands, leaned in, and whispered, "Don't let him cheat you. And don't let your sister out of sight." She bent to touch her nose to Graciela's. "Stay with your sister."

Candelita's eyes followed Mamá out of the store. What would Villa's supporters do to someone who helped a Chinese man? She took a calming breath, but the air felt sharp.

She pointed at a barrel of pinto beans and asked the grocer, "Por favor, how much for three pounds?" Later she'd be unable to recall the price, only that she protested it was too high, the way she'd heard Mamá do a hundred times. In turn, he complained about the cost of war, a bargaining tactic she'd never heard before. A rattling distracted her. She turned to see Graciela plunging her arms into the beans. She, too, loved to feel that smooth stony coolness engulf her warm skin. But she was no longer a child. She was in charge.

She slapped Graciela's arm. "Don't touch!"

Graciela jerked her arms out of the barrel, tucked them behind her, and backed away, but she didn't look scared or angry, merely puzzled. Candelita stepped back too, struck by the feeling something bad was coming. The hairs on her neck tingled, urging her to hurry out of the store. She gave up haggling and cut her order in half, hoping Mamá wouldn't be angry. She rocked from foot to foot as the grocer wrapped her purchases in newspaper. Then she pulled Graciela outside.

They paused outside the door, shading their eyes till shapes came into focus: Mamá and Benito behind the wagon with their heads together, the plaza's empty bandstand circled by stunted trees and a dirt paseo, the two old cowboys slouched on their bench. A man entered a door across the plaza, letting laughter escape along with the lament of a mariachi—a saloon. Aside from that and the church bell's occasional clang, all was still.

Nothing was coming. She was being silly.

Mamá walked back to the store as Benito crossed the plaza in the opposite direction. Graciela yanked free to run after him.

"Get back here!" Candelita scurried after her, hampered by the bundle of groceries.

Benito caught Graciela as she leapt into his arms. "¿Qué pasa, calabasa?"

"Candelita won't let me shop."

He grinned, and she wondered how he still could, after being humiliated in the store. "Tell you what: promise to be good for your sister and I'll give you money for jamoncillo."

Her mouth watered at the memory of caramel, though the thought was soured by envy. In her family, between the educated firstborn son, the charming second son, and the baby, the only role left to her was dutiful daughter. Dutiful daughters never received treats for behaving.

Benito set Graciela down and drew a coin from his pocket. She reached for it, but he withdrew it, pointed it at her nose, and said, "Share with your sister," making Candelita ashamed of her thoughts.

"Sí, Tío Benito." Graciela snatched the coin from his fingers and skipped back to her.

Candelita took her hand, ready to rejoin Mamá, but the mariachi's voice rose again. She turned to see two men walk out of the saloon, leaning together, unsteady. Drunks could cause trouble. As if Benito shared her thought, he shoved his hat down over his eyes. The pair passed him without a glance. She exhaled. Then thunder shook the earth.

Graciela pointed at a dust cloud on the edge of town. "Horses!"

Two men wearing sombreros rode the dust, and their voices ripped open the quiet, "¡Viva la revolución!" They shot pistols at the sky, sharp reports that set her heart galloping fast as the horses.

The two drunks in the plaza turned tail and scrambled to regain the cover of the saloon.

She dragged Graciela back toward the store.

"Want to see the horses!" Graciela whined.

"Are you crazy?"

The hoof-beats closed in behind them, then stopped. Her heart did the same.

"¡Buenas tardes, chinito! Where're you headed?" The man's voice was like bitter coffee covered up with too much sugar.

She turned around so fast Graciela stumbled into her. The Villistas, one on a pale mount, the other on a dark, grinned down at Benito, whose back was to them. The trio was no more than twenty feet away. Nearby, the two old cowboys leapt from their bench and ducked toward a barbershop, where a man in an apron held open the door and waved them in.

"Did you hear me talking to you, chinito?" said the rider on the pale horse.

Benito didn't turn, his only response a slight hunch of his back.

Chino meant Chinese, and in her experience people added the letters i-t to a word to indicate something small or precious—chinito—but the man's mouth stole the sweetness from the word. He had an overbite like snake fangs and bandoleras crossed his heart. The other man would've been handsome if his nose didn't bend sideways.

Snake Fangs walked his horse around Benito. Bent Nose followed. They holstered their guns, which still gave off a powerful smell: the smoke of war. They dismounted to face Benito. The horses went still as statues, as if they smelled what she smelled.

Candelita's feet stuck to the road.

"You're hurting me!" Graciela's piercing voice startled her.

She looked down, dismayed to notice she was mashing her sister's fingers. She let go and patted her hand. "Sorry, mija."

"Are you deaf, chinito?" Snake Fangs said. "I asked where you're going."

Benito kept his head down. "Nowhere."

Snake Fangs stepped up to Benito, hand cupped to his ear. "I can't hear you."

"Maybe we could hear you if you didn't hide under that hat." Bent Nose held out two fingers and flipped Benito's hat off. It tumbled to a stop against a tree. Nobody moved to retrieve it. "¡Híjole! I see why you want to hide that ugly face. So, where'd you say you're going?"

"Nowhere."

"You hear that? He's going to Corralitos," Snake Fangs said. "This devil-eyed pendejo is going to work in the mine where they fired you."

"I'm not a miner," Benito said as if this were a normal conversation. "I just sell supplies."

"To your chinito friends, no doubt."

"I have Mexican friends, too."

"Hear that? He has Mexican friends. Ever hear of a chinito with Mexican friends?"

"No. I think he's lying," Bent Nose said.

Benito clenched his jaw and lifted his head, then quickly lowered it again.

"Does that make you angry, pinche cabrón? Go on, show us how angry you are!" Bent Nose stooped down to peer up into Benito's lowered eyes, then grabbed the back of his neck and shoved him to the ground. "Too scared? Then maybe you should dig a hole back to China."

To her dismay, Benito gave a girlish giggle. "A hole to China! Very funny!" He made a show of digging dirt with his hands. "This might take a while…" She felt ashamed for him, his inability to defend himself, but couldn't make herself look away.

"Are you laughing at us?" Bent Nose said.

"No-no. I'm laughing at *me*. Silly me, too weak to dig even a thimble of dirt."

"That's how el chinito fools you," Snake Fangs said. "He pretends he's weak, acts like a clown. But he's the devil and he's laughing at you."

Benito jumped up and ran. Snake Fangs gave chase, and her stomach went tight as his long legs closed the distance. He grabbed Benito round the waist, threw him down, and kicked his belly. Bent Nose kicked him, too. In the gut, the head, the groin. Every time he covered part of himself, they kicked another. Every time he broke free, they jumped in his way, one pointing a gun while the other kicked some more. At first, he made no sound. Then, he roared, a guttural bellow so bottomless she wasn't surprised both men halted mid-kick.

They bent over their knees to catch their breath.

Benito shrank into a ball, gasping, hands over his face, blood leaking between his fingers.

Then Snake Fangs walked to his horse, took a black canister from his saddlebag, and returned. He unscrewed the top and poured liquid over Benito. The smell drifted to her: kerosene. What was he doing?

"Please, don't kill me! I promise to leave México!" He wept, breath quivering—the quietest sound of all, yet she yearned to block her ears. She clutched the groceries.

Snake Fangs lit a match. Her mouth went dry.

That's when Graciela found her voice. Her little sister rose on tiptoes, balled her fists, opened her mouth wide as the future, and screamed—louder than anyone she'd ever heard. The unholy sound echoed off plaza walls, across the meagre bean and corn fields, to the desert where no one would hear. As if her voice directed the wind, a gust blew out the match. All three men gaped at the girl, who, having discovered her voice, continued to scream and scream and scream.

The sound turned Candelita's arms to water. The sweaty newspaper package tore, and the groceries fell to the dirt. Eggs cracked, beans scattered, potatoes rolled.

Graciela ran to Benito, crying. "No-no-no! Leave him alone!"

"¡Chingado!" Bent Nose said. "We can't burn him in front of the little girl."

Mamá ran outside with the shopkeeper, grabbed Candelita's shoulders, and shook her, wearing an expression beyond rage or terror. "Didn't I say to watch your sister?!"

Candelita bolted after Graciela to try and make things right, but Mamá snatched her braid, hauled her back, and locked both arms around her. Together they watched Graciela dart from Benito's side to kick Snake Fangs in the shin. He jumped back and raised a fist.

"Only a coward strikes a child!" came a raspy voice. Behind the Villistas appeared one of the two old cowboys she thought had run into the barbershop.

"What will you do about it, abuelo?" Snake Fangs' hand waited in midair.

The old grandpa pulled a knife from his belt and held it before his face like a cross. "Don't act like you don't know me, Felipe Luna. I know you and your friends stole our neighbors' winter food stores, and Señora Castañeda's liquor. Stole my granddaughter too, to be a cook or nurse or God-knows-what for your héroes."

"Rosa fights for the cause. Villa doesn't kidnap the weak. He defends them."

"Maybe *Villa* does, but I know *you*, Felipe. Even as a boy you were a bully."

"So now you'll turn the tables with your little knife?" He exchanged a look with his partner, and they laughed. "Bien, defend your granddaughter's honor—*after* I kill this animal."

"You don't understand"—Candelita was baffled to see the shopkeeper step in front of Benito—"This 'animal' supports the revolution."

"How do *you* know?" Snake Fangs said.

"He's a friend."

"Unfortunate choice of friends."

Before she knew what was happening, a jagged red doorway opened in the shopkeeper's chest as a gunshot turned her ears inside-out. Everything after that sounded muffled. Mamá dropped to his side, eyes and mouth wide, and pressed both hands to the red door. Then Snake Fangs stared down at a knife sprouting from his chest and dropped his smoking pistola. Bent Nose aimed a gun at the grandpa who'd thrown the knife, but before he could fire, a spout of dirt shot up between them—another bullet. From where? Bent Nose didn't stay to find out. He ran toward the horses, but they were already galloping away.

Meanwhile, men burst from the saloon, the barbershop, and several buildings Candelita had thought empty. More men ran down the main street to pour into the plaza, voices rushing like a flood. They carried shovels, axes, sickles. Brandished rifles, guns, knives. Ready for revolution—except this one was all backwards. Bent Nose pointed his gun at one group, then another, and another. For one terrible second he pointed it at Graciela, who was tugging Benito's hand, trying to coax him off the ground.

Without thinking, Candelita leapt between her sister and the gun. She'd promised to protect her. She braced herself for a bullet's sting, but before Bent Nose could fire, a flurry of arms and legs closed in.

The two Villistas curled around their centers, but feet and fists broke through. Down came shovels and axes, rifles and knives. Bent Nose's head split open in a spray of blood. The mob tore into both men like a pack of coyotes tearing into two dogs. A ragged torso appeared between kicking feet. Something small flew overhead. A finger? A bare foot stomped her ankle so hard she feared it might break. They had to get out of here before they got killed in the chaos.

She pressed through the crowd to Graciela. Together they pulled and pushed Benito as he struggled to rise. She reached under his arms, straining to lift him, till a man pushed her aside and slung Benito over his shoulder. It was Papá! He shouted something she couldn't hear.

She didn't need to, just swung Graciela over her shoulder and followed him through the crush.

Mamá still knelt over the shopkeeper—Señor López—whose empty eyes stared at heaven, where time passed differently than on earth. Papá didn't break his stride but shouted to Mamá as he passed. She seemed to snap out of a trance, leapt to her feet, and ran after Papá.

They hurried to the livery, where Miguel sat on the wagon's buckboard, El Presidente's reins in hand, and Lalo sat astride Feo, hugging the horse's neck. Both animals' ears twitched in alarm, but they waited patiently for Papá to load Benito into the wagon and for Mamá and the girls to scramble in after him. Papá then joined Lalo astride Feo, kicked his flanks with spurless boots, and galloped off. The wagon lurched after him, knocking Candelita on her back.

Blankness veiled her sight, tempting her to sink into its soft white cloud. She blinked and turned to see Mamá rocking Graciela in bloody arms. Mamá's lips moved as if she sang, Graciela's mouth strained as if she wailed, but Candelita heard nothing save a persistent ringing. To her other side lay Benito, stinking of kerosene, face a map of war. She sat up, lifted his head into her lap to prevent it banging against the boards, and looked around for something to bind his wounds. The blankness would have to wait. She was needed here.

14. Angel Island

1911 – San Francisco, California

The nurse jostled the bedpan out from under Yan Chi, sloshing dark blood onto the floor. He feared the Kei Lun had disemboweled him. Maybe it had taken the form of this nurse, taller than most men he knew, golden hair curled into a dragon's mane, mouth full of big white teeth: a beast carrying him away bit by bit to an underworld that reeked of antiseptics.

He rolled over in careful increments: head, then torso, then buttocks and legs. His skeleton vibrated pain. The cot creaked as if he were still onboard ship. He finished the journey to his left side and found himself staring at his neighbor's face. Lee Chung Hong's blue eyelids were closed, and his lungs crossed an ocean with each breath, as if he too remained at sea.

Whenever they both woke, they talked. Whenever he woke alone, he played a guessing game: what was killing Chung Hong and how long would it take? Malaria in a week? Yellow fever in three days? Rat plague in twelve hours? He looked worse than the other patients in this hospital, and he was older than most arrivals here at Angel Island. Chung Hong was thirty-five.

Like Chung Hong, Yan Chi was slated to be deported because he was sick. Also like Chung Hong, the only reason he wasn't deported yet was because doctors declared him too sick to sail. Turned out he'd brought unwanted stowaways with him, so well-hidden he hadn't known they were there: hookworms. Parasites were forbidden to immigrate to America. No one cared about Yan Chi's claim that he was born here. Unless he paid for medicine to kill the worms, the Americans would ship him home.

Yet all his money was gone.

Bing Sam was right: he never should've trusted the men in steerage. He'd sewn his money inside his pants, but diarrhea and vomiting had withered his body till the excessive bulge of his ban zau became suspicious. The morning he woke to discover his money gone, he suffered the added indignity of wondering which fellow voyagers had groped him while he slept. He swore accusations at several suspects only to receive blank stares in reply.

His brother's response to the note he sent to Chinatown expressed surprise he was here at all. The letter he'd mailed from China to announce his coming must still be at sea. Nonetheless, he thought borrowing from his brother would be simple, until Tsi Chaum replied that he too would have to borrow the money.

Yan Chi could not, would not, recross the Pacific.

He looked past Chung Hong, past the green walls, through the window that framed his limited view of Gold Mountain—which was no mountain, just a line of fog above a wedge of sea barely visible through the island's eucalyptus and pines. A burst of sunlight turned that slip of America to flashing gold coins. Ah, to reach out and pluck that gold from San Francisco Bay...

He must've spoken that last thought aloud because Chung Hong opened one eye and croaked, "You think they call it Gold Mountain because you'll find gold here? Maybe in your grandfathers' day. Now you must provide your own."

"That makes no sense."

"If you want sense, go back to China. If you want Gold Mountain, you must pay for it. If you cannot pay, you must steal it."

"How can I steal anything when I'm trapped in this bed?"

"Don't worry, your brother will bring money. San Francisco tongs are eager to help the desperate. But, after you get out of here, never again let anyone see your desperation. Instead, find others more desperate than you. You must always appear to know more, have more, be more. Make friends, ask what they need, get it for them. Stack up favors till others owe you more than you owe anyone. That's how you steal gold—because power is the new gold in America."

"What makes you so sure?"

"I've lived here a long time."

"Then why won't they let you in?"

"Because I'm sick and they fear contamination. I've lived in the Beautiful Country most of my life, but I wasn't born here. They can make me leave anytime they want."

His words were enough to renew desperation, but Yan Chi did as he suggested and offered Chung Hong his first favor: "If they let me into America before you, I'll help you stay."

Chung Hong stared at him so long—yellowed eyes unblinking, breath stilled—that Yan Chi thought he'd died. Then he took a long, watery breath, "Would you be willing—" He erupted into a coughing fit. Yan Chi struggled to reach the water glass by the man's side, but he waved him off. "Would you be willing to transfer your promise of help?"

"What do you have in mind?" Yan Chi asked.

"It's not me I worry about. I'll either get well and talk my way back into America, or I'll die and my troubles will end. But my son waits for me in Angel Island's Yellow House. Hoi Sam doesn't know how things work here. Without me to speak for him, they might send him back."

"You wish me to help him stay?"

"If you do, I'll owe you, and my son will honor the debt."

He weighed how much this reciprocity might buy him against how likely it was the dying man's story was a lie. Old Mr. Ma once said:

America is a game of chance. If so, Yan Chi must learn to gamble. "You have my word, Chung Hong. But don't lose hope. You may live."

He berated himself for ever letting himself grow weak. A weak man's fate belonged to others. Enough. From now on, he thought, I'll always be first to offer help, never first to take it.

Yan Chi never saw the money his brother paid the immigration men, only tasted the bitter potion it purchased, which seemed designed to complete his disembowelment. Doctors sent him to the overcrowded men's dorm to recover. He spent three weeks shuffling to the overflowing toilets and back, shitting liquid, waiting for the poison to kill either him or the worms.

Around him, a herd of young Chinese men milled in a steamy haze of body heat, bet future earnings on card games, or swung from chandeliers—until one swing too many felled an amateur gymnast in a pile of plaster, glass, and laughter. The few longtimers kept to themselves. Some carved poetry into the dorm walls of the yellow clapboard house:

The young children do not yet know worry.
Arriving at the Golden Mountain they were imprisoned in the wooden
*   building.*
Not understanding the sad and miserable situation before their eyes,
They must play all day like calves.

Several calves clomped out to the yard for volleyball. Though it was a Western game, it reminded him of home. In Baba's day, Overseas Chinese brought volleyballs back to Toisan, and village boys had been playing since. Seeing such a familiar sight unnerved him more than anything else at this island prison. They invited him to join. He declined, said the doctors ordered him to rest. One boy called him a *no fu*, and he laughed. Running away to America made them all either *cowards* or heroes, but if a man kept his mouth shut nobody needed to know which.

To his annoyance, one boy wouldn't drop the subject. "Yan Chi is no coward! He traveled as far as any of us, alone, almost dying on the way!" Lee Hoi Sam always defended him, no matter how often he asked him to stop. The fifteen-year-old's chin, voice, and arms were soft as a girl's, attached to a body limp as a noodle.

Three teens stared at Hoi Sam's face—so earnest above his bobbing throat-knot—and broke into laughter. "Yan Chi," the eldest said, "why couldn't you leave your wife home and spare us her lover's lament?"

"She doesn't belong to me." He rolled over in his cot to face the wainscoting, his back to them all, and silently re-read the characters a previous occupant had carved into the wood:

Our national shame is hard to forget, and we become prisoners.
What joy is here for heroes? We must soon unite...

Hoi Sam, unable to take a hint, treated his turned back as an invitation to talk. "How can you endure such disrespect?"

"It's you who are upset, not me."

Hoi Sam shrugged, then swung up to the bunk above his, kicking his head in the process.

Yan Chi slapped his foot away.

"Deoi m zyu!" Hoi Sam apologized. "Sorry you got stuck with someone so clumsy!"

If only he could bleed the boy's neck like a chicken to stop his squawking. He regretted taking responsibility for this fool that Chung Hong had called "son"—though he looked nothing like him. But the older man's last words clung to him: "I'll rest easier in the afterlife knowing he can count on you."

It unnerved him the way Hoi Sam acted so indebted though Yan Chi had yet to help him. He was turning the tables, making Yan Chi appear indebted to *him*, all the while wearing the face of a long-suffering wife. Yan Chi preferred to be left alone. Hard enough in this room built for 50 but packed with 200; impossible with an unwanted champion following him everywhere.

That night Hoi Sam's screams woke everyone again as the boy leapt from his upper bunk and thumped to the floor next to Yan Chi. The others threw insults across the room: "*Sau pei!*" "*Yau mou gaau lan cho?*" "*Fan choeng*"—tossing in the classic *foreskin, fucking,* and *pig guts*—along with a slipper, wet towel, and bar of soap, all of which missed Hoi Sam and hit Yan Chi. He stuffed the soap under his pillow. Might come in useful.

Yan Chi sighed at the sight of Hoi Sam still cowering on the floor. "What is it this time?"

"A spider big as my hand!"

"It was only a nightmare."

"Are you sure?"

He stood, whipped Hoi Sam's bedding off the upper bunk, and shook it. "See? Nothing."

Another dorm-mate called out, "Can you two lovers please fuck more quietly?"

Yan Chi yanked Hoi Sam up off the floor by one rubbery arm. "Get hold of yourself. Want them to tear you apart and suck out your insides like a shrimp?"

The boy hung flaccid from his grip, whimpering, "My ankle, I think it's broken."

Yan Chi carried him to the infirmary like a toddler.

Hoi Sam begged forgiveness the entire way, "Deoi m zyu! Sorry I acted like a baby. I'll try harder to follow your example."

"What example?"

"You don't care what anyone says. You like being alone. You prefer the dark."

Was that how others saw him? The idea pleased him.

The injury was only a sprain. Back in the dorm, Yan Chi gave up his lower bunk so Hoi Sam could rest his ankle. After it healed, he let this new arrangement stand. It wouldn't do for his clumsy new friend to jump again and crack his head. He might come in useful someday.

The interrogation room was empty of furniture, save a white metal table and five wooden chairs. Yan Chi sat in the only open seat, edges carved with tiny half-moons left by the nervous nails of other detainees. He must remain certain of his right to be here, or he'd never convince *them*. He relaxed his hands atop his thighs. Unguarded, unconcerned, undisputable. He belonged.

The four other people in the room tried to catch his lowered eyes, but he didn't let them trick him into disrespecting their authority. Two white men in military uniforms questioned him, while a white man in suit and tie scratched squiggles onto a notepad—English words, he assumed. The fourth person was a Chinese translator: a woman, to his surprise, wearing a blue-striped Edwardian dress with broad collar, as if she hoped to pass for a British schoolteacher from Hong Kong. She was pretty, though older than he, maybe twenty-five. All four wore spectacles, including the woman. He wondered if America's soft life weakened the eyes.

He struggled to focus on their questions while thoughts flapped round his skull like moths. Why was this room colder than the dorm? Was it because there were fewer people or was it a tactic? Why did the woman keep smiling? Could he trust her translations? Could he trust the wriggling words in the stenographer's notebook?

If the stenographer's words recorded the truth, they might read something like this:

Interrogator #1: What is your full name?

Yan Chi: Wong Yan Chi.

Interrogator #1: What is your nationality?

Yan Chi: I am an American Citizen.

Interrogator #2: (snorts, shakes head)

Interrogator #1: (rubs eyes, shrugs) Where and when were you born?

Yan Chi: I was born in San Francisco, California in 1890.

Interrogator #2: Uh-huh. Do you have a birth certificate?

Yan Chi: No. I used to have one, but it was lost in the Great Fire of 1906.

Interrogator #2: Right. Of course. Why didn't we think of that?

Yan Chi: I'm not sure, sir.

Interrogator #2: That was *not* a question for you. (He seemed to say more, but this was all the translator provided to Yan Chi.)

Yan Chi: I'm sorry, sir.

Interrogator #1: (chuckling) No need to be nervous, Mr. Wong.

Yan Chi: I'm not nervous, sir. (He didn't correct the pronunciation of his family name, though the man used the wrong tone, making it sound ugly and inauspicious.)

Interrogator #1: Do you have records to prove your San Francisco residence after 1906?

Yan Chi: No, I left San Francisco before the Great Earthquake and Fire. My parents sent me to China when I was young, for a Chinese education. That's why I don't speak much English.

Interrogator #2: In America, it helps to know English.

Yan Chi: (in English) Yes, sir. I know a little.

Interrogator #2: You mean "little," not "litter." *Litter* means *trash.*

Yan Chi: Yes, sir. Trash. (Was this an insult? If so, Yan Chi must not act offended. If he showed anger, they might consider him a threat and deport him.)

Interrogator #1: What are your parents' names and what is their present address?

Yan Chi: My father's name is Wong Wing Chong and my mother's name is Fong Lai Syut. My father and mother died in China during the famine in 1907.

Interrogator #2: (throws down pen)

Interrogator #1: Your father and mother returned to China? When?

Yan Chi: A few months before San Francisco's earthquake.

Interrogator #2: That's quite a coincidence. Why did they leave America?

Yan Chi: To visit family. They planned to return, but the fire left nothing to return to.

Interrogator #2: And *you*? You have something to return to?

Yan Chi: To rebuild my father's dream.

Interrogator #1: (laughs, pounds desk) Good for you, Yan Kee!

Interrogator #2: (not translated)

He didn't correct Interrogator #1's odd pronunciation of his name, because the man seemed to be on his side. He didn't need to understand Interrogator #2 to know the man believed he was a liar. He itched to strangle him for his insulting attitude. So what if the man was right? They forced people to lie with their unfair laws. Americans were happy to welcome Chinese when they needed their precious railroads. Now Ellis Island let Europeans in by the droves while at Angel Island his people must play this stupid game. He deserved a reward for playing it well.

After about an hour, his inquisitors fell silent. He was unsure what to make of this. Interviews of other detainees sometimes went on for hours, days, even weeks. Most of the others who'd been led out of the dorms before him hadn't come back, but he didn't know if that was because they were allowed through the Golden Gate or sent home.

Interrogator #1 scribbled on several papers. Interrogator #2 stamped them.

The translator said, "Welcome home to America!" with a smile that bared all her teeth.

He looked from her to the men in confusion.

"You're free to pack your things and board the next ferry," she assured him.

His brother must've paid extra. He hurried out before they could change their minds.

That afternoon he dragged his trunk off a ferry, craning his neck to find Tsi Chaum. Their eyes met amid a tangle of shouting and laughing Chinese men, a few of whom were hugging and crying—in public. To avoid such a display, he stood behind his trunk, keeping its bulk between him and his brother. Tsi Chaum reached across the trunk, took his hand, and pumped it up and down. Yan Chi matched his grip and rhythm, just as his brother had taught him. Shaking hands, like an American. He smiled, face so tight he realized he hadn't smiled in weeks.

His brother lifted one handle, he lifted the other. Together, they walked into America, grinning like old friends instead of the strangers they were, carrying secrets between them.

15. Electricity

1911 – Juárez, Mexico

What an odd way to discover she could be proud of her big brother: for dressing up to look like he was her big sister. Miguel sat next to her on the buckboard wearing Mamá's red skirt, flowered blouse, and blue rebozo—he draped the shawl to hide his short hair *and* the bulging Adam's nut at his throat. She remembered the time he stole Tía Eloisa's lacy orange panties from the clothesline and splashed through the acequia, giant chones hitched up to his chest, their red-faced auntie chasing him with a chancla. The memory shook Candelita with a nervous itch to laugh, till his elbow pressed a warning into her ribs. He lowered his eyes, pretending feminine modesty, as the wagon rolled to a stop at the military checkpoint on the outskirts of Juárez.

She wore Benito's cowboy hat pulled low over her eyes as if to shade them from the afternoon sun. He'd lent it to her when her family moaned she was no good at lying because her big eyes always gave her away. Mamá gave her a stern look from astride Feo, where she sat with Lalo. Candelita took the hint and lowered her eyes like Miguel's, picking at a thread in her skirt till it threatened to unravel.

She was more worried that Graciela—seated on Miguel's lap to hide his lack of breasts—would get them in trouble with her chatter.

One of the soldados approached Benito on the driver's side, and her gaze drifted to the rifle slanting across his chest. His face was grimy with dust that suggested the end of a long day. Three more government soldiers propped up the shack behind him: one stood and caressed the pistol at his hip while the other two sat on the ground, rifles slouched against them as if the weapons themselves were bored. None looked much older than Miguel.

"What's your business in Ciudad Juárez?" the dusty soldier demanded.

"You don't recognize me, Emilio?" Benito said with the warmth of an uncle.

Emilio slapped his own cheek, and his voice rose in pitch, "¡Señor Chung! ¿Qué pasó?" Benito had told the Riveras he passed this checkpoint often, but a week after his beating in Ascensión he still looked a fright. His face remained purple, green, and scabbed.

"I had a disagreement with El Presidente," he explained, and Emilio reared back in dismay. "Not that president," Benito assured him, shaking the reins. "My mule, El Presidente?"

"Ah, sí-sí-sí!" Emilio chuckled, then cut himself short, "Pues, much has changed since I last saw you, and not just your face. You'll understand if I check your load?"

Benito shrugged. "Of course. These are dangerous times."

Emilio stepped to the back of the wagon. Candelita's family stared straight ahead as if their necks were nailed to their shoulders. She held her breath, waiting for the creak of a crowbar, the surprised shout of the soldier finding Papá squeezed inside the largest barrel, the angry declaration that he was under arrest because of the federal leva. A man they'd met on the way here had said the price of fleeing the draft was a bullet to the head. Papá and Benito carried guns of their own, but it would be two against four. Would they shoot it out right here?

She closed her eyes and mouthed a silent prayer: Madre de Dios, we've come so far. Blessed Virgin, please don't let it be for nothing. Her dried lower lip cracked as she prayed.

"What's in the barrels, Señor Chung?"

Startled by Emilio's voice in her ear, she opened her eyes to see him standing on her side of the wagon. Her clasped hands shook. She unclasped them and tucked them under her thighs.

"The usual supplies," Benito answered. "I couldn't sell anything in Corralitos, thanks to those malditos insurrectos."

Emilio nodded, toed the dirt with his boot, and tilted a look up at Candelita. Had her nervousness given them away? She couldn't let him ask Benito to open the barrels.

In one decisive move, she looked Emilio in the eye and unmasked her terror. "Have you seen the terrible bandidos?"

His lip twitched as if her outburst amused him. "Me? No, señorita. But they do come and go through Juárez. They recently stole a train."

She allowed tears to fill her eyes. "We've been so scared."

He reached up to pat her knee. She tried not to flinch.

"Are all these children yours, Señor Chung?" His gesture took in all the youngsters, but his gaze fixed on her. "This one doesn't look like you." He tipped up the hat she wore, revealing her eyes. "She's too pretty." His grin revealed white teeth flecked with chewing tobacco.

She swallowed her disgust and attempted the secret smile she'd seen older girls give the boys during the Sunday evening paseo back home, each hoping to win a stroll with her would-be novio. "You're a true caballero, to say such a thing to a girl so dusty from a long journey."

He held her gaze till her stomach twisted. It struck her too late that she didn't know the rules for this game.

Graciela's voice rang out, "Are you a Villista?"

Emilio seemed to notice her for the first time, then guffawed, spewing wet tobacco. "Hear that?" he shouted to the other soldiers. "The little one thinks I'm a Villista!"

His comrades laughed. Benito joined them, followed by Mamá, Lalo, even Graciela.

Only she and Miguel stayed silent, sweaty arms stuck together.

"No, chiquita," Emilio chuckled. "I'm no Villista. If I were, I'd never let my Chinese friend pass, would I, Benito?"

Benito shook his head, agreeing.

"Welcome home, amigo, to you and your family." Emilio waved them on with a flourish.

The checkpoint shrank behind them, and Benito tossed a cautious question into the back of the wagon, "Are you all right, Eduardo?" The reply from the nearest barrel was too muffled to make out, but at least it indicated her father hadn't yet smothered to death.

The further they got from the checkpoint, the more she shook. She glared at Graciela, whose only response was a deepening of the question mark between her eyes. Hadn't Ascensión taught her the danger of drawing attention? Of course not. It had only taught her the power of her voice. Candelita feared her bold little sister would keep testing that power, like a man shooting bottles to improve his aim with a gun.

Miguel must have felt her shaking, because he pulled her to his side and rocked her, as if the skirt he wore imparted to him the mothering skills of a woman. "We're safe now, hermanita."

He'd picked on her all her life, and she often thought things would be easier without him. Yet she felt a surge of gratitude that the soldiers had failed to recognize he was male even though her mother had said many times, *Miguel is all boy*. She studied his eyes and swallowed a laugh.

He frowned. "What?"

"It's not fair. You have longer eyelashes than me!"

He pushed her away.

She shook a fist. "Careful! You might find out I'm stronger than you…sister."

"I don't doubt it…brother." He pushed Benito's hat down over her eyes.

They grinned at each other, as if sharing their first real secret. What that secret was, she couldn't say, but she wondered what other secrets it might lead to.

It wasn't as if they stepped out of the desert into the city. More as if the city lay buried under the desert, and one-by-one its bones rose from the grave: a camp here, adobe hut there, a saddlery, brick homes, a crooked line of shops. They passed other campesinos headed the same way, scattered at first, then a line, thickening till it plodded like a funeral procession: horse-drawn wagons and donkey carts, men pulling barrows and families on foot.

It gave Candelita a start each time her sister called out, "¡Buenas tardes!" A few people said it back, but most just stared or ignored her. It was a relief when she gave up. Graciela kicked the floorboard. "Juárez people are mean! I want to go home."

"They're just tired, mija," she said. "Our friend Benito is from Juárez and he's not mean. Anyway, most of these people don't live here. They're on their way to El Paso, like us."

"Are El Paso people nice?"

She wished she knew. Miguel said americanos hated mexicanos. Benito said Americans were friendly, but if so, why wouldn't they let him in? Papá had never seen America but knew men who had. He said they called it, "The Land of Dreams." She pictured the border like the edge of sleep: one side restless with monsters, the other peaceful as a Sunday siesta, but hard to guess which was which.

The line of refugees slowed to a crawl as a cross floated into sight. It rose from a whitewashed adobe tower, painted ruby by the setting sun. "That's the Mission of Guadalupe," Benito said. "Welcome to Juárez."

A small military band played a waltz from a nearby bandstand, keeping time as two opposing forces circled the mission plaza in an odd paseo. Dozens of soldiers strode clockwise while a handful of nuns scurried counterclockwise: men and women who would never flirt, never court, never marry. The plaza itself stunned her: drenched green vegetables and herbs stood at attention around tiny trees with strange fruits. In their midst squatted a round brick cistern, water glinting gold in the sun. The sight made her dry tongue thicken. They'd left Ascensión so fast they'd been forced to ration water. She hadn't drunk a sip since morning. Picturing Papá trapped in the barrel was all that kept her from leaping down from the wagon and splashing into the cistern.

Benito slowed El Presidente to a trot as they turned down a boulevard lined not with adobe but colonial towers of red, white, and gray. Despite the army, hundreds of ordinary people bustled through el centro, the biggest gathering of humanity she'd ever seen. So this was a city. Dusk crept over it all till a line of glass globes burst into stars, as if a constellation had joined the exodus. Her family and other nearby campesinos gasped as night turned into day.

Her mother crossed herself. "What's happening?"

Lalo slid down Feo's flank and ran from streetlamp to streetlamp, swinging around each pole. "E-lec-tri-ci-dad!" He called out each syllable as if opening a box of marvels.

"They put in the lights for the meeting between President Diaz and the President of the United States." Her family turned to Benito, who sat up taller. "So many campesinos crowded the city, I thought they'd start the revolution that night. But they simply came to see the lights."

Although the lights were miraculous, they weren't what Candelita was most eager to see. She craned her neck this way and that until Benito laughed and pointed.

"The border's right there."

"Where?" She squinted but saw no river or bridge, only buildings. "All I see is the city."

"That's it! Except, you see that cluster of buildings? They belong to two cities, not one."

She refused to believe it so long as she couldn't see the Río Bravo, which Benito said the americanos called Río Grande. Was it possible the famous river that formed the border was neither fierce nor large—but invisible? She stood up for a better view, but all she could make out were two rows of crosses linked by ropes. Benito explained those weren't ropes but wires running across the bridge, some for telephone service, others for the trolley that, until recently, had carried people back and forth across the border.

She imagined Jesus hanging from all those crosses, crucified over and over.

A loud honk like a goose's call followed by a crack like gunfire stunned her into falling back in her seat. She clutched Miguel and braced herself, sure it was a canon and revolution was upon them. A black coughing carriage without a horse rumbled past and people scattered, men cursing, women shrieking, children giggling. She closed her eyes against a flurry of dust, then opened them again to the sight of Lalo laughing up at her.

"Did you see? An American automóvil! El Modelo T. Didn't I say America was magic?"

Graciela looked ready to laugh or cry, hard to tell which. "Why is magic so loud?"

"Magic is loud so you'll pay attention and won't miss it," Benito said.

Candelita wiped the dust from her eyes and silently vowed to pay attention.

Darkness fell as they zigzagged past shops and homes, from el centro to the colonias beyond. They stopped in a quiet neighborhood, at a small red brick building where two windows blinked through sleepy blinds.

"We're here," Benito said. "This is my store, and my home: El Emporio Chung."

Candelita looked from face to face, as did the others, uncertain eyes asking each other if arriving could be this easy. They all climbed down. Her legs shook like a newborn colt's.

A young Chinese man in a clerk's apron ran out of the shop, bowed to Benito, and sang to him, a hum of musical notes she realized must be Chinese. His anxious gaze flitted toward her family as he pointed toward el centro with slashing gestures—which clearly did not mean "welcome home." Benito sang back to him till the clerk's eyes widened and he cast a sidelong stare at the rear of the wagon.

"Go inside," Benito told Maria and the children. "Hang Lu and I will unload the barrel."

As one, they ignored his instructions and rushed to the wagon's rear.

The two men lowered the heaviest barrel from the wagon, pried it open, and tipped it over. Her father slumped out, blinking as if it were day instead of night. The family surged forward, and Miguel held out a hand. Papá waved them back, growling from his curled position on the ground. He rolled onto hands and knees, half-rose, and clutched his thighs in a bow-legged stance. He arched his back, then paced (or rather, inched), lifting one leg at a time like a dog marking territory, muttering curses. He didn't seem at all grateful to have survived.

Once Mamá saw he wasn't dead, she said, "Children, inside! Your father's unfit for company."

The bell above Benito's shop door rang like the one in Señora Garcia's tienda in Mata Flores. The familiar sound comforted Candelita, though the buzz of electric lights unsettled her. She'd never seen such a pretty shop: clean white shelves stacked with jars and cans covered in red-and-black squiggles like artwork. She couldn't identify a single item, which made her dizzy. She tiptoed across the clean wood floor, embarrassed when she looked down to see she'd left a trail of dirty toe-prints. Mamá whispered, "Don't touch." The warning was unnecessary. They milled in the center of the room, arms glued to their sides, gaping.

The clerk scurried past and slipped through a curtained doorway to a room beyond. He returned carrying a tray with a pitcher of water and many glasses. He set it down, poured two glasses, and carried them out. Candelita volunteered to pour the rest, slopping water on the floor in her eagerness. Despite her thirst, she drank slowly, remembering the lessons of the desert.

A rustle drew her attention, and everyone turned to see a beautiful, big-featured woman emerge from the curtains, arms spread like a performer taking a stage. Her generous skirt of orange, pink, and yellow flowers swirled with a desire to dance. Benito's wife, Isabel. She halted at the sight of her husband stepping into the shop, her hand to her mouth as if to stifle a scream.

"I'm fine!" he bellowed as if loudness would prove it. "It looks worse than it is."

She stepped forward and touched a finger to the edge of one swollen eye. "¿Qué pasó?"

"I caught the wrong end of the revolution."

She threw her arms round his neck and kissed each bruise like a chicken pecking corn, ignoring every flinch. He patted her arm, smirking as if this affectionate assault both pleased and embarrassed him. Then she scolded, "Didn't I tell you not to go? What will happen to Marcela and me if you die? Why did my parents let me marry such an idiota?"

"Which question would you like me to answer first, mi amor?"

She pulled a towel from her waist and swatted his shoulder.

"¡Ay!" he moaned.

She rubbed his shoulder, contrite. "Sorry. Did I hurt you?"

He laughed, and she balled up a fist and hit him.

"You see why her parents were grateful any man would take her?" he appealed to the others.

The children snickered.

"I see I've failed to teach my parents manners," a feminine voice chimed in so gently it was hard to believe she was related to these two. "Papá, are you going to introduce us?"

Candelita turned to see the voice's owner, and her body felt weightless as a balloon. She'd grown accustomed to Benito's foreign look, the unexpected angles, planes, and circles. Marcela's face was something else: a harmony of Mexican earth, Chinese starlight, and notes in between. Her black hair was pulled back in a vast white bow like a flag of surrender. The girl, who looked both much younger and much older than fifteen, glided over the floor to her father, bare feet leaving no mark and making no sound. Did she have the power to levitate?

"Welcome home, Papá!" Marcela's fingers alighted on his arm, delicate as a butterfly's feet. She blinked hard as she looked up at his battered face but said nothing of his injuries. He laid a hand atop her head, and she pivoted beneath it to look straight at Candelita, eyes brimming with affection as if they already knew each other.

Candelita was still deciding how to return such a gaze when her father walked in. Benito introduced everyone. Soon they were all talking at once, shaking hands, bowing, hugging, and blurting the first unpracticed versions of their stories.

Graciela soon lost patience with this. "When do we eat?"

"Graciela!" Candelita said. "Don't be rude."

"I'm not rude, I'm hungry."

She snuck a hand behind Graciela and pinched her arm.

"Owww!"

Marcela laughed so loud and long, the sound was a revolution unto itself. Candelita let go of her usual shyness with strangers and gave in to an uncontrollable urge to laugh with her.

Mamá cut her short by addressing Isabel, "I'm sorry. We know you didn't expect guests."

Isabel's fingers snapped duets in the air, dismissing her concern. "It's our pleasure."

Marcela walked over and sat on her heels in front of Graciela. "Papá often brings home guests, so we always have plenty of food to celebrate his return. Do you like soup?"

Graciela nodded. "Cocido's my favorite!"

Candelita's stomach growled, and she darted an embarrassed glance at the others. All the travelers were in bad shape: bloodshot eyes, dirty sunburnt faces, the stench of old sweat. Yet a fresh scent of unidentifiable herbs, citrus, and flowers drifted her way. Must be Marcela, still squatting in front of her sister, who was jabbering about the city lights. Ashamed of her own bad breath and unwashed stink, Candelita stepped back.

But Marcela rose, took her hand, and halted her retreat, sending warmth tingling through her till she felt she herself might burst into electric light. The older girl drew their joined hands to her womanly breasts. "I've been waiting for you."

She didn't question this. She too felt as if something long awaited was beginning.

Graciela frowned, no longer the center of Marcela's attention, and ran off to try her luck with the adults.

"Come." Marcela's hypnotic voice drew Candelita on with a pressure as gentle yet firm as the fingers twined in hers.

She followed Marcela through the dark curtains at the rear of the store, into a room so splendid she wondered if Benito was rich. Unlike the shop's stark white electric lights, here oil lamps cast a soft golden glow over every glorious thing: walls papered with blue forget-me-nots, a wide-hipped rose-garden sofa and overstuffed chairs, polished dark wood tables and floors. Multicolored rugs swirled with warm geometry under her chilled feet.

"This is our parlor," Marcela said. "But let me show you my room."

"You have your own room?"

She wondered, is this how people live in China? Whether it was or not, she crossed the threshold into a new world. Much as she missed home, this was a world she already didn't want to leave.

16. Laundry

1911 – San Francisco, California

One day in San Francisco and already strangers owned him. It wasn't Yan Chi's brother who came up with the fifty dollars for his hookworm treatment, an extra fifty for dysentery, plus another fifty for "other costs." He should've known, but he was too infatuated with American ideas like "freedom" to suspect someone could steal his before he had it.

His brother's partners—identical twins big-bellied with success—called it a "loan." But they wouldn't offer him the chance to pay it back the way he'd hoped: by working off his debt at their store, Two Brothers Grocery. Instead, they insisted he take over one of their family obligations. Their uncle expected one of them to help open a restaurant a thousand miles away on the Texas-Mexico border, in a city called…Paso? A place neither twin wanted to go.

Neither did Yan Chi. He was tired of travel. Besides, why leave this city that jingled with American coins and its Chinatown that rang with familiar sounds, so he could take a train to a desert town he never heard of, to cook and serve food like a wife?

To get out of it, he told the twins he'd promised Bing Sam on his deathbed that he would help his family by taking over his role as partner in a local tailor shop.

He gave a humble bow. "I promise to pay you back with my earnings there."

The twins exchanged a look and nodded in sympathy.

"Of course, you must honor your promise to your departed friend," said one twin.

"Do you know how to find his shop?" said the other.

"No, but Chinatown isn't so big. I'm sure I can find it."

"Your elder brother knows where." The first twin turned an earnest face to Tsi Chaum. "Why don't you take Yan Chi to the tailors' now. Make sure he doesn't get lost."

He thanked them, relieved they chose to be civil. He only hoped Tsi Chaum would help him talk his way into his dead friend's partnership. On the streets, his brother hurried two steps ahead through Chinatown's crush, which thwarted his efforts to ask for more information about Bing Sam's shop before they arrived. It was all he could do to keep up.

It was like walking through any coastal city back home: haggling voices, sizzling woks, briny smells. Yet something felt very different. What? Not the clothes. Men wearing long dark tunics and long braided queues were familiar sights in China. Many of these men topped them with broad American hats, but he'd seen those in China as well. The sickening sweet scent of opium drifting through unmarked doors was familiar from his Hong Kong sojourns. Men smoking cigarettes was also common in both places. These Overseas Chinese raised more moon gates, pagodas, and red-and-gold lanterns than anyone in Canton. But that wasn't it either.

His brother turned down a narrow street, past a warehouse that leaked steam clouds, just as a woman's screech pierced the building's wood planks. A door with a smeared glass windowpane swung open and smacked him in the face. A squealing toddler dodged out.

He snatched the child before it could slip into the crowd, crouched to stare into the boy's astonished eyes, and saw the answer to his question. "Children!" he blurted. "And women! That's what's missing. There are hardly any here." He wagged the boy's chin. "You must be a god among men, ah?"

The boy grinned, dipped his chin, and bit deep into the web between Yan Chi's thumb and forefinger. Yan Chi fell onto his rear and howled. The boy fell with him, razor teeth still gripping his hand.

"Let go, beast!" He squeezed a chubby arm with his free hand and shook the creature till its teeth let go. Then he drew his arm back, ready to hurl the wicked thing as far as possible.

A hand clamped over his. "Brother, no!"

He looked up to see Tsi Chaum flanked by a circle of staring men. He rose to face them, still clutching the boy's arm but also patting his head. "I must return the poor child to his mama."

"I'm his mama!" A red-faced, wet-haired young woman pushed through the men, wrested the boy away, and hid him behind her. She screeched, "What kind of monster hurts a child?"

"Waa! You have it backward! Your child attacked me."

This only enraged her more. "He's half your size. How dare you blame my baby!"

He started to retreat from this mother-son opera just as the boy wriggled free of her, leapt forward, and gave a parting kick to his shin before darting through a gap in the crowd.

His mother chased him, shouting, "Come back, you monster!"

The circle of men burst into laughter.

He first checked to make sure the boy's teeth hadn't punctured his hand, then joined their laughter—till he noticed Tsi Chaum was not amused. "What's wrong, daai go?"

In answer, his elder brother stepped into the warehouse, through the door where the boy had emerged.

Wary, Yan Chi followed him into a tiny shop front. Inside, the air sweltered. A pudgy, freckled, blue-eyed woman stood at a counter watching a sweaty, bald, middle-aged clerk slide beads across an abacus with a practiced thwick-thwock. The Chinese clerk spoke in English, and she handed him money: green bills and silver coins. No gold. He handed her a bundle of shirts, and she left.

"Gee Sing, nei hou maa?" Tsi Chaum said. So, his brother knew this clerk.

"Hou hou! Sik zo faan mei aa?" the clerk replied.

"Yes, we've eaten, thank you. I'd like to introduce my brother, Yan Chi."

Yan Chi bowed, but Gee Sing picked up his hand and shook it. He resisted the urge to pull away from this unwanted intimacy, reminding himself handshakes were normal in America. "Welcome to San Francisco," Gee Sing said. "Bing Sam told me good things about you."

"Thank you, though I'm sure he exaggerated." He tried to hide his confusion. Why were they here? Was this the tailor shop? He looked around the cramped space. Where were the suits? Why was it so hot his back dripped sweat? The air smelled of soap. He glanced through the door behind Gee Sing. Steam clouds floated in the room beyond. What was this place?

"My brother has bad news," Tsi Chaum said.

Yan Chi turned to address the clerk, "Ah, yes. I sailed with Bing Sam from Hong Kong, but he died onboard ship. Did you know in such a case they throw the body overboard?" His brother kicked him in his already injured shin, and he yelped in pain, "Aiya!" But he took the hint and said, "Bing Sam was brave to the end. I'm sure he found honor with his Ma ancestors." Why did his brother care how he spoke of Bing Sam? Who was this man?

Gee Sing's sunken eyes retreated deeper into his skull, as if he'd just received news that his own son died. Gee Sing reached behind him, found a stool, and sank onto it. "This is too bad. He was my best worker, and a dear friend."

This only deepened Yan Chi's confusion. Bing Sam hadn't been a business owner but a worker? This clerk had been his boss? He'd had a "dear friend" in America?

Just then, the biting toddler ran through the door, feet thundering past into the foggy room beyond.

His mama stood in the doorway, looking from Tsi Chaum to Gee Sing. "What's wrong?"

"Bing Sam died."

"Waa!" She covered her mouth with both hands, then shook her head. "What a pity."

Yan Chi turned back to Gee Sing, still confused. "He made suits for you?"

Gee Sing studied him, looking equally confused. Then he cupped his own chin and nodded. "I think I understand." He cocked his head at the woman. "Give us a moment, lou po."

She was his *wife*? He would've guessed daughter. She followed her son into the next room's fog, looking down at her feet, just as Yan Chi's mother did when men wished to talk.

Gee Sing beckoned, "Follow me, please," then stepped into the fog too.

Yan Chi followed into white clouds so hot, thick, and wet he struggled to breathe. Veiled in steam, three red-faced, red-handed men worked amid vats, machines, and a persistent roar. This was no tailor's shop. He crossed his arms at Gee Sing: a question. Gee Sing pointed at the workers to indicate, *Watch*, then tucked his arms behind him.

One worker stirred a wood pole in a vat of steaming water suspended over a fire. He used the pole to lift out a dripping white sheet. Two other workers grabbed the ends of the sheet to twist it over the vat, squeezing out most of the water. Then one cranked it through a wringer, while the other pulled out the steaming tongue of cotton and dropped it into a bin full of sheets.

Gee Sing pushed the bin to another room, and he followed again. In this cramped space, four men pushed irons over damp shirts on boards, spurting more steam spirals into the air.

Beyond that stood a kitchen where the wife mopped her damp face with a rag and fed her son with chopsticks. She'd tied him to a chair with a diaper to prevent another escape—though who could blame him in this heat? She nodded at Yan Chi, a truce. The boy smacked her arm till she turned back to him and poked another morsel in his mouth. He raised both arms in victory.

"My son," Gee Sing chuckled, then lowered a hand to sweep Yan Chi back out front.

He sucked air like a survivor of drowning. The front room felt almost cool by comparison. "What is this place?"

"This is my hand laundry," Gee Sing said.

"Laundry? Where are the women?"

"Chinese women? In America? M hai! My wife is one of the few. Rich American women will pay someone to do their laundry, but most Americans won't work in a hot place like this. So Chinese men do it. It's the best job many of us can get."

Yan Chi turned to his brother. "I don't understand. Bing Sam said…"

Tsi Chaum shook his head. "Bing Sam was ashamed."

"Only ashamed in *China*," Gee Sing said. "Here, we know his job wasn't shameful. He was a good worker, good friend, good son. He did what he had to. In America, he was proud."

Yan Chi nodded, impressed: Bing Sam had fooled him. He'd thought his friend dull and lacking imagination, but he'd invented an elaborate fiction complete with handmade silk suits, employees who did his bidding, a red brick American house. And Tsi Chaum had kept the secret.

On their walk back to Two Brothers Grocery, he had one question left, "Did you lie about the buffalo too?"

"No, they're real, though I've never seen one. Wait…" Tsi Chaum rummaged in his pocket, pulled out a coin, and handed it to him. "Except here."

It was stamped with the raised image of a bison. He rubbed a thumb over its ridges.

Maybe he would see one in Paso, which his brother assured him was still the Wild West. Whether it was or not, he must go. Unless he wanted to slave in that torturous hell called a "laundry," it was the only sure way to pay his debt to the twins. The more he thought about it, the more it grew on him: the allure of a new life in a place where men made their own rules.

He wouldn't be sorry to leave Tsi Chaum. They were brothers, but little else connected them—neither friendship, nor understanding. Tsi Chaum believed in community, in family duty, in returning to China someday. Yan Chi believed only in himself. If he were alone, far from anybody who knew his past, then he'd be free to become whoever he wanted to be.

17. Candlelight

1911 – Juárez, Mexico

Candelita floated amid islands of candlelit bubbles and told Marcela her story of the desert crossing. She didn't consider herself a storyteller—that was Mamá's territory. Then again, Marcela was the first person who ever asked her to tell one. How could she say no after her new friend drew her this warm bath in this big white porcelain tub? She was used to filling a bucket at a well, heating the water over a fire, then dumping it into a cramped washtub. *This* water came hot out of a faucet, mixed with cold from another faucet, no need to haul buckets. In gratitude, she held nothing back, revealing her every misstep and sinful thought on the journey.

Marcela bathed her in acceptance, laughing even when she said nothing funny, as if they'd been friends all their lives. She trailed off, struck by the picture they made together, lounging in the amber light and beeswax scent of the candle flickering in the mirror: Candelita naked under bubbles, Marcela dressed in lace to her chin and sitting atop another wonder…a toilet, with a lid! In Mata Flores, people squatted over a pit next to a desert willow so full of purple blooms it looked like a bridal bouquet. The willow grew from the last pit they'd buried. As if Marcela read her thoughts, she dropped a coy glance at the toilet and covered her mouth. The moment their fit of giggles subsided, it began again, shifting the steam in the air.

Marcela wiped her eyes and said, "Your brother was staring at me."

Candelita stopped laughing. "Lalo?"

Marcela gave her an admonishing look. "No. Miguel."

She grew wary. Strange, she usually didn't mind sharing with her siblings, but she felt as if this girl belonged to her. She shrugged. "I'm sure many people stare at you."

"Because I'm different."

"Because you're beautiful." The words spilled out without a thought.

"Not everyone sees me that way. But yes, maybe I'm beautiful because I'm different."

Candelita giggled again. She'd never heard any girl call herself beautiful before.

Marcela took the soap and washcloth from her, rubbed them together to make suds, and lathered circles into her back.

She closed her eyes to focus on the ebb and flow of Marcela's hand. "Do you like my brother staring?"

The cloth paused. She sensed that Marcela was indifferent to staring but felt a softness for Miguel. Not romantic softness, something else. What? Uneasy, she shifted, sloshing water.

"He can stare if he wants," Marcela said. "He's just a boy."

"He's almost your age. When he gets older maybe you'll like him staring."

"He'll always be a boy." What did she mean by that?

The water grew chilly. She shivered.

Marcela rose, grabbed a fluffy pink towel from a brass stand, and spread it open for her to step into. "You'll be my sister," she declared, as if that decided it.

Candelita toweled off under her steady gaze, which revealed absolute faith that she returned the affection—which she did. She'd heard of brujas who controlled people's minds. Was Marcela a witch? If so, she didn't care.

Marcela pulled fresh clothes from a brass hook and handed them to her, not hand-me-downs but a stylish new set she said was hers to keep: a long, straight, deep-blue skirt and turquoise blouse with flowers embroidered into the collar. The bodice held extra space for Marcela's more mature breasts.

Candelita slapped the empty puff of fabric, flattening it against her meager chest to release a gust of air. "Maybe someday I'll live up to it!" They laughed again.

Marcela picked up the candle, led her across the hallway to her room, and lit a lamp. She sat her at a vanity and pulled up a stool beside her, their reflections in the mirror so bright it seemed they might ignite.

Candelita shuddered, remembering the man who poured kerosene on Benito.

"You're safe now." Marcela rested a cheek on her shoulder. "You take care of everyone. I know."—but *how* did she know?—Now *I'll* take care of *you*." She ran a soft hairbrush through Candelita's hair, pressing a palm to her head to prevent pulling. "You're beautiful too, you know."

"Not like you."

"Of course not. Everyone carries beauty differently. My mother says intelligence is more important, though she warns me never to tell boys this. In your case, beauty is better."

This didn't sound flattering. Candelita frowned.

Marcela went on, "Your beauty is like your name, a candle: solid and cool by day, soft and bright by night. When it's dark, you'll always make others feel safe and warm."

Now it sounded like a compliment, but one she didn't want. "*Will* it be dark?"

"Darkness always comes. But don't worry, the light always returns."

For dinner, they sat in tall-backed chairs at a long table. Candelita's plate alone sat surrounded by as much silverware as her entire family used at a typical meal. She was stunned anyone owned enough candles to cast so much light, and she'd never been warmed by coal-fired braziers before. Mamá looked dumbfounded when Isabel apologized for the cramped set-up: an antique oak dining set butted against a raw plank on sawhorses, both families elbow to elbow. Yet the smells of cocido, rice, and beans steaming from terracotta bowls felt comforting as home.

Marcela said a mercifully quick grace, everyone loaded their plates, and the hungry travelers chewed loud as goats—except Mamá, who ran her fingers over the hand-embroidered tablecloth, with its braided green vines, colorful fruits, and gold bees.

"Exquisito," she said.

"My mother sewed it when I was a girl." Isabel waved her glass of red wine at the cloth with such a flourish that Mamá reached out in alarm, but Isabel didn't spill a drop.

Mamá picked at her food in tiny bites and sips, all the while scolding Lalo and Graciela about manners she never required before: "Keep your elbows off the table! Stop slurping! Don't grab, ask!" This only startled them into spilling more.

The more they all ate, the clearer it became: Mamá's hesitance to dig in wasn't politeness but self-preservation. Isabel's cooking was as eccentric as she, an odd mix of over- and undercooked flavors. How could she get cocido wrong? It was *soup*. Candelita's spoon dangled mid-scoop as Marcela caught her eye. The two pressed napkins to mouths, pretending to cough.

Isabel tipped Mamá a confidential look. "Marcela has made a friend. We all have."

This time both women raised their glasses.

With that, Mamá settled her elbows on the table and bit a hunk of thick tortilla, the only part of the meal that tasted as delicious as it smelled.

Pleasantries aside, the men dominated the conversation. Their talk didn't help digestion.

The clerk was gone for the day, but Benito translated the news he'd greeted them with earlier: "Hang Lu says insurgents are gathering near Juárez again. Some hide in the foothills. Others wait in El Paso, where they can buy arms to smuggle over the river. Americans patrol the border to enforce their so-called neutrality, but some get paid to look the other way."

"Surely they can't catch them all anyway," Papá said. "It's hard to watch an entire river."

"Will the Americans try to catch us?" Lalo asked.

"Don't worry," Benito said. "They don't stop Mexicans going to America, only American guns coming to México."

"You do want the rebels to get the arms they need, don't you, Señor Chung?"

Mamá laid a hand on Miguel's arm. "Mijo, we're guests." No wonder she'd insisted on sitting next to him.

He eased his arm free of her grasp.

"It's all right." Benito held up a hand. He then addressed Miguel much the way he addressed Papá, like an adult, a tone that scared her. "I support the rebel cause: fighting against a corrupt government that kills whoever disagrees with them, against ranchers who steal land from the poor, against mine owners who drive workers like animals. In China, my countrymen fight the same evils. But I fear what war will mean for my family."

She followed his gaze to Marcela. What would happen to her new friend?

"You believe in the cause but don't want the revolution to succeed?" Miguel said.

To her astonishment, Marcela answered him, "The revolution will succeed, but victory won't last because men who overthrow power also want power. The real victors protect their families. Men like our fathers."

"You mean men who run away or get beaten? Ow!" Miguel yelped and jerked sideways. Mamá must've kicked him under the table. He scowled but said no more.

Marcela spent the rest of the meal pretending not to look at him. She appeared not angry but worried. Candelita's family always fretted over Miguel as if he were a boy lighting firecrackers that might blow off his fingers. But Marcela looked at him like he was a bundle of dynamite, with the power to blow them all apart.

Propped against Marcela's brass headboard, tucked under a colorful quilt, wearing one of her white flannel nightgowns—Candelita barely breathed. She didn't want to miss a single note of her friend's soothing voice reading from *La historia de mi vida*, a real-life story by a deaf-and-blind woman in America. That such a woman wrote a book impressed her, but what enthralled her most was that Marcela owned this book, and several others, waiting on a shelf for her to read anytime she wanted.

"Helen Keller lived in the dark but found the light," Marcela said. "Isn't she inspiring?"

"You're inspiring."

"Why?"

"You're so smart."

"Thank you, but that's a God-given gift. It doesn't count until I do something with it."

"I'm sure you will."

"My mother says if I'm smart I'll find a smart husband and give him smart children."

Was that all Marcela's education was for? For weeks, she'd been jealous of this girl. For the past few hours, she'd yearned to be just like her. Now, she wasn't sure. She imagined Marcela standing next to Miguel in a wedding gown, its train trailing down a church aisle, pew after pew. She traced it to its end, where Miguel lit a fuse.

Her body jerked out of the dream. "Anyway, you'll probably marry a Chinese man."

She didn't realize she'd muttered her sleepy thought aloud till Marcela replied, "There won't be many Chinese men left alive in México if Pancho Villa has his way."

"I didn't know there were so many Chinese in México."

"I don't know how many in the whole country, but in Juárez we have hundreds."

"I don't understand. Colonel Villa fights for the people, and your father gives food to the people. Why aren't they friends?"

Marcela laid a warm cheek atop her head. "It doesn't matter that my father supports the rebels or feeds the poor. All some people see is a foreigner who eats while Mexicans starve."

"I wish you could come with us to El Paso."

"The Americans hate the Chinese too."

"But you look Mexican."

"I can't leave without my father. We're trapped."

Candelita would feel the same if it were *her* Papá. "My father traps rabbits. He baits a snare with a little carrot. The rabbits can't resist so they get caught. But sometimes one escapes."

"How?" Marcela asked.

"It chews off its own foot."

"That's a little drastic, don't you think?"

Both girls drew a deep breath and held it. Then their giggles burst through the quiet house. Nobody shushed them. They were the only two awake.

Candelita didn't know what woke her. Not the singing crickets, nor Marcela's steady breathing, nor the distant murmur of the city center. The air shifted around a new shape moving through the house: the sharp angles of a boy who wanted to be a man. She heard a bump, a trip, a curse. She'd often wished her brother gone, but much as he frustrated them all, her family would be incomplete without Miguel. A door snicked closed at the other end of the house.

She had to stop him.

She slid out of bed like a snake escaping its skin, trying not to bounce the springs, then turned to make sure Marcela's face remained slack with sleep. She crept across the house, willing the sleepers to hear each creak as nothing more than a mouse. If they all woke and tried to stop Miguel, he'd surely feel cornered and bolt.

She squeezed out the kitchen door onto cool, packed earth, and looked down at her bare feet in the dark, regretting that she was about to undo her beautiful bath by blackening their soles. She peered into the distance where rolling black curves blotted out the stars, the foothills where rebels prepared to strike. She lowered her gaze to the few houses on this street and spotted a stick-like shadow moving away from her between red brick and whitewashed adobe.

Miguel.

She didn't know why she loved that stupid troublemaker, but then she never thought about why she loved any of her family. Family was a fact of life. That fact used to feel safe. Then the desert taught her that the sunbaked, corn-breath, talk-talk-talk people who shared her life were bits of a wider world, bits that could be torn away at any time. She couldn't bear the idea of such a hole.

She followed him toward el centro's glow, which he must pass through to reach the foothills. They both avoided the middle of the streets, slinking along walls to avoid notice. She had no idea what to say when she caught up to him—an arrogant scholar who once lectured her that the sky wasn't blue, a big brother who bullied scared siblings, a son who considered obedience a vice. For Miguel, the revolution began at home. Yet, Mamá said lost sheep were the most precious, so the most irritating Rivera was now most precious of all. Darkness was about to take Miguel, and she was her family's candle, so she must light his way back to them.

He looked back, and she darted into an alley. Why did she fear him spotting her? It would be worse if he got away. She stepped out again.

He was gone.

She was alone. In a strange city. Full of soldiers. She hadn't paid attention to their route here and didn't know the way back. She stood pressed against a brick wall, its chill penetrating her nightgown, and gave a strangled sob. Don't panic. Think.

She took a deep breath—and heard men laughing. She followed the sound to another alley, where Miguel was sneaking toward the gap at the other end. That gap opened into the plaza, where a circle of soldiers stood, talking over each other, passing around a bottle. She tiptoed fast to catch up with Miguel. He whipped around, and she was staring into the barrel of a gun. They both froze, eyes locked.

"¡Mierda!" The gun shook as he lowered it: Papá's Colt Single Action Army pistol.

"¡Miguel, idiota! You almost walked into the federales. Why'd you come this way?"

"I was trying to lose whoever was following me. Why *were* you?"

She was no longer sure. She'd thought to keep him out of trouble, keep her parents from worry, keep her family together. But had part of her simply wanted to see where he'd lead her?

"Why are you deserting us?" she asked.

"What do you care?"

"What do you mean?" She prodded his foot with her big toe. "You're my brother."

His ferocious hug scared her. "I love you too, hermanita! But I'm doing what I must."

She pulled away. "No, you're doing what you want without thinking of anyone else, like always." This prompted no reaction. "You'll break Mamá's heart." There, that should work.

He only stood up straighter. "She'll get over it. In the end, she'll be proud because I'm standing up for justice to make a better future for México."

"With the gun you stole from Papá?" She pushed her finger against the pistol. "Is this how you stand up for justice, by becoming a common thief?"

"There's nothing common about me, hermanita." His white smile bit a hole in the dark.

A sliver of light escaped the plaza to illuminate the resolve in his eyes, and—something else. What? Whatever it was, it made him look like a man, and she didn't like it. If *he* grew up, she couldn't remain far behind. She wasn't ready.

Then the voice of an actual man boomed off the alley walls: "Who's hiding back here?"

Startled, she looked up to see a silhouette towering at the plaza end of the alley. Miguel wheeled around, raised his gun, and fired. The shot went astray.

The silhouette, a federal soldier, ducked round the corner and called out. "Spies in the alley!"

More soldiers shouted. Boots drummed in their direction. Miguel said, "Run!"

She did, without hesitation, Miguel at her heels. At the near end of the alley, she turned right, trying to head back to Benito's house. Was this the right way? The boot-falls receded.

A hand grabbed her arm and pulled her behind a shop. She opened her mouth to scream, but a hand clapped over it, so all that escaped was a calf-like moo as she stared into the face of—Marcela? Like her, the older girl still wore a white nightgown and no shoes.

Marcela took her hand and led her out, not into another alley, but onto a wide street where electric lamps were still lit. "Don't run. Walk. And let's sing."

"Sing?! Don't you know the federales are chasing us?"

"That's why we must act like we're *not* the ones running away, just two silly girls who came to see what the fuss was about."

Candelita looked around in alarm. "Wait! Where's Miguel?"

"He ran toward the hills." Marcela nodded in the opposite direction.

She turned to run after him. Could still hear men shouting and running in the distance.

Marcela yanked her back and spoke in her ear, voice low but firm, "He's determined to join the rebels. You can't stop him. Your family will lose one child tonight. Don't make it two."

She nodded and let Marcela lead her away. Tears dripped from her chin. How long had she been crying? "Why did I come? I only made it worse."

"No, you didn't." Marcela squeezed her hand where it hung between them. "A soldier needs to know people at home love him. You showed him that. It'll make him a stronger fighter."

"If he survives tonight."

Death. That was the look she'd seen in her brother's eyes, the thing that made him look older. Not as if he feared death or longed to kill, but as if he now carried death inside him. A moment ago he'd stood in front of her. Now he was gone. Maybe forever.

Candelita looked at Marcela in wonder. "How'd you know where to find me?"

"I followed you. You're not as sneaky as you think. So, what shall we sing?"

She sang the only song she could think of, the lullaby about the barefoot angels. Marcela chimed in, so loud and off-key she was tempted to shush her to avoid drawing attention. Then she realized their nightgowns were beacons in the dark and soldiers would likely stop them anyway. Maybe it would distract them from Miguel. She decided to trust her friend.

Several soldiers did pass by, and a few stared, but none asked why they were there. Maybe they assumed the pair they were hunting really were spies and therefore must be men. Or maybe they feared the girls in white were not of this world but two ghosts singing in the night.

18. Oranges

1911 – San Francisco

Yan Chi sat on a barrel in the storeroom of Two Brothers Grocery, bowl to mouth, and used his chopsticks to shovel down rice, salty fish, and pickled cabbage—eager to gain back the weight he'd lost at sea. He didn't want the cowboys in El Paso to see him as weak.

Customers' voices drifted from the shop in a meaningless ramble until he overheard a name he recognized: Hoi Sam. The voice didn't sound like Hoi Sam himself. Still, he dreaded the possibility the boy would take him up on his promise of help. When he'd made that promise weeks ago, he'd expected to start a new life in San Francisco with his big brother's support, and to build his own power and influence on that foundation. All that had changed. His coming journey to Texas posed enough uncertainty without adding the fate of a simple-minded boy he'd rather forget.

Eager to avoid whatever the stranger's voice portended, he crept out the back door into the alley just as a hand fell on his shoulder. He turned to face his brother. Tsi Chaum didn't ask where he was going but pressed what felt like a tiny cigarette into his palm.

He opened his hand and stared at a thinly rolled American dollar. "What's this?"

"What does it look like?"

"A dollar. But why are you giving it to me?"

"Look again. It's a note from your friend at Angel Island."

"I have no friends at Angel Island."

"Listen, Yan Chi, because this will be important to you in the future"—Tsi Chaum often used that phrase, as if to remind him he always lagged behind his big brother in life—"*Everyone* at Angel Island is your friend. This is yin and yang. When you arrived you were yin, now you're yang, later you'll be yin again. Yesterday you received, today you give, so that tomorrow you may receive again. That dollar contains a question. Find the answer and send it back."

Yan Chi unrolled the dollar, revealing tiny Chinese characters scrawled around its edges. He gave his brother a skeptical look. "Won't I risk getting deported?"

Tsi Chaum scoffed, "Even if Americans could read it, nobody would ever tell them who wrote it. We look out for each other here. If someone did report you, it wouldn't stick. We all look alike to gwai lou."

"What if I can't find the answer?"

"We both lose face. Find the answer." His stern tone was pure Baba, duty undeniable. He strode off, leaving Yan Chi alone to read the tiny scroll.

He would later learn that Angel Island's interrogators had called in one of Hoi Sam's so-called cousins in San Francisco, then tested Hoi Sam's ability to match that stranger's memories of their supposed village in China. Hoi Sam followed his father's dying advice: "If you're not sure of an answer, say, 'I'm sorry, I'm tired and don't remember.'" As expected, the interrogators ended the session to let him sleep on it, which gave Chinatown till morning to send an answer. Hoi Sam had slipped six one-dollar bills to one of Angel Island's cooks, a man who lived in Chinatown. One of those six bills was the curling note he now held.

Hoi Sam had correctly answered questions for days: "How far is your village from the bamboo grove? How did your neighbor Lee Sin

Ick die? Does the wife of your mother's uncle have bound or natural feet?"… Written in the margins of the unrolled dollar bill, was the only question Hoi Sam couldn't answer: "Where does Lee Yik Dun live in Gong Yi?"

He ducked into the shop to ask if his brother knew anyone from Gong Yi. No, but the twins did. They directed him to a restaurant two streets over, where he stood in yet another steam cloud as the dishwasher told him the answer: "Third house, fourth row."

Back at the store, one of the twins—he couldn't tell them apart and had no interest in trying—invited him to sit behind the desk in their cramped office, then pushed a pen, inkwell, and blank receipt toward him with a conspiratorial grin. He didn't smile back, refusing to give the twins any more of himself than they'd already bought. The twin shrugged and walked out.

He dipped pen in well and drew the answer on the receipt. He followed his brother's advice, "Make the characters as tiny as possible." So, he was shaking out a hand cramp when Tsi Chaum walked in and dropped a full gunnysack on the floor with a thump. His brother reached into the sack, pulled out an orange, and set it before him.

"Thanks," Yan Chi said and reached for the plump, ripe orange.

His brother slapped his hand. "Not to eat. This is the envelope to send your answer." He held up a hand to stave off questions. Then he drew a small knife from his apron, flourished it like a magician, and slid its thin blade deep into the orange, releasing a mouth-watering whiff of citrus. He pulled out a square of tinfoil, picked up the receipt with its miniature calligraphy, and held them side-by-side as if to perform an illusion. Mystification turned to understanding as he folded the receipt over and over into a tiny square, wrapped it inside the foil, and used the knife to push the miniature package into the orange's center. He curved one hand into a basket, balanced the orange on his fingertips, and rotated it before Yan Chi's eyes. Aside from a tiny pucker, the fruit looked as it had when he'd started. He put it in the sack with the others. "Now, when the cook returns for an answer, we sell him the oranges."

"Very clever, daai go." Yan Chi nodded with unfeigned admiration.

Before sunrise, the cook returned with more dollars—regular ones. Yan Chi gave him the oranges, plus a receipt for twice what the man paid. The rest of the day, he both worried and hoped the cook would give Hoi Sam the wrong orange. Even if the answer reached him, he still might fail the interview. The boy had no talent for subterfuge. If he passed, there'd be no escaping his intolerable gratitude, which was sure to include a request for more help.

Yan Chi considered bumping up his departure to El Paso—planned for next week—to the next day instead, just to avoid the oaf. But an unexpected feeling stopped him: curiosity.

Next day, Yan Chi was stacking a sidewalk bin with more fat sunny oranges— "Valencias" a small sign called them—when he felt someone behind him. He turned, startled to see Hoi Sam inches away. He was already learning the American habit of keeping one's distance. He stepped back to make space, which Hoi Sam filled with a bow. He retreated again, but still got a head to the gut, jostled the bin, and sent a dozen oranges rolling to the ground.

"M hou yi si!" Hoi Sam gave an apologetic bow, then dropped to the sidewalk to crawl after the runaway fruit.

"Mou man tai," Yan Chi sighed, pretending not to be annoyed, then joined the chase.

"Careful, Yan Chi, they'll bruise!" both twins shouted from inside.

"It's my fault!" Hoi Sam popped up, balancing several oranges under his weak chin.

Yan Chi plucked the fruit from below the boy's chin, one by one, and dumped them into the bin. Then he crossed his arms with an unspoken question: Well?

Hoi Sam bowed again, careful to keep his distance this time. "My friend, I've come to thank you. I'm forever indebted to you for helping me land in America."

"There is no debt," he replied.

But this buffoon never took hints. "Then I'm at your service in the spirit of brotherhood."

Why hadn't he avoided this embarrassing display by escaping on an earlier train? One reason: Hoi Sam's father had promised, if Yan Chi sowed favors, then he'd reap power. Hoi Sam didn't look capable of conveying much power, but he was young. With time, maybe Yan Chi could make something of this quivering pile of gelatin still bowing before him.

Yan Chi straightened his spine and bowed in return. "How can I refuse such a gracious offer? But your generosity may take you farther from home than you expected, my friend."

Hoi Sam lifted his face to reveal something unnerving: his eyes pierced Yan Chi with a look no longer dull but sharp. "I see," Hoi Sam said. "Where are we going?"

19. The Bridge

1911 – Juárez, Mexico

"What were you thinking, stupid girl?" If only Mamá would slap her, it might sting less than her words.

Candelita knew it was really Miguel her mother wanted to punish, that she was only taking it out on her as the one person who'd witnessed him running away. So she accepted the tongue-lashing without complaint, not wanting to further shame her family in front of their hosts. Benito, Isabel, and Marcela exchanged awkward glances at the far end of the dining tables.

Her big brother was always trouble, but who knew he could make her life harder by disappearing? Who knew it would hurt so much to be called stupid? Then again, being "the smart one" had done Miguel no good.

Now her mother was repeating herself, "Why didn't you tell us instead of running after him by yourself? We could've stopped him!"

Her mother had already said this, and she'd already agreed that would have been smarter. In fact, she'd been agreeing with her mother on everything since her initial confession about an hour ago. All she had confessed was that she'd followed him and tried to convince him to come back but that he'd run off anyway. She didn't tell them he'd had Papá's gun, pointed it at her, fired it at a soldier, or that last she heard he was fleeing an unknown number of drunk federales. When her parents asked which way he ran, she was at a loss.

She'd made Marcela promise not to tell them she'd been there too. She worried dragging Marcela into her family's troubles would end their friendship, or that her friend would say too much and make matters worse. Marcela met her gaze across the room, eyes silently conveying that she need only say the word and Marcela would gladly share the blame.

Candelita said nothing, just watched her mother's mouth move, no longer following what she said. Maybe I am stupid, she thought.

Her father's roar broke her trance. He trampled the dining room like an injured bull, pounding a table, kicking over a chair, throwing a glass to shatter against a wall. He stopped as suddenly as he began, maybe remembering these things didn't belong to him. He still swung his head like a bull, shoulders hunched, ribs heaving, but his voice fell. "He's only a boy. He doesn't know what he's doing. I must find him and bring him back."

Benito's voice quieted to match his, "Think about what you're saying, my friend."

Papá ignored him, strode from the room, and returned with his pack. He rummaged inside with increasing agitation, then turned it over to spill its contents on the floor: dirt-stiffened tarp, sweat-yellowed clothes, rusty knife... He dropped to his knees and pawed through it all, panting hard, then swept everything aside. "¡Chingado!"

"What in the name of the Sierra Madre are you looking for?" Mamá clutched her hair. This was bad. She rarely evoked the name of the *Mother Mountains* instead of the Blessed Virgin unless she was scared.

"Our idiot son took my gun!" Papá rose, fists clenched, and paced. "I told the children never to touch it, and *he's* why! I tried to teach him to fire it, once, but he almost shot me by mistake!"—this was news to her—"That pendejo never listens! Pinche know-it-all. If I don't find him, he'll get himself killed!" It was a relief to hear her brother get his share of blame, but it didn't stop her from being terrified of Papá's red eyes—more terrified *for* him than *of* him.

Mamá threw herself at him, wrapped every limb around him, and pounded a fist against his back. "You can't go! You'll only throw away your life too! Don't abandon us, mi corazón! I'll lose my mind." She didn't cry or howl but moaned, deep and low, like a wolf in mourning.

They sank to the floor, locked in combat, Mamá pummeling him, Papá squeezing her so hard his muscles shook.

The Chungs filed out in silence, into the kitchen, leaving her alone with her parents.

She looked over her parents' heads to Marcela's room, where Graciela was ordering Lalo round and round. Their game was unclear, but it appeared she was pretending to be a queen, and Lalo her slave. It surprised Candelita, the indignities he endured at the whims of their younger sister, especially since Miguel often ordered *him* around. She would've expected him to jump at the chance to boss someone else. Instead, he was always eager to please Graciela, the baby at the bottom of the family pack. Lalo caught Candelita staring, and he looked from her to their parents on the floor then back again, his eyes holding hers with a frankness that said he understood more than he let on. He walked to the door and shut it with a firm but quiet click that said: Leave Graciela to me, I'll leave our parents to you.

She realized she was now the eldest. She looked down at her parents where they lay clutching each other at her feet. How had her whole family changed places with just one member gone?

Then Mamá dragged her down with them and rocked her hard. Her mother's tight embrace was suffocating, as if Candelita must not only endure Miguel's punishment but also his burial.

Her parents waited for her big brother to come to his senses and return to the Chungs'.

She and Marcela sat up late each night in bed, reading aloud to each other from Marcela's books, then lying in the dark tracing stories on each other's backs with their hands. An ache pulsed between Marcela's hands and her back, different from what she'd felt with Juliana, but yearning all the same. Marcela was the only person who looked her in the eyes anymore, who touched her with affection and without hesitation, who never spoke a word of blame.

She'd be happy to stay here forever. If Marcela lived in Juárez, she wanted to live here. If Marcela went to El Paso, she wanted to go there. If Marcela married, she would marry, and they'd live next door to each other the rest of their lives. If she looked into those accepting eyes every day, she might get over her guilt at losing Miguel. If those lively but gentle hands shared their stories with her each night, she might believe in safety again.

"I've only known you two weeks, Candelita, and already I know you by heart," Marcela said. "I don't want you to leave either. But you must. Do you know that Madera, Villa, Zapata, and all the leaders of this revolution do all their planning in El Paso? Whenever they return to México, they usually pass through Juárez. And do you know what everyone here in Juárez is saying? That the biggest battle of the coming war, the one to decide México's fate, will be fought right here. So, you see, it's not safe to stay."

Next day, her parents came to the same conclusion.

They left after midnight to avoid drawing the neighbors' attention. Unlike in Mata Flores, this time Candelita was allowed to say goodbye to her friend, yet she couldn't bring herself to speak. Benito, Isabel, and Marcela lined up in the kitchen to wish them all luck before they slipped out the back door. She hung at the rear, then threw her arms around the necks of each Chung one by one, pressing her cheek to theirs as if her cheek were a word she couldn't voice.

She followed her family into the alley, but a fist gripped her heart and refused to let her go. She turned back just as Marcela squeezed out the door, alone, as if she'd expected this.

Candelita kissed her cheek. "Thank you for saving my life."

"Sisters always save each other. You'll see." Marcela kissed the part in her hair.

Goodbye felt wrong after that, so she said nothing more, just ran to catch up with the others.

Candelita wasn't used to feeling lonely when surrounded by family. Was it her big brother's absence that made her feel this way? Or leaving first one and now another friend behind, both of whom called her *sister*? Maybe it was dread of that long dark line: the border.

Papá led the way. For once, this didn't inspire confidence. He carried Graciela on his back—a back already broken by a bronco—and the extra weight made him walk hunchbacked. Mamá brought up the rear, her steps no longer strong and certain but hesitant and shuffling. Lalo took the middle with Candelita, and his white teeth seemed to float in the blackness, grinning as if this were a game. Except for his smile, they all looked invisible in the dark.

Feo was gone. A local farmer had agreed to buy the horse from Benito, but when he delivered Feo, several *federales* were waiting to conscript the horse for military duty. Benito didn't dare argue. So Papá made no money on that horse after all, and the Riveras were on their own. They carried almost nothing. Benito had promised to send their few things later.

They wouldn't be crossing the Paso del Norte Bridge as they'd hoped. It used to be simple, *más o menos*, to walk across that wooden bridge with a nod and a smile at customs officials. Or so Benito said. Not many Mexicans had crossed recently. The insurgents blew so many bridges throughout the interior, no trains were carrying civilians to Juárez anymore. If her family tried crossing the main bridge with so few people on it—day *or* night—they'd draw attention. They didn't dare risk Papá being drafted now, not with America in reach.

They headed for the El Paso Brick Company's footbridge. Americans and insurgents watched that smaller bridge too but were less likely than federales to question them.

The river that marked the border seemed longer and wider in the final hour of night. Papá meant to cross before first light. But he hadn't known it would take so long to reach the smaller bridge, much farther from Benito's. A glow on the horizon threatened to reveal them as they approached the six grain silos of the Globe Mills towering across the river.

At first, Candelita couldn't identify what changed. The river sounded muffled. Then she heard a snort, a stamp, a splash. She wouldn't understand until later what these sounds meant. Though the rebel army had a reputation for superhuman machismo, their ranks were made up of nothing more astonishing than men and horses, both of which needed water. They had cut short an attack near the railroad stop at Bauche to come to the river and drink.

Just as the federal army predicted.

She recognized the first gunshot for what it was. Instead of screaming or running, she relaxed, tempted to curl up on the ground and sleep the sleep of the dead. She'd waited for this moment so long, it came almost as a relief. For an instant, she thought the sun rose, but the light burst and faded in flashes, followed by blasts and yells. Not dawn, but battle. Mamá shouted something in her ear and shoved her. Then she lost her mother's voice and hand at her back, lost sight of her father and sister ahead, lost her little brother's smile in the dark.

Alone, she tripped through cold mud, hot clouds, and the pounding of war. Worlds ended all around her as she tried to find the only world she knew. But it was gone. Her family was gone.

The growing dawn revealed the bare feet of rebel soldiers running past, heads hidden in smoke. One face lurched out of the haze, eyes jittering in their sockets. This one wore a uniform. A federale! He grabbed her, dragged her under a bush, and held her tight, not as if he were a lover but a child. "Mamá! Mamá!" he cried, shaking. She stiffened, consciousness shrinking until animal instinct burst from her, snarling and kicking to free herself. He gripped her arms and searched her face in the growing light as if to assure himself she was real.

"What're you doing out here?" he shouted. "Are you crazy?"

"Yes!" She leaned forward, clamped her teeth into his neck, and bit till she tasted blood.

He released her. She scrambled to her feet, ran blind into the stinging smoke, and crashed into someone else, knocking them both down. It must be Lalo, no soldier could be that short. They lifted each other to their feet and ran hand in hand, which felt clumsy, but she feared letting go and never finding him again.

"Don't worry, hermana. I'll protect you." He squeezed her hand as if pumping courage from his heart to hers.

Even in the midst of her panic, this amused her. "Who do you think you're talking to? Mamá wants *me* to protect *you*."

They caught up to a three-headed shadow at the river's edge. It was only Mamá and Papá clutching each other with Graciela between them.

"We're here, Papá!" Lalo called, his voice strong, like the man he would become.

"Thank God," Mamá said. "Stay close."

The family moved as one though bullets flew around them.

Lalo stumbled into her and said, "I'm tired."

"We're almost there." She wrapped an arm around him till they leaned together like drunks staggering home from a party. He smelled like smoke, but the whole night smelled that way.

The footbridge was straight ahead. Papá approached, looked left and right, then peered across. The bridge was wrapped in smoke, but

El Paso's lights beckoned in the distance. She thought she glimpsed americanos across the river, heard them shout to the fighting soldiers. She didn't understand what they said or which side they shouted at. Maybe both. Their weird laughter stunned her, more like the howls and yips of coyotes.

"Perfect," Papá said. "Everyone's distracted by the fighting. Follow me."

Her family stayed close together as they stepped onto the swaying bridge. She gripped one of the guide ropes in one hand, Lalo's hand in the other, but he fell, yanking her off balance. She tried to pull him up, but he hung from her hand as if he wanted her to swing him for fun. She feared he'd drag her into the river. "Lalo, stop goofing off!" She yanked again, but he knelt as if praying. Then he pitched forward, dragging her down with him. Panicked, she pulled him away from the edge. He fell into her lap, eyes staring up at her in confusion, then past her…at nothing.

"Lalo!" she screamed. "Lalo, what's wrong?!" But she knew, felt the wetness pool in her lap, saw the darkness spread from his shirt to her skirt. If this were daytime, it would be bright red, the color of the door they'd left behind, the color of home.

"Mijo, wake up," she whispered. "It's just a bad dream." She tried to wake, too, but she was stuck on that bridge. Part of her would always remain there, kneeling with her baby brother on those boards, a splinter driving into her knee, though she couldn't feel the pain, not yet.

She looked up to see her parents and Graciela huddled over her, staring down at Lalo. Graciela untucked her head from Papá's neck and demanded, "Get up, Lalo! We're going to America!" Papá pressed her face into his chest, and she fell silent. No one else spoke.

The sun rose, revealing them to anyone nearby who cared to look. The bridge creaked under their unmoving weight. They were in no hurry to cross anymore. Lalo's blood glistened, a liquid jewel in the light of a new day.

Papá handed Graciela to Mamá, then lifted Lalo in his arms and carried him across the unsteady bridge to El Paso. Mamá followed with Graciela. Candelita stood, spilling blood from her skirt. It dripped through the gaps between planks, splashed into the shallow river below, and floated away.

At the bridge's far end, two uniformed men rushed toward her family, shouting. Frightened, she almost turned back, but these were American soldiers, not part of the fight in Mexico. She didn't understand what they shouted, but they beckoned her to hurry.

Not yet. She bowed her head. "Miguel, don't you dare die now. Live. Find us." Then she ran to America, trailing red footprints behind her.

PART TWO
THE BORDER

20. Yankee Doodle

1912 – El Paso, Texas

"Dos Chop Suey!" Candelaria ducked whenever Yankee's voice boomed out of the kitchen like a cannonball. He was the only nonwhite in El Paso who didn't shrink his voice to fit white ears. He tossed the dishes onto the shelf with a clatter, two chipped plates where blue dragons circled a heap of soy-drenched pork, vegetables, and rice. His big boxy head appeared in the pass-through, one eye closed against the steam so he appeared to wink as he said, "Taste better hot!" His face was not handsome or friendly like Benito's, yet it held the certainty of a man in charge. His tall white hat, like the ones hotel chefs wore, made him look less certain, its top tilted to one side as if he pondered a perpetual question.

She kept her own persistent question to herself: why did so many customers laugh when they heard Yankee's name?

She grabbed a plate from the pass-through, only to jerk her hand back in pain. "Ay!"

"Care-ful. Hou hou hot!" He wagged a finger. "I always tell you!"

"Sí, you tell me: 'Plates hot, use towel.'"

He reached a hand through the shelf. "Lemme see."

She held her palm up as if to have her fortune told.

"*Mano* no burn-ee. Okay-aa!" He gave her red palm a stinging pat, then turned to pour sesame oil into his wok. It smoked and crackled like gunfire. At fourteen, two years since the border, she'd finally trained herself to stop jumping at the sound.

She reached for her waist to grab the towel tucked between her puff-sleeved white blouse and ankle-length navy skirt, tossed the towel over her hand, balanced the plates on top, and carried them out. It was hard to understand Yankee's blend of English, Spanish, Chinese, and gibberish, but easy to figure out which orders went where: she was the only waitress, the Louis Café held only six tables, and the mostly white clientele ordered mostly chop suey, worried anything else might be too spicy. Her mother sometimes threw together pork, vegetables, and rice, but nothing like this. Her mouth watered at all of it. She was overdue for a break.

She set down both plates in front of the two americanos at table four, arching away from the armpit-smell of the one with the straggly beard.

"Skittish ain'tcha? Well, don't be shy about *mas cer-ve-zas!*" He over-enunciated every word as if she were deaf, then raised one of their four empty beer bottles and wagged it at her.

She smiled, snatched the bottle from him, flipped it in the air, end over end, and caught it, as if this was their private joke. "Yes, sir. *More beer.*"

After a year in El Paso, and a few months at the Louis Café, she knew enough English to serve her customers well, and her regulars tipped big. The stinky Beard Man was no regular, but she'd seen him a few times, and she knew how to deal with his type. It was his quiet, soap-smelling, clean-shaven companion who worried her, staring like he'd just as soon scoop out her insides with a fork and devour them. She evaded his gaze as she collected the rest of the bottles with an irritable clank and hurried away.

The Soap Man's whisper followed her, "Can't make a lazy Mexican go faster, Charlie, even if ya dip 'em in soy sauce. But when they look like that spicy señorita, who cares?"

Her English was limited, but she got the idea. Pues, he thought she was lazy? Fine, she would be lazy. She paid special attention to her next two tables: poured them extra water and tea, offered free dumplings, made sure they had all they needed. The drunks at table four could wait.

Lunchtime at the Louis Café wasn't as scary as war, but it wasn't peaceful either. The lunch crowd was male-only: not just white, but Chinese and Mexican too. Most drank booze, and a few had a secret third hand—hands that smacked, pinched, and squeezed, hips, waist, and breasts, then slipped into hiding before she could react. Some men didn't bother playing innocent, and that was worse. Because if she dared pull away or object, her tips went down.

She didn't risk complaining to the three Chinese men she worked with, worried Boss-man would fire her. She suspected he knew, though he was never in the room when the hands appeared. Yankee's friend, Sam, the skinny bookkeeper whose real name was Hoi Sam, once looked her in the eye while a customer fondled her braid. Sam's gaze was sympathetic as he pinched the muscle of his own soft arm, as if to say, I'd defend you if I were stronger. As for Yankee, he was always turned toward the wok because it always happened during the lunch rush—at night, most of her regulars went home or sought female company elsewhere.

She never so much as hinted about this battle of hands to Mamá, who might forbid her to work at all. Her family needed her tips now more than ever.

Coming to El Paso hadn't prevented the Mexican Revolution from wounding her father after all. The only work he'd been able to find in this city was as a teamster, driving wagonloads of boxes between the Southern Pacific freight house and Shelton-Payne Arms Company. Everyone knew Shelton-Payne sold arms to both sides of the revolution. It marked the first time she felt ashamed of Papá. How could he flee a war only to turn around and help sell it?

Whatever his reasons, one day his back gave out while unloading a crate of rifles, which toppled onto his left foot, crushing all but his biggest toe. A few days later Juárez was taken by General Pascual Orozco—who most Americans would forget—and Colonel Pancho Villa—who everyone would remember. It all came too late for her father. His four crushed toes turned black, and an American doctor amputated them to prevent gangrene. No charge. The doctor, a rebel sympathizer, treated her father like a hero though he'd never fought in a single battle.

Papá lived. But with his limp, nobody would hire him. Meanwhile nobody would hire Mamá because she carried her fifth child and was starting to show. Candelaria, the only child left to them who was old enough to work, gave up her dream of attending school in America. She had no time to cry over this, too busy hunting for jobs all over town, until that hope too began to dissolve. No businesses wanted help from thirteen-year-old Mexican girls, except shops owned by Mexican families who already had daughters.

Louis Yang, whose employees called him Boss-man, had been reluctant to hire her too. When she walked in to ask for work, he closed his eyes and beat a palm against his bald head as if to pound her image from his memory. Then Hoi Sam strode out of the office into the empty dining room, pointed at her, and shouted at Boss-man in rapid-fire Chinese, tone so intense she feared he was accusing her of a crime. She got ready to run. But Boss-man simply wriggled his mustache in disgust and relented: "You come tomorrow. Try one week. Tips only. No keep up, no stay." She turned to give Hoi Sam a grateful smile, but he'd already ducked back in the office.

She was a terrible waitress, at first: couldn't keep up, broke glasses, spilled soup and burned her arm, dropped a plate of barbecued pork on one customer when another tripped her (some men had secret feet too). Despite all that, within a week business was on the rise at the tiny café on South Mesa Street. They came from downtown, the Globe Mill, the laundries, railyards, Segundo Barrio, and Chinatown.

(Not that Chinatown had an official location, just scattered shops and rooming houses on Oregon, Mesa, and Stanton.) Every day she was on shift brought a lunch rush to the Louis Café. Some days, customers waited in line. All men.

Marcela was right when she said Candelaria was more beautiful than she knew and that this would prove important. She'd never admit this to a soul besides Marcela, but there was no denying she was the reason men lined up at this rough intersection of El Paso's White, Mexican, and Chinese worlds, hungry not for chop suey but for a look at the "spicy señorita."

At the end of her first week, Boss-man folded his arms. "Slow, clumsy, too much mistakes. But customers like you. You stay." Her second week, she stopped dropping things, and he shrugged. "Still slow, too much mistakes." Within a month, she developed a juggler's dexterity, able to balance seven plates. He nodded, but still said, "Always too slow-slow-slow." She learned this was his way of saying he liked her.

Although she avoided talking to her parents about work, Mamá still complained about "that job": said she stank when she came home, asked why she couldn't work in a family-owned Mexican restaurant, warned her to be careful around "those Chinese bachelors."

"Wait…now you hate Chinese people? Benito Chung is Chinese, and he's our friend."

"I don't hate them. I don't know them. But not all Chinese men are Benito, and the ones in America are bachelors. They have no women, unless they have bad women. That can make any man dangerous."

What made their women bad? She didn't ask. Mamá's list of things a bad girl does was long: from running like a "wild Indian," to talking to strangers, to talking with her mouth full. Mamá sometimes called herself an Indian, she knew Candelaria couldn't work without talking to strangers, and her whole family talked with their mouths full. But it was a bad idea to argue with Mamá, almost as bad as arguing with a drunk, although sometimes neither could be avoided.

Candelaria made table four wait as long as she dared before she delivered more beer to Beard Man and Soap Man. Although Louis Café was a Chinese establishment, they sold Chihuahua's Cruz Blanca beer, because working-class men liked the price and better-heeled gentlemen thought the plain white label gave it a revolutionary mystique.

The Beard Man snatched one of the bottles from her before she could set it down. "Thought I'd die o' thirst waiting for your shitty bean-eater beer, señorita."

"Sorry, so busy!" she said, voice syrupy as miel. "But the food's good, no?"

He shrugged. "Can't deny Yankee makes the best chop suey of any chinaman I know."

"I'll tell him what you said." She forced a smile. Yankee's mouth always went sour when people called him that, so she knew he hated it as much as she hated when Anglos talked as if Mexicans should be ashamed to eat beans. She turned to leave, felt a hand spank her rear, and scooted away in surprise. She spun around, too late to catch the Soap Man red-handed, though he was gulping beer as if it were the last drink in the desert. She kept spinning like a dog chasing its tail, then walked away muttering, "Must be the ghosts again." Let him think she was crazy.

Yankee beckoned her to the pass-through, cast a glance at table four, and muttered, "Slowly slowly with the beer. They're drunk."

"Probably—they say your chop suey is the best."

He snickered. Then he crooked his finger to coax her closer and whispered. "Time you learn secret about chop suey: I never hear of this strange dish until America. You know what *chop suey* mean? *Chop leftover.*" He suppressed a grin, clearly anticipating a reaction.

She shook her head, confused. "Leftover?"

He paused, then tried to translate it into Spanish. *"Comida vieja?"*

The favorite dish of white customers, the dish the drunks at table four thought was so tasty, was *old food*? She gave a surprised snort of laughter, then covered her mouth, too late. Usually, Yankee's face had a sternness that made him look like he might be as dangerous as the Chinese bachelors Mamá warned her about. Now he was laughing with her, eyes crinkling like the twisty ends of candy wrappers, reminding her of Benito.

The Beard Man shouted, "Hey, Yankee, is that your Yankee Doodle sweetheart?"

The Soap Man guffawed, spewing rice.

A Mexican at the next table slapped the Beard Man's back, laughing, "Yankee Doodle!"

She fought an urge to run out of the café.

Several regulars broke into song, soon joined by the rest, until some dozen men, White, Chinese, and Mexican alike, all sang together:

I'm a Yankee Doodle Dandy
A Yankee Doodle do or die
A real live nephew of my Uncle Sam
Born on the Fourth of July

Customers had sung this song to Yankee before, though she was too embarrassed to ask why. Just another inside joke in this male lair, she guessed. But this time was different. The pair at table four stood, hats over their hearts, and drowned out the others:

I've got a Yankee Doodle sweetheart
She's my Yankee Doodle joy...
Yankee Doodle came to Texas
Just to ride her chonies
And gave her his Yankee Doodle boy!

This time only the drunken pair laughed, falling back into their seats.

The rest fell silent, until one regular mumbled, "Now now, there's ladies present."

Did those men sing the word *chonies*? *Panties?* Why? She turned a puzzled look to Yankee.

To her surprise, he bent over his knees and belly-laughed. "Very funny!" Didn't sound like he meant it.

A couple of men tittered. The rest fell silent.

The air thickened, like it had before the battle at the river. She felt a disturbing urge to giggle. Without thinking, she untucked the towel from her waist and whipped it at the Soap Man. The *snap!* split the air like a shot. Too late she regretted her instinct to break the tension. He grabbed the towel's end to reel her in like a fish, pulled her into his lap, and pressed his baby-smooth cheek to hers. She inhaled his feminine perfumed soap laced with garlic and beer.

"Gal, you need a *real* Yankee Doodle. Haven't ya heard? Chinamen have tiny doodles."

His bearded friend hooted and slapped the table, knocking a bottle to the sawdust-covered floor where it rolled downhill with the floor's slant, chiming over each warped wood board.

"Enough!" Yankee's voice filled the room.

Even the regulars, used to his big voice, looked taken aback.

He strode up to table four and crossed his arms, eyes hard and black as coal but ready to explode into flame.

"Enough what, Chinkee Doodle?" The Soap Man tightened his grip on her as he lurched to his feet, lifting her with him.

Boss-man and Sam appeared out of nowhere to flank Yankee. All three Chinese men stood so close to her and the Soap Man that if anyone stepped forward, they'd all collide. In response, the Soap Man leaned back, forcing him to loosen his hold on her waist. She took the chance to leap forward, stumbling into Yankee's arms.

"No need to get jumpy, little gal. I was just playin.'"

Yankee pushed her behind him and presented his left side to the drunk, one foot forward, one back. When she was a little girl, her father once took her to a bullfight, and the torero stood like that to face the bull. Unlike the bullfighter, Yankee smiled, though his eyes didn't crinkle this time. "Lunchtime over. Back to work-time now. You no wanna get fire."

Chairs scraped, coins jangled, feet shuffled, as men paid and left without waiting for bills.

Candelaria, eager to escape this macho standoff, made a move to collect the money.

Sam shook his head at her and pointed at the ground. Stay put, his finger said.

She did.

"Ain't got no job, Yankee," the Soap Man said, face downcast. "Damn foreman let me go."

"Sorry, Pete. Maybe good day to *find* job. No can find one here."

How did Yankee know his name? She wished he hadn't said it. It'd be hard to forget.

Pete's face went as still as if he lay in his own coffin staring at the lid.

The Beard Man stood. "C'mon, Pete. Yankee's right. Even if he wasn't, I heard he knows that Chinese fightin' and he ain't had no slew o' beers like you."

Pete's jaw worked, as if he'd just remembered some leftover chop suey in his mouth and was giving it a chew. "Hey, Yankee, I was only kiddin'. You know me!"

"Yes, Pete, I know you. Beer make you kidding all the time. No problem. But lunch over. Come back tomorrow."

Pete backed away till he stumbled into his bearded companion, who grabbed his arm and shoved him out the door.

In the silence that followed, Pete's voice drifted in from outside, "Yankee Doodle my ass! Fuckin' uppity chink. I coulda laid him out."

"Yeah, yeah, okay. But then they'd kick us out permanent, and that chink makes the best damn food in town."

Her face flushed on Yankee's behalf. Yet she didn't feel grateful to him but angry. She didn't ask him to rescue her. Would he resent her now for causing him trouble? She refused to look at him as she rushed from table to table to slide money into her apron pocket. Her hands shook, and several coins clattered and rolled across the floor. Yankee bent to retrieve them, poured them into her cupped hands, and closed her shaking fingers over them. She lifted her eyes to his and tried to look thankful, but his eyes said he wanted more than that.

He leaned close, murmuring, "Today when you finish, I walk you home." His breath smelled, not of garlic or beer, but something sour.

She shook her head. "No is necessary." Then she walked to Sam at the counter and piled the gathered paper dollars and coins in front of him. "Sorry, they go before I do the bills."

"No trouble. If you give me your order book, then I will add the total that belongs to Boss-man and subtract the tips owed to you." Sam's English remained formal as always, which still struck her as odd. He looked more Chinese than Yankee, with his long braid, silk cap, and dark tunic. Yankee always wore chef's whites at work and a dark American suit to walk home. Even Boss-man wore a Western button-down shirt. Yet Sam's English was better than any of theirs. His educated tone reminded her of Miguel, though Sam was gentler, almost feminine.

She handed him her order pad so he could add the checks. "Thank you, Sam."

Worried lines pulled down his delicate mouth. "Please allow me to accompany you home tonight. It's not safe."

She glanced at Yankee, hesitated. "Maybe."

He gave a curt nod and turned back to the pile of money.

Yankee helped her clear tables, but she didn't feel relaxed with him anymore. She kept catching him staring, and he wouldn't look away.

Maybe she should walk with Sam, who was closer to her age and never gave her long looks that made her uncomfortable.

She moved toward Sam again, about to accept his offer, when she caught a flash of light, a stray sunbeam glinting off metal. Had he just swept some of her coins into his pocket and not the cash box?

Sam looked up at her and smiled, giving no hint she'd caught him at anything. Must've been her imagination. Yankee treated Sam like a little brother. In turn, Sam trailed Yankee like a loyal dog. And everyone respected Boss-man. Sam was too kind and trustworthy to steal, especially from a man he respected. Wasn't he?

Either way, she decided not to let Sam walk her home after all. It might give him the wrong idea. She'd walk alone as usual. It wasn't far.

The dinner crowd was thin that evening. The few who showed up confirmed gossip was spreading: *They say a Chinese cook at the Louis Café punched a white man…I heard he was a Chinese boxer, and he beat the white man…My buddy said he killed two guys.* She lamented the lost tips, but at least the police didn't come—Boss-man said he paid "good money" every month to avoid that. It was still light outside when they closed, making it easier to convince her coworkers to let her go home alone.

From now on, though, she'd ask her father to come escort her home. She wasn't sure how well he could defend her, but his foot had healed so well that his limp was unnoticeable at first glance. Strangers who saw them arm-in-arm would be unlikely to guess his weakness.

As for Yankee, he'd proven himself capable of protecting her. But Mamá had warned her that sin tempted even the nicest of men. And she couldn't help wondering, if he escorted her home, would she need someone to protect her from *him*?

21. Courtship

1912 – El Paso, Texas

Candelaria's father didn't walk her home from work next night like he'd promised. He claimed he was coming down with something: his chest felt heavy, throat tickled, teeth itched. "Besides, when I walk far it hurts my foot, or what's left of it. Back and forth from your work is almost a mile." She should've known. Ever since he'd lost his job, whenever anyone suggested he leave the apartment, he always had an excuse.

She gave Mamá a pleading look but found no help there either.

"Your father knows what he's ready for."

Maybe they'd change their minds if she told them about the drunks at the café. But then they might accuse her of doing something to encourage those men, or worse, forbid her to return to such a dangerous workplace. So she only said, "Weren't you the ones worried about me walking alone at night?"

"Aren't *you* the one who convinced us it was safe?" Mamá said. "Pues, you were right: you walk through Segundo Barrio, where we have good neighbors who watch out for each other. Besides, you've worked there all summer. Why is it suddenly a problem?"

"It's getting darker now."

But her mother had a point. Her path home did take her past several homes of friends, cousins, or cousins of cousins. In Segundo Barrio, eyes were everywhere: the stoops, the streets, the kitchen windows. Her neighbors were too nosy to let anything happen to her.

The problem was, she'd told Boss-man her father would walk her home from now on.

When she tried to leave work, after sunset, he said, "Wait-wait-wait! Where's your Papá?"

"He meets me outside."

"M hou laa! No-no. You wait inside."

"Papá says outside."

"Then I wait with you."

Unused to fibbing, she didn't know how to wiggle out of this. She let him stand out front with her in the lengthening shadows of the boarding house and shops across the street, hoping he'd grow bored and retreat to his office, or that Sam or Yankee would call him inside for something. Maybe she'd see a male neighbor down the road and run to him, pretend he was her father. Boss-man had never met him and wouldn't know the difference. Awkward minutes passed. She grew frustrated, stuck in this situation caused not by her but by men—good guys, bad guys, no importa, all of them were trouble.

Boss-man did get sick of waiting. But instead of leaving her alone, he opened the café door, poked his head into the glimmer of its single rice-paper lantern, and hollered for Yankee to walk her home.

She protested, "Please, no need—"

He put up a hand to shush her. "You know I have daughter in China?" She shook her head.

"She lives with her mama but has many uncles, so she will not walk alone. Here *you* have Uncle Boss-man, and I say *you* will not walk alone." He patted her hand. "I trust Yankee like my son. He will care you."

"Do ze!" She relented with an affectionate smile, grateful for his concern.

Except now she was forced to wait for Yankee, who insisted on changing clothes first. By the time they left, dusk had fallen, and

Yankee—in his navy-blue suit, red bowtie, and black bowler—must've looked more like a wealthy gringo than a Chinese cook to the Mexicans they passed. Heads turned to glimpse the unusual sight of such a man walking a Mexican girl through Segundo Barrio, though most were careful not to stare.

For two blocks, she and Yankee didn't speak except to agree the evening was pleasant.

"Warm but not hot," she said.

"Cool but not cold," he said.

Their only common language was English, and speaking it all day took such effort it gave her a headache by day's end. Silence felt easier.

The closer they got to her home, the more neighbors she knew, and therefore the more people stared—long enough to notice it was a Chinese man walking with the Rivera girl. At first, she'd been relieved not to walk home alone. Now she worried about gossip.

In Segundo Barrio, Mexicans and Chinese often worked together, visited each other's shops, talked on the street. A handful of Chinese men even married Mexican women. But most El Paso Chinese were bachelors who never approached women of any kind, at least not in public.

Once Mexican girls got their figure they rarely walked with boys unless their brothers, sisters, aunts, or uncles chaperoned or hovered nearby. Walking alone with a strange man of any nationality was a quick way to a fast reputation. She lowered her face and picked up her pace.

"You okay, Candelaria?" In his accent, her name would've sounded unrecognizable, except that he said it the way Benito did, which made her smile.

"I'm okay. Only thinking about the bad men yesterday. Thank you for your help."

"No need to thank. Why you work in city? No father to care you?"

"Yes, but Papá, he…hurted the foot and cannot work."

"Ah-ah-ah! What a pity."

"Yes." Not knowing what else to say, she blurted the question so long on her mind: "Excuse me, why people always sing the Yankee song to you?"

He smirked. "A joke on my name. Yankee Doodle is song about man who love America. Yankee means americano."

"Ohhh. Yankee is no Chinese?"

"No. My Chinese name is Yan Chi. Americans no can say, so say nickname: Yankee. Makes them laugh: Chinese man have American name, hahaha."

She smiled. "Maybe *I* need a nickname. Maybe Candy is more easy to say?"

"No, no. Pretty girl need pretty name: Candelaria."

She pressed her lips tight to hold in a giggle.

"What? I no say your name right?"

A chuckle escaped. "It's okay. I like how you say my name. I like to laugh."

"Me too. Too much serious no fun."

She cleared her throat. "Sí, tienes razón."

"What does that mean?"

She tried to think what her words meant in English. "I don't know."

They burst into mutual laughter.

She looked around, hoping they didn't draw attention, relieved to notice they'd reached her tenement at 5th and Mesa, where it was too dark for others to see their faces. Electric streetlights gave way to the wavering light of candles, lanterns, and woodstoves, sifting through rows of screen doors. Each doorframe was painted a different color, the only way to tell them apart. Two abuelitos sat on neighboring stoops and chattered in the shadows. They paused to nod at the young pair. She glanced at their screen doors—one blue, one yellow—and realized that, in her distraction, she'd passed her family's tenement.

She turned to Yankee and dipped her head to indicate the green door behind him. "Mi casa… My home."

He turned to stare at the door, tensed, waiting. Did he expect her to invite him in?

She toed the gravel in the road, ashamed of the way everyone here lived on top of each other. In Mata Flores, everyone had their own house, however small. Yankee wore a fancy suit. Maybe he had more money than them. But didn't he live in a rooming house with Sam? It must be lonely to live in a foreign country without his family. She took a deep breath. "Please, come meet my family?"

He hesitated. "Thank you, but they no ready for company."

"My father must thank you for to walk me home."

He gave a small bow. "Excuse me, but *I* no ready for company."

She was about to say he looked fine in his suit, when it struck her that wasn't the problem. Her family would speak Spanish. He'd feel awkward.

"Candelita, who're you talking to?" Mamá called in Spanish through the screen door.

"It's Yankee, the cook from the restaurant. He walked me home."

Mamá lowered her voice, "¿Un chino?"

Candelaria darted a look at him, hoping he didn't understand, but she could tell he did by the way he pretended to study the tenement across the street. She stepped closer to the door to murmur to her mother without being overheard. "Be nice, Mamá. Some customers at the restaurant caused trouble yesterday. The boss insisted Yankee get me home safe."

Her mother gripped her own jaw as if it threatened to fall off. Then she opened the door, wedging it wider with her pregnant bulk, letting the thick aroma of boiling beans slip outside. She flapped a hand at Yankee as if to both welcome *and* dismiss him. "Bien, bien! Invite him for dinner then."

Candelaria gritted her teeth and turned to Yankee. "My mamá invite you to dinner."

"Gracias, señora." He tipped his hat at her mother. "But I eat at work. Now I go home."

"Thank you for…walk my daughter…home!" Mamá said in halting English. Only Candelaria knew the effort this cost her.

But Yankee was already walking away. Probably for the best. Much as she wanted her mother to give him a chance, she wasn't ready to do the same.

Her mother's belly still blocked the doorway like an accusation, but Candelaria pushed past her into the undersized, under-furnished, under-lit apartment. Stinging smoke engulfed her from the crackling wood stove where they cooked even in summer.

Mamá swatted her with a kitchen towel. "Walking with a man at night? What if someone saw you?"

"Do you prefer a man to attack me at night? Boss-man sent Yankee to keep me safe."

"Never mind, never mind!" Mamá waved her towel in the air, scattering smoke that made them both cough. "I'm glad that cook left, because your father and I have something to tell you."

Candelaria blew a deflated fart of air through her lips. The homey aroma of pintos now soured in her stomach. She was used to bad news but hated that it was always served with dinner. Although Boss-man gave her free meals, she always saved room for dinner at home. It was the only time her family still laughed together, even if most of the laughter came from Grace.

Grace. That's what they called Graciela now, because Papá said it sounded American and as the youngest she had the best chance to grow up American. Grace was sitting on his lap, both of them sunk into the old sprung couch the last tenants left behind. She was showing him the hand-clapping game she learned from a neighbor girl.

Then she saw Candelaria, jumped off his lap, and burst out, "The mean landlord is making us move!"

"Hush!" Mamá said. "Did anybody ask you?"

Candelaria looked from her mother to her father, waiting for confirmation before she panicked. Her eyes landed on the kitchen table, where a lantern cast stingy light on a stack of towel-wrapped tortillas and a sheet of paper scrawled with thick, angry black writing. An eviction notice. She'd seen one before, nailed to the door of neighbors who fell behind on rent. Mamá followed her gaze to the paper, snatched and crumpled it, then shot a look at Papá, who avoided her stare to look at Grace, whose sheepish eyes remained on Candelaria.

"Why didn't you tell me?" Candelaria said.

"You know your father and I are both unable to work right now."

"Candelita, you're a big help," Papá said. "But your little restaurant job will never be enough to pay for food and rent both."

"Then we'll return to México?" She tried not to sound too hopeful, tried not to give away her secret: that every night she dreamed of going home, of friends and cousins left behind, of speaking her own language whenever she wanted. Of strumming old corridos on her lost vihuela.

"No, we'll stay in El Paso," Mamá said, "but we'll move to Chihuahuita."

"Into one of those filthy huts by the river?!"

"Maybe not!" Papá said. "We have time… One month to pay."

"Except by then we'll owe *two* months' rent," Candelaria said.

Mamá slammed the crumpled notice on the table. "Enough!"

"I didn't know." Papá slumped forward on the couch, arms atop his knees, palms raised. As if he were still carrying Lalo across the bridge. "I didn't know."

Mamá rushed to his side, and her pregnant bulk sank into the couch until the springs screeched a threat to give way. "How could you know? How could anyone know?" She combed his hair with her fingers, turning it white with the flour from her tortillas.

Papá raised his head. "I may yet find a job. I can still work with my hands, you know."

"Of course," Mamá said. "And after this baby is born, I'll work too, God willing."

At that, all four of them crossed themselves. For Candelaria, this was habit, nothing more. She felt sure God had stopped watching over them ever since the dark morning they left Mata Flores. Her sister mirrored her motions, crossing herself in the wrong direction: right-to-left instead of left-to-right. Candelaria snorted in amusement or irritation; she wasn't sure which.

Grace stared up at her, face bunched up like an old woman. "Don't be scared. Papá says all the bad things already happened. So no more bad things can happen."

22. Underground

1912 – El Paso, Texas

Yankee followed New Moon deep into Mr. Yee's Underground House of Forgetfulness, down dark, narrow stairs to her windowless room of red silk scarves and jasmine-perfumed sheets. He didn't choose her because she was the new girl, or because she was only fourteen and might be the virgin she claimed to be, or even because she was El Paso's only Chinese prostitute. For him, Mr. Yee's Mexican girls held the exotic allure of the new, as did the white working girls in the Tenderloin District (only a few of them finicky about Chinese clients). To him, all women were either a curiosity or a curse—his countrywomen no more or less than any other.

No, what drew him to New Moon was the patch over her left eye, a black mystery in an otherwise pale and ordinary face. Beneath it, he imagined a tunnel to the other side of the world. He never forgot the bride he left buried there. In dark places, he still looked for her.

Some said New Moon lost her eye when a customer grew careless with a cigarette. Others said she bit off a man's ban zau, and in his rage and pain he plunged a knife into her socket. One drunk told him she gave the eye to a witch in return for perfect golden lilies—convinced the world's tiniest feet would win her the world's richest husband. "A cruel trick by the witch," the drunk said, "because who'd marry a one-eyed girl?" Yankee found the idea tempting. A one-eyed wife would command attention, which could open opportunity—if only she weren't a whore.

New Moon lay back on the bed and spread her legs in the air like a circus freak. Her one good eye looked right through him, with neither desire nor distress, only acceptance of whatever he might demand as he stood before her, pants open, erection balanced in his hand like a blade. Yet it felt as if her missing eye fixed on him.

He gestured to her eye patch. "What happened?"

She sat up, propped on her elbows, as if seeing him for the first time. "An ember from a wok stove flew up when I was a child. Funny, nobody ever asks."

"I want to see."

Without hesitation, she lifted the patch. The flesh looked sunken but otherwise a normal closed eyelid, as if one eye dreamed while the other remained awake.

A sensation gripped him that the dreaming eye was Mei Yin's, a ghost eye hiding elsewhere in the room, watching. His ban zau went soft. He gazed down at it in disappointment, then leaned over New Moon and lowered the patch back over her eye. "You can't help me."

She didn't give up but instead slid from the bed, knelt between his legs, and clasped his sleeping cock between her hands like a child at prayer. She closed her single eye, but that didn't help. Somewhere in the room was an eye that saw him, and before that eye he felt ashamed.

Before he came to the border between America and Mexico, he'd never worried he might be ugly. In China, he hadn't known his head was large, eyes slanted, cheeks round. In Toisan, if he hadn't been handsome, he'd at least been eligible: forehead high with intelligence, eyes bright with persuasion, cheeks well fed by hard work and good luck. The looks of a provider.

In El Paso, that man was gone. Many Westerners saw him as celestial but inhuman, a beast of burden, unwanted now the railroads were built. Newspapers blamed him for everything from prostitution and gambling to opium dens and public drunkenness. True, Yankee liked bars, games, and women, as did many bachelors of all races. But often in America, the mere sight of a Chinese conjured fear born of myth, like a dragon come to life, bent on rape and murder.

He decided the key to overcoming such phobia was to craft a new myth for himself: king to the scattered men of Chinatown, servant to Whites, ally to Mexicans, eunuch to all. If he wanted a life in America, it seemed marriage wasn't in the cards. Even here at the edge of things, who'd let a daughter marry the unworthy creature they saw in him? Demon, dragon, clown, washer "woman," kitchen help, railroad slave. If he married a woman not "of his kind," this too would mark him as deviant. Yet New Moon was the only unmarried Chinese woman in this city.

Still, he couldn't imagine facing long nights alone for the rest of his life. He came often to the House of Forgetfulness, to warm himself inside one or another of Mr. Yee's dolls—all of them Mexican except this new girl. He limited himself to entering only their mouths. He sometimes feared they might bite, but the possibility of losing his manhood to the diseases between their legs scared him more.

Now, sitting on this thin mattress, studying New Moon as she knelt at his feet—pale skin, tiny breasts, miniature feet, absent eye, every part of her insubstantial as an apparition—he knew her mouth alone wouldn't satisfy him. He wanted to thrust into every tunnel inside her until he found his way home. But his *ban zau* refused to rise, flopping in her hands like a baby bird.

He slapped her hands away. "Stop!"

"If I don't finish, Mr. Yee will get angry."

This moved him. He was no fiend, just a lonely man denied the bride he once wanted, all because he'd failed to be a hero. "Mr. Yee won't know," he declared. He lifted her hands from his member and cupped them together like a beggar's. He held up a finger, indicating *wait here.* Then he slid off the bed, crawled across the cheap rug to the chair where he'd thrown his suit jacket, and rummaged in the lining for a small stack of paper dollars. They never felt like real money to him, never conjured the image of gold.

He turned to the girl, her hands still cupped as if awaiting a drink of water, and counted ten one-dollar bills into her palms. Her lone eye gazed up wide and wet, awaiting his command. So he sat back against the bed and commanded her. "Tell me how you came to America."

"You won't like such a sad story, sir."

He sighed. "No, you're probably right."

"But it will make my heart happy to hear yours."

He cocked a doubtful eyebrow. Then he realized she meant it, because now that he'd paid her she preferred to delay serving another customer. So he began, "I was on duty in our village tower, watching for bandits…"

The night after Yankee walked Candelaria home, her father took over that job, for weeks, picking her up out front, never coming inside. After that, she changed toward Yankee: made excuses to talk, giggled, sighed, asked for help she'd never needed before: "Please, Yankee, can you get the napkins down? You're more tall than me… Please, Yankee, can you open this jar? I'm too weak…" Was it possible that since he'd saved her from the drunks, she saw him the way the young people of Gong Hau used to see him: strong, smart, heroic?

Although Candelaria was Mexican, she was more like the girls back in Gong Hau than New Moon was. Gong Hau mothers didn't bind their daughters' feet, which would prevent them from working the fields. Like Gong Hau girls, Candelaria walked with two flat feet planted on the earth, and this steadiness captured his attention in ways the mystery of a one-eyed girl could not. He imagined Candelaria bucking beneath him, naked back arched, thick hair freed from its usual ponytail, breath coming hard and fast. He'd yet to mount a real woman this way, but he heard Mexican girls were wild mustangs eager to be broken and tamed.

At the thought, his cock rose and did not fall.

One day she asked, "Please, Yankee, come with me to the storage room? I have fear of the rats."

In the dark storage closet, he pulled the cord on the overhead bulb, and the light sent a plump shadow scuttling for cover.

"¡Ay, los ratones!" She buried her face in his neck, and he breathed in her rich scent of cinnamon and clay.

He lifted her chin, hoping to look into her eyes and see the straightforward, no-nonsense girl he'd walked home the other night, but she squeezed her eyes shut. He would barely have to shift to cover her mouth with his. He hesitated.

She opened her eyes, not liquid with desire but glassy as the porcelain dolls in the display windows of The Popular, the bright white department store downtown. "You too nice, Yankee."

Was he? Why was she flirting like some working girl from the Tenderloin District? Suspicious, he leaned away from the kiss she seemed to be offering and stepped back to survey the shelves above her head. "What you need?"

Her face flushed and fingers fidgeted as she turned to search the shelves too. "Here it is! The Dutch cleanser." She bent to reach the bottom shelf, grabbed the small can with the picture of the blue-and-white peasant woman, and hurried out without a backward glance.

Next day, he spied her talking to Sam at the cashbox, leaning close, voice loud. "Sam, I don't know if I add the numbers right on this check. Please look?"

Sam leaned away. "Why don't you ask Yankee?"

She cupped a hand around her mouth as if whispering a secret, though Yankee could hear her plainly, "He only knows the Chinese numbers."

Sam snatched the check from her so fast it tore. He didn't bother with the abacus, so the math must've been easy. Nonetheless, she watched his pencil move across the paper as if admiring an artist sketching a masterpiece.

She dimpled. "Thank you, Sam. So smart!"

She delivered the check to her table, hips rolling as if she crossed a ship at sea. Was she putting on this show for *Sam*? The rest of the day she was a fabric-swirling dance of arms, legs, breasts—gliding, bending, twisting. Yankee's chest rose and fell with each juggle of her plates, each swipe of her towel, each toss of her ponytail.

He was irritated to catch Sam watching too. It made sense. Sam was closer to her age. But he told himself his devotee would never make a move without consulting him. He need only tell Sam *he* had his eye on the girl, and the boy would never look at her again.

Sam turned to see him staring at her. Yankee winked, proof of his confidence. Then Sam peered at the wok behind him and said, "You're burning the pork." Startled, Yankee turned to give the sizzling meat and vegetables a stir. He'd once called this "women's work" but had since grown proud of his talent for cooking. Odd, the meat wasn't burning. Why did Sam say it was?

He glanced up again to catch Sam looking from him to Candelaria, his face tight with a look Yankee had never seen in him before. Was he jealous? Was he stupid enough to think he had a chance with her?

If anyone was to get burned by that unpredictable little flame, it must be Yankee. He was a man. She was a girl. He knew what he wanted. She did not. He would teach her what to want.

Next time she went to the storage room, he followed. Without word or gesture, he yanked her against him and kissed her, hard, sampling her salty lips with his tongue. She stiffened but didn't resist. He let go so suddenly she stumbled against the shelves. She planted her feet, breathing hard, and stared into his eyes with what looked like a challenge. She pressed the back of her hand to her mouth but didn't wipe away his saliva.

"Now you know how it is," he said.

"Yes, Yankee, now I know." She propped one defiant hand on her hip, then lowered the other hand from her mouth and held it out. "Please hand me the mop?"

He did. Her hands shook, revealing that her boldness was a pose—which impressed him all the more.

His blood pumped with the possibilities that follow a kiss, but first he must think. He mustn't let Candelaria derail his future. He couldn't marry a Mexican. He'd lose status with his people. Her people might not even allow it. And if he wanted less than marriage, it was simpler to pay.

He avoided her for the rest of her shift. After she left, he cleaned the kitchen fast and then leaned into the office, where Sam sat at Boss-man's cluttered desk tallying the day's receipts. Boss-man was gone for the night.

"Hurry up," Yankee said. "We're going to Mr. Yee's."

"But it's Thursday."

"One weeknight won't hurt you."

He changed into his suit in the office while Sam counted cash and coins. Then he sat on the desk, foot wagging impatiently till Sam put the money in the safe and spun the dial.

Yankee was used to Sam tagging along with him down the alley to Mr. Yee's. Despite the boy vowing he didn't care for strong drink, opium, gambling, or entertainment women, he once declared he'd never let Yankee risk such a rough crowd without an ally. It would've been difficult to exclude him in any case: they shared bachelor quarters in the rooming house above Mr. Yee's. Besides, Yankee had come to accept Sam as family, or at least, an unavoidable fact of life.

They stepped from the alley into the peeling clapboard boarding house, past the naked lightbulb on the landing, down uneven stairs, into the tropical weather of Mr. Yee's. Tobacco and opium raised clouds; laughter and dice thundered; cards and candles flashed lightning; and liquor rained over it all. Another stairway continued deeper underground to the girls' private rooms—including New Moon's. In this dark den under the city, men of varying fortunes, Chinese, Mexican, and White alike, slouched together like uneasy comrades, draped with the limbs of irritable Mexican girls.

He scanned the room for New Moon's lone eye, but she must be busy downstairs.

At a few low tables, pairs of Chinese gamblers hunched over wood boards carved with the squares of the elephant game, known here as Chinese chess. Drunks crowded round the players to shout conflicting advice.

Yankee earned legendary winnings at this game, not only cash but also tokens of other men's luck: a rabbit's foot from a White, a little wood saint from a Mexican, a red silk knot from a Chinese. Some claimed the charms gave him power over those he defeated. Rumor had it he carried a knife black with the blood of a fellow Chinese he'd caught cheating, who he buried in the desert. As far as he knew, the man simply caught a train to New York, but he said nothing to dispel the tall tales, knowing they unnerved his opponents.

A human growl went up at one table, where a red elephant toppled a black king. The young loser strode away, leaving an open seat across from the winner: a withered old ye ye he'd never met. Though the old man was Chinese, he dressed like a Mexican peasant, sported an American military pistol, and smoked a hand-rolled cigarette like a Texas cowboy.

Yankee slid into the open seat and tossed in his coins, a larger bet than most men would dare with an unknown opponent.

The grandpa yawned and stacked a matching wager. He leaned on a cane though he was seated, using one hand to set up the black-engraved discs while Yankee set up the red.

Yankee whipped him the teasing grin that used to throw Uncle Fu Ying off his game.

The old man didn't smile back, only gestured to Yankee's phalanx: red first.

Yankee sacrificed a pawn, then sat back and waited for his opponent to reveal himself.

The old man remained hard to read, move after move. He favored his elephants, diagonal shuffles revealing nothing.

The circle of men gathered around them grew.

As always, Sam stood wordless at his side, never shouting advice like the others. Yet he felt the boy's body react to every move, vibrating when he gained ground, still as a lizard when he missed a trick. He never worried others might read Sam's tells. Nobody paid attention to Sam.

Yankee sent his army charging toward the river, while his enemy inched forward and then retreated as if afraid of water. It called to mind Candelaria's teasing dance, skipping from table to table in the café. "Where's your courage, grandpa? Come into the open and fight," he said as he ran down his opponent's horse with his chariot.

The old man tapped his finger on a cannon, considering. "You're a cook, aren't you?"

Yankee had been called a woman too often to care. "And you? A retired railroad slave?"

The old man shrugged, stopped tapping his cannon, and shifted a pawn. "What if I am? I know you used the tracks I laid to make your way to this city."

"All that's in the past, Ye Ye. How will you make your way in the future?"

"My future lies with my sons, who live in the land of my father."

Sons. Something Yankee could never have unless he returned to China for a wife. He grabbed his double whiskey, which sat sweating next to the board, and gulped it down. He surveyed the room, pausing at a Mexican girl's nipple peeking from a loose Chinese robe. Then he saw her. The waif, New Moon, eye-patch aimed at him, lone eye staring inward. She scratched her back against a post, acting indifferent as a cat but clearly aware of his attention.

He turned away in irritation. He couldn't marry her, or claim her sons, or even fuck her without risk. What was the point?

His thoughts returned to Candelaria, who only worked because her father couldn't, and who therefore couldn't afford to be choosy. Yankee was a foreigner, yes, but so was she. Most Chinese men in this room either had futures across the sea or none. That need not be his fate. He would plant his seed in America, in the only soil available to him. If that soil wasn't Chinese, so be it. She didn't know it yet, but she was a bridge to the future he wanted, in the American frontier, where a pawn could become a king. He smiled at his decision.

On the board, he sidestepped his enemy's cannon, one move from checkmate. Then his right shoulder grew cold. He looked over that shoulder to see Sam shake his head.

"Yes, Yankee, you've lost."

What?! How?

He turned back to the board, eyes darting from square to square till he saw the black chariot in the corner, lying in wait for the wrong move he'd just made. He clenched his fist. The circle of men gasped, sucking air from the room. He opened his fist, picked up his red king, and handed it to the old railroader. Men exhaled and money changed hands in a flurry of laughter and shouts. His jaw clenched as he pushed his lost coins across the table, the price of letting women distract him. He rose and offered his hand to the railroad man, who shook it with a grip callused and strong, letting his cane clatter to the floor—sly bastard.

Yankee smirked but bowed. "Good game."

The railroader's lips twitched. "You might fare better without women on your mind."

Startled, Yankee couldn't help laughing.

Before he could say more, Sam draped an arm over his shoulder and steered him to the bar. "This is a topic I've been meaning to discuss with you."

"My bad chess?"

"Paying attention."

"To what?"

"Candelaria."

Yankee grinned. "I'm already paying attention to her."

Sam held up two fingers to the bartender who scurried to pour their usual: straight whiskey for Yankee, plain soda for Sam.

Yankee tossed back his drink.

Sam moved his glass in small damp circles atop the bar. "You mustn't marry her." Once again, he proved cleverer than expected, not only at games but also mind-reading.

"Marry? Who said 'marry'?"

"It seemed the next step."

He patted Sam's cheek so hard it was almost a slap. "My boy, there are other steps. Satisfying steps. Why do you care? Don't tell me *you* want her?"

"Of course not!" Sam looked so appalled at the suggestion, it was clear at once: he loved Yankee, only Yankee, and would put no one before him.

His friend's devotion moved him. "Good. Though I wish you did desire a woman—some *other* woman. I worry about you, Sam, who seem to want nothing of your own."

"I have what I want: a good job, saving for my future in the land of opportunity." Sam swigged his soda as if it were something stronger. "It's you I worry about. I know you're a powerful man, and it makes you lonely. I know you're a man of appetite, always hungry. I know you want Candelaria, so I checked on her."

"You mean you spied on her." This didn't disturb him, only roused his curiosity. Was she hiding something? How much could a fourteen-year-old girl hide? He hadn't yet had his way with her. Did someone beat him to it? Did she hope to trick him into raising another man's child?

Sam portioned out his next words in careful bites. "I inquired. Segundo Barrio is poor in money, but rich in gossip." He bowed his head. "I was only looking out for you."

"Yes, yes," Yankee grew impatient. "What did you find?"

"Her family will soon be evicted from their home."

He puzzled over this, then grinned with dawning elation. "She believes I can save them?"

"All I know is, one or two old women saw you with her and *they* believe you're rich."

Yankee slammed his empty glass onto the bar, and the bartender scurried to refill it. "But this is good news, Sam! It means in El Paso I'm known as a man of worth."

"Among Mexicans." Sam sounded unimpressed.

"A man must start somewhere. If I marry Candelaria and we have healthy, educated children, the Chinese will see my value. When I buy my own restaurant, white men will come to see my pretty wife. With the money they pay, I'll buy more restaurants. I'll build an American empire." He took in Sam's worried look. "I mean *we'll* build an empire, my faithful friend."

"You don't care that she doesn't love you as you love her?"

He smiled at his friend's naiveté. "I don't love her. I want her. It's not the same."

"Of course. I must be too young to understand."

Then it hit him: Sam *was* jealous—not of Yankee but of Candelaria. He shrugged. It would pass. Sam always gave him the better portion of every room, every meal, every opportunity. Surely he wouldn't begrudge Yankee a wife. He reached for Sam's arm, missed, reached again, and grabbed on, perhaps a little drunk. "You're a good friend. I'll be careful."

Sam held up the dregs of his soda in a toast. "To trusted friends!"

Yankee tipped his glass toward Sam's, but he frowned. Bing Sam was the only other man he'd ever trusted, and Bing Sam had died. He waved the melancholy thought away. "All this talk isn't solving my immediate problem. My ban zau is as swollen as a horse's."

He slapped Sam's back, stood, and swayed toward New Moon. This time, ghosts would not turn him soft. Candelaria would be his queen, but he would be king. And a king could afford a concubine.

23. Honorable Intentions

1912 – El Paso, Texas

Yankee stole kisses from Candelaria in the storage room several times after their first encounter, though it was never clear whose idea this was. Once, he tried shifting his hands from her face, shoulders, and back, down to her breasts, hips, and thighs. She pushed him away. "That's enough. I must save that for the man who marries me." But as she backed away, she took a deep breath that swelled her breasts. He wondered if she did this on purpose, to entice him to say the word, the golden key to unlock her forbidden places: marriage.

Yet it was someone else he must say the word to, not Candelaria but her father.

The first few times her father arrived to walk her home, she ran outside to greet him before he had a chance to enter the café. All Yankee could make out from a distance was his faded straw cowboy hat. Then, one hot autumn evening, a late rush slammed the café. Afterward, Yankee was helping Candelaria clear dishes, both of them working in companionable silence, when he looked up to see her father in the doorway. The man was as slight and dry as a desert breeze, maybe ten years older than him but twice as tired. He held the hand of a tiny girl, who must be his other daughter.

"¡Buenas noches!" Yankee said.

Candelaria looked up to see who he was speaking to, and her eyes widened in dismay. "Papá! I'm almost done. Please, wait outside!"

Her father gave her and Yankee an odd look before he limped away, favoring his right foot.

Yankee wondered who she was ashamed of: her Chinese suitor or crippled father? Or was this about the little girl?

Candelaria soon left, and he stepped outside to watch the three of them walk away. She tucked her arm at her father's elbow, and it was hard to tell which of them was supporting the other. As for the sister, she bobbed around them like a bird, scurrying ahead and back, head stretched forward on her neck like a roadrunner. How he envied her innocence, her freedom from memories, obligations, or plans.

Next night they came again. He tried to avoid scaring off the father by retreating to clean the kitchen, leaving the dining room to their family. Still, he listened, smiling. He missed the idle chatter of family life, and the little roadrunner's giggles were an unselfconscious explosion of joy, the likes of which he hadn't heard since Mei Yin.

The third night, Candelaria introduced them, and he couldn't resist lingering in the dining room with these people who acted unaccountably happy together. Grace whirred through the room in a blur that threw him off-balance, sending whatever he'd hoped to say to her father out of his head. She charged his way, slid to a stop, and stared up at him, head cocked. Her boldness amused him.

"You never saw a man like me before?"

"I know a man like you. His name's Benito. Are you his brother?"

He chuckled. "No. My brother is Tsi Chaum. He lives in San Francisco."

"At the ocean?"

"Yes."

"I'm going to the ocean!"

"Are you?"

"One day. Benito says it's big, like the desert. Do you know Benito?"

Candelaria looked up from the table she was swabbing with a rag. "Chinese men don't all know each other, apestosa. You don't know every Mexican, do you?"

"So? I know a lot."

"Gracielita, no bother Mr. Doodle." Their father sat in a chair tilted against the wall, hat tipped over his eyes.

Candelaria clapped a palm to her face. "¡Ay, Papá! Not *Doodle*. Mr. *Wong*, Yankee *Wong*."

"Sorry, Mr. Wong." He returned the front chair legs to the floor with a slam and offered Yankee a guarded smile.

"Is okay, Señor Rivera." His smile was equally guarded.

"You know, Mr. Wong, our name, Rivera, is a name with much history. Many years ago, in Spain, it was Ribera. How do you say? Riverbank."

"Very auspicious. Water is life," Yankee said. "Wong is old family name too. *Wong* means yellow. Also, *Yellow King*. Long time ago, *Wong Dai* is father of China."

Grace pressed her fists into her hips. "You're not a king."

"Ay, Grace!" Candelaria said. "Don't be rude."

He laughed. "Not rude. Honest." He bent to Grace's level. "I'm no king, I'm Kei Lun."

Grace scrunched her face. "Who's Kei Lun?"

"Kei Lun appears when a wise king comes. Kei Lun is part dragon, part deer, part horse, and part ox. He protects—"

"Dragon?! Can you fly?"

"If you want."

"Fly with me!" She held up her arms.

He'd never been one to play with children, but it felt impossible to say no to this one. He crouched down to her level and pointed to his back, inviting her for a ride.

She patted his shoulders as if feeling for wings, then climbed on. Her thin arms enfolded his neck, wiry legs clung to his sides, flimsy ribs pressed into his spine. He molded his palms around her bare heels to protect them. Her shrieking giggles bounced off the ceiling as he flew her between tables, roaring like a dragon—an imaginary one, not the raging Kei Lun he had met.

On their third flight round the room, Candelaria said, "¡Basta, Grace! Get down!"

He pulled up short and snorted and pawed the ground like an ox, hoping to make Candelaria laugh. Instead, she stared him down, not with a doll's eyes anymore but those of an alley dog: feral, territorial, with a promise of violence.

"Don't let my sister be the boss-man," she said. "Already she's spoiled."

He set Grace down. "Long ago, I know one girl like her. Not spoiled, just strong."

She shrugged and turned away from him to her sister. "Okay, apestosa, help me fill the soy sauce."

"What's soy sauce?"

"Mmm…like salt but wet," she said. "Here, you try." She sprinkled a dash on the girl's finger.

Grace licked it, scrunched her face, and gave a hop of delight.

He laughed, but Candelaria frowned at him, shook her head, and tipped a pointed glance at her father. He did not look amused—probably didn't like him being so forward with his daughters. She was trying to help Yankee save face. He retreated to the kitchen, hoping he hadn't offended the man whose approval he needed to marry her.

Mei Yin had loved him even though he was a creature of mismatched inhuman parts, but he'd never kissed her, barely even touched her. Candelaria was easier to kiss and hold, but she was harder to win. To his surprise, he liked this challenge. She would make a practical wife, who'd marry him without illusions, who'd stand by him long after youthful desire, dread of poverty, or whatever had driven her to him—was gone.

None of this meant he was "falling in love," one of many American things he saw no point in—like using different words for "him" and "her" or how Coca Cola only tasted good until the bubbles went flat. This was simple: he needed her, she needed him. He needed a wife to make him respectable, so he could open the city's most successful café and raise sons to pass it down to. She needed a husband to take care of her because her father no longer could. He would forget Mei Yin's ghost, marry this sensible living girl, and father a dynasty. All without crazy American ideas like "falling in love." Only a fool would hope for such a painful accident.

He'd planned to plant himself in her father's mind like a seed, tend it, and watch it grow. But that would require courting her as Westerners did: finding excuses to walk her home again, finagling invitations to dinner, flattering Señor Rivera. That could take years. He was supposed to get married two years ago. No more waiting. It was time to take control of his destiny.

Two nights later, Yankee pulled his silver pocket watch from his pants pocket and thumbed the crown, springing the case open to reveal the crystal. Just past eight: closing time. He set the watch on the corner of the desk where Boss-man sat scribbling in a ledger, then he shut the door, sealing them together in the office. He yanked off his chef's whites, reached for his new suit jacket, vest, and dress shirt, dangling from a hook on the door, and changed.

Boss-man was supposed to be tallying the day's receipts for Sam, so Sam could clean the kitchen for Yankee, so he could prepare for an audience with Señor Rivera in the dining room.

Instead, Boss-man pushed his chair back and said, "You're being hasty. You should wait."

"You're the one who encouraged me to walk her home." He rummaged in his suit pocket for his flask and took a swig. The whiskey burned his already churning stomach.

"Yes, but there's a vast distance between walking her home and marrying her."

"I waited too long once before. I won't make that mistake again." He swung to face Boss-man with determination, but the way it set the old man back in his chair, maybe his face suggested a more violent feeling.

"Of—of course, it's not for me to say," Boss-man stuttered. "I only want you to be happy. But please do one thing?"

"What?!" Yankee's voice came out strangled.

"Your bowtie looks drunk, son." The older man crooked a finger, beckoning him closer.

He leaned down to let him straighten it. Then he flung open the door, strode to the sink to wet his hands, and slicked his hair. He glanced at his reflection in the mirror over the sink. Already balding at twenty-two? Even more reason to act now. He wasn't getting younger.

Sam appeared at his side to hand him his bowler hat. With that, he stepped into the dining room, clasping the brim before him.

Candelaria was sweeping the dining room floor when he entered, but her broom swished to a halt the moment she glanced up at his navy-blue serge suit. She looked him up and down, then turned an alarmed look at her father, napping at a table by the door, head pillowed on his arms, hat sliding off. Her reaction threw him. He hadn't told her his plan. Still, wasn't this what she hinted about every time she pulled away from him in the pantry, insisting she was waiting for marriage?

She threw a panicked glance at Grace—who was intent on discovering how many napkins could be squeezed into an overstuffed dispenser—then she shot Yankee a pleading look. Was she worried the silly little piggy would get in the way?

He bowed to whisper in her little sister's ear, "Grace, if you and sister help Sam wash dishes, then I give you dragon-ride after."

Grace cupped a hand to his ear, though her loud effort to whisper was comical. "Dragon first!"

"First I talk with your Papá," he said.

At that, Señor Rivera sat up and scrambled to retrieve his hat, too alert to have been truly asleep.

Candelaria set her broom in the corner, lifted her sister under the armpits, and carried her toward the kitchen.

Grace's legs pedaled the air in protest. "I can walk by myself!"

She set her down and bowed. "Excuse me, princesa. Before, you like for me to carry you."

Grace ran to the kitchen.

Candelaria's final glance at Yankee held neither encouragement nor discouragement. She turned away and trailed her sister into the kitchen.

Yankee pulled up a chair across from Señor Rivera and set his hat on the table. Señor Rivera took off his cowboy hat and set it down facing the bowler, though he kept his seat facing sideways. Up close, he looked younger, though his eyes were bloodshot as if he hadn't slept well. He ran one hand through sweat-pasted hair and looked at Yankee as if he were a knife-wielding bandit about to rob a slice of his flesh. So, the older man knew what this was about. Yankee no longer had the element of surprise in his favor.

In China, when a daughter married, she no longer belonged to her family. This wasn't the case in America. It was the only reason he had a chance, because when he married Candelaria he'd join her family—and the Riveras needed another breadwinner. On the other hand, the weakness of her father's position must make him apprehensive. Yankee hated owing anything to any man, and assumed her father felt the same.

"¡Señor Rivera, tan en-can-ta-do-ras sus hijas!" He pronounced the compliment in careful, practiced Spanish as he gestured toward the man's daughters in the kitchen.

Señor Rivera said nothing but cast a scornful glance his way. Maybe his Spanish was wrong. Or maybe it was too forward to call his daughters enchanting.

He cleared his throat and tried again, still in halting Spanish. "Candelaria is…a nice woman."

Her father's eyelids lowered like a sleepy lizard's, but in a way that suggested he was growing more alert, not less. He folded his arms and spoke in Spanish even slower than Yankee's, as if he not only doubted the younger man would understand but felt sure he was an idiot. "*Candelita* has many good qualities, but she is no woman. She is a girl." Yankee had never before heard anyone use the diminutive of her name.

"Excuse me. My Spanish bad. *Candelita* is a nice *girl*. She works hard. She is quiet. She has respect."

Her father gave a slow nod. "I'm happy she behaves herself. She says the men who work here behave like caballeros."

"Sí, señor. I'm a man of good family."

"Good. If I suspected you did not respect her, I'd keep her home." He set his elbows on the table and leaned toward Yankee. "¿Me entiende?"

"Yes, I understand."

Yankee didn't assume Señor Rivera was trying to discourage him, only pushing for the best possible offer. The man had lost two sons, half his foot, and his job. He needed sons to care for him in old age. An unmarried daughter was a burden. He had no choice but to let her go. Maybe he wanted to make her appear more valuable by pretending he could afford to keep her. Or maybe he worried Yankee wouldn't take good care of her.

Yankee searched for the right words to put him at ease but knew neither the English nor Spanish for ideas like *honor*, *intention*, or *support*.

Maybe Boss-man was right and he should've waited. He struggled on, "I want to say…I have a good job…I save money…Soon I buy a restaurant…Soon *I* am boss-man. A man needs a good wife. It is my idea… No, it is my wish…my question…"

"You want to marry my daughter?"

"Sí. Esposa. Wife."

Señor Rivera looked down at the table and breathed deeply. With each inhale he seemed to consider the idea, and with each exhale to reject it. He looked up, focused on a point past Yankee's ear. "You and my daughter are of different cultures."

"Yes…" He'd expected this. Still, it was hard to push down his anger. The man thought a Chinese was not good enough for his daughter? He wanted to throw the unspoken insult back at him, to suggest *she* wasn't good enough for *him*. But then he'd lose. He fell silent.

The sound of clattering dishes and Grace's chattering birdsong drifted from the kitchen.

"Please understand, Señor Wong, these differences are no problem for me. But other people can make life difficult—for both of you."

He thought of the jump-rope rhyme little American girls sang: "Ching chong chinaman sitting on a fence…trying to make a dollar out of fifteen cents!" Thought of children who ran at the sight of him, warned by their parents that chinamen stole bad boys and girls and dragged them to underground lairs to eat them. Thought of the two drunk white men he saw follow another Chinese down an alley one night, pushing, kicking, taunting. The man didn't run, fight back, or utter a sound, only struggled to keep walking as if they didn't exist. The attackers' violence didn't upset him nearly as much as the victim's muteness. He'd hurried out of that alley to escape notice. He'd felt ashamed, not only of himself but of the man he'd left behind.

He imagined a mob chasing his future children. Rage shot through him. He stood so suddenly he toppled his chair, and said in English, "I'll protect Candelita. No one will hurt her. America is home of the brave. El Paso is city of many cultures. We live in new times. If two people marry, the world must respect." His fists were clenched. He loosened them.

Señor Rivera sat back, staring, until his eyes lost their wariness. He spread his arms wide and flipped his palms upward to show their emptiness. "Candelita has no *dote.*"

"Excuse me, what is *dote*?"

"I have no money or gifts to give you for my daughter."

"Ah, *dowry!*" He'd learned this word from Sam of all people. He hoped Señor Rivera's use of this word suggested he was ready to accept his daughter marrying a Chinese. "Don't worry. Candelita is a good girl. She works hard. She will give babies. This is enough *dote.*"

"If she says yes, then I'll give you my blessing—in two years."

"Two years?!" He didn't bother to hide his dismay.

Señor Rivera turned his chair to face him and sat up with knees spread, feet planted, arms folded, indicating he wouldn't negotiate this point. "I told you, my daughter is not a woman. She's a fourteen-year-old girl. When she turns sixteen, then you may marry her."

Yankee paused. New Moon could satisfy his physical needs, yes, but that wasn't enough. If he were to keep spending money on women, it should be an investment: in a wife who'd give him a family and help with his restaurant, not a prostitute who could give him nothing.

Both men started at the sound of a dish shattering, a scolding voice, a rising wail. Sam appeared in the kitchen entry, looking helpless. Yankee shook his head, indicating that whatever the problem was it was up to Sam to fix it. Sam gave him a sullen look and retreated.

The wailing cut short, then changed to giggles. Grace's tiny bird legs appeared, flying past the kitchen door, then out of sight, then flying past again. Sam was swinging her in circles in the space between wok and sink. "More!" she shrieked. Sam and Candelaria laughed with her. Yankee felt an urge to run into the kitchen and tell them all to shut up because they weren't helping his argument—acting like children, just as Candelaria's father said she was.

Señor Rivera laughed too, but it sounded less like amusement and more like his signal that this conversation was over. "She'll wear him out. We should go. Candelita!" He grabbed his hat, crushing it as he rose to head toward the kitchen.

"Señor Rivera?" Yankee blocked his path.

The other man lowered his chin but raised his brow. "¿Sí?"

"She is a little girl only if you say. If she is a wife, then she is a woman. For a father, less children means less worry."

Her father pulled himself to full height—which made him only as tall as Yankee—and looked him dead in the eye. "Children are a blessing."

"They're important to Chinese too. So, I give you gift: Your family will be my family, my fortune your fortune, and if Candelita gives me children, then I give you lucky money."

But Señor Rivera was looking past him. Yankee turned to see Candelaria standing behind him, gazing up at her father like a penitent child. Was she ashamed he was the best suitor she could get?

Her father dug his boot-heel into the floor and stared at its toe, maybe contemplating the space where his actual toes used to be. "When you have daughters, you'll understand." He held up two fingers. "Two years," and offered his other hand to seal the deal.

Yankee shook it, having pushed as far as he dared. "Please, now I am Candelaria's novio, may I visit her, Eduardo?"

Her father looked startled but said, "Yes. Tomorrow is Sunday. Please join our family for dinner. And please, don't call me Eduardo."

"Sí, claro, Señor Rivera." He let go his hand and bowed.

He turned to Candelaria with a hopeful smile. But her eyes remained fixed on her father, who turned his back on her, limped to the café window, and looked out. She remained rooted to the spot, eyes brimming. Yankee didn't move, unsure how to reassure her with her father there.

Señor Rivera called out without turning around. "¡Graciela!"

Grace sprang out of the kitchen, ran past her sister, and flew into the arms of her father, who carried her out the door without looking back to see if Candelaria followed.

If his future father-in-law was going to take this attitude, Yankee didn't know how he could wait through two years of it.

24. The Virgin

1912 – El Paso, Texas

Candelaria despaired at the prospect of waiting two years to marry Yankee. Her family needed another working man now or they'd lose the roof over their heads, such as it was. But the justice of the peace wouldn't allow her to marry *any* man, let alone a Chinese man, unless her father came to the courthouse to speak for her. She hoped to discuss a way around this with Yankee. But next time she saw him was at Sunday dinner, and her parents wouldn't let them out of sight.

At dinner, Yankee and Grace were the only ones who spoke more than a few words, as if he was as oblivious as a five-year-old about how much this match worried her parents. Afterward, he suggested they all take a stroll. Papá said his foot hurt. So only her little sister and hugely pregnant mother went along, waddling behind them like nosy dueñas.

Yankee whispered, "I have an idea so your papá will let us marry sooner."

"Shh!" she hissed. "Not here."

"Here is good. At café, too many people listen."

"Mamá always is listening, everywhere."

He shook his head. "She isn't now."

She looked over her shoulder. He was right. Mamá's attention was on Grace, whose babbling drowned most other sounds. "Okay, tell me."

"We will make a baby."

She clapped a hand to her mouth and halted. "No. Papá. He will… angry."

"Yes, but what will he do?"

"I will bring dishonor to my family."

"But what will he *do*?"

"I don't know. Throw me from the house?"

"No. He will let us marry, so no dishonor."

Maybe. Her neighbor, Augustina, got married and had a baby five months later. She couldn't marry Yankee in the church anyway because he wasn't Catholic, so what did it matter? Would she burn in hell? He said there was no hell, that people made up hell to scare other people into doing what they wanted. She was shocked to hear him say so, though she often wondered this very thing. But what if she got pregnant and he changed his mind about marrying her?

He answered her unspoken question. "In China, a man cannot break his word. The ancestors will know. He will lose face."

He took the same risk she did? This was hard to believe. She could think of nobody as defenseless as a pregnant woman. She pictured her mother giving birth in a gush of blood, inside a smoky hut, along the icy edge of the Río Grande, her baby just one more mouth to feed in Chihuahuita—at this thought her hand convulsed in his. She swallowed her doubts and nodded.

"You'll do it?" he asked.

"Yes. We will make a baby." Except her voice went up at the end, like a question.

In answer, he took her hand and rubbed his thumb over the back of it.

She cast a sidelong glance at him. It was the first time she ever saw him smile with his whole face. Was this what love looked like? She didn't feel like smiling. She didn't love him. Not like that. She wanted to—he was her novio, the man she was to marry. She remembered Angel handing her the bouquet of purple salvia, her arm linked in his as they strolled the Sunday paseo in Mata Flores, the stars under her skin when her lips brushed his.

Yankee kept rubbing her hand with his thumb till it tickled. She pulled free and scratched, till she realized something else nagged at her: a hole in his plan. There was no place in the city where a Chinese man and Mexican girl could go together unnoticed. She told him this, and he dumbfounded her again, by leaving it up to her to solve the problem.

"I trust you," he said.

But did *she* trust *him*?

Not exactly. Not the way she trusted Papá. Not the way Papá trusted her. And she was about to break that trust. Never before had she defied her father so completely. She told herself she was doing it for him, for all of them. A gift unlikely to make him proud.

In the coming nights, she lay on the narrow mattress she shared with Grace, mentally scouting locations to surrender her virginity. As usual, her sister proved distracting, thrashing with nightmares that bruised Candelaria in the oddest places: behind her knee, below her ear, along her hip bone. She warded off one after another of Grace's feet and fists as she stared at the ceiling, trying to imagine a safe place where she and Yankee might go at night:

Not his boarding house.

Not her family's apartment.

Not a hotel, where no unmarried couple would be admitted, much less a mixed-race couple, much less a man with a girl of fourteen.

Not an abandoned camp in Chihuahuita, where a non-Mexican would attract notice.

Not an empty train car at the railyard, where young americanos went to spoon but where she and Yankee would look out of place.

They needed a remote, unlit, secret place where their presence would go unremarked. The map in her head insisted no such place existed. Unless she considered…the border itself.

They agreed to seal their promise on Isla de Córdoba. It wasn't a true island but a peninsula surrounded on three sides by the Río Grande; a sliver of Mexico trapped in America; a patch of wilderness nobody owned. Nobody went there at night. At least, nobody who could afford to notice them.

Candelaria waited for silence to bury the city, for her parents' breathing to grow heavy, for Grace's thrashing to subside. Then she slipped into a dark skirt and dark sweater and floated across the dark apartment the way her friend Marcela might—light as air. She felt for her chanclas amid the other sandals near the door, looped them through the fingers of one hand, then used the other to inch the door open. The hinges squeaked. She held her breath, squinted at the cracked open door of her parents' room, and listened.

Papá snored on.

But Mamá called softly, "Careful, mijita," her voice a startling caress in the dark.

She knew? And gave her blessing? It marked the first time she knew her mother to grant permission for anything important without consulting her father, much less in a whisper while he slept—implying this was *their* secret. That whisper broke a fact of her life. She couldn't ask what it meant without waking her father. So she said nothing, just reached for her mother with the beats of her heart while the rest of her went on its way.

Her eyes burned with unshed tears as she slipped out into blurry moonlight, so at first she didn't recognize the man on the corner. He wore a loose cotton shirt, red-and-brown woven blanket slung over his arm, face so tanned that in the half-light Yankee looked Mexican. She slipped on her chanclas, holding his shoulder for balance, inhaling his familiar smells of sesame, ginger, and that sour tang she had yet to identify. Then he crooked his elbow. She pretended not to recognize the invitation to take his arm. It would feel awkward on such a long walk.

For the next hour, they silently traced the crooked black line of the Río Grande, the edge of America.

At a sharp left turn of the river, she removed her chanclas again to wade through the chilly water, a trickle this time of year but still challenging to cross. Mud sucked at her toes and rocks jabbed her soles. On the opposite bank, the chanclas went back on, but her muddy feet threatened to slip out of them, so she hung onto Yankee to avoid tumbling into thorny brush. She looked up at him. In the moonlight, he looked handsome, like a hero, like a lover.

People said that bandits camped at Cordova Island, but he said not to worry because such men treated it as neutral ground where everyone pretended not to see each other. She could swear she heard distant footsteps and whispers, but if so, they blended with the river's soft music. The swirl of stars overhead painted the palo verde trees' yellow blooms into lanterns, but they didn't shed enough light to reveal whether anyone else shared the island this night.

Yankee spread his blanket under a scraggly desert willow, its pale pink blooms dangling over them like eavesdroppers. She sat rigid at his side, not wanting to appear frightened, or eager, not sure if she felt either. Her arm tickled where it brushed his, but she resisted the urge to scratch. Their muddy feet wafted a smell of decay to her nose.

She told herself a man who loved her was about to take her virginity, that this was the Garden of Eden, that they were Adam and Eve. She looked up at the River of Stars, pulled her knees to her chest like a child, and asked if he knew the story of The Cowherd and Weaver Girl.

"Everyone in my country knows this story," he said.

"Please, tell it to me?"

"If you lie with me." He pulled her back onto the rough blanket and nestled her head in the crook of his shoulder.

Her heart threw itself against her chest as if ready to run home without her. A twig dug into her side, but she dared not shift against him, worried he'd take it as a signal to start making love to her. She wasn't ready. She tried to listen to the story.

He told it differently than Benito. The fairies had no wings, the children didn't cry, and the queen who kept the star-crossed lovers apart didn't sound wicked at all—she asked why.

He explained, "What will happen if Queen of Heaven let stars live anywhere they want?"

She thought about it. "Travelers will get lost at night?"

"Exactly. Very smart."

His unexpected praise put her more at ease. He must have felt her relax against him, because he turned and kissed her in a way he never had before: soft and slow, till their breath became one. He had searched her mouth with his tongue before, but this time it hesitated as it touched hers, like a question. For the first time, she let him reach under her blouse. His fingers traced her breast, thumb brushing her nipple like a ripe strawberry that might bruise.

A pulse twitched between her legs. Startled by her own response, she bolted upright.

He sat up, held her shoulders, and gazed into her eyes. "What's wrong?" Beneath his husky murmur she heard a deep rumble, like an approaching train.

"Promise you won't hurt me."

"I promise."

He went on patiently, his kisses a long, slow drink of water, like a lost man in the desert who hesitates to quench his thirst. He suckled her nipples like a baby. She stifled an embarrassed giggle, but she liked it. It made her prickle hot and cold all over.

He reached under her skirt, up, up, up to her private place, which not even she had touched that way before. Liquid seeped from her, and she was ashamed to think she'd accidentally peed. He pulled down his pants, guided her hand to his pito. She'd seen one before—on a dare, she and Angel had traded peeks in the cornfields—but she'd never touched one. She didn't expect it to leap against her hand like a wild animal. Wasn't *he* supposed to put it inside her? What did he expect *her* to do with it?

She pulled her hand away.

He guided it back.

So she stroked it, like a pet, something she might tame.

He yanked his shirt overhead, then slid her blouse off and pressed their warm skin together. His heart knocked at her chest, insistent as a soldier at the door. Her heart fled into her throat, made it impossible to breathe. Was this how love felt, like dying? Her thighs parted, and her wet opening reached up to welcome him. Yet as he tried to enter, she felt sure his key wouldn't fit the lock, a crooked little gap so tucked away she hadn't been sure it existed till now. She braced herself, scared he would split her open.

He broke his promise. It hurt.

He forced her legs wider apart so he could bury himself deeper, bruising her inner flesh, filling her with pressure until something snapped. He pushed inside again and again till she felt cramps that made her want to double over, except she couldn't because he was on top of her. She wanted to ask him to wait, stop, slow down, but his chest pushed the wind from her and all she managed was a moan. He moaned too, but she realized for him this meant pleasure.

They were speaking two languages, and he didn't understand hers.

In some distant part of her she sensed pleasure waiting, but it remained out of reach while she lay crushed under the weight of this sudden stranger. She wanted to cry, but the feeling was too deep. He shuddered and spurted inside her, or maybe it was she who burst open and bled. Before she knew it, he rolled off, leaving a dull ache between her sticky thighs.

The ache spread, carrying her mother's whisper, "Be careful, mi-jita." She had thought those words a blessing, but maybe they were a curse. Why had her mother let her wander into the night to suffer this emptying of herself? Wasn't it a mother's job to protect her daughter? Papá never would've betrayed her to this fate.

Yankee wrapped himself around her limp body. "You okay?"

"I don't know..." She tried to hold back tears, but it was no use. Her face became a floodplain where rivers multiplied, crossed, and recrossed, drowning the person she used to be.

He turned her face to his. He looked puzzled, not by her tears but by her very features, as if he expected someone else. "Don't worry. First time for woman always hurt. Better next time."

She didn't believe him. He'd already broken his promise not to hurt her. She shivered.

He tightened his arms around her. "You cold?"

Before she could answer, he pulled the blanket over her, leaving none for himself, and this tenderness was more than she could bear. This time it was she who shuddered, in surrender. She huddled against him and let him hold her. Who else did she have to comfort her now?

25. Childbirth

1913 – El Paso, Texas

Candelaria and her mother panted hard, warm breath bouncing off greasy walls till the bungalow was stifling. She knelt with her head pillowed on a kitchen chair while Mamá stood behind her, pulling the ends of the blue rebozo wrapped around her belly to ease the cramps, rocking her side to side. She'd gone into heavy labor at sunset, a lifetime ago, vowing not to yell and upset her new neighbors. They were kind but not what she'd call friendly, not once they'd seen her with her Chinese husband, and she didn't want to push their goodwill.

Each pain grew more pitiless than the last. Still she refused to voice the scream inside her.

Was this what her mother had tried to warn her about, with her whispered "Be careful," that first night she'd snuck off with Yankee? More stolen nights had followed. Within three months, she got pregnant, forcing her parents to let Yankee marry her. By then, Papá had found enough odd jobs to prevent the eviction that set her on this path. Yet he forgave her right away, while Mamá grew distant, till they barely spoke at all.

Even now, she was relieved Mamá stood behind her rather than before her, so she didn't have to meet her eyes.

She wished Papá had never promised her to Yankee. But she was angriest at Mamá, for making no effort to stop her that night, for never warning her against marrying a man who rarely laughed, who didn't speak her language, who she knew little about. For failing to at least warn her of this bottomless pain—then again, she never would've believed it.

The only advice Mamá gave now was, "Push!"

To which she shouted, "I hate this pinche baby!"

The pain passed, the rebozo slackened, and she collapsed to her side. Her mother dropped to the floor with her and said, "I promise never to tell the baby."

They both burst into laughter.

After that, the pains came harder, her shouts grew louder, but her bitterness at her mother faded.

She knew women often died in childbirth, but only now, when her belly, hips, and changuito filled her mind, did she fear she was too small to give passage to an entire human. Why had she thought she could save her family by having a baby? For nine months, she carried this insatiable beast, and it was about to repay her by tearing her in two. If she died, who'd take care of it? Not Yankee. Her family would have another mouth to feed and one *less* worker instead of one *more*. Stupid, stupid, stupid girl.

Only one thing mattered now. "Mamá, if I die, please take care of my baby."

"Mija, you won't die. I had Miguel when I was only two years older than you are now, and I lived to have four more."

Four more? She unleashed a wail that surely reached beyond Segundo Barrio to cross the border. In response, her mother hummed a lullaby in time with the rocking of the rebozo across her middle. Mamá's shawl had held all her children at one time or another, and now it carried Candelaria again—across the desert, through the red door, to the dirt floor of the home they'd left behind, where she hid from the pain for a time.

Upon returning to her body, she said, "Where's Yankee?"

"I sent him away. Men are no good at a time like this."

She had a good idea where he was: at Mr. Yee's with his putas. She didn't tell Mamá.

She never accused him of unfaithfulness. She *had* tried to catch him in a lie, by expressing doubts in herself, "Soon you won't want me anymore, now that I'm big and fat."

He'd pulled her onto his lap and wrapped his arms around her, tapping long fingers atop her belly like a drum. "You're more beautiful than ever, round with our son"—he was certain it was a son. "Haven't I shown you again and again?"

It was true, the larger she grew, the more attentive he grew: bringing flowers, pressing lips to her belly to tell stories to the baby, cooking to fulfill her cravings for odd combinations like Chinese tea and Mexican capirotada. He laughed when she put sugar in green tea. She laughed when he added candied ginger to bread pudding. They laughed together. Their lovemaking gave her more pleasure than she'd hoped. Often, she ached for it, even when he came home from Mr. Yee's sweating sour whiskey and sweet perfume.

Sam obliged himself to tell her every time Yankee went to that brothel, shaking his head at his friend's ill judgment, acting as if he expected gratitude for the information. She was only thankful her husband didn't perform entire sex acts in front of his chatty friend.

Yankee often had his way with her *before* he went to Mr. Yee's, as if to mark his territory before leaving, often doing things that shamed her. He sometimes put his pito in places on her body where it didn't belong. One time he insisted she treat him like a baby, rocking him and calling him mijo while he suckled her breasts. How could he do such ungodly things to her and still come home smelling like the musk of others? Was this natural?

She alternately feared and hoped to discover they weren't really husband and wife since a justice of the peace had married them, not a priest. In the six months after that, Yankee became both hero and villain, surprising her with acts of tenderness followed by pure mean-ness. He abandoned her to hours of silence so lonely that his bellowing afterward came as a relief. He accused her of being lazy, her parents of eating all their money, her six-year-old sister of having no common sense. Candelaria once chuckled at his Spanish and he charged at her, snarling, teeth bared, hands like claws. When she screamed, he rolled his eyes, "Don't be silly, I'm only teasing." He said she was too sensitive because her parents spoiled her. Did they?

Or did she marry a bad man? She wasn't sure she wanted to know. Too late now.

He declared he planted his son in her that first night, as if this proved his virility, and promised to father many more. He never beat her, thank God, but he might kill her yet with his appetite. If not this time, then the next. How many times could she survive this?

The next pain mounted till she screamed, "Please, God, let me faint!"

God ignored her.

The baby held fast. She understood how it felt: not wanting to leave home. But what if it suffocated? "Mamá, if you must, call a doctor to cut the baby out. I don't care what happens to me." The moment she said it, she knew she didn't mean it. It seemed unfair a stranger she'd never met might survive at her expense.

"Your baby will be fine," Mamá said. "You've only been pushing for five hours."

Seemed like fifty.

Mamá reached into the bowl for the wet cloth, wrung it out, and laid it across her forehead. The ice melted, the water turned lukewarm, but it didn't matter. Only the movement mattered: her mother's hands withdrawing and returning, driving away death, calling forth life.

An hour later, The Queen of Heaven ripped her in two with her hairpin, blood poured from the gash, and The Stranger emerged, a gory sacrifice. Her mother scrubbed him with fresh steaming rags, de-claring, "Cleanliness is the luxury of the poor." He disagreed, bawling so loudly it was clear he inherited Yankee's lungs. Mamá wrapped the infant in a blue blanket with hand-stitched bees—a gift from Isabel and Benito—and placed him in her arms.

She gazed into his big black eyes while her mother soothed her changuito where he'd torn her open, patting it with a wet poultice of leaves, herbs, and red caliche.

She looked down at the muddy concoction in alarm. "Isn't that dirty, Mamá?"

"No. Humans and animals carry disease, but our mother, the earth, is a healer."

"I thought Mary was our mother."

"Sí, claro. But before she gave birth to our Lord, Mother Earth gave birth to her."

"Isn't that blasphemy?"

"Pfft! Blasphemy is for men, who don't carry life inside them. What do you think 'dust to dust' means? But let's keep that between us—and your daughters when you have them."

"Must I do this again?"

"Unless your husband loses interest. But his hunger's too big for that, don't you think?"

She snorted. "How do you know?"

"I'm your mother. Also, every morning you walk the way your father did when he was breaking horses."

She chuckled, stopping when she felt her skin split again.

Her mother touched her arm. "Careful. You need rest." She cupped The Stranger's tiny head. "I'll tell this one's father the same, or he'll answer to me—I don't care if he says it's not my business. He's kind to help us, but he doesn't own us."

Did Mamá only say that because she feared the opposite was true? Had he used this baby to buy them all?

For now, they were free, two women with nothing to excuse or explain. Together they taught The Stranger to suck her nipple and laughed when the greedy boy refused to let go. He tugged at something deeper in her than her husband ever did, though he looked twice as foreign.

"Isn't he different from any baby you've seen?" she said.

"It's true. I've never seen anyone like him."

"Is he ugly or beautiful, do you think?"

Mamá tilted her head. "It's hard to tell when they first come out. Their heads always look like mashed fruit. But beautiful, I think."

"Will looking unusual be good luck or bad?"

"Good, I'm sure. This child is two in one. His face will open the door to a new world."

"Or close the door to an old one."

"No importa," Mamá shrugged. "There's no going back now."

True. Candelaria often imagined returning to Mata Flores, but when she pictured walking up to their old casita, she was a giantess who no longer fit through the tiny door.

She couldn't believe Mamá had left her nine-month-old son with Papá so she could midwife Candelaria through ten hours of labor—though in the early stages he did run Salvador crying down the street for Mamá to feed. Already Candelaria couldn't imagine being parted from her little Stranger for one minute. She grew impatient waiting for Mamá to fetch the others to the bungalow to meet him.

The tiny bedroom felt crowded with the addition of Papá, Grace, and tiny Tío Salvador, yet a hole opened inside her. Not everyone was here. She blinked away tears, lifted The Stranger and said, "Look what I made, Papá."

He took one look at her son, then his eyes sought hers and, in one swift wink, told her she remained his little girl. She was glad. Someone should hold onto her childhood.

"Can I hold him?" Grace asked.

Papá directed her to first sit in the oak rocker (a gift from Marcela and her husband, a young Chinese merchant in Juárez). Then he tucked the baby in her arms. "Careful with his head!"

"I know how, Papá!" Grace insisted, indignant.

He hovered over her, forehead wrinkled, studying the baby's face. "He looks like Lalo."

As if those words summoned him, her little brother appeared after all. All his old pranks gleamed in The Stranger's eyes. Her mother was holding tiny Tío Salvador but leaned down to press her nose to The Stranger's head, inhaling his newborn scent, like a stream after fresh rain. She suspected Mamá thought not only of Lalo but also Miguel. A chill shook Candelaria. What if her son grew up and ran away? What if he were killed? How had Mamá survived such horrors?

Her father laid a finger in The Stranger's palm, and the baby gripped it as he sang:

Naranja dulce, limón partido.
Da me un abrazo que yo te pido.

Sweet orange, sliced lemon too.
Give me the hug I ask of you.

Lalo used to love that silly rhyme.

"Look!" Grace said. "He's making sour lips. He wants a lemon."

Her family's laughter multiplied against the close walls and ceiling. Whenever Lalo was around, everybody laughed. If she named the baby Lalo, maybe she could keep this laughter close. But her husband wouldn't like it. Lalo was short for Eduardo, her father's name, and Yankee made it clear: she belonged to him now.

Candelaria woke to the familiar fumble, shove, and rattle of the front door, tight on one side, loose on the other, no matter how often Yankee and Papá planed, sanded, and argued over it. Yankee teetered into the bedroom, lit by the sepia sunrise that snuck past the shades he bought at The Popular. He'd rejected Mamá's homemade curtains, sewn from discarded pink tutus she found behind a dance studio: "No. Our home will look like a whorehouse." Now his gaze fell on Mamá dozing in the rocker, one hand on the baby's cradle, also from The Popular.

His sway told her he was drunk. She wanted to warn him not to wake the baby, but he'd grown fond of yelling, *Don't tell me what to do!* Her chest tightened as he grinned at her, finger to lips, and rocked the cradle, jostling both The Stranger and her mother awake.

The Stranger's cries were impressive.

Mamá gave Yankee a grudging smile. "Your son says, 'Good morning.'"

He reached into the cradle and lifted The Stranger, whose tiny cries cut through her. She pushed herself up, ready to jump to her feet and snatch the baby away before Yankee dropped him. To her surprise, he put a protective hand under the infant's head and cuddled him to his chest, as tender as Papá with his own babies. She fell back onto the bed, scolding herself for overreacting. The Stranger continued to cry, till Yankee's voice exploded:

"I knew I would have a son!"

The Stranger's wide-open mouth snapped shut, stunned to silence.

"*You* would have a son?" Mamá folded her arms. "Who do you th—"

Candelaria cut her off, "Proud new baba, did you also know what you would name your son?"

"Bing Sam," he blurted as if he'd spent his many hours at Mr. Yee's making this decision.

"What does it mean?" Mamá sounded genuinely curious.

He hesitated, as if he didn't want to tell her. Then he said. "*Bing Sam* means something like *shining forest*. But, for me, it's just the name of my...brother from China who passed away."

Mamá nodded understanding. But, although Candelaria sympathized with honoring a lost brother, she didn't want to erase the blessing her mother had bestowed when she predicted this baby wouldn't be rejected as different but accepted as something new. A true American.

She said, "Will you also give our son an American name, for luck in America?"

"I don't believe in luck. A man makes his own luck."

"But *your* American name—Yankee—it has made you friends, no?" He pushed out his lower lip. "True. And these Americans will never pronounce his name right. So, Wong Bing Sam, what is your American name?"

Yankee gazed into his son's eyes, while she studied *his*. How different he was from the first Chinese man she'd met. Benito's voice could be as big and commanding as her husband's. But where Yankee unsettled people with unpredictable moods that swung from charm to bluster, Benito relaxed those around him with the easy ebb and flow of his humor and strength.

She knew the name she wanted, but she pretended to deliberate: "Bing Sam, Bing Sam...Ben Sam? Ben? What about Ben?"

"Yes, very American... Or Benny! That's how Americans do it."

"Ben-nee, like Yan-kee! Perfect." She gave him her brightest smile.

"Welcome to America, Benny!" Yankee declared.

Mamá gave her a tender look, a look that recalled not only their dear friend but also the last time their family was whole: the journey across the desert to Benito's home, before the border. Tears threatened, prompting her to turn from her mother to her husband. He was chuckling into his son's solemn face, his own face boyish with wonder.

Yankee never spoke of his mother, who must love him, as any mother loved a son. Unless she was bad, like *La Llorona*, the ghost who drowned her children in sorrow and revenge. This possibility roused in her an instinct to protect her husband. If she could always remember him as he was at this moment, face filled with both fatherly adoration and boyish innocence, maybe she could fall in love with him yet. She was only fifteen. Surely it wasn't too late.

26. Partners

1914 - El Paso, Texas

"Gon bui!" Yankee shouted. He and Estefan Wu raised their small white cups, slammed them into the table, and tossed baak zau into open mouths. They downed the clear liquid in one gulp, rolled their shoulders, and roared, as if this weren't a toast but a contest to impress their young tea-sipping wives. Waa, how rice wine opened the sinuses!

He pressed a hot cheek to the wall's cool white tiles, trying to keep his café from tilting, He must maintain control. This after-hours dinner with Candelaria's friends was turning into more than a casual visit.

Yankee's new restaurant on South Oregon Street straddled a world neither here nor there: shiny white tiles to convince white customers his place was clean, red-and-gold decor to remind Chinese customers of home, and hand-painted salt and pepper shakers Candelaria had bought at the mercado—to please Mexican customers while maintaining his Chinese color scheme.

"You see?" she'd said. "Little red chiles and gold corns!"

He called it the International Café.

Tonight, it smelled the part. The chow mein he'd made for the day's customers now collided with the chicken mole he made for their after-hours guests: his wife's half-Chinese/half-Mexican friend, Marcela, and her Chinese husband, who went by the improbable name of

Estefan. Though they mostly looked Chinese, the couple from Juárez mostly spoke Spanish. He didn't mind. His Spanish was improving, and he felt smart for choosing a wife who spoke a language so useful in his new world.

At first, Estefan's self-important lecture on the import business made Yankee want to join the ancestors. "Salt is the key to make Overseas Chinese feel like they never left home: salty dried fish, salty dried plums, salty-sweet lychee…" He alternately chopped the air with one hand and trapped Marcela's hand with the other, slapping it for emphasis every time he bragged about his troubles (endless paperwork, unreliable employees, bribes), smoothing her fingers whenever he confided the rewards (helping his fellow Chinese, shameless markups, bribes).

At first, Marcela hung on his words, portrait of an adoring wife, dabbing her mouth with a napkin in a way that suggested hidden appetites. Yet her eyes followed Candelaria's every move as the younger girl popped up and down to heat tortillas, serve seconds, clear dishes, pour tea, wipe spills. A warm current flowed between the two girls, leaving the men in the cold. Estefan didn't seem to notice, just played quacking duck to his wife's floating swan, tittering at his own jokes, forcing Yankee to laugh in self-defense, until…

Marcela gave a sudden, single clap, startling him out of a daze. "Candelita, your dinner was more delicious than anything my mother makes!"

Both women grinned as if this were a private joke. Candelaria's grin revealed two dimples on one side, none on the other. He'd never noticed this imperfection before. Why? Did she reserve the extra dimple for Marcela? "I can't take credit for dinner. Yankee made it."

Marcela turned to him, eyes round and shiny as new pennies. "Pollo en mole? But you make it better than a Mexican!"

He bobbed his head in humility. "Candelaria taught me. Our son gives her no rest, so I often cook. But she made the tortillas, an art I'll never master."

"If you pay your wife any more compliments, I'll suspect you don't like her." She winked at Candelaria.

Was she mocking him?

Estefan railed on about his business problems: "It's hard to find partners in America. Chinese customers on your side of the border are eager for our products, but Americans make it hard for new Chinese business to enter the country."

Yankee grew wary, sure the man was about to ask for money.

Instead, Marcela chose that moment to announce her father recently opened a new Juárez hotel for wealthy travelers—American, European, and Mexican. "He also specializes in *Chinese* travelers who wish to keep their travels secret."

Yankee sighed loudly at the illogical change of subject, convinced women should never try to talk business.

She failed to pick up the hint. "It's not safe for Chinese travelers to show their faces in Chihuahua, not with Pancho Villa as governor."

Estefan shook his head. "It's not safe for any of us."

She nodded. "That's why we hide them in the hotel basement."

Yankee sat up. "Excuse me, what?"

"I said, that's why my father hides our Chinese guests in the *basement* of his new hotel."

He leaned forward. "Really? Why?"

"My father has lived in Juárez long enough to make friends among both Mexicans *and* Chinese. Now many Chinese ask for his help to cross the border to America, where they believe they'll have a better chance."

Estefan sat back, hands folded across his slim belly, and watched his wife talk the way other men might watch an opera star perform. He seemed unashamed, even proud, of her interest in business and politics. But then, why not? Her father was one of the most successful Chinese men in Juárez, where her husband ran a thriving import business despite anti-Chinese sentiment. Her boldness hadn't hurt them.

He admired the way her arms swept the air, as if at any moment she might dance to emphasize her point: "It's against American law to let in more Chinese, yes? This is unjust. The Statue of Liberty loves immigrants, no? Yet American politicians only love foreigners from the West, not the East." She was magnificent.

Though she addressed Yankee, she seemed to read Candelaria's reactions like a book she knew by heart. In turn, Candelaria's eyes blazed at her with something beyond worship. Here was the key to unlock the mystery of Marcela and tap into her family's power. That key was his wife.

He took her hand, interlaced their fingers, and leaned toward Marcela, bringing Candelaria with him. "Tell us more."

But she shook her hand free of his and leapt to her feet. "Café con leche, everyone?" She hurried to the kitchen before anyone could answer.

Why so fidgety? Maybe Marcela made her jealous. She'd certainly flustered *him*. The over-sweetened coffee-and-milk Candelaria served gave him the jolt he needed to wake from her friend's spell and stop acting like a moonstruck boy.

Estefan was saying something about El Paso's Mounted Guards: horsemen who patrolled the border to keep the Chinese from crossing into the United States.

Yankee picked up the thread. "I know of these patrols! They're why Mr. Yee pays Mexicans to carry goods across the border."

"Until a few years ago," Estefan said, "darker Chinese could slip into America by dressing like Mexicans who cross the Santa Fe Bridge every day. Then the Commerce Department cracked down. Now they stop many of us for questioning—" He nodded to Marcela, who picked up the thread:

"—but they don't stop *me*. Our business often brings me to El Paso to buy supplies we can't get in Juárez, thanks to the return of war. Because I'm half-Mexican, I cross with less trouble. What's more, because, well—" She looked at Estefan.

"—because my wife is so beautiful, dare I say exotic, she has captivated the customs agents at the bridge." He gave her a lingering look. "In the best way of course."

"I'm fortunate my husband is too much of a man to let this trouble him."

Estefan flung an arm round her shoulder and pulled her to him. "If Mexican men knew the power an attentive husband has over his woman, they'd feel more threatened by competition from Chinese men."

Yankee had heard this joke before, from two other Chinese men with Mexican wives, but he laughed as if it were the funniest thing he'd ever heard. With his head thrown back, it took a moment to catch Marcela's inquisitive look at Candelaria, who gave a quick nod in reply, urging her on. Who was in control here? Surely not Candelaria, barely more than a girl.

Whoever gave the cue, Marcela dropped all pretense of wifely humility and grabbed the table with both hands, a general focused on a battle plan. For the first time, she looked him in the eye. "My father has heard that, in El Paso, the Chinese have underground tunnels to hide and transport illegal opium and prostitutes as well as legal alcohol and guns. Is this true?"

Three faces turned to him. He sucked in his breath. Noticed the nervous rise and fall of Candelaria's breasts. Was she the source of Marcela's information? Did it matter? If Candelaria was smarter than she looked, he should be proud—she belonged to him.

He exhaled. "There are a few tunnels, one at Mr. Yee's and at least two more. But they don't go *everywhere*. They certainly don't go under the river, though I've heard that rumor too."

"I didn't think so." Marcela smiled. "That would be impractical."

"And dangerous," Estefan said. "Imagine if the tunnel weren't deep enough, the horror of walking a passage to freedom only to have it cave in on you in a flood!"

Marcela gave him an affectionate nod and moved on, "I have friends in the horse patrol and among the bridge's officers. So long as we don't move atop the bridge, we can pay them a small *propina* to look the other way while we move *beneath* the bridge. Not under the river, mind you. Through it." Her words swirled through him in cross-currents of opportunity versus danger.

"The river is powerful," he countered. "Every year, people get swept away. Children disappear."

"True," she said. "But when the river is low, it's possible to cross the shallow sections with ropes and strong men. Once the immigrants make it across, though, they can't move to their next destination right away or move freely in El Paso. That's where you come in. Our clients will pay to hide in your tunnels until we send them elsewhere."

She and Estefan, and likely her father, had thought of everything. Estefan explained that many Chinese felt they had a better chance crossing the river than passing the test of Angel Island. Yankee couldn't blame them.

He lost track of the conversation after that. It wasn't the plan that compelled him so much as Marcela's voice, now gentle as a breeze, now a storm-driven wind. Estefan nodded in rhythm with her, like a metronome, until Yankee nodded along.

"So," Estefan said, "shall we help our fellow Chinese and make money while we're at it?"

Yankee turned to direct his answer to Marcela, but she'd scooted next to Candelaria, arm-in-arm, leaning close to whisper in her ear. Together, they giggled, though Candelaria covered the sound with her hand. Sharing a secret? About him? He didn't like her spending time with a young wife who led her husband by the nose. If he said no to this deal, he could put a stop to their friendship. If he said yes, he might be giving two girls more say in his destiny than he cared to give anyone.

Yet the allure Marcela exuded was musky with power.

"How much will these immigrants pay?" he asked.

"Perhaps we should discuss that over more baak zau." Estefan picked up the jug and wagged it to demonstrate its emptiness.

"Yankee also has a bottle of Kentucky bourbon." Candelaria was full of surprises.

He grabbed her chair and rocked her onto her feet. "Just what I was thinking, my love!"

She scuttled into his office and returned, fingers of one hand clasping four short glasses, the other hand gripping the round-hipped bottle of honey-gold he kept on a high shelf. Out of her reach, or so he'd thought.

He accepted the Maker's Mark from her like a caress. Then, eyeing the four glasses, he said, "Why don't you girls go down the street to visit our son and his abuelita?"

Without pause, she set two glasses before the men and took the other two away.

Marcela rose to leave, tipping Estefan a smile so subtle he knew the couple had already settled on a bottom line. Yankee grinned. This was a game he was good at. She kissed Estefan's cheek, and he imagined the feel of her wide mouth, soft but with a slight sandpaper rasp so there'd be no forgetting it.

Candelaria returned from the kitchen, and he yanked her against him, jutting his jaw out for a kiss. She hesitated, and he guffawed, "Don't be shy in front of our friends!"

She pecked his chin, then scurried to the door with Marcela. "Wait till you see how big Benny is!"

"Ahhh," Marcela's face brightened with comprehension. "Benito, like my father!"

Candelaria's glance bounced to Yankee and away. "Benny is easier for Americans than Bing Sam. How's *your* son?" She elbowed Marcela out the door and shut it behind them.

Benito? So, Marcela's family had invaded his before they even met. If his next child were a girl, would his wife suggest an American name like…Marcy? He saw it now: the true negotiators of this deal had just left, Marcela leading the way no doubt. No matter. Her father and husband controlled the purse strings, and now that he knew they let her make decisions, she'd never catch him off guard again.

As for Candelaria, let her hoard her little secrets like coins. She'd earned them, and he was too smart to let it bother him, so long as he made money.

27. The Tunnel

1915 – El Paso, Texas

The Santa Fe Bridge was half a mile downriver, yet its lamplight rippled up-current, glimmering like stars, threatening to give away the four shadows that waded toward Yankee: a dark constellation of men clinging to a rope. The first shadow was José—all the guides went by "José." This one emerged dripping, planted his feet in the muddy bank, and leaned back against the rope wrapped around his torso. Yankee never knew who was tethered to the other side. He stared past José at the rope shuddering atop the water, waiting for three young Chinese men to rise from the Río Grande as if from an American baptism.

Shadow Number Two—a thin, shivering Chinese youth—tripped out of the river with a splash. Yankee leapt forward to grab his arms and steady him, and he gasped at the unexpected touch. Yankee pressed a finger to the noisy boy's lips.

"Deoi m zyu," Shadow Number Two apologized, his whisper louder than the splash.

Yankee rolled not just his eyes but his entire head, clamped a hand over the boy's mouth, and half-carried him to the Chinese farmer waiting atop the riverbank. The farmer loaded him into a donkey cart full of leafy vegetables, pantomiming for him to crawl beneath the greens and try not to bruise them. The boy misunderstood and lay atop the produce, mashing it. The farmer repositioned him but didn't complain. Why should he? He made more money from the smuggling fee Yankee paid than he did from his crops.

Yankee turned to head back down the bank, but the farmer grabbed his arm, pulled him close, and tapped his own ear to indicate he heard something. Yankee listened, heard clopping hooves. They looked around, but the early morning dark revealed nothing. The hoof-beats closed in. He scrambled downslope, too late to stop Shadow Number Three from crawling out of the water. But he yanked José's elbow to stop Number Four. José gave the line a single hard tug, alerting the final man to halt midstream. José then ran his end of the rope to the river's edge and tied it around a submerged boulder. He pulled a bottle from his pocket, took a swig, and swayed toward town, now no more than a wandering drunk.

Meanwhile, Yankee reached toward the man who'd just crawled out, yanked him halfway up the bank and, sinking one foot into the mud, whipped him up to the farmer like a slingshot.

The clatter of horseshoes on tar changed to thuds on dirt, closing in, trotting from road to riverside, the sound of an approaching border guard on horseback. No time to hide this traveler inside the cart, so they shoved him underneath. Yankee and the farmer proceeded to haggle over produce as if this were normal on a riverbank in the dark. The hooves slowed. Yankee and the farmer barely turned, as if only mildly curious about who approached.

A Mexican led an old swaybacked horse, bowed by saddlebags loaded with vegetables and fruits. "¡Buenos días!" He reined the nag to a stop and tipped his battered straw hat.

"Good morning," Yankee said.

The Chinese farmer said nothing, mute with caution…or anxiety.

"I thought you were Roberto," the Mexican farmer said in English. "He has a cart like yours. We often set up next to each other at the market."

Yankee chuckled, nodding rapidly. "Ah-so, no-no-no. This Mr. Chen. He no Mexican, he Chinee. Best price. Best quality. Maybe you likey Chinee food?"

The Mexican backed away. "No entiendo," he said, though he'd spoken perfect English the moment before. He tipped his hat again and clucked at his horse to move on.

Yankee kept talking to him in pidgin as he left, "Mr. Chen good farmer. Maybe you teach him grow Mexican food and he sell at market too. You savvy?"

The man didn't look back.

The second he was out of sight, Yankee scrambled down to the river's edge and waved a white handkerchief, the only signal they'd all agreed they were likely to see in the dark. He peered into the river, tried to pick out the silhouette of the only traveler still standing in cold water to his waist, saw nothing but vague reflections rippling in the current.

In six months, they had brought three dozen men across, minus the one swept away after unexpected rain swelled the river. He'd found the body washed up downstream, eyes staring through a veil of water, fixed on the stars above as if he still might find America there.

Now Yankee held his breath—until José skidded past him to splash into the water, untie the rope from the rock, and haul in slack as if his own life depended on it. The rope was taut, but that meant nothing except that the man on the opposite bank still held his end. The man in the middle was either following the rope or gone. Yankee swayed forward and back, willing him across.

A silhouette separated from the night and transformed into a man, hunched, stumbling, pawing the rope.

Without thinking, Yankee waded in up to his thighs, heedless of the noise or chill, and reached out as if for an embrace. The stranger let go the rope and collapsed against him. Yankee gripped his arms and walked backward, leading him from the water as if leading a waltz.

He couldn't make out his features, a puddle of dark-on-dark. They fell onto the bank, and the man landed atop him, knocking the wind from him, soaking him, wracking them both with shivers. Close as lovers, he made out the stranger's eyes, watery with the end he'd glimpsed.

Yankee shoved the man off him, staggered to his feet, and stared into the river. It looked shallow, sounded unhurried, smelled of nothing more deadly than mud. Yet decay was near. It clung to him, so even though he hadn't met death, he was sure death knew all about him.

Yankee strode down the alley, restraining an urge to run, trying not to draw the attention of early risers. Though he and his partners had loaded his three shivering clients into the cart without getting caught, the close call rattled him. He couldn't rest till all three made it to the tunnel. He reached his small adobe house, the only building on this alley not devoted to commerce, burst through the back door and past Candelaria, startling her from her doze at the kitchen table.

"What?! Did another one drown?" she asked, voice loud in the pre-dawn quiet.

"No! Shhh!"

He didn't pause to explain but barreled through the house, out the front door, and across the courtyard, to charge through the back of the International Café. Inside the dark restaurant, he picked his way among tables topped with upside-down chairs, their legs in the air like a battlefield of dead horses. At the front window, he knuckled Candelaria's crooked homemade curtains apart, and peered through the hand-stenciled word *CAFÉ* into the threat of dawn.

The donkey cart had beaten him here, and now sat out front. Sam and the farmer stood on its far side, haggling over its mangled produce—as if this were just another morning getting ready for customers. They blocked much of the cart from view of the few businesses across the street: a laundry, a restaurant, a grocery. The neighbors on this side were a cheap hotel and saloon, full of people who couldn't afford to talk to police. Through the café window came the muffled rising and falling tones of the two men bartering, which covered the snick of the trapdoor in the cart's bottom. Nobody but Yankee was likely to spot the shadows scrambling beneath the wagon to crawl under the raised square of boardwalk abutting it. The wood square slid shut, leaving the boardwalk seamless again.

If anyone in this slice of Chinatown noticed that the farmer's cart dripped water, or that his load shrank more than could be accounted for by the vegetables in Sam's basket, none would report their suspicions. Who would look out for them if not each other?

He stared at the floor, as if he could see under it to the men waddling through the tunnel below. Sam entered the front door, rested his basket on a table, and nodded at him. Yankee stepped forward to inspect the greens, lifting a cabbage head, a broccoli bunch, a snow-pea pod.

He poked out an approving lower lip. "Not as bad as I expected."

"Only the best for you, boss."

"Good man!" He slapped Sam's back, knocking him into the basket, dumping half the greens on the floor. "Sorry. You can pick that up, can't you?"

He didn't wait for an answer but rushed back to the house. At the door, he paused to pull his flask from his pocket, took a sip to calm his nerves, then hurried inside.

In the baby's room, he opened the built-in wardrobe and slid aside a trunk, revealing a trapdoor in the floor. He opened it and whispered into the dark hole below. "On chyun laa!"

He heard shuffling, saw a pair of eyes blink up into the bedroom's lamplight: the last crosser, who'd waited in the river longest. His chest rose through the opening and Yankee gripped his icy hands to pull him up. The man leaned against the wall, hugging his body as if to hold himself up, while the other two climbed out. Yankee pointed them to blankets, towels, and clothes stacked next to the empty crib, inviting them to dry off and change for breakfast. Baby Benny was with his grandparents, where he always spent the first night when Yankee's "cousins" arrived—not real cousins, only related to him if they got caught.

He returned to the kitchen, where Candelaria dozed again, head pillowed on her crossed arms atop the table. He touched her shoulder.

Her body jerked, head popped up, eyes wide. Ready. "Did they make it?"

"Barely." He explained the close call.

She didn't throw her arms around him or say, You're so brave! No. She pressed a hand to her chest and said, "Thank God we don't have another death on our hands." What did she mean, *our* hands? *She* never faced life-or-death at the river as he did. She only waited at home.

He shook off his irritation, reminded himself she was sensitive. She'd been so upset by the crosser who drowned, she'd suffered nightmares for weeks, whining in her sleep. He couldn't get it out of his head either, though he'd seen nothing, heard no splash or shout, no sound but the river. He hadn't even been sure the immigrant was gone till they hauled in the rope.

He shouldn't have told her. Women weren't built to carry men's burdens.

His voice softened, "They'll be hungry."

She shuffled to the stove, struck a match, and lit a burner with a whoosh-and-pop of gas. Pulled a bacon slab from the icebox, peeled away a half-dozen slices, and laid them across the pan. The bacon shriveled and crackled as he stepped behind her, wrapped his arms around her, and rocked her. His erection rose against her hips, soft and spreading with a new pregnancy. The danger of the river-crossing always increased his desire.

"Not now." She bumped him away as she tilted the pan to slide grease down its face.

He let her go. Begging implied weakness, and she had a point. What he wanted to do to her, he couldn't do in front of the cousins.

She turned to heat the comal, and he shook his head, chuckling. There was no convincing her that, unlike him, most Toisanese men didn't find comfort in tortillas warm from the griddle.

The men shuffled into the kitchen, and he told them to eat without him. Though his stomach rumbled with hunger, he was in no mood for conversation.

He decided to check supplies. Back in the baby's room, he lowered himself through the trapdoor into the wide end of his tunnel. It smelled ancient and looked primitive, but its tapering walls of cracked yellow clay and chiseled white limestone were solid and new. He did a visual inventory of the food tins and canteens, stacked against the largest wall in case the cousins needed an extended stay. Further down the narrow end of the tunnel, closer to the café, opium and liquor hid in the bottoms of boxes topped off with restaurant supplies.

At first, they'd used Mr. Yee's tunnel. But the Temperance League's complaints grew louder last election, and Chinese "dens of iniquity" were the first targets for raids. An easy way for the mayor and sheriff to act tough on crime while turning a blind eye to establishments enjoyed by whites, or by those Mexicans whose votes they bought.

Yankee and Sam dug this tunnel from the café to the house, with the help of their Chinese dishwasher and two old bunkmates from the Chinese dorm. Mr. Yee paid to divert most of his opium to Yankee's tunnel, a safer location due to the International Café's respectability. Only drugs and booze stayed in the tunnel. Human cargo slept on the floor of Benny's room.

As usual, the plan was to bring Benny home after breakfast. He'd sleep with Yankee and Candelaria for three nights, until the men moved on to their next destination. If anyone came to call, they'd send the men back into the tunnel and plop Benny in his crib to avoid suspicion.

The arrangement's only drawback: whenever cousins stayed over, Candelaria evaded his advances. He let it go, since she let him have his way most other nights. She even seemed to enjoy lovemaking as much as he did.

Yankee climbed out of the basement, slid the trunk back over the trapdoor, and only then realized he was shivering, his clothes still soaked from the river. He hurried across the short hall to his bedroom, peeled off his clothes, and crawled into bed, where he lay listening to the cousins eat. They were more silent than most, the only sounds that of chopsticks and Candelaria offering more tea. She addressed them with easy familiarity, as if they were real family and not human contraband who could get everyone in this house arrested if they were discovered.

Yankee woke to the cousins' chorus of snores and Candelaria's singing drifting from the courtyard. Spanish lyrics always eluded him, even when he recognized the words, but he was stunned to feel tears close as she sang a folk song praising the colors of the rising sun.

De colores, de colores brillantes y finos se viste la aurora,
De colores, de colores son los mil reflejos que el sol atesora...

He rose to follow her voice outside, sure he'd find her singing to the baby. Then he remembered, she'd left the boy at her parents', saying, "Your cousin who waited in the river? He looks funny, all pale and blotchy. What if he gives Benny a disease?" He was too tired to argue. Besides, the baby cried a lot, so it would mean one less noise to keep him up that night.

He found her singing to no one as she hung the cousins' wet clothes, bending to pull them from the basket, rising on her toes to pin them to the clothesline. The heels of her bare feet were stained purple from stepping on the olives that fell from the old tree shading the courtyard. He hung back in the shadows, moved to catch her in this private joy which seemed to have no source but herself. Then she saw him, stuck a clothespin in her mouth, and the song vanished.

He closed the distance, plucked the clothespin from her lips, and kissed her. Lingering, tasting every part of her mouth, trying to awaken her as she had him. She pulled away, again.

Before he could protest, she said, "While you slept in, I talked to Marcela."

He stepped back, wary of her accusatory tone. "About what?"

"She says she's been paying Estefan's tong fees to Sam instead of to you."

"And?"

"She says you told her to."

"Good to know she'll do *something* a man tells her to." Where was she going with this?

"Why has she been paying Sam and not you?"

"I don't have time to run around collecting fees from half the Chinese on the border. Sam's my right hand. Everyone in the Chee Kung Tong knows this. What's the problem?"

She blew a puff of air, disturbing a loose hair. "We talked about this."

"Don't talk to me the way Marcela talks to her husband. He might like it, but I don't." In truth, her flashes of rebellion made him crave her more. But he wasn't about to tell her so.

"We agreed to trust nobody outside the family with money."

"Surely you didn't mean Sam? He's my most loyal friend."

"Yes, yes, he owes you his life," she recited like a schoolgirl repeating lessons.

"Even if he didn't, he's afraid of his own shadow. He'd never risk betraying me."

"He's brave enough to risk smuggling men into America."

Yankee considered this. "He wouldn't take the chance of losing a profitable partnership. He knows I'd make him regret it if he stole from me, or my friends. But tell me, why don't you trust Sam?"

She hesitated, eyes darting around the courtyard as if for an answer. "He always looks startled when I walk into the office. He never talks about his life outside the restaurant. When I ask about it, he changes the subject. What does he do when he's not with you? And…sometimes he stares at me funny when he thinks you're not looking."

He snorted. "We need to find Sam a wife."

She turned to hang more laundry. "That's not what I mean. I don't think Sam will ever marry. I don't think he cares about that."

Maybe she was right. Sam never talked about, looked at, or paid for women. Yankee never saw him eyeing men either, nothing to indicate his pendulum swung the other way. But how could a man have no interest in sex? Sam was just shy.

Why did she care who took the payments? Did she expect him to let *her* do it? Sam had warned him she wanted his money, but he still took pride in that. It wasn't as if she could steal it. No businessman in town would take more than a few dollars from a young wife without telling her husband. And she couldn't run away, not with a babe in arms and another on the way.

Still, she wanted something. What? He studied her, distracted by the way the wet laundry soaked her blouse so it clung to her nipples. He pulled her to his chest till they were both damp. "Fine. I'll tell Marcela to pay *me* from now on. Now come nap with me." He slung her over his shoulder, laughing.

If her giggles seemed equally amused and panicked, it only excited him more. He carried her to the bedroom, tossed her on the bed, and pushed into her resistance till it gave way. The box spring from the Sears catalogue squeaked till it drowned all sound, from her first whimper to his final groan. He liked her confused look at the end, as if he'd made her forget herself.

Only once they'd finished did he notice the other sound: a man vomiting. Yankee hurried across the hall and found him leaning out Benny's open window, retching into a bush. The cousin who'd waited in the river. It was true: he looked pale, almost transparent, like ice.

The cousin assured Yankee his wife's Western-style breakfast had simply disagreed with him. But when Yankee helped him off the floor, he noticed that, though the man's hands remained cold, his body radiated heat. He felt his forehead. Fever. He led him to the indoor toilet to vomit again, then across the house to a cot in the spare room. No sense getting the others sick.

Candelaria packed a bag to stay with her parents, saying she wouldn't risk catching something that might leave Benny motherless. He agreed, wishing he could go with her.

Next morning the other two cousins blended into the lunch crowd at the International Café, then left the restaurant like any other customers and caught a train to the next city. The sick one stayed behind, with a headache and body aches so severe he couldn't get out of bed.

By day three, the sick cousin's neck hurt so much he couldn't sit up. Yankee had to feed him. When he labored to breathe, Yankee sent for his herbalist. The herbalist had cured Yankee, his wife, and in-laws of fevers, coughs, and stomach pains. He said he'd never seen this illness before, but he confidently prescribed *white tiger*: a pale tea of gypsum, rice, and licorice root.

It didn't help.

Yankee couldn't call an American doctor, who might report him for harboring a fugitive. He crossed the courtyard to the café to do something he'd never done before: ask Sam's advice.

"Take him to the hospital. It's wrong to let him die to save our skins." That was Sam's first argument. "Besides, if he stays long enough, we might all catch it." That was the second.

But he returned to the room to find the cousin struggling for air, gurgling as if drowning, as if he'd never made it out of the river at all. Yankee watched transfixed as he exhaled his last.

Unable to bear the house's sudden stillness, he walked to his in-laws', anxious to bring his wife home. But she refused to return till the body was gone. She did step outside and sit with him, on the stoop of the new, larger apartment he'd rented for her parents and siblings.

"He came to us for help," Yankee said, not looking at her.

"He was probably sick to begin with." She took his hand and held it between both of hers. "You did your best."

He would always be grateful to her for that.

On Sunday before dawn, as the last Saturday revelers passed out and the first churchgoers woke, Yankee and Sam rolled the body into an old sheet. The farmer returned with his cart, and a shovel, and again hid the man under Chinese greens. They rode him out of town, past the Franklin Mountains but before the pecan orchards, to a stretch of New Mexico desert where they dug an unmarked grave for Li Wing Kee. At least, that's what he'd called himself. Nobody knew his true name, not even his two fellow travelers, who were surely in Oklahoma by then.

28. Friendship

1915 – El Paso, Texas

Her deep breathing didn't fool Yankee. He found it endearing, how bad Candelaria was at faking sleep. Her back stiffened when he rubbed against her plump little rear. Sometimes he let her get away with this. Usually he tickled, caressed, and prodded, teasing her until she gave up the deception.

This time she whispered, "Remember, Marcela's staying tonight."

He sighed. "Must she stay so often?"

"She's the only one who can safely cross to El Paso for her family business."

"But doesn't she have other friends to stay with?"

"She's more than my friend. She's family. And her husband's your partner. Don't you always say relationships are important in business?"

"Yes, but a happy husband is important in marriage."

"She might hear us."

"She's on the other side of the house."

"Sometimes you're loud."

"You're not quiet either, mi amor. Are you worried your friend will be jealous you're married to a real man? Not like that Estefan."

She turned to face him. "I like Estefan."

Damn Estefan. Damn Estefan's mannish wife. Damn his own wife's moods. Without warning, he rolled onto her, lifted her nightdress, and entered her before she could object. He reveled in the tease of her arching away, followed by the exquisite pressure of him opening her up. She cried out, once, and he couldn't tell if it was from pleasure or pain. Let her friend hear. Let her know who was in charge of this house.

After Candelaria's initial cry, she fell silent, though she shook as he punished her from the inside out. This was his right as a husband, and she was wrong to deny him. She shuddered, and he was sure she felt as excited as he did.

Afterward, she continued to tremble but made no sound except an intermittent gasp. He realized she was weeping, and it struck him with remorse for his roughness. He flung an arm over her and rested his cheek atop hers. "I'm sorry if I hurt you. But you're my wife. And you're so pretty. How can you expect me not to want you?"

He didn't ask the question he wanted to ask: "Why don't you want *me*?" Did she see him the way so many Americans saw him, as a dragon, or a clown?

Something woke him. What? He opened his eyes to blackness. He hated this hour, the fulcrum between night and dawn, nobody awake but him, the world and everyone in it pulled out from under him like a magician's trick. He reached for Candelaria and discovered he was truly alone. The sheets felt cold on her side of the bed. How long had she been gone?

He heard a distant murmur. She must be soothing the baby. Odd, he hadn't heard Benny cry. The baby's colicky shrieks usually ended all possibility of sleep, tempting him to smother the child.

He rose, crept across the hall, and eased open the nursery door. Benny lay asleep in his crib, breathing those fast little gasps that always made him chuckle. She wasn't there.

He returned to the hall, uncertain. The floor felt chilly underfoot. The murmuring resumed, two voices, which conjured an image of fish talking underwater. Candelaria and Marcela were talking in the spare room on the other side of the house.

In the middle of the night.

He tiptoed to the room, hoping to catch them in their girlish secrets.

The door was shut except for a crack. He sank to the floor and pressed one eye to the gap. The room was so dark he couldn't make them out. They spoke Spanish, always hard to understand when he first woke. Their whispering made it more difficult, plus the fact they hadn't turned on a lamp so he couldn't see their body language. Finally, words took shape.

"Why didn't you ask us to help you?" Marcela asked.

"It wasn't only me who needed help," Candelaria said, "but my whole family."

"My family loves your family."

"You have your own problems. How long could you keep helping us?"

"Why him?"

"Yankee liked me. And I liked him…I mean it, I did." Why did she sound defensive? Was it so hard to believe a woman might like him? "At first, he reminded me of your father, who was so kind. And his laugh sounded strong. He came farther than we did to get to El Paso, yet he already knew so many people, already belonged. I believed he could help us make a home here."

The bedsprings complained as one of them shifted on the narrow bed. "And now?"

"He still takes care of us: me, our son, my family. But…"

"But?"

"He frightens me. Sometimes I'm sure he'd rescue me from anything bad. Other times I think he might tear me to pieces. I'm even more afraid it's a sin to think like this, because he's my husband. Except we didn't marry in the church, so maybe he's not my husband? Maybe I'm going to hell."

"God would never send you to hell. You're His little candle that lights the dark."

"You see me that way because you love me."

"You have it backwards: I love you because you *are* that way."

Peering one-eyed through the crack, he saw a pale misshapen moon floating in the center of the room. It was the shape two young pregnant women in nightgowns made as they wrapped their arms around each other in the creeping dawn. Was Marcela kissing his wife's cheek? Why did she linger? Candelaria sighed, a sound so full of longing he felt an answering sadness.

She sat back with her hand on her belly. "I love being a mother. Sometimes I love being a wife—when he's sweet. Even when he's not, sometimes he makes me feel things I never knew were possible. But he wants me to fulfill my vows all the time, and I don't always want to. He stinks of liquor, or women's privates, or, I don't know, some kind of sickness on the inside. Then I want to run away, but I can't. If I make an excuse, he…he hurts me."

This was how she saw him? How she cut him down behind his back? In the silence that followed, their breathing seemed loud. He tried to pick out who took the short shallow breaths, and who took the long shaky ones. Did it matter?

"How does he hurt you?" Marcela asked.

Candelaria took Marcela's hand, curled it into a fist, and pulled it between her thighs, like a punch. Marcela didn't yank free and instead opened her hand. Candelaria didn't shy from her touch as she had from his. His heart filled his throat, choking him. Then Marcela gently withdrew her hand. "I see. Maybe it's Yankee who'll go to hell…"

He tensed, ready to burst through the door and send *her* to hell.

"I think he's angry because he senses the truth." Candelaria sat up.

Marcela sat up with her, and echoed his own question, "What truth?"

"I *can't* love him."

"Because he's mean."

Candelaria shook her head.

"Why then?"

"Because I love you."

"I love you too."

Candelaria folded her own legs beneath her, took Marcela's hands, and leaned forward till their foreheads touched. His breath caught at the sight of their double silhouette, two mirror images in the dark. "No. I mean, I love you the way I'm supposed to love my husband."

Marcela sucked in a deep breath. "There are many kinds of love, my friend. You married a man who's also a beast, who thinks love is something you can take. The love you and I feel is shared without fear or duty. That's why you believe as you do."

"Are you sure?" He thought Candelaria pressed her lips to Marcela's. Slow, soft, silent.

Marcela's lips seemed to part until they shared one breath. Or maybe it was a trick of the shadows.

He wished for more light, to see better. Not because he was aroused, though he was, but because he'd been sure his wife belonged to him and now he saw he was wrong. If he paid attention, this pair might answer questions he never knew he had. He watched them lean together in the dark while he waited—for illumination.

Marcela slowly pulled away but kept hold of Candelaria's hands. "You and I carry a part of each other nobody else can, but the love you're talking about, I've found it in my marriage."

"I'm sorry. You must think I'm a bad woman." Candelaria started to rise from the bed, but Marcela laid both hands on her shoulders to stop her.

"No, I know you're a good girl. My mother once told me that, long ago among her people, there were always some women who loved women, and some men who loved men, and nobody thought it was strange. It made sense to me, because we most love the person whose heart talks to our heart, so maybe sometimes our body wants to talk to their body. For you, I think it's simpler: I think you're lonely. I think you'll always love someone who sees your light the way I do. I'm sorry you didn't marry such a man."

"It's my fault. I gave myself to a man I didn't love, to trick my parents into letting us get married. Now God's punishing me for my lies. I don't deserve love."

"Everyone sins. And everyone deserves love. I don't know if you'll find love in your marriage. But I promise this"—Marcela gripped her shoulders—"Some friendships hold as deep a love as marriage. That's how it'll always be between you and me." She lay back on her pillow and Candelaria followed, her head on the older girl's shoulder.

"But Marcela, I'm so lonely when you're not around."

"Let me tell you a secret: I love Estefan, but sometimes I feel lonely even when he's with me. Sometimes that's the way of love."

"When I was a girl in Mata Flores, I never felt lonely. I was too stupid to know I was happy. Why didn't my parents warn me growing up would be so sad?"

"You're not grown up yet. You're only seventeen."

"But I'm married. I have a baby."

"It takes more than that to be a woman."

"Like what?"

"I don't know. When I find out I'll tell you."

To his astonishment, they collapsed into giggles, pulling their pillows over their faces to stifle the sound, transformed into girls again.

He longed to laugh with them, but if he made his presence known they'd surely stop. If he entered they'd exclude him. He could no longer bear to look. He crept away from the door, leaned against the wall, and tried to blink away the dry stinging in his eyes. It might be a relief to cry, but tears didn't come.

29. The Resurrection

1920 – El Paso, Texas

Candelaria was used to guests appearing on their doorstep at odd hours. Most shouted through the screen, swung it open, and let it bang shut behind them without waiting for an invitation: her parents, siblings, cousins, and of course Marcela. The Chinese immigrants they concealed usually stayed in the tunnel—ever since the one who died in the house—but a couple of times after hours, Sam let them walk through the courtyard to knock at the front door. Something felt different, though, about the impatient person leaning on the doorbell this autumn night.

By unspoken agreement, they all ignored the uninvited caller. They were settled for the night: Yankee on the couch drinking his highball; thirteen-year-old Grace tucking the girls into bed in their room (the old spare room); herself perched on the ottoman, singing *El Corrido de Gregorio Cortez*, strumming the new guitar Yankee gave her for their sixth anniversary.

An extravagant surprise, this guitar. At first, he'd complained she sang too many sad songs, "Always someone running from the law, someone getting shot, someone dying." Now he often requested them. Especially this one, after she explained Gregorio was a hero who only killed to defend himself and his brother from the americanos who wrongly accused them. Yankee's favorite part: it took more than 300 men to capture him.

"Don't stop." He waved her on. "You make gunfights sound soothing after a long day."

She resumed Gregorio's lament in a lower voice:

Decía Gregorio Cortez
Con su pistola en la mano:
"No corran, rinches cobardes
Con un solo mexicano."

Then said Gregorio Cortez
With his pistol in hand
Don't run, you cowardly Rangers
From one lone Mexican.

The bell rang again.

Yankee set down his drink with a sharp clink, rose to peer through the parlor curtain, then strode to their bedroom, grumbling. He emerged wearing his old suit jacket. No bowtie, just the jacket. Why? He hated to bow and grin for the white political flunkies who stopped by to drum up Chinese support for this or that, no matter how much he liked their cash. And he rarely dressed up for callers of any kind. Curious, she stopped playing to listen.

He cracked the door. "Good evening, sir. What can I do for you so late?"

"Sorry, I think I have the wrong house." The visitor had a Mexican accent, not unusual in Segundo Barrio.

"Why don't you tell me what you want, and we'll see?" Yankee opened the door wider.

She still couldn't see the man's face, only his leather jacket and fedora. Odd combination: too expensive for a laborer, too modern for a rancher. She'd yet to ever see a Mexican door-to-door salesman. She hoped he wasn't one. Yankee once threatened to shoot the only salesman to ever get past Sam—ah, that's why the suit jacket. Yankee reached behind him, under his coattail, for the Browning pistol he smuggled home from his brief stint in the Great War.

The stranger sounded wary. "I'm looking for Candelaria Rivera. Folks tell me she lives behind the International Café. The man in the restaurant sent me back here."

"Who are you?"

"Her brother, Miguel."

"Candelaria has no brother named Miguel."

The hollow clang of her guitar startled her as she dropped it on the floor. She ran to Yankee and wrapped her hand around his where it gripped the pistol behind his back.

Her voice was half-whisper, half-shout, "Don't shoot him, mi amor!"

He stepped aside, eyeing her as if she too were a stranger at the door.

She edged past to stare up at the tall man standing in the lamplight from the parlor.

He removed his fedora, thick black hair springing up despite the obvious effort he'd taken to slick it down. His eyes were no longer the angry black coals they once were, now watery with doubt, and his slim shoulders were no longer squared for a fight but round with defeat. Still, he looked the way Papá once did, before the frontera.

"Miguel?"

"Candelita?"

She opened her arms for a hug, then dropped them and backed away. For nine years she'd told herself Miguel was dead until she'd come to believe it. This man must be an imposter, come to destroy the bit of peace she'd carved out in life.

She turned to Yankee, whose hand returned to his gun. In seven years of marriage, his face had become a mirror of her memories, his body a map of her history. And she? At twenty-one, she was both harder and softer than when they met, like a bolillo, the crusty French rolls she dipped in her morning coffee, a true El Pasoan now. She must look like a stranger to Miguel too, no longer his well-behaved sister from Mata Flores. She missed that girl. That decided her.

She finished flinging herself at his neck, knocking off his hat and locking him in such a stranglehold it might've been less violent to let Yankee shoot him.

"Didn't you say your brother's name was Lalo? Didn't he die in the revolution?" Yankee's voice was thick with suspicion. "You said you saw it with your own eyes."

Miguel pulled free of her and looked in confusion from her to Yankee. "I can guess why you didn't tell people about me. But Lalo? Is it true?"

She looked past him into the dark, hoping another ghost might appear. Her eyes returned to his. Her lips trembled with rage. She leapt forward and, without thinking, slapped him so hard he stumbled. "¡Cabrón! If you'd stayed with us, we would've left Juárez sooner and Lalo would still be alive! I chose to believe you died too. You deserve to be dead for leaving us to wonder. For leaving us without another pair of hands when Papá lost his job and we had nothing. *Nada, me entiendes?*" She gave Yankee an uncomfortable glance and stopped.

Yankee went still, like he always did before he exploded. She wouldn't blame him. What would anyone think of a wife who kept a whole brother secret? Then again, she knew almost nothing about Yankee's family in China. He always said, "I don't dwell on the past." He glanced from her to Miguel with a smirk. Was it possible he enjoyed watching her lose control?

"I'm sorry, Miguel"—her voice cracked with the effort to compose herself—"but why did you wait so long to find us?"

He shrank, into the boy he'd been last time she saw him. "I *was* dead. Dead as the men I killed. How could I come back? I'm sorry, I never should've left. But I see now, once I left, I should've stayed away."

He didn't collapse so much as fold himself onto the new paving stones of the courtyard.

The men he *killed*? Maybe he *should* have stayed away. Too late now. She knelt with him on the stones. He pillowed his head on her breast and sobbed. She rubbed his back in small circles, the way she did with seven-year-old Benny when bullies beat him up.

Yankee cleared his throat. "It's cold out here. Let's finish this little reunion inside."

She and Miguel helped each other up. Then he offered a hand to Yankee. "And this is?"

"My husband, Wong Yan Chi."

She expected him to say, *Call me Yankee*, like always, but just then Grace emerged from the back bedroom in a huff. "Shhh! I just put the girls to bed! What's all the noise?"

"A ghost." Yankee winked at Grace.

Candelaria frowned at him for making a joke of it.

Grace pointed at the gun he held, now dangling by his side. "You always shoot ghosts?"

Candelaria blurted, "Miguel's come home."

He emerged from behind her with a little wave.

Grace gasped, then ran at him, only to trip over the guitar Candelaria had dropped. She fell into the center table, cracked her head on the edge, and rolled to the floor. Everyone froze.

Grace curled into a ball, hand to her forehead, and moaned, "I think my skull's broken."

Yankee and Candelaria hurried toward her. Yankee swept her into his arms, laid her on the couch, and put a pillow under her head. "Move your hand and let me see, little bird."

Since when did he call her that? More important—was Grace bleeding?

"This must be Graciela," Miguel said, "Still the center of attention, I see."

"Until *you* showed up," Yankee muttered.

Candelaria almost laughed, but only said, "That cut looks bad. I'll get something to clean it. Meanwhile, viejo, I don't think you need this anymore?"

She picked up the pistol, which he'd set down on the table, and carefully de-cocked the trigger while Miguel cocked an eyebrow at her. Surprised she'd learned to handle a gun? Or that her husband let her? Her heart pounded as she wondered one more thing: was Miguel still carrying Papá's old Colt somewhere inside that leather jacket?

Her parents welcomed Miguel home without hesitation, threw their arms around him as if he'd never given them a day's trouble. Mamá stuffed him with sopa and tortillas till his belly grew so tight Papá punched it—just as a joke. His amusement at their attention was infectious, a side to him she'd never seen, as if Lalo had left that role to him.

"Maybe I should've visited you first," he teased their parents. "Stupid me, I started at Candelita's. She used to be so sweet."

"Nine years changes things, mijo," Papá said.

Miguel turned quiet and thoughtful after that.

Yankee agreed to let him stay at their house, which had more room than her parents' apartment. Mamá and Papá were back to raising four kids: Grace, eight-year-old Salvador, six-year-old Anita, and four-year-old Frank.

Miguel spent hours at Candelaria's kitchen table, drinking black coffee till his hands shook, while she caught him up on the lives of the Riveras.

Those hours yielded only vague answers about what he'd been up to since running from the federales in Juárez, turning left when she'd turned right. He said he'd fought with the rebels no more than a week before he knew he was in over his head, a boy in a man's war. After that, he crossed the border and caught a train to Los Angeles, where he'd been living since.

"Why didn't you come find us?" she asked.

"I was ashamed."

She pressed for details about his life in the City of Angels. He gave sketchy answers. Said that, till recently, he lived with "friends" and worked with "businessmen," as an assistant with unnamed skills who solved unnamed problems. "Guys in L.A. call me a troubleshooter."

Upon hearing that word, she panicked. She could forgive him, yes, but she refused to risk her children. Yankee proved a worrisome enough father without adding a criminal uncle. "No!" She jumped to her feet. "No-no-no-no!" She grabbed Miguel by the ear, dragged him to the back door, and shoved him into the alley. "No gunfighters around my children."

"Not that kind of shooter."

"Tell me you don't still have Papá's gun."

"But—your own husband has a gun!"

She slammed the door in his face.

30. The Survivors

1920 – El Paso, Texas

Candelaria's long-lost brother moved into their parents' crowded apartment. Next day, he had Grace carry a note to her, written in Spanish, explaining the English word "troubleshooter" meant "problem-solver" not "gunfighter." She didn't reply. The day after, he sent another note, explaining he only kept their father's old pistol for protection. She didn't respond to that either. Then another, saying he tried to return the gun but Papá told him to keep it. He sent many notes: asking if she remembered how the mountains of Mata Flores looked "like the arms of a mother," if she remembered how they all used to sleep in a pile like puppies and she kicked him in her sleep, if she remembered the time Lalo kept a cockroach in a matchbox as a pet.

This went on for a week, till he wrote a note in English, which he knew she couldn't read. So Grace read it for her.

Dear Candelaria,

Sorry I was mean when we were kids. You deserved a better brother.

Please forgive me,
Miguel

She dictated a note for Grace to carry back. She was only literate in Spanish and felt ashamed of her sixth-grade scrawl, while Grace attended eighth grade, wrote in both languages, and had penmanship like art. Assuming Grace wrote what she told her, the note contained no apology or forgiveness, only:

Dear Miguel,

Please join us for dinner at our home. We still have much catching up to do.

Sincerely,
Candelaria

Despite her invitation's chilly tone, Yankee berated her for encouraging him. He said she'd been right in the first place, that her brother could be a bad influence on the children. "I don't believe his explanation for that 'troubleshooter' business either. He does carry a gun."

"*You* own a gun."

"I don't carry it all the time. And didn't he steal his?"

"You just don't like my brother."

"You're the one who threw him out." He flung his hands wide in surrender. "Do what you want. But remember, just because he's grown up, doesn't mean he's changed."

Yet Miguel had changed. The argumentative boy once so sure of himself had grown into a withdrawn man with twitchy eyes and uncertain limbs, leery of adults but kind to children. Benny, Cecilia, and Mary adored him. Of course they did: they were seven, five, and eighteen months, while Miguel was an overgrown child who never complained even when all three at once hung from his neck, arms, and legs, or searched his pockets for the endless toys and treats he hid there. Where did the money for those things come from? *Troubleshooting?*

She didn't ask. She couldn't lose another brother. Not again.

He didn't move back in. Not exactly. He split his time between their parents' home and hers. Woke late each day and retreated early each night, to the Rivera sofa or baby Benny's room—where Yankee set up a cot for him though he pulled off the mattress to sleep on the floor. She heard him slip out the kitchen door late most nights and crash back through it before dawn. Otherwise, he rarely left the two homes except to traverse the streets between. He didn't even pretend to look for a job.

"Do you think he's hiding something?" Yankee asked one night in bed.

"What if he is? He's a grown man. He's entitled."

Still, she asked herself the same question.

One morning after Yankee crossed the courtyard to work at the café, Mamá burst through the kitchen door, babbling hysterically. Candelaria guided her to the sofa and tried unsuccessfully to make her lie down. She could make out little more than the two words Mamá kept repeating: Blue Death. Miguel had the flu, and not just any flu.

"La gripe española?" Candelaria whispered as if that might prevent it from being true.

"What else?" Mamá said. "He has a high fever. He says it hurts to swallow."

"I thought the epidemic ended."

"Me too. What will we do? We can't lose him again, like we almost lost you." Funny, she'd expected Mamá to mention Lalo.

She put her hand to her own chest, tight with a memory of struggling for air. It was why they called it the Blue Death, because in the end so many turned blue. For the first time in her life, she took her distraught mother in her arms and rocked her like a child. Once she'd calmed her, she packed a bag and sent her son to the café to tell Yankee she was going to Mamá's to help take care of Tío Miguel.

Moments later, Yankee crossed the courtyard back to the house, pulling Benny with him so fast his feet barely touched the ground. "What's this nonsense? Who'll take care of our kids?"

"Grace will. It's only a few days."

"That makes no sense. Then why can't she look after your brother?"

"Grace likes to help, but she's no good in a crisis."

"I need you here!"

"Don't go, Mommy!" Benny's whine echoed his father's as he clung to her waist.

She gave Yankee a pleading look, though she felt sure it was no use.

To her surprise, he swung Benny up into his arms, wiped his tears, and said, "Don't cry. Be a big boy for Baba. Auntie Grace will stay with us, and Mommy will be back soon."

As always, his booming voice stunned Benny into stone stillness.

Yankee surprised her further by kissing her cheek and saying, "I understand you must do this to repay your own luck. We're all lucky you're alive."

She squeezed his hand. He really could be sweet sometimes. Still, his sudden change of opinion made her suspicious, and she almost stayed. Then she looked at her mother, leaning against the kitchen door for support, walked over to lend her shoulder, and led her home.

The epidemic had killed hundreds in El Paso, hitting Segundo Barrio hardest. She'd lost three cousins—plus two neighbors she'd never much liked till she realized they would never again say hello as they passed on the street. She'd been terrified when Yankee shipped to France, to a town she'd never heard of, to cook for General Pershing—or so he claimed. He said, "Cook is the only job the U.S. Army will trust to a Chinese man." She begged him not to volunteer, fearing he'd be killed, but he insisted it was for her and the children, that it would prove him a patriot and make it harder to ever deport him. Then came the reports: countless soldiers dying in Europe, not from the war but from the flu.

She was the one who fell ill. He told his commanding officer he received a letter from home saying his wife was dying. This may or may not have been an exaggeration. She'd never been sicker.

By the time the army shipped him home, she was better but still weak and tired. He sent her mother home and took over her convalescence, as well as cooking, cleaning, and looking after the children, leaving Sam to manage the café. She heaped him with genuine praise for his devoted care, but within days his help made her feel useless, until she begged him to return to the restaurant and leave housekeeping to her.

Since then, they'd retreated into largely separate lives. Most days, they only saw each other briefly each morning and for a couple of hours before bed each night. The more time they spent apart, the more she enjoyed him when he was around. Yet if she never saw him again, it wouldn't destroy her like losing Miguel, or any of her family who came with her from Mexico.

Her brother's fever was so high her mother bought extra ice from the iceman to break into pieces and rub him down, trying to cool him off. He said little as they fussed over him, only whimpered when they shifted him to change his sweat-soaked sheets.

That first night, she sat up and watched him sleep fitfully, repeatedly waking himself with hacking coughs.

After one coughing fit, she said, "We should take you to the hospital."

"No. I'd rather die at home."

"Don't act like a woman," she said, though she'd never heard a woman complain half so much. "You're not dying."

"Maybe it's what I have coming," he said. "How do they say it? 'He who wants to die won't complain if he's buried standing up.'"

"Why would you want to die?"

That's when he told her the only thing he ever would about his time with the revolutionaries, pausing his story only to cough. "You know how I wanted to fight for the campesinos? Pues, one night we went to the river to get water, for ourselves and the horses. Just before dawn, the federales made a surprise attack. In the dark, with all the smoke, I couldn't see who I was shooting at. I thought it'd be easy to recognize the enemy because so many of our men didn't wear boots, only huaraches or no shoes at all. Then I saw a barefoot man lying on the ground. I ran to ask if he needed help. He was dead. He wore a thin manta shirt like mine and was barefoot like me, but a comrade dragged me away, said he wasn't one of us, said he saw him fighting for Diaz' army. Conscripted, or he would've had a uniform. See, he *was* a campesino."

He paused for an alarming coughing fit. She held her breath, waiting.

"I got scared—not of dying, but of killing the wrong people, or *any* people. I hid in the smoke and ran away. I crossed a small bridge into El Paso. Then I hopped a train to Los Angeles." He closed his eyes and slept for a long time.

For a moment, she forgot how to breathe and choked a little on her own saliva. For all she knew, Miguel was the one who'd shot Lalo. She must never tell him. Not now, when he might be dying. Not ever, or it might break him. Then she realized, she'd already told him what happened to Lalo, so he probably already thought of that. No doubt it was why he'd avoided talking about the revolution, until the fever loosened his tongue.

By morning his fever broke, and though the coughing intensified, the worst was over. He always got away with everything more easily than her. Or did he? Neither of them ever again discussed the skirmish at the river. Maybe he forgot telling her. But she felt sure neither of them would forget the battle itself. From then on, every time she remembered running with Lalo to the bridge, she pictured Miguel there too, his face shrouded in smoke.

That changed memory bonded her to her big brother in a way that wasn't possible with anybody else. Maybe that was why, long after he got well, she returned to visit him daily. Grace reassured her she didn't mind watching the kids after school. And so long as Candelaria only walked over there while Yankee worked, she figured it made little difference to him.

31. Happy Wife, Happy Life
1920 – El Paso, Texas

Yankee spent his brief months in the Great War farther behind front lines than he'd ever admit to anyone, especially his wife. In the port town of Saint-Nazaire, he worked as a cook with a black labor battalion. To the army, he and those men had one thing in common: others didn't believe they could be trusted in a fight. The only battle he saw was a mess-tent brawl over a potato shortage. Still, he met men who'd seen action. Most wore a look much like Miguel's from the moment he appeared at Yankee's door: an odd combination of deep inward stare and watchfulness. When he first saw Miguel's leather flight jacket, Yankee assumed he was a fighter pilot, till he re-membered Mexicans weren't allowed to fly in the war.

He decided the jacket was a pose and Miguel couldn't be trusted. But there was no convincing Candelaria, determined to see the best in her prodigal brother.

Yankee didn't blame her for never mentioning him before. He un-derstood too well the desire to leave ghosts behind. He also under-stood her urge to take care of Miguel when he got sick. The day he'd received his father-in-law's letter telling him Candelaria was dying, his own terror had surprised him. He'd shipped home as fast as possible. But military paperwork and transport ships didn't move as fast as flu. By the time he arrived in El Paso two months later, he resented her for being so damned healthy. But, to his pleasant surprise, she welcomed him back with more enthusiasm than he expected, as if she'd missed him too.

Nine months later, Mary was born.

After that, he let Candelaria become the axis on which his life turned. Why not? She ensured his children were fed and disciplined and schooled, his immigrant "cousins" warm and hidden, and White and Mexican leaders from the Five Points Businessmen's Association entertained as needed. Her cinnamon-spiced café de olla and low-cut green dress from The Popular helped clear the path for approval of his second restaurant downtown. And every night, she kept him safe from Kei Lun, nestling Yankee between her strong arms and soft breasts.

Until now.

Once Miguel got over the flu, Yankee expected his wife to return her attention to life with him. But she continued to hover around her brother as if he were one of her children. She found him jobs he didn't stick with, bought him clothes because he'd only brought a duffle from L.A., and coaxed him out of dark moods, sometimes late into the night.

Yankee didn't accuse her of favoring her brother over him. Jealousy was for weak men. But one night as they climbed into bed, he said, "Isn't it time you let Miguel live his own life?"

"You don't understand," she said. "I didn't tell you this before, but… last week he threatened to kill himself. Imagine what it would do to my parents to lose him."

"Imagine what it's doing to this family to lose *you*."

"You exaggerate. I'm always either here or at my parents' a few blocks away. I get Benny and Celia to school and keep baby Mary with me. After school, the children play outside. Mamá, Grace, or me are always around if they need us. I make your breakfast, wash your clothes, pour your whiskey. I massage your feet while you talk about your day."

"I miss you when you're not here."

"I'm here now."

"Really?" He lifted her nightdress and cupped her bush, which felt rough and uncontrolled compared to the well-brushed waves on her head. She tried to scuttle free, but he tightened his grip. "Doesn't feel like you're here."

She sighed. "Must you always start down there?"

"You didn't used to mind."

"How would you know?"

"And you never used to talk to me like that."

"I'm no longer the girl you married."

"Not since Miguel arrived. Is he why you won't give yourself to me?" He slid two fingers inside her, challenging and coaxing her at the same time. "Do you dream of letting him in here?"

He understood her shocked eyes, but her slap felt like an overreaction.

He sat up, puzzled, and slapped her back.

The heat of the exchange stirred him, but before he could make another move, she rolled off the bed, snatched her robe from the bedstead, and backed toward the door. Moonlight from the window illuminated her eyes. They held a new calm, as if she knew his thoughts and they no longer concerned her. That hurt more than her anger. She slipped out and closed the door, not with a slam but a nudge, though he knew that was only to avoid waking the children. Soon another door snicked shut across the house and he assumed she was headed to her parents', to Miguel.

Yankee didn't follow her. Whatever Miguel was up to, it would come out. Then she would see that scoundrel wasn't worth the trouble. He didn't really think Miguel was her lover. Even if she wanted something so unnatural—Marcela or Miguel—she'd never go through with it. Though she'd broken with her church to marry him, at heart she remained a Catholic, afraid to sin. When she missed what only Yankee could give her, she'd be back.

Come morning, Yankee found out Candelaria had never left. He looked up from his tea just in time to catch her slinking from the girls' room into the kitchen. That made her third night in a row sleeping with Cecilia and Mary. He shot her a look he hoped suggested indifference while still hinting at potential rage. Let the uncertainty unsettle her, like her refusal to share their bed unsettled him.

"Good morning," she mumbled.

"Good morning!" he bellowed cheerfully, relishing her startled jump.

She tiptoed around him the rest of the day, which he would've found endearing if he weren't so annoyed. It wasn't as if he were a violent man. He only hit her after *she* hit *him*.

When dark fell, she went to the girls' room to listen to their prayers and didn't come out but slept with them all night—again. Same thing the next night, and next, till it became routine.

Soon, she flaunted another change. On Sundays, after she took the children to Mass with his in-laws, it wasn't unusual for Grace to come home with her to chatter in the kitchen while the children napped. But one Sunday, Grace sat at the table, opened a scratched schoolbook with blue-and-white swirls—one of Benny's old McGuffey primers— and began teaching Candelaria to read in English. Surely the idea was Grace's, never one to keep thoughts to herself. The sound of Candelaria quacking English one syllable at a time got on his nerves, but Grace made up for it with her sweet chirpy voice. It was kind of her to teach her sister, and he decided it was harmless. Until they increased the tutoring to twice a week.

One Sunday afternoon, he waited till Grace left, then walked into the kitchen and blurted to Candelaria: "Why?"

"I'm tired of my younger sister reading everything to me: letters, newspapers, books, even signs. In America, everyone reads in English, including Mexicans. Miguel says in Los Angeles even Mexican *women* read in English."

"Here we go again: 'Miguel says this, Miguel says that.' I'm tired of what Miguel says. Miguel isn't a wife and mother. Miguel doesn't understand you don't have time for books."

"Marcela reads books."

He snorted but let it go, remembering his baba's advice: *Happy wife, happy life.* He was no good at happiness but tried not to stand in the way when his wife pursued it. He reminded himself of what he'd heard Marcela tell her the night he listened to their secrets: that Candelaria would love a man who saw her light. Maybe the English lessons would light her up again.

Soon the sisters graduated from reading the childish morality tales of the McGuffey Reader to whole novels, about spirited girls who saved the day: four opinionated *Little Women* from New England; angry Francie Nolan from Brooklyn; and *Jane Eyre*, a smart-mouthed English orphan. Sometimes he lingered in the parlor or lay in his bedroom with the door open, pretending to read his Chinese newspaper while he listened. Much as he didn't understand why the sisters were obsessed with the lives of people who didn't exist, he couldn't help liking the girls in those stories. They reminded him of Grace, the most dangerous girl of all—not because of her effect on Candelaria, but because of her effect on him.

He began having his own fantasies about his feisty sister-in-law, fantasies that would have shocked the girls in those books. Grace was thirteen now—only one year younger than Candelaria had been when she'd married him—and still unaffected by the adult ups and downs that turned his twenty-two-year-old wife serious and made her immune to his charm.

How could he admit to Candelaria that the real reason he didn't want her sister in the house so much was because she tempted him? In no world would giving in to that temptation lead to good. Occasional visits to Mr. Yee's girls were one thing, his wife's sister was another.

New Moon remained his favorite consolation. Her body no longer interested him, worn out by too many men, but it comforted him to sit in a room full of Chinese silk, to talk with someone who spoke his language, to watch the delicate movements of a woman raised back home. This helped him overcome the greatest temptation posed by Grace, who, though she wasn't Chinese, reminded him of his favorite ghost: Mei Yin, once the loudest and least ladylike but also the most natural and unspoiled of all Gong Hau's waiting brides.

Surely Candelaria didn't suspect or she wouldn't invite Grace so often. Then again, she seemed careful never to let her little sister out of her sight. The pair cleaned house side-by-side, slapped tortillas side-by-side, even slept side-by-side in the girls' room—putting Mary in Celia's bed so they could share the other. When Candelaria went to the market and left Grace to mind the children, it struck him that she left her in charge of as many kids as possible—brothers, sisters, nieces, nephews, cousins—as if to surround her. Yankee was grateful to them all for unwittingly helping him stay on the path of fidelity.

He contented himself with the role of Grace's doting brother-in-law. Which was all he had in mind the next time he woke in the early dark to sit in the kitchen with Candelaria, who liked to drink coffee while the house was quiet. He asked her to pour him a cup, which she did without comment. He rarely took morning coffee, but he had something to say, and sharing her ritual seemed a good place to start. He did appreciate the bracing brew, which woke his senses in a different way from tea. However, he took his black, while she turned hers into a sickening-sweet dessert full of milk, sugar, and cinnamon.

He took a sip, grimaced at the bitterness, and announced, "I've been thinking. Your sister should come work for me at the International Café. Now that we're opening a second restaurant, we need more waitresses. This way we keep the money in the family." He nodded, pleased with his prepared speech, certain she'd appreciate him looking out for her sister's interests.

"No!" Her vehemence surprised him, and maybe her as well because she quickly lowered her voice. "Grace must finish school."

"Of course, my love. She can help before and after school."

"That's when Grace helps me around the house, especially with the little ones, mine *and* Mamá's. *You know* my mother hasn't been well since Sarah was born. We can't spare Grace."

"If you really need help, maybe we can hire a girl."

"If you can afford another girl, then hire one for the restaurant and leave Grace alone." Her eyes gleamed in the dark with the fierce twin fires of Kei Lun, protector of the innocent.

Kei Lun had not stalked him for some time, and those fire-possessed eyes made him leery. Yet it felt unwise to let his wife control all the decisions. He proposed a compromise: he'd pay Grace to deliver food from the café to the Chinese immigrants in his tunnels. Yankee and Sam were smuggling more men than ever, and the café's two waitresses delivered their meals.

"No!" she repeated, her Kei Lun eyes narrowed. "I won't expose my sister to those wifeless men."

"She won't be alone with them. She'll just carry trays to their door. It's a chance to earn money—something your parents can't give her."

Her eyes surrendered. Kei Lun's fires vanished, letting Yankee escape again.

With that, things fell back into the places they belonged. His grandfather once told him this was the way of Confucius: *Men should not speak of what belongs inside the house, but women should not speak of what belongs outside.* He gave Grace more to do outside the house, so she spent less time with Candelaria inside, and Candelaria came back to his bed.

Grace worked for him a few days a week whenever his endless cousins passed through. Two to three times a day she would visit the café, pick up a food tray, and drop it off at the new oversized "outhouse" on the courtyard's south end.

The outhouse had two stalls, one carved with a crescent moon, the other a star: moon for men, star for women, though no women went inside. In fact, nobody ever entered the outhouse through the doors, always locked from the inside as if they were occupied. The two holes in the floor led not to shit-buckets but to the tunnel through which his traveling cousins came and went. He made up for the tight quarters with mattresses and blankets, and they seemed as grateful to stay in the fake shithouse as anyone who'd ever stayed in Benny's room. If café customers asked to use a toilet, they were invited to use the one in his house. Nobody took him up on it.

In return for Grace taking over "outhouse duty," it pleased him to give her extra pocket change. He encouraged her to treat the money as hers to enjoy, since he and her parents already provided her food and shelter.

"Anything you want," he said. "Candy, movie tickets, maybe a new hat?"

They were standing in the courtyard, and he didn't notice Candelaria listening from the doorway until she called out, "Let her decide for herself what she wants to buy!"

Upon seeing her frown, he walked over, pulled several bills from his pocket, and folded them into her hand. "Here, buy yourself a hat too. You deserve one for all you do to take care of our family, and your face deserves one for all it does to make the world a prettier place."

She flashed him her rare smile with the two dimples on one side, lending truth to his compliment. "This is too much money for a hat," she chastised, though she didn't give it back.

The sisters came home from their shopping excursion wearing stylish, cloche hats, charming bell shapes that fitted snug to their heads and flared at the ears. Candelaria's maroon felt with violet silk ribbon lent her a glamour that suggested wealth. Grace's was covered with multicolored silk flowers that looked as if a host of butterflies had landed on her head. He asked them to step into the courtyard and model their purchases in the golden afternoon sun. They spun and posed, arms akimbo, giggling.

He clapped with delight. "You look like movie stars."

"Flattery will get you nowhere," Candelaria said but smiled wider than before.

He kissed both her dimples. Then, to include Grace, pinched her cheek.

A frown flashed across her face, but then she propped a hand behind her head and batted her eyes. "You see, I can even make my eyes flicker."

"Like an actress in the flickers!" he chuckled.

Candelaria pushed disapproving fists into her disappearing waist, "You look like a tonta who got something in her eye."

They all laughed harder than the joke deserved.

32. Into Temptation

1921 – El Paso, Texas

Yankee never attended Sunday Mass with Candelaria and her family. He refused to be a hypocrite. Thank God she stopped trying to talk him into it—pestering him to go just to please her parents, keep her company, set an example for the kids. He knew she was skeptical too, about God and Heaven, saints and spirits. He suspected her favorite thing about church was time away from him. He didn't mind. He enjoyed the rare opportunity to have the house to himself.

In their home, she attempted to honor both Chinese and Catholic traditions, in ways he found both touching and amusing. She erected an altar to his ancestors in the hall, where she lit incense, poured rice wine, and watered flowers before his grandparents' red name-tablet. To all this, she added a portrait of Jesus, His Sacred Heart exposed— His flaming, bleeding, thorn-wrapped heart. That heart gave Yankee nightmares.

His father-in-law once explained the blood of Jesus could save him from hell. Yankee pressed him with questions until his answers grew confused. When he asked how Jesus could be God's son if God had no marital relations with Mary, Eduardo turned helpless eyes to his wife.

Maria crossed herself. "Madre de Dios, pray for my heathen son-in-law."

Candelaria assured him this meant she liked him. "When Mamá stops praying for you, that's when you should worry."

Every Sunday, all the Riveras walked to Mass together, then ate a late breakfast at the Rivera home. But one weekend, Grace came down with a cold while sleeping at his house. Come Sunday morning, sneezing and feverish, she begged to stay behind from church.

Candelaria hesitated to leave, till he said, "Don't worry. I'll look after Grace."

She held his gaze for one long moment, then gave a stern nod. "Make sure she rests."

With that, she shooed Benny and Celia out the door. She trailed behind, tussling with baby Mary to stop her from yanking the bonnet off her outraged little head.

Yankee tried to read his newspaper and let Grace sleep, but it was impossible to concentrate with her explosive sneezes shaking the house. He might as well ask if she needed anything. Candelaria often laid hot compresses on the children's chests when they were sick. He pictured doing this for his fourteen-year-old sister-in-law, then dismissed it as a bad idea.

Candelaria also laid cold cloths on the children's foreheads. That was innocent enough. He went to the kitchen, filled a bowl with water, used a pick to hack ice from the icebox into a bowl, and tossed in a kitchen rag. He made his way to the girls' room with the bowl, trying not to slosh water on his polished wood floors.

He opened the door to find Grace asleep. If he laid an icy rag on her forehead it was bound to wake her. He set the bowl on the nightstand that sat wedged in the corner between her bed and Celia-and-Mary's bed—maybe she'd need it later. Her snores bubbled like a boiling kettle. He sat on the other bed and leaned over her to listen, unsure if the alarming sound was a problem.

He studied her face: dark circles under her eyes, nose red-rimmed, lips chapped. Laid a hand on her forehead, the way his mother did with him as a boy. She felt warm but not hot. Her breath smelled of castor oil, cocido, and tortillas, his wife's holy trinity of answers to every ailment.

Grace stirred and opened her eyes, which looked glassy and confused to see his own eyes inches away. She yawned. "Yankee?"

He smiled. "I came to see your health."

She started to laugh, then sneezed instead. Too late she covered her nose. "Sorry."

"No problem." He made a joke of pretending to wipe sneeze droplets from his face, then pulled a handkerchief from his pocket and handed it to her.

She blew her nose so hard it honked like a goose. They both chuckled.

She held out his hanky to return it, but he waved it off. "Keep it."

"You're a good brother," she said, waving the used hanky as proof.

"You're a better sister."

"I am?"

He patted her plump cheek. "Of course. You help my wife make a clean home, you help take care of my children, you help feed my Chinese cousins… And you make me laugh."

"Yes, well, I'm very funny."

He didn't realize he'd let his fingers linger on her cheek till she brushed them away.

She sat up to look around as if she were only now waking. "Where is everyone?"

"Mass."

"Oh, right." She flopped back. "And you don't go because you don't believe in God."

He thumped his thumb against his chest. "I believe in me."

She pointed her index finger at the sky. "But you're not God."

"How do you know?"

She sat up on her elbows and peered into his face. "You look nothing like Him."

He didn't know if it was because she made him laugh or challenged his godhood, but he couldn't help kissing her. Hardly a kiss really, barely touching his cool lips to her feverish ones. She jerked her head with a whine, of dismay or pleasure, he didn't know which. Candelaria had been the same age when he'd first lain with her, but the air between them had never swelled with this much heat. He kissed Grace harder, pressing her to him, and felt her heart leap.

"What're you doing?" Her words came out muffled against his mouth.

"What I've wanted to do a long time." His tongue snuck between her lips like a secret. He grasped the tail of her nightgown, reached underneath, and sought a path to her breasts.

She pushed him away. "Stop! You're my sister's husband." She slapped his back and shoulders until he released her so suddenly her head bumped the wall. She stared at him, startled.

He rubbed the back of her head. "Oops. Are you all right?"

She crawled around him and climbed out of bed.

He pulled her back, not ready to let her go. "Wait."

"Ow! You're twisting my arm."

"I'm sorry. Let me see." He drew her into his lap and stroked her arm. "Don't be scared. How many times did I hold you when you were small? How many years are we friends? You know I'll never hurt you on purpose. I love you." This felt so true it surprised him.

She hitched in a congested breath. "You love me because you're my brother."

"Except I'm not your brother, not really." He tugged her head to his chest, and she gave the slightest resistance before letting it rest there.

"Feel how my heart's running, Grace. It could never run so fast unless I loved you more than a sister."

She yanked her head away, gave him a wild look. "My sister will get mad."

He pictured the thorns that pierced the terrifying Sacred Heart. "She doesn't have to know. This can be our secret. A secret between friends."

"I never keep secrets from my sister, and you shouldn't keep secrets from your wife."

He didn't like where this was going. Might she tell? He shouldn't have kissed her, but he couldn't resist. He wished he hadn't, but it was too late. It wouldn't be good for anyone if Candelaria found out. She'd hate him—this thought upset him more than he expected. "That's why you can't tell her. She'll blame you for flirting. You're the one who asked to stay behind."

"Because I have a cold." She looked so hurt he felt bad.

He patted her shoulder. "I know you didn't mean anything by it. But tell me you don't like it, even a little bit, when it's just the two of us." He kissed her cheek. "If you let me, I'll show you what love is. I can make you feel good…better than a new hat." He nuzzled her neck.

"Please stop," she rasped. But she never screamed or cried or called for help, so he knew she didn't mean it. He felt sure she only fought herself, her desire, her sin. Like all the Riveras, she believed in the notion of sin.

He turned and leaned into her, his weight pressing her into the bed. She closed her eyes. He couldn't resist kissing her again. Her fevered body stiffened, dry lips tightened, small fingers clutched her nightgown against her thighs. Her modesty increased his desire. He kissed her all over, untwined her fingers from her nightgown, lifted it. Suckled her breasts, her belly, her jade gate. He returned to her mouth, and she bit his lip so hard she drew blood. The shock of it only excited him more. He entered her gate till it gave way, moved inside her till she gave up, flinging her hips against his as if she wished not only to surrender but to impale herself on him.

Release came too fast and too hard, like unwanted rain.

Only then did he notice something sticky. Blood. He felt this mark of her virginity wash him clean, return him to his youth, ready to begin a new life. A better man this time.

Then his climax receded, and he drifted for a time, until he felt her chest hitch under his, heard her single choked sob. Had he hurt her? It wasn't what he'd meant to do. He rocked her and this time she let him, tears drenching his chest till she emptied of water. He smoothed her tangled hair behind her ears. "You can't help who you love, little bird."

What time was it? Her family would return soon. He suggested she wash up, but she didn't move. He had to carry her to the bathroom.

No time to draw a bath. Instead, he sat her on the toilet, wiped all traces of tears from her cheeks and blood from her thighs, rubbed a wet cloth over her with tender care until she looked…untouched. He threw the stained sheets in the laundry basket, slid fresh sheets onto the bed, and instructed her to tell her sister she had her monthly. She nodded, silent.

No point hurting Candelaria. What was done was done.

He tucked her back into bed, rubbed her arm till she fell into deep sleep—as if nothing happened. Then he wrapped his hand around her slack arm and knew he was wrong: she wasn't asleep but unconscious. She'd given him everything in one moment. Nothing was left.

He cursed the Kei Lun, guardian of the innocent, for failing to protect Grace from the evil inside him. Why didn't the beast stop him as it had the night he conjured Mei Yin, eager to consummate their love in the graveyard? What good was such a savior if it only rescued ghosts?

33. Prohibited

1922 – El Paso, Texas

Candelaria grew suspicious when Yankee became thick friends with Miguel after all that time warning her not to trust him. She tried to be grateful for his change of heart. Told herself she was overreacting because she was pregnant again. She loved her first three pregnancies, but a fourth was bound to put any woman in a bad mood. She should be happy to see Miguel cheer up, and to hear Yankee stop complaining about the time she spent with her brother.

To be honest, she was jealous. Not because their late-night talks in the café looked interesting. Nor did she yearn to drink and gamble with them across the border at scandalous places like Trivai, Big Kid, Bagdad, or smack on the border at the filthy Hole in the Wall on Cordova Island. But sometimes she resented that she and Grace must always stay home with the kids—not just her three but often their four siblings too—while the men did as they liked.

In the months after local prohibition, El Paso men had done most of their drinking in Juárez and that had worked fine. Why not keep that up under national Prohibition? Why did men have to change something easy and make it hard?

The night Miguel arrived in his new Model T, to give Yankee a ride to their watering holes, she scolded him for wasting money to show off. But he said he got the car for a steal, that he needed it for handyman jobs, that now he could give their family rides to shopping, errands, visiting, whatever they needed.

She was inclined to see things his way, till the morning Marcela visited over coffee and said she'd seen the car.

Marcela expressed the usual admiration, then asked an odd question: "Why does it have thick bars underneath?"

"Does it? I never noticed." Candelaria puzzled over why it mattered.

"Yes. I've never seen a Modelo-T like that."

Nine-year-old Benny piped up. "I know what those bars are." The two women turned to him, all ears.

"Smugglers use them so their Fords don't bounce crossing the river. That way their engines don't get waterlogged, and their cars don't get stuck in the mud when Prohibition agents are on their tail."

Candelaria was stunned. "How do you know these things?"

"My friends told me."

"How do your friends know these things?"

Benny shrugged.

She shook herself out like a dusty rug. "Your uncle isn't a smuggler."

He shrugged again. "If you say so, Mamá."

She itched to slap him for smarting off—so like his father   but she didn't want to discourage her son from giving her more information in future.

That night she waited in the courtyard for Miguel and Yankee to finish another late conversation in the café. They talked by the glow of a hurricane lamp. Then the lamp went out, and as Miguel exited out the front, she stepped into the dark kitchen—and barreled into Yankee on his way out the back. They both gasped in surprise. He flicked on the lights, and she put up a hand to shield her eyes.

"What're you doing?" he said. "What if I mistake you for a robber and stab you?" He gestured to a butcher block full of knives.

She ignored that and got to the point, "I've learned to live with your lawless ways, but must you drag my family to hell with you?"

He lowered his chin at her like she was stupid—she hated that look. "You really are blind where your brother's concerned."

"What're you talking about?"

"Miguel was a gangster long before he arrived here. Don't tell me you buy his story about 'troubleshooting' business problems? What kind of *business* do you think he's qualified for, a Mexican deserter with an eighth-grade education?"

"But he came back, to his family, to start over."

"Bullshit, mi amor. Miguel came back to find cheap Mexican tequila to compete with American moonshine."

"Baloney! If that's all he wanted, he could've stayed in L.A. and gone to Tijuana."

He grinned at her ladylike swearing like it was cute—she hated that look too. "His last boss does business in Tijuana. Miguel wants his own territory, his own connections. He heard you had money. He heard you married me."

"But…he looked surprised when he met you."

"That doesn't mean he *was* surprised. Our partnership, it was your brother's idea."

Yankee explained that it wasn't a bad idea. Prohibition was an opportunity for them all, and he and Miguel needed each other to make the operation work. Miguel needed his connections, and he needed a Mexican to blend in at the border. She let him explain, because it never paid to cut him short when he was impressed with himself. But she didn't hear a word. She was too furious with Miguel for pulling her family into his lies.

One night, Candelaria invited her brother to supper while Yankee worked late. She planned to wait for the kids to go to bed, then give Miguel a piece of her mind. Grace made this easier by complaining she was tired and going to bed early. But Yankee must've warned him, because instead of lingering to chat, he stood, said he needed to go meet friends, and grabbed his coat from the rack. Irritated, she grabbed his fedora from its hook, about to throw it at him, when something caught her eye. She rotated the hat till she found two tiny, singed holes in the crown. She held it up to a lamp, sending light through the holes.

Her hands shook. "What's this?"

He snatched it and studied the holes with a befuddled look, until his features fell with comprehension. Then he shrugged and poked out his lower lip. "Moths?"

"I'm not stupid, Miguel. Yankee told me everything."

"Everything about what?"

She yanked the hat away, shoved it back onto the rack, and crossed her arms at him.

"It was your husband's idea," he said.

"That's not what he says."

"He didn't hate the idea. Take it up with him." He grabbed his hat again as if to leave, then stepped back into the kitchen, sank into a chair, and poked his fingers through the holes. He blew a fart with his lips. "The other night while I crossed the river, they shot at me." He told her he'd been chased, not by American agents or Mexican cops but El Paso moonshiners who hated competition. "Good thing I got an empty head or they mighta hit something."

She reached out to shove him but jumped at the sound of a stifled giggle. How long was Grace standing there? Her sister had become silent and invisible lately, slipping into rooms without her former chirp and scurry, sneaking like a burglar.

"I thought you were tired," Candelaria said. "You should go to bed."

"And miss hearing all about the bootlegging?" Grace poured herself a cup of coffee, lots of condensed milk, and settled into a chair across from Miguel.

Candelaria remained standing. "Who said anything about bootlegging?"

Grace shot her a look that said, Are you kidding? Little know-it-all.

Candelaria pulled out a chair for herself, with an angry scrape. "Coffee will keep you awake."

"And stunt your growth." Miguel winked, then poured himself a cup, black as usual.

Grace gave him a sharp look. "I'm not a little girl anymore."

"Why are you in such a hurry to grow up?" he said.

"Why not? You were." Grace's response threw her. She was often bossy but rarely sarcastic. What was going on with her? Her woman's time? A crush on a boy? That would explain her new secretiveness.

"True," Miguel said. "I was in too big a hurry to grow up. Running away was a mistake."

"And now you've made the grown-up decision to become a bootlegger?" Candelaria said.

"Why not?" Grace said to her. "Your husband does it. Where do you think he got the money for your icebox, your radio, or those fancy flowers in your courtyard?"

"My gardenias?"

He had given her the little potted bush for their seventh anniversary. The fragrance made her dream of tropical islands. It was such a romantic gesture, she'd let him plant their fourth baby in her that night. Gardenias were thirsty flowers, hard to keep in the desert, imported. Expensive. She'd assumed the money came from the restaurants, and from helping his "cousins" come to America—which she considered a good deed though it was illegal. Then again, opening a second café *did* cost a lot. Plus, there was the money he gave her parents. Why did she never ask how they afforded it all? Did she not want to know?

Miguel chimed in, "Then there's the money for your children's shoes, schoolbooks, toy trains, dolls. And remember, we have Mamá and Papá's needs to consider too."

"*Are* you thinking of our parents? What they'll go through if you're arrested, or killed?" She spoke with less force now, uncertain of the ground beneath her.

"Life's a risk," he said. "You can't protect us all."

"What was it like when they shot at you, Miguel?" Grace clasped her coffee cup in both hands and leaned forward, as if they sat around a campfire telling made-up stories.

"You think getting shot sounds fun?" Candelaria said.

"I don't know." Grace gave a catlike shrug, as if to goad her. "*Is* it fun, Miguel?"

He leaned in too, his tone confidential, "I'll tell you this: getting shot at is no fun, but the chase? I'll admit, sometimes it makes me feel more alive."

"Because you could die?" Grace's eyes shone as if death were the height of adventure.

"Because *who* could die?" Yankee exploded into the kitchen with annoying good humor.

"Miguel almost got shot smuggling tequila," Grace said.

He didn't act surprised that Grace knew. "Don't worry, your brother's a skilled driver. He'll never get caught."

"Haven't you seen enough on that river to know better?" Candelaria said.

"Yes. I've also seen your brother drive. In water. He learned at the Los Angeles viaduct."

"The what?" she said.

The others laughed, making her want to grab her broom and chase them out of the house. They all thought she was stupid, did they?

"I wish I could go with you," Grace said to Miguel.

"Are you crazy?!" Candelaria said.

"No. Why would you say that?" The girl shot a hurt look, not at her but at Yankee.

What was that about? She tried to catch Yankee's eye, but he was studying Grace as if more concerned about her than she was. Flustered, Candelaria turned to Miguel. "Must you always tear the family apart?"

Miguel splayed an open hand against his chest. "Me?"

"Fine. If you *men* want to risk your lives, I can't stop you. But Yankee, know this: I'll never let you drag my son into this! Never." She didn't add her next thought: *Even if I have to kill you.* The idea so chilled her, it jolted her to her feet.

She ran to the girls' room and shut the door. There, she stood watching Celia and Mary sleep, arms and legs grappling as if wrestling in their dreams. The second bed was empty, though Grace would be coming back to it. She considered going to her own bed, but it was also Yankee's bed, where she'd be subject to his demands.

She had no place in this house to escape, to be alone with her thoughts, to call her own. This never occurred to her till now.

34. The Smuggler's Box
1922 – El Paso, Texas

Candelaria woke to the awareness that Grace no longer lay in bed next to her. At first, she assumed Grace went to the toilet, but that must've been some time ago because her side of the mattress was cold. Her sister had acted angry earlier. Why?

She crept out of the room, careful not to wake Celia and Mary, then padded into the parlor, hoping to find Grace reading a book by lamplight or brooding in the dark over whatever had hurt her feelings. Not there. She squinted into the dark kitchen, glided past the master bedroom where the open door signaled Yankee was out late, poked her head into the empty bath, then opened the door to Benny's room. Her son snored like an out-of-tune accordion, which would've made her chuckle except her worry was mounting. Because Grace wasn't here either.

She stood in the parlor listening to the grandmother clock tick-tick-tick on the mantel, until it sank in that both hands were tipped past the wrong side of midnight.

Where was Grace?

She grabbed her red rebozo, then laced her boots with shaking fingers as she remembered Grace's excitement at Miguel's descriptions of smuggling tequila across the border. No. Grace could be headstrong, but she'd never go that far. Anyway, Miguel would never take her with him. Grace must be at their parents'.

She went to the back door, then hesitated, afraid to leave her children alone at night. What if one of them woke and needed her? She was only going to her mother's right down the street. If she needed to search farther, then she'd send Mamá back here to watch them. She stepped into the night's cold breath and hurried past shuttered shops and darkened homes. She cringed at the thud of her boots against tar, and then dirt road.

In contrast, she pondered the strange quiet of Grace's steps these days. Even after their desert journey, the Riveras were typically a noisy lot, Grace most of all. It used to be that her heavy footfalls woke babies, her wild arms flung wreckage in the marketplace, her giggles scattered flocks of birds. These days she slunk along walls as if she feared human contact, clung to shadows as if she feared light, tucked her limbs close as if a monster lurked at every turn.

What was stalking Grace? Candelaria shivered.

At her parents' tenement, she opened the unlocked door and tiptoed through the parlor where the boys, Sal and Frankie, lay panting on the sofa as if they'd fallen asleep mid-chase. She slipped into the bedroom where Grace often slept with eight-year-old Annie. But Annie sprawled across the space where Grace should've been, mumbling to herself. Worry turned to panic.

She lingered in her parents' open doorway and listened to their snorting, grumbling duet, surprised at how much it calmed her. Baby Sarah slept in an open dresser-drawer at Mamá's side, suckling a nipple in noisy dreams. Candelaria yearned to crawl inside her family's outrageous noise, to squeeze between her parents like she used to when nightmares woke her.

"Mamá?" she whispered. *I'm afraid*, she thought but didn't say.

No answer.

"Mamá!" She shook her mother's shoulder. *I'm afraid*, she mouthed without a sound.

Mamá's hand snaked out to clutch her as she hissed, "Did he kill you?"

"What? Who? No. Mamá, Graciela's missing."

"Missing? No. She must've come here. Did you check the girls' room?"

"She's not there."

Mamá stood up, instantly alert, feeling around the foot of the bed for her robe.

Papá stirred, muttering a creaky, "What time is it?"

"Somebody kidnapped Graciela," Mamá's voice remained hushed.

"Who?! Where?!" Papá leapt out of bed and fell. Sometimes he forgot about his bad foot.

"Shhh! Nobody kidnapped her, Papá. I think…" she hesitated, unsure how much to say.

"Tell us!" Mamá cinched her belt tight around her stout middle.

"Miguel drove to Juárez, and I think she hid in back of his Model T."

"Ridiculous," Papá said. "Why would she do that?"

"I don't know." She sank onto the bed, then leapt back to her feet, unable to endure a moment's stillness. "Yankee and I will look for her. Mamá, will you watch my children?"

"Sí, claro."

"I'll go with Candelita and Yankee," her father said.

"No, Papá! Someone has to stay with my brothers and sisters." She didn't want him to know his son-in-law wasn't home, or to find out where he really was.

"Bién. I know I'm a worthless cripple." He sank onto the edge of the bed, head in hands.

"Don't be a tonto. Candelita's right. Besides, if Grace sees you and thinks you're angry, she might run off again. Don't worry, we'll find her." Mamá kissed the top of his head.

Candelaria did the same. Then they hurried out the door together.

At the edge of Chinatown, her mother pulled her into a violent embrace, then thrust her out to arm's length and commanded, "Go get your husband and find our precious girl."

How had it come down to her, the stupid girl? Surely Mamá couldn't forget what happened last time one of her children ran off and Candelaria followed.

This wasn't the first time Candelaria poked her head through Mr. Yee's doorway to holler for her husband. What did she care what anyone in such a place thought of her? It *was* the first time she stepped past the threshold. The House of Forgetfulness didn't look like the demons' nest white people said it was, didn't look much different from any other El Paso saloon she'd glimpsed before Prohibition: smoky lamplight, wood bar, scarred tables. She did notice three differences: most (though not all) of the men were Chinese, the smoke carried an added cloying sweetness, and here the putas entertained clients underground instead of upstairs.

"You cannot go down." A grim-lipped, barrel-chested Chinese bouncer blocked the stairs, black tunic flipped open to reveal Levi's topped by a holstered pistol and ready hand.

She planted her feet, arms akimbo. "My sister's missing, my husband's the only man who can help find her, and if you want to stop me you'll have to shoot me." Though her whole body shook, she shoved past him and scurried downstairs without looking back.

In the downstairs hall, she flung open doors one after another, to curses, roars, and thrown bric-a-brac—flung by Mr. Yee's Mexican girls, not their customers. The fourth door was half-open, letting her husband's deep voice roll into the hall, and letting her get a good look. Unlike the other men, he was fully clothed, reclined in a chair with his legs on the bed, bare feet touching the miniature red slippers of a Chinese woman who looked older than her. The woman sat against a headboard littered with red pillows, body slung with a red robe, plain face interrupted only by a red eye-patch. She and Yankee were laughing so hard they didn't notice her. In other rooms, lamps were dimmed with scarves, beds disarrayed. In this one, cheerful golden light revealed a bed without a wrinkle.

She had steeled herself to catch her husband in any number of compromising positions, except this one: enjoying a conversation with another woman. The tableau—cheerful, warm, human—filled her with loneliness, standing unseen under the glare of an exposed bulb in the hall.

Yankee's Chinese dialect was complex as a secret code, and she'd never learned much, so she only understood a quarter of what she heard. It was enough to fill in the blanks:

"Then what did she do?" Yankee asked the one-eyed woman.

"Her teacher said, 'You will learn life isn't fair.' Then my daughter said, 'My mother already taught me that.'"

He guffawed, toeing her leg till she joined him. "I hope my own girls grow up so clever."

Candelaria flung the door wide. "If you ever come home, maybe *you* can teach them."

The pair stopped laughing and turned. The woman cast her single eye sidelong at Yankee. He remained seated but tipped his chin to Candelaria, the same way he tipped his bowler hat to strangers. She wanted to crack the room's gold lampshade over his head. He addressed her in his language, calling her *wife*, "Why'd you come, *lou po?*"

She replied in hers, in less endearing terms, "Grace is missing, hijo de puta."

His smile vanished as he shot up from his chair. "What happened? Where is she?"

"I hoped *you'd* tell *me*. I think she hid in Miguel's Model T, in the smuggler's box. Remember when he bought it, he bragged it had room to fit a whole person? You even talked about using it to smuggle the Chinese cousins. I think he drove her to Juárez without knowing."

"Why?"

She resisted a perverse urge to laugh at his flabbergasted face. "Last night she said such a trip sounded exciting—" She hesitated. The prostitute leaned toward Yankee, as if *she* were the concerned wife and *Candelaria* an embarrassing relation come to beg. It was too humiliating to continue. "I refuse to discuss this in front of your...friend."

He turned to the other woman and said in English, "Excuse me, New Moon, I must go."

She closed her only eye and bowed her head, demure as a fine lady. "Of course. I hope your girl is safe."

Yankee swept past Candelaria and down the hall.

She turned to New Moon, who met her gaze with infuriating calm. Candelaria had only one question, and asking it would waste time. All she could manage was, "Grace is not his daughter."

But New Moon answered her unspoken question, "My daughter is not his either." This was such a relief she almost thanked her, until New Moon added, "Yankee just likes my stories."

Her teeth clacked shut at this polite little cruelty. Impossible to respond. She slammed the door between them and ran after her husband.

He was pacing the alley. "What took you so long?"

"Are you kidding?"

He waved the subject aside. "You're sure she went with Miguel?"

"She's not at our house or my parents'. She said smuggling sounded 'fun.' Where else would she be?"

"Spending the night with a friend?"

"When has she ever done that?"

He pulled his pocket watch from his vest and squinted at it in the amber light of a streetlamp. "If she hid in the smuggler's box, he won't find her till he meets our Juárez supplier."

She bit her upper lip. "Then what?"

"He has three choices." He cocked a thumb to indicate choice one: "Leave the alcohol behind and bring her back across the bridge tonight." Thumb and forefinger: "Spend the night in Juárez and bring the tequila across the bridge in the morning—with your sister in the front seat to help him tell an innocent story and avoid being searched." Thumb, forefinger, middle finger: this time he locked eyes with her but said nothing.

Her eyes widened with comprehension, "Or drive *through the river*, tonight, with both her and the booze?"

He wobbled his head, neither nodding yes nor shaking no. "Maybe."

"Can we get to him before he does any of those things?"

He checked his watch. "We'll never make it. It's almost three a.m. He always crosses the river between three and four. Whatever his decision, he's already made it. Come on." He bowed to her, deeper than New Moon had bowed to him, and held out a gallant hand.

To her shame, the gesture gave her a flush of pleasure. "Where are we going?"

He broke into an infuriating grin. "It's clear you're not content to stay home, so we're going to the river to wait."

Hand in hand, like young lovers, they walked beyond the halo of city lights to a dark spot along the river's southwestern reach. There, they sat against the twisted base of a forlorn olive tree. She let him keep her hand, though it made her feel no less alone.

They didn't wait long. Yankee's whisper cut through the lazy summer shush of the Río Grande, "He's here." He pushed off of the olive tree's lumpy roots and onto his feet, then reached down to pull her up with him.

She followed him to the river's edge. "I don't see anything."

"Listen."

She leaned forward and held her breath. Despite the low current, the river yielded a new sound like a thousand tiny wings flapping. In the dark water, a boxy shadow split a double wake of white foam. The headlights were off, but she soon heard the Model-T engine's rattle.

She followed Yankee's gaze up and down the bank, steeling herself for headlights to blast open the night, for federal agents to shout, "Department of Revenue!" For bullets to whiz past until one found her—the moment she'd been waiting for since her first night on this river. Maybe she deserved it. Mamá kept trusting her to watch Grace, and she failed every time.

The car climbed to the top of the low bank until she made out a single shape in the driver's seat. Miguel. Where was Grace? Hunkered down in back? Yankee began to raise his arms to wave but stopped short, grabbed Candelaria, and yanked her to the ground with him.

"What're you doing?" she said.

Before he could answer, three pairs of white beams caught the mud-spattered car in a web of light. Miguel cut the engine and rose halfway from his seat, one arm flung over his eyes, a gun in that hand. But there was nothing for him to aim at except the onslaught of light. He waited.

"¡Hola, Chuco! ¿Qué pasa?" a man's nasal voice called from behind the lights. Why did the invisible man call her brother by the nickname for El Paso?

Miguel slowly peeled his gun-arm up from his eyes and rested it atop his head, so he could peer into the lights. "Nardo, is that you?"

A man in a suit the same color as the night stepped into the light. "Good ear, hermano."

"I'll never forget the voice of the man who told me to get out of his city or die."

This could only get worse. Where was Grace? She craned her neck. Yankee pushed her back down.

"You take things too seriously, Chuco. You know I like to joke."

"Yeah," Miguel said, "and your pistola likes to deliver your punch lines."

"My gun likes to laugh, it's true, but never at your expense. Not after you saved my life."

"Are you sure you didn't come to pay me back for the other thing, jefe?"

"You mean to ask *you* to pay *me* back? I'm sure my life is worth the money you took, como un reward. I mean, what would my cash mean to me if I was too dead to enjoy it?"

"I guess the same thing it'll mean to me after tonight, boss." Miguel's gaze darted along the arc of lights as several silhouettes stepped in front of the headlamps to aim at him. With guns. Was he about to die like Lalo? What did this pendejo river have against her family?

Nardo turned to his companions. "¡Eh, cabrones! Put down your guns. You're giving our friend the wrong idea." The silhouettes stopped aiming at him but stayed put. Nardo turned back to Miguel. "Sorry if our little surprise scared you. I just happen to be in town visiting a cousin, and he mentioned I might find you here."

"Which cousin is that?" Miguel asked.

"Does it matter? They're all assholes." They both erupted into rolling laughter. She didn't get the joke. "Anyway, I came here because I was thinking, since you *borrowed* my money to finance your new business, you might want to give me your first payment in person, and maybe give me a taste of your new product—to thank me."

Miguel shrugged at Nardo's men, "How can I say no?" With his gun-arm still flung over his head, he opened the Model T's door and stepped out. She heard multiple guns cock. She closed her eyes and plugged her ears…but nothing happened. She unplugged her ears and opened her eyes. Miguel held both hands up in surrender, dangling his gun from one finger and dropping it on the front seat. "What's mine is yours."

Nardo turned to his men and made a slicing motion across his throat with the blade of his hand. The cabrón was going to kill him anyway? But the men simply cut all the cars' headlamps, submerging them in darkness. It took a moment to adjust to the natural light of the moon, but she made out Nardo striding to Miguel. The unlikely pair threw their arms around each other and slammed one another's backs. She sat back on her heels in relief. Next to her, Yankee snorted in disgust.

"Good to see you, my friend," Miguel said.

"You too, Chuco." The darkness had shrunk Nardo, who now appeared shorter and wider than her brother, not the menacing figure he had appeared in the headlights.

The two friends, or enemies, or whatever they were, muttered together. Nardo waved his gun at the back seat to indicate the other men should take whatever was there. Was he taking Grace along with the tequila?! She lurched forward, but Yankee hauled her back. She let him, realizing she couldn't save Grace if she herself died. As it was, the men only hauled out three cases to load into their cars. No sign of Grace. She exhaled.

Less than two minutes passed as Nardo's men loaded the cases into the cars and climbed in.

Nardo walked to his car, leaned inside, and emerged with a bottle, which he waved at Miguel. "For your hospitality, Chuco. Get drunk on me." He tossed the bottle.

Miguel caught it, hugging it to his chest so it wouldn't fall. "So, you're in El Paso then?"

"I'm in El Paso *now*. As for *then*, who knows? I like to visit my cousins. I have lots of cousins. And I like knowing I can count on old friends like you for a drink or two when I come. ¿Tú casa es mi casa, eh?" He chuckled at his own joke.

"Igualmente," Miguel said, and they both laughed harder.

"Vámonos!" Nardo slid into his car's passenger seat and shut the door.

The three cars rattled off until they became one with the dark.

Miguel sagged against his driver-side door, opened the bottle Nardo had tossed him, and took a swig. Yankee strolled toward him while Candelaria hung back to shake out her legs, which had fallen asleep while she crouched in the dirt.

"So, brother-in-law," Yankee said, "did you plan to tell me they took that bottle too?"

Miguel wiped his arm across his mouth but betrayed no surprise at seeing Yankee. "Just sipping a little off the top for my nerves. I planned to split shots with you while I told you about the stolen cases. Want your share now, partner?" He offered the bottle with a grin.

Yankee ignored it.

Miguel cocked his head. "What's wrong, brother?"

Why didn't Yankee get to the point? She strode up to join them.

Miguel snapped to attention at the sight of her, then turned his head aside as if to receive a blow. When none came, he leaned in for a closer look at her, then offered her the bottle. "Looks like you need this more than he does."

She slapped the tequila aside, chest heaving, eyes burning. "Where's Grace?"

"Grace? How would I know?"

"Don't play games!" She pushed past him to the car's rear and stared into the back seat. The black fake leather upholstery was flipped back, its secret metal compartment gutted—nothing but an empty hole. "Where is she? Does this car have another secret box? Open it!"

He rested a heavy hand on her shoulder. "Sis, you can see as well as I can, there's no more room under that seat. What gives?"

She opened her mouth to answer, but nothing came out.

"Grace is missing." Yankee's voice was heavy. "We thought she'd be with you."

"I haven't seen her since last night. Missing? You're sure?" Miguel's alarm sounded real.

Candelaria sank against the car.

Her brother put his arms around her. "Don't worry. Grace would never leave home."

With that, she knew where Grace was. The same place she'd go if she could. She pulled free, took his face between her hands, and looked into his eyes, so like Papá's. "She *did* smuggle herself with you. Before you went to your supplier, you had a drink in Juárez, didn't you?"

"Yeah, but…"

"She waited till you went into the saloon, then she climbed out and went on her way."

Miguel followed her gaze across the river, as if their sister might appear on the other side.

"On her way where?" Yankee asked her.

"Home."

35. Wayward

1922 – Juárez, Mexico

Candelaria pushed into the heave of people riding the streetcar, bargain-seekers who crossed the border at dawn. Most were women and girls from Segundo Barrio, carrying empty sacks or bags sewn from old skirts. They chatted in Spanish, scolded and soothed children, or sat in focused silence—already mentally haggling with vendors at the Juárez mercado on the other side of the Santa Fe Bridge. Most Frontera women simply walked across, but Candelaria panicked at the very thought of ever crossing a bridge on foot again.

Either way, crossing the border always frayed her nerves, especially coming back. She was terrified customs officials would refuse to believe she was an American, drag her off the trolley, and force her into the fumigation showers at the U.S. Customs building, where they sprayed Mexicans with delousing chemicals. She heard this gave people a terrible cough. Worse, two of her female cousins told her they had to strip naked while the male agents stared and laughed at them. She tightly clutched her purse, which held the papers proving she wasn't a dirty Mexican but a clean American, by virtue of her marriage to Yankee, who even had a letter from Uncle Sam thanking him for his service in the Great War.

Anglo women rarely caught this early run, especially without husbands. But two young güeras sat across from her, arm-in-arm, whispering. Sisters, she thought. Overdressed for the hour: in tiny hats, dresses cut to reveal silk stockings, and pointy shoes dyed navy blue. It used to surprise her when people called skin like theirs *white*. To her, Grace's skin looked lighter. This pair wasn't white. What then? Pink? Porridge? Sand? Whatever the color, it guaranteed nobody would question them when they returned.

Damn her big brother, who refused to come with her, blaming a rumor that Prohibition agents were looking for him. Damn her husband, who also refused, claiming a Chinese man would draw attention. Damn Papá, who stayed home too: "If Grace wants to run away, how can we force her to stay?" What was wrong with the men in her family?

Going *into* Mexico is easy, she thought, eyes fixed on the river for the brief minutes it took to cross. She stepped off the trolley into the crowd—stomach rolling like she'd just taken a carnival ride after a bad hot dog—and started the long walk to Marcela's. She stopped when a familiar but unexpected voice called, "Candelita!" Amazement flooded her as Marcela floated toward her, then relief as they hugged fiercely, not letting go till the crowd thinned.

"I came as soon as I could," Marcela said.

"But how did you know I was coming?"

Marcela's reply was matter of fact, "I have friends at Mr. Yee's. One of them…"

She held up a hand. "Better I don't know. Pues nada, I'm grateful you're here."

Marcela cupped warm hands to her chilled cheeks. "What happened?"

"You don't know?" It was easy to assume Marcela knew everything.

"I only know Grace is missing and you think she came to Juárez. I brought Estefan's truck, just in case. Where are we going?" That was more like it.

"I'll explain in the truck," Candelaria said.

Estefan used his ugly Model TT stake-bed truck to haul dry and canned goods from the railroad, so it was built for strength not speed. Candelaria grew impatient as first an automóvil and then a horse passed them. At least it gave her a chance to search the faces of the waking ciudad. El Paso's sister-city dwelt in a sleepier era than its twin; this side of the border still favored foot traffic. Then all traffic dwindled as Marcela steered west although Candelaria had yet to suggest a direction.

"We aren't starting at your house?" she asked.

"You said Grace was headed home." Marcela gestured to the road where it changed from tar to dirt. "This is the way."

"We're driving all the way to Mata Flores?"

"Of course not. Grace won't go all the way there."

"She sounded eager for danger."

"She only talked that way so you'd save her."

"From what?"

"That's what we must ask when we find her."

Candelaria threw herself back against her seat with an infuriated sigh. She'd spent her whole life waiting on the answers of others.

Though Marcela had washed the windshield before setting out, the dirt road kicked up a fresh coat of dust. Candelaria leaned out the cab's open side, hoping the clear view would help her spot Grace sooner, among the shrinking number of walkers on the dwindling road.

The buildings at the edge of Juárez tumbled into the earth, then so did the hills, till the military checkpoint loomed alone in the desert ahead. The last time Candelaria stopped here, more than ten years ago, she'd been terrified her father and Miguel would be drafted, Benito shot, she and her mother attacked—though back then she had only a vague idea what that meant. She wiped sweaty palms on her skirt, told herself she had nothing to fear this time. The post's new soldiers were not the federales of the past. *The people* had won the revolution.

Marcela slowed the truck as they approached the guard shack. The tiny building was fortified with a low bulwark of bricks and sandbags, and one soldier leaned across them. Behind him, a trio slouched against a wall, eating and smoking. Another handful played cards under a scraggly tree. Their guns were not in hand but tipped or fallen like abandoned toys. Spending a decade alert for the call of war must make any army tire of it, but these soldiers seemed too young for that.

Marcela braked the truck to a halt, and two guards strode toward it, rifles across their chests at the ready. They looked irritated at the interruption.

Marcela murmured to Candelaria, "Do you trust me?"

"Always."

"Then let me do the talking."

One guard strode to the driver's side, the other to the passenger's side.

"Buenas tardes," Marcela smiled at the one on her side.

He didn't smile back. "Buenas. Where are you from?"

"Juárez."

"El Paso."

"My sister is visiting." Marcela laid a hand on her arm.

Right. Let Marcela do the talking.

"Two women traveling alone?" His mouth puckered as if at something sour.

Marcela shrugged. "We're not driving far."

The one on Candelaria's side stepped back to peer into the wood truck bed. It held only a coiled rope and empty crate, yet she feared he'd accuse them of a crime.

"We're going to see our other sister," she blurted.

Marcela's guard dropped his chin to peer across the cab at Candelaria. "Where is this other sister?"

"Actually," Marcela said, "we hope you might help us with that."

His face opened into childlike curiosity. "Help? How?"

"We're looking for her. A young girl."

He broke into a grin. "Hear that, Diego? They're looking for a girl."

Candelaria's guard returned to her side. "Really? What does she look like?"

She shot an apprehensive look at Marcela, who nodded. "Fourteen, small, fair, with freckles…"—she hesitated—"…and dark circles under her eyes." It was true, but when had those arrived?

"Her name wouldn't happen to be Graciela?"

"You've seen her?"

"Seen her? She's here."

Candelaria jumped out so fast, he jumped back to avoid getting knocked down. "Grace!" she shouted, looking all directions at once. "Gracielita!"

The soldier clasped her elbow. She pulled away, startled.

"Don't be scared." He lowered his rifle. "I'll take you to her."

She let him steer her into the shack. What she saw there twisted her gut. Grace sat on a crate, leaning forward on her hands, murmuring to a grinning soldier who sat sideways to her, tipped back in his chair with his feet on a desk. She was leaning so close her breasts almost brushed his shoulder. Candelaria knew her sister liked attention but had never seen her flirt so brazenly.

"Graciela?" Her voice sounded faint in her own ears, as if she didn't expect an answer.

Surely Grace saw her come in, yet she was slow to tear her eyes from the young man, giving him a crooked little smile before turning to her. "What're you doing here?" Why wouldn't Grace meet her eyes?

"I could ask you the same thing."

"These nice soldiers won't let me go farther. They say it's not safe. Right, Arturo?" She gave him a playful push.

A blush crept over his face as he gave a helpless shrug.

Candelaria gaped at her sister, who seemed replaced by a stranger. "Grace!"

"What?"

"Do you have any idea of the terrible things that can happen to a girl traveling alone?"

"At least nothing terrible did happen, thank God," Marcela said from the doorway. "Maybe we should go elsewhere to talk?" She drew Candelaria's gaze to the original two guards who'd followed them to the shack, plus the dozen or so others outside.

"Of course." Her throat thickened with shame as she addressed all of them, including the one at the desk grinning at Grace like a baboso. "Thank you for looking after my sister." Then she grabbed Grace's wrist and dragged her outside. The girl neither resisted nor helped, just shuffled behind, reminding her how frustrated she used to feel being in charge of Grace when she was little. Her sister was never one for obedience. But this?

At the truck, she clutched Grace's shoulders and shook her. "What's gotten into you? How could you shame yourself with a strange man?"

Grace shook herself free, lifted her face to the painful blue sky, and gave a howl of such primitive suffering it set Candelaria on her heels. Without thinking, she wrapped her arms around her sister, surrounding her with her body, as if shielding her from an unseen attacker. "Sh-sh-sh," she said, and thought but did not say, It's just a bad dream, mija.

A tense silence filled the truck cab as Marcela drove them to her home. Grace, who sat in the middle, stopped crying, though she wiped her nose on the back of her hand till Marcela handed her a handkerchief. Candelaria tried to put an arm around her again, but Grace cringed, so she let go and kept her eyes on the city. Grace seemed to stare into a scary place only she could see, but Candelaria feared if she looked into her eyes, she might see it too.

Candelaria felt a comforting familiarity returning to Marcela's home. Marcela, her husband, and children lived in her parents' old place behind the store, no longer called El Emporio Chung. Renamed La Calidad, the shop gleamed with tile, chrome, and glass, and sold a mix of dry goods and groceries for both Chinese and Mexican tastes. Her parents had moved into their new hotel, closer to el centro. Marcela led them through the shop, where Estefan and their ten-year-old son, Tonio, were helping customers. Candelaria waved while Grace stared down at the black-and-white checkered tiles underfoot.

"Where are Pedro and Regina?"

"I sent them to stay with my parents, so we'd have peace and quiet to talk. Come, let's go to the kitchen."

Another need Marcela anticipated. If she had her friend's special powers, she would've sensed Grace was going to run away. She could've stopped her. She lingered in the parlor as Marcela walked ahead. "You always think of everything."

Marcela walked back to her. "It's easier to know what to do when it's not happening to you. Come-come, I'll make tea." She opened and closed one hand, coaxing her.

Grace's hand crept into Candelaria's and squeezed, as if to encourage her too. As if Candelaria were the one in trouble and Grace would take care of her now. After her outburst at the checkpoint, it made no sense. She studied Grace, hoping for clues, but though she still held her hand, Grace appeared absorbed in admiring the room's newest addition: a Victor Victrola phonograph record-player cabinet. Their friend must be doing well.

She pulled Grace into the kitchen, where Marcela heated a kettle of water. Together, they set tea things on the little wood table, bustling around each other in silence. Then they settled in a circle behind blue-painted china teacups and breathed the comforting aroma of cinnamon tea. Candelaria and Marcela talked about their kids: who was smartest in school, who was the biggest help, and, their favorite topic, who got into the worst mischief. She found it hard to laugh. Not because their friendship was any less comfortable than before, but because Grace uttered no sound except to blow on her tea.

Several times Candelaria took a deep breath, impatient to ask questions, but Marcela shook her head. Let her speak in her own time, Marcela's eyes said. Fine. She pretended Grace was simply listening as they exhausted every topic: how Marcela's Victrola sounded like a whole orchestra in her parlor, how Candelaria's gardenias made her courtyard smell like heaven, Marcela's relief the revolution was over, Candelaria's mixed feelings about Miguel's return.

Out of nowhere, Grace pushed away her untouched tea, and said to Marcela in a small voice, "You knew I'd return to Mata Flores?"

"Not me." Marcela raised her cup to Candelaria. "Your sister."

"But how?"

How *had* she known? Maybe, like Marcela, she contained mysteries of her own. Maybe family was the mystery. She shrugged. "You're my sister. I myself often go home in my head."

Grace pressed her hands to her temples. "I don't even remember Mata Flores."

"Maybe that's why returning in your mind isn't enough," Candelaria said.

Grace studied her face as if searching for what to say next.

Marcela folded her hands, pressed them to her lips, and exhaled. "Graciela, whatever you need to tell us, we won't be angry. It's clear you're struggling, and we won't add to your burden." She turned an admonishing eye on Candelaria. "Right?"

"Right."

She sensed Grace was about to say something unthinkable, but it was true, she didn't want to dole out consequences. Grace wasn't her daughter, but her sister. It wasn't for her to judge, only to stand by her.

Panicked at the thought of losing another sibling, she forced herself to say, "You're the one in our family who knows me best, both who I was before *and* who I am now. I've known you since you were born. We're more than sisters, more than friends. We hold each other's stories. Nothing will change that."

"That only makes it worse." Grace buried her face in her hands.

Candelaria placed a hand atop her head. In turn, Marcela rested a hand on Candelaria's shoulder, linking them in a chain. Grace looked up, eyes filled with an ache vast as Mother Earth. Hers was no longer the face of a girl, but a woman.

"Is this about a boy?" Candelaria asked.

"No. A man."

"A man?" Her stomach dropped. She'd kill any man who hurt her sister.

Grace turned to Marcela with the familiar question mark between her brows.

Marcela nodded as if Grace had already explained everything. She placed her free hand atop Grace's, closing the circle. "It's all right. Tell her."

"I think I'm going to have a baby. Yankee is the father."

Candelaria felt like she was waking from a fever dream. She'd thought Yankee had already hurt her as deeply as possible with his demands on her body and soul. But family was her soul. She pulled Grace's forehead to hers, long hair mingling, fingers laced together, tears pooling between them. Torn halves of a whole.

"I'm sorry, Candelaria."

"No. I'm sorry. Our family crossed the border to escape a monster: the war. I had no idea another monster waited on the other side. And I invited him into our family."

"No you didn't. I don't know what he is, but he caught both of us."

"I promise I won't let him or anyone else hurt you again, Graciela."

Marcela held up a cautioning hand. "Monsters always hide among us. You can't promise rescue. You can only promise love."

Night crept in but they kept their circle around the kitchen table, hand-to-hand, shoulder-to-shoulder, knee-to-knee. This, Candelaria realized, was the answer to Marcela's mystery. She was no bruja, no fortuneteller, no angel. She was a woman. They all were, these three, made not only to carry life but also life's stories. Stories not only of monsters but of love. So long as they survived to fight for love, the stories were not over yet.

36. The Sacrifice

1922 – El Paso, Texas

They shoehorned themselves into the combined kitchen and parlor of her parents' tenement: Mamá, Papá, Miguel, Grace, and herself standing on one side of the table, Yankee on the other. Despite the greater number of Riveras, Candelaria felt all the disadvantage of their position. They'd sought to meet Yankee in Rivera territory, but this too was Wong terrain. He paid for the roof overhead. Their heat, water, and clothes came from Miguel's pockets, but Yankee lined those pockets. Papá's maimed foot meant he couldn't find reliable work to feed his family, so Yankee sent free food from the café. And Candelaria? She was born a Rivera, but marriage made her a Wong. To stand against her husband might be to stand against her own interests.

The unofficial leader of Chinatown, Yankee carved out his own outsized corner of Segundo Barrio. He not only owned two cafés but also imported Chinese delicacies, sundries, and herbs to sell to fellow immigrants. His bootlegging enterprise brought alcohol not only to Mr. Yee's but also to speakeasies and dens throughout the Southwest. Overseas Chinese near and far knew that whispering his name could unlock the backdoor to America.

How could a five-foot, pregnant, unwed Mexican girl like Grace stack up against all that?

Still, Papá stood on what was left of his feet to defend the honor of his daughters. "I never should've let you court Candelita when she was only a child. I should've known you were a threat to her—and all my girls."

"It was a one-time mistake, Eduardo," Yankee said. "I would never—"

"¡Cállate, *Yan Chi*!" He spit out her husband's Chinese name like a curse. "I'm not stupid! I've seen Grace change. She was a happy child, a sweet little bird with bright feathers and bright ways, until you crushed her." Papá had never made her prouder.

The Riveras all stood taller. Except Grace, the only one seated, in a swaybacked easy chair of faded rose chintz, studying her hands where they rested on her still-flat belly. Her face alone was rounder. How had Candelaria missed that first sign of pregnancy?

"I'm not educated, but my son is," Papá said. "Miguel, tell Yankee what you told me."

Miguel's tone was resentful but careful. "You can go to prison for what you've done."

"I didn't force her."

Mamá slammed a hand on the kitchen table. "¡Mentiroso! How dare you lie to us?"

"It doesn't matter if you forced her or not," Candelaria snapped. "My sister's a child."

"If you want to send me to jail, first you must prove I did anything. Do you really want to put this innocent girl through that sort of ordeal?" He pointed at Grace, finger shaking, while she remained motionless in the chair.

"When the baby's born everyone will know it's yours." Miguel's lip curled in disgust.

"I'm not the only Chinese man in town."

Mamá splayed her hands around her head as if it couldn't contain his words.

Candelaria stepped behind her, hands on her shoulders, and glared at her husband. "Shame on you!"

"Even if the cops won't charge you," Miguel said, "we'll make sure you can never show your face in El Paso again without disgrace."

She swallowed hard. What of her sister's disgrace? Her own? Her children's? She sank into the armchair next to Grace, who took up almost no space at all, as if instead of pregnancy causing her to grow it was shrinking her. Candelaria squeezed her hand. Grace squeezed back. It was Candelaria who insisted they include Grace in this meeting, declaring she deserved a say in her fate, though now she seemed incapable of speech. They should've sent her to the house with the other children. No young girl should hear this sort of talk.

Yankee lifted his hands, palms down, and bobbed them in a request for calm. "Listen. You have a right to be angry. I made a terrible mistake, and your daughter will suffer for it. I'm truly sorry." He turned to Grace, voice cracking, eyes shining. "As your brother-in-law, I should've protected you, even from myself. Forgive me, little bird."

There it was again, the endearment he only used with Grace—though Papá was now calling her that too. Was Yankee in love with her? Candelaria's stomach churned. A girl half his age? If so, that made it twice as vile. Did anyone else see it? She looked around the room and found Miguel staring back. A vein in his neck throbbed. Soon he would explode, something she'd long expected but never witnessed. She was eager to see it now.

Yankee knelt before her and Grace in the chair. "I need you both to understand…"

Someone pounced, punching his ears, neck, and shoulders with such force it was as if her entire family pummeled him. "¡Pinche carajo! Get away!" He curled into a ball, arms shielding his head, which only inflamed her more. Here was the biggest boss of Chinatown, and he was a fucking coward! She didn't realize she herself was the one beating and kicking him, until Papá pulled her off. She swung at him too, nearly knocking him down. Her sight returned, revealing Miguel and Mamá backed against the wall gaping at her, Yankee crouching stunned at her feet, Grace chewing a cuticle, Papá trapping her in a bear hug.

"That's not helping, mija." Papá's voice fell even softer than usual.

Yankee rose from the floor, one hand warding her off. "I know I deserve greater punishment. But that can't happen, because to punish me is to punish all of you. Think about it." He turned in a slow circle to face them all, and their faces fell as his words sank in. "If you lock me up, put me out of business, or run me out of town, who'll take care of this family?"

Miguel stepped forward until they stood chest-to-chest. "I will."

Yankee held his ground. "How? After you, Candelaria, and Grace, your mother has four other children. Candelaria has three of her own, and now"—here she shook her head at him, but he wouldn't shut up—"she has another on the way. Your father can rarely get work, and none of your brothers are old enough for decent jobs. Will you support a dozen people on your own?"

Miguel leaned into him so his next words sprayed Yankee's face. "Fuck you."

Yankee didn't wipe away the spit, didn't reply, didn't move. He waited.

Miguel's fists clenched and unclenched.

"He has a point, mijo." Papá let go of Candelaria and stepped between the other two men. "My son also has a point, Yankee. A man defends his family. I have two other daughters. I can't let them grow up believing we'd do nothing to protect them. What do you suggest?"

Yankee rubbed his chin as if to summon an answer. That told her he'd planned for this moment. He had rubbed his chin that way when he'd asked her opinion about opening a second restaurant. The moment she'd expressed approval, he'd revealed he'd already bought a place. Now, as then, she had no choice but to listen. "If you five keep this secret, Eduardo, I'll provide dowries for all your daughters—a larger sum for Grace, who'll need more to attract a husband once she has the baby. And she'll return home to you. I'll never be alone with her again."

Papá nodded, retreating with each nod until he fell to the couch. "One more condition. We won't seek public retribution if you'll accept our private punishment."

Yankee gave a curt bow. "What do you have in mind?"

"Let Miguel finish what Candelaria started—" He turned to her mother who completed his thought:

"—Let my son beat you."

Candelaria felt as if someone had opened an icebox on a too-hot day. She backed away from everyone until she felt sticky wallpaper behind her.

Tears filled Yankee's eyes. She'd only seen him cry twice before: the first time they made love after she almost died of the flu, and earlier today when she told him Grace was carrying his child. Good, let him cry. She'd pitied him too long: his boyish need to be worshipped, his ineptitude at affection. She could no longer afford pity. Grace needed her, so did her own children, her parents too. She was the only softness that stood between him and them.

For a moment, she hoped Miguel, former soldier and "trouble-shooter," would beat her husband to death. But that would fly in the face of the reason they'd chosen this sentence. Her big brother would hold back because he couldn't carry this family alone. It was the best they could do to show Grace she remained theirs and they were still hers.

Grace gave no sign of what she thought or whether she heard any of it. Miguel led his brother-in-law to the alley. Her parents huddled on the couch, listening to boots and fists pound flesh and bone. Grace sat alone, quivering with each animal blow and answering grunt, until it dawned on Candelaria they were making a mistake. Miguel might beat him bloody, but Yankee would recover. They'd *all* move on, except one.

Grace sank into the sprung coils of the rose chintz armchair, looking trapped as a prisoner in an electric chair. Candelaria ran to the alley to stop her brother, but it was too late.

37. God's Hotel

1923 – El Paso, Texas

Yankee insisted Grace's baby must become his first offspring born in a hospital, everything stainless, antiseptic, and modern. He still believed Chinese herbalists superior to Western doctors. His own herbalist had cured his appendicitis with a bitter tea of rhubarb, peony bark, and salt crystals—which shriveled his appendix to nothing. But the complications of Grace's pregnancy called for a miracle. To him, *miracle* and *science* were interchangeable. Traditional Chinese medicine honored ancient wisdom, but Western medicine invented the future. He wanted Grace and her baby to have all the future money could buy. He refused to have their deaths on his conscience.

Not that Grace or her baby promised happiness to either the Wongs or the Riveras. Mother and child were sure to be outsiders among outsiders. His in-laws learned this the hard way the day they took Grace to Sunday Mass after she started to show. Of course, he wasn't at the church to witness what happened, but Candelaria told him when she came home:

She said the Mass felt like an inquisition, one that replaced old-fashioned interrogators and torturers with a congregation that stared and whispered…or worse: ignored the Riveras altogether. Afterward, the priest pulled her family out of the receiving line to rebuke them in undertones that bounced off the ceiling, pronouncing their guilt to the gold-winged angels, blue-robed saints, and gossips in the vestibule. The padre accused Eduardo and Maria of flaunting their daughter's sin.

Candelaria replayed the exchange:

"The priest said, 'Her presence might tempt girls to believe God approves of fornication.'" Her mouth puckered around the word *fornication* as if it were dirtier than any common word for the act. "So Mamá asked the priest, 'Did you not accept her confession and forgive her sins?' He said that wasn't the point. He said, 'God places many souls under my care, and I can't let your *unfortunate* daughter become a weapon of Satan in our church.'" She flung the words at Yankee like holy water at a demon.

He knew she expected the story to prompt more repentance from him. He also knew nothing he said would make her forgive him. All he said was, "This priest of yours is full of convenient excuses for cruelty."

"Unlike some men who need *no excuse* for cruelty," she said.

He stepped into her spitting rage, inches away. "Don't be afraid to say what you mean."

She didn't flinch. "You know what I mean. And I'm not afraid of you anymore."

Had she ever been? He was the most powerful Chinese man in America's Wild West. So why did this little woman make him feel small? He strode out the front door and slammed it, then crossed the courtyard into the café's hum and committed another sin in the eyes of his wife's church: worked on Sunday. Nobody expected Chinese businesses to close, and some Christians avoided cooking after church. Why shouldn't he feed them? It was their God, not his.

After that Sunday's ritual humiliation, many neighbors no longer allowed Grace near their families, as if her pregnancy were a disease their daughters might catch, her lost maidenhead a temptation to their sons. Her parents tried to protect her from judging eyes by confining her to their apartment for her final three months of pregnancy. During that time, Yankee saw her only four times.

The first time, he stopped by her parents' to look for Miguel, and his mother-in-law made him wait outside. He saw Grace sitting near the screen door, reading. He felt sure she chose the spot because it received the most sun, which she rarely saw anymore. She was seven months along and looked like a pale stick insect that swallowed the moon. Miguel met him outside to talk business, but Yankee also asked how Grace was feeling. Miguel said she threw up a lot. Yankee didn't know if this was normal, only that his wife was never sick so late in pregnancy. She'd recently given birth to their fourth child at home, as easily, he thought, as a chicken lays an egg.

The next three times he saw her were when he and Miguel kidnapped her for appointments with an obstetrician, over Maria's protests: "What kind of doctor specializes in looking at a girl's privates? No more perverts near my daughter!"

He scoffed, "Don't be ridiculous!"

On the other hand, he did order Grace to ignore the doctor's prescription of bed rest, which he also pronounced, "Ridiculous! She's already withering away from lack of sun and exercise."

Then, early one morning, her nine-year-old sister, Annie, ran to Yankee's house, banged open the screen door, and hollered that Grace was in labor. The whole Wong family hurried to the Riveras': Yankee, Candelaria, Benny, Celia, Mary, and even baby Rose, who Candelaria carried everywhere. At the Rivera apartment, he dismissed the midwife his mother-in-law hired and demanded Miguel drive Grace to the Catholic hospital, Hotel Dieu: God's Hotel, the only place the church would welcome her, so long as Yankee paid for the privilege.

Miguel looked relieved as he ran outside to get his car.

Maria protested, "What, and have my daughter around all those sick people? It's unnatural."

"So is such a sickly young mother," Yankee said. "These are the terms of my continuing to give you extra money to take care of her and her baby."

In this, Candelaria was his ally. "It's a *Catholic* hospital, Mamá. They have priests and nuns. And Grace might need a doctor. You know her pregnancy isn't normal."

To Yankee's surprise, Candelaria asked him to carry her sister to the car—though it probably shouldn't have surprised him, since Eduardo was lame, Sal was eleven, and Miguel was driving. He eased her from her bed, and she moaned so softly, he doubted this labor was real. Nonetheless, he carried her to the Model T idling out front. They all arranged her in back with her head in her mother's lap and feet in Candelaria's lap. Yankee sat in front with Miguel. Eduardo and the children watched unsmiling from the sidewalk as the car pulled away.

From outside, the old red-brick mansion of Hotel Dieu looked more hotel than hospital, and he worried it wouldn't be clean. Then he and Miguel carried Grace between them, panting up the stone steps into the entry, where the relief of clean white tile greeted them. They shouted for help, and a pair of orderlies took over, leaving nothing to do but wait.

"Waiting is for women," Miguel said and marched out.

Yankee took one look at his wife and mother-in-law, their faces an impenetrable wall, and marched out after him.

He turned down Miguel's offer of a ride home. Yankee felt too wound up to stay cooped up in the house and too tired to work in the café. He decided to take the day off, stroll near the hospital, and return to check on the girl. Estefan and Marcela Wu had recently moved to El Paso and opened a store several blocks away. He walked there, just for something to do.

The West Orient Grocery's aisles were too narrow, its shelves packed with too much inventory. The moment he entered, he perspired with claustrophobia and the urge to exit. But Estefan was there, unoccupied with customers, so he felt obliged to say hello. Waang dim, it might relax him to speak his own language. Not that their common culture had bonded the two men. They rarely paid social calls without their wives.

As usual, Estefan acted more excited to see him than he was to see Estefan. Yankee told him Grace was in labor and that he'd stopped by hoping to find a gift.

Estefan nodded, brow furrowed, as if trying to make sense of this. "Yes, Marcela went to the hospital. We're all worried about Graciela." He wagged his chin. "But I'm sorry, we don't carry too many baby things…"

"No, not baby things. A gift to cheer up Grace. She's been very sick." A bin of California oranges caught his eye. "There! Sunny and sweet, to make up for the sunshine she's missed."

Estefan shook a finger at him, "Wait, I have an idea!" He led him to a stack of wicker baskets. "For the oranges. Ladies love baskets. No charge for your wife's sister, poor thing."

Why did he say it that way? Marcela must've told him who was the secret father of Grace's baby. Eager to escape, Yankee dumped oranges into the basket as Estefan lamented his business woes, something about undercalculating floor space and over-ordering merchandise.

Yankee pointed to a man reading labels in the rear aisle. "I think that customer needs you."

"Where?!" Estefan swung round. "You see! It's all stacked so high, I didn't see him."

He rushed to the back while Yankee bustled out the front, tossing a "Do ze!" over his shoulder.

The basket of oranges weighed a few pounds, the morning was heating up, and Hotel Dieu stood a mile distant. So he did something he usually avoided: hopped a streetcar on bustling Stanton Street. He preferred to walk most places. He didn't own a car—driving made him nervous—and he hated trolleys because of the staring. But this day was made for exceptions...

The trolley was packed with people heading to work, mostly Whites and Mexicans, who left extra space around him as he stood holding a pole, basket between his feet. Most riders cast their eyes everywhere he wasn't, till two young boys jumped onboard. They gaped at him and whispered. Upon overhearing them use words like *chinaman*, *dragon*, and *dare you*, he bent to laugh in their faces, a booming, maniacal, "*BWA-HA-HA-HA*," as a keeper of dragons might. They stumbled backward, ran down the aisle, and leapt off the moving trolley, giggling as they tumbled into the street. No doubt he'd regret it later, but for now he gave a satisfied nod and ignored the other passengers' stares.

By the time he reached the hospital with the overweight basket, he'd worked up a rare sweat. He craved a swig from his flask, but his hands were full. He pressed on to the waiting room, where Marcela now sat between his mother-in-law and Candelaria, who was breast-feeding baby Rose. He envied that baby, not just the breast but the peace in her drowsy eyes.

Candelaria looked up at his sweaty face and pile of oranges, coughed a single laugh, and muttered to Marcela, "I told you."

Marcela suppressed a smirk and squeezed her knee.

His mother-in-law snorted, "Hmph."

The wall of women was widening against him.

He handed his mother-in-law an orange. She accepted it, held it to her nose, and inhaled without comment. She peeled the fruit and shared wedges with the younger women, all three ignoring him. He settled in a chair against the opposite wall, facing them over the stupid basket.

For the next few hours, the women exchanged their own childbirth stories, napped on each other's shoulders, and diapered and rocked and fed Rose. Then an irritable white nurse walked up to them, said

Grace was asking for her mother, and led her down the hall—but not before Maria leveled Yankee with an "I told you so" glare.

Hoi Sam came twice with food for them all, prompting a temporary truce.

Yankee dozed off and on, occasionally pacing to wake up his numb ass. Miguel was smart to leave, but a superstition took hold of Yankee: so long as he stayed here, worrying, Grace would live, but if he went elsewhere and took his mind off her, she might slip away.

Around hour four, Candelaria handed baby Rose to Marcela and crossed the room to him. "Go home. There's nothing you can do here, and no telling how long this will take."

"I'm responsible. I'm staying."

"*Now* you want to be responsible."

"I cannot keep apologizing for the past. I can only do the right thing now."

"The right thing for who?" She didn't wait for an answer but crossed the room to rejoin the others.

Being a pariah was exhausting. Again his eyes drooped into sleep.

His pocket watch ticked away almost twenty-four hours. Still the baby refused to come. The doctor emerged to say he feared Grace was too small to deliver it and might require a Cesarean section. While the family argued—Yankee convinced of the scientific logic of lifting the baby from a large opening instead of forcing it through a small one, the women aghast at the horror of slicing into Grace—the baby dropped farther until it was too late to cut it free.

After Grace's thirty-fourth hour of labor, her mother reappeared, gray-faced, to announce Grace had given birth to a small but healthy girl.

Yankee couldn't help thinking it was too bad. After going through so much, Grace now had a daughter who would become a burden, rather than a son who'd someday take care of her. So much was stacked against them both, that when a nurse with a clipboard asked who the father was, he gave his name—over the protests of Candelaria and her mother.

"Don't you know when to stop?" Candelaria said.

"Haven't you taken over enough of our lives?" her mother said.

"Wait, let's think about this," Marcela said.

The other two women gaped at her apparent betrayal.

At that moment, only Marcela understood him: in China, a child without a father's name was a child who didn't exist. If Yankee's ancestors watched from the afterworld, then he wanted to keep their eyes on the most unfortunate of his offspring. So, he gave his new daughter his family name. Grace had already chosen her given name. A Christian name, a Mexican name: Esperanza. The nurse asked if he approved.

"Of course. It's a perfect name. Exactly what she needs: Hope."

"The mother wants to see you," the nurse said.

The other three women rose.

"Sorry, only the father."

The trio gave him a unified stare. He knew better than to smile in triumph. Just picked up his basket of oranges and followed the nurse down the hall. She pointed to a door and left.

Out of nowhere, Candelaria flung herself between him and the closed door. "Wait."

If he'd learned anything, it was this: it often paid to listen to his wife. So he did.

"If you say or do anything to my sister other than what a brother-in-law would, Miguel will drive the kids and me home to Mata Flores to live. Nobody will welcome you there."

He wanted to say he didn't care, didn't love her, the kids were a headache. But that would be a lie. He took a long look at her—muscled arms folded under milk-heavy breasts, hair spilling in tangles after a sleepless night, eyes glaring with determination—more beautiful than ever. The house would be lonely without her, without them all. What good was an empire without a son to take over or a daughter to take care of? Benny was finally starting to make interesting conversation. Yankee was teaching Celia to cook. Anyway, he'd already made his choice.

"Don't worry. I'll respect her as a brother-in-law."

She stepped aside but remained next to the door like a sentry. He struggled to balance the basket against one side of his body while opening the door with the other.

Yankee set the basket on the nightstand and rearranged its oranges, averting his eyes from the distressing sight of Grace and her baby. Grace lay so slight in the bed she barely raised a bump in the sheets, and her eyes looked like bruises. Worse, she held a nightmare creature in her arms. The baby's body was puny as a newborn squirrel, but its monstrous blockhead had nearly split Grace in two, which in turn mashed its face into a hideous red mask of outrage.

"So," he said, "maybe I *am* Satan after all."

"Pobrecita, she had a hard day. That's why she looks cursed. But I'm sure she'll grow into a beautiful blessing."

"A child that's a blessing? I've yet to father such a thing."

"But you and Candelaria have four beautiful, healthy children."

"Hmph! Bottomless wells of need, every one. They give us no peace."

The question mark between her eyes narrowed to an angry exclamation point. "Don't worry, Yankee, this one won't burden you. My parents will take care of her."

He wasn't worried about who'd care for the baby so much as what would become of Grace. The mischievous girl of the past was receding, leaving an ancient spirit in her place. He laid a cheek atop her head, and noticed her hair no longer smelled of tortillas but antiseptic. Her body stiffened, and he knew she'd never soften for him again—as she had more than once, despite what he told her family. Just as well. If he were wise, he'd keep his word to her sister.

He stepped back. "I'm sorry, I didn't mean…"

"Brother, I've given birth to your child, so I must forgive you. I *do* forgive you. You are as God made you. I don't know why."

"You know I don't believe in God. I am as *I* have made me. I don't know why either."

She nodded, not as if he made sense but as if the topic was a waste of time. She pointed at the oranges and brightened. "Are those for me?"

"What? Oh. Yes." He picked one up and thrust it at her.

She shrugged to indicate she had her hands full with the baby. "Peel it for me?" He dug in a thumb and unfurled a long curl into a trashcan while she revealed why she'd asked to see him. "I'm going to need to get out of the house sometimes, or home will become a prison. I also need money to take care of Esperanza. When I get better, may I work at the International Café?"

"Candelaria will never let you work for me."

"She must. What other boss will let me keep my baby close so I can feed her?"

He puffed his cheeks and blew a gust of air. "Okay. I'll ask your sister."

"Let me ask her. She'll listen to me. And please do one more thing for me? Forget Esperanza is your daughter. You're her uncle, that's all."

He cocked an eyebrow. "Anything else?"

"Yes." She looked at the baby as if it were in charge. "If you ever hurt me or Esperanza, this time I will tell my sister. And if she doesn't kill you, I'll find someone who will."

He clenched his teeth. The chastisement of women grated.

Worst of all, in the next moment, she acted like he didn't exist. She directed her next words only to the red spawn in her arms, which looked nothing like him. "Be a good girl," she cooed, as if an infant could understand such instructions.

The peeled orange still sat in his palm. He split it in two, looked for a place to set the halves, then gave up and set them atop the unpeeled oranges, out of her reach. He wiped his sticky hands on his slacks and left. On his way out, he held the door open for Candelaria to go in.

In China, he could have two wives, and nobody could keep him from any of his children. But though he was born Chinese, his papers declared him American. His wife was born Mexican, but their marriage made her American. Their children were American, his businesses were American, he was emperor of an American dynasty. Therefore, he must act American, which meant keeping up appearances, which meant walking out of God's Hotel and not looking back.

38. Consumed

1924 – El Paso, Texas

Yankee only rang the little chrome bell when orders were up for café customers. For the three underground *cousins*, he bellowed, "Grace!" For the lone patient in the sick shack, he gave no signal at all, simply set aside a small copy of the larger underground order, which was: a platter of pork lo mein, bowl of wor wonton, and pot of rice.

Grace popped into view at the pass-through shelf, saw the extra order, and sighed wistfully. "So, Cousin Man Fai still stays in the sick shack?"

In answer, he held up a stern thumb and forefinger. "Second tray, second trip."

She avoided his eyes as she moved the three larger dishes to a large tray.

"Hurry-hurry, before my delicious food gets cold." He waved her off.

He watched her carry the first, larger order across the courtyard to the house. He smiled. She'd filled out in the year since she had the baby, and though she walked fast she couldn't control the roll of her hips, so like her sister when *she* was seventeen. In no time, she rushed back to prepare the smaller tray for the worrisome young man in the sick shack.

Yankee had a reputation for helping Chinese men in need, and sick ones with nowhere to go often appeared at his door. Healthy cousins were back to staying in the tunnels and eating meals in the house. Recuperating cousins like Man Fai stayed in the fake shithouse, one at a time. Yankee attended to their every comfort: providing food, supplies, and even his herbalist for free. When sick cousins needed a hospital, he paid for that too. He gave starting-out money to those who lived, and most did. Those with TB remained in Texas or other desert climates. All the survivors found ways to return the favor: with contacts, illegal booze, hard-to-find goods, hiding places, quick loans.

Man Fai seemed like a survivor.

Grace's lips twitched in a secretive smile as she picked up his tray.

"Just drop off the food and leave him alone," Yankee said. "He needs rest."

"He needs company. Nobody talks to him but the Chinese doctor. It's like he's in jail."

She scurried out with the tray, and he called after her, "Keep your distance!"

His eyes tracked her to the shed. It still looked like a double outhouse—one door carved with a moon, the other a star—but inside, it was now a single shed with a cot, blankets, and a woodstove for cold nights. She set the tray on a large stone next to the star-door, knocked, and stepped back. A muffled cough drifted from inside. The young man opened the door, no longer coughing but beaming, the picture of health.

Yankee couldn't hear their talk over the wok sizzling behind him. Still, he watched them so intently, it wasn't till he smelled shrimp burning that he turned to stir it, swearing over the ruined seafood, which cost a pretty penny. It only had a few black spots, so maybe it could be saved. He kept stirring blindly as he leaned toward the door again to glance at Grace. She flung her head forward, laughing at whatever Man Fai just said.

Yankee wished this task didn't fall to Grace, now a regular waitress at the International Café. But when he'd tried to coax his other workers to carry meals to his visiting cousins, the other two waitresses and second cook had exchanged looks. They'd said they were happy to serve the underground men but not the ones in the "sick shack."

"Some of them have consumption," the cook said.

"You don't have to go near," he replied. "Just drop off the plates." They all remained silent.

"If I fire you, that won't be good for your health either."

"I can find another job. I can't find another life," the cook replied.

"Never mind. My sister-in-law is happy to help those in need." He flapped his arms at them. "All right, all right. Back to work."

Sam offered to do it but wasn't always available. He managed the accounts for both restaurants now and spent a lot of time at Yankee's Chinese Café, too long a walk.

Last time Yankee visited Man Fai at the shed, the young man said he owed his improving health to him, which swelled Yankee's chest with pride. Then Man Fai added, "And thank you for sending your kind sister-in-law to visit me. She lights up dark days," which swelled Yankee's chest with the desire to smash the boy's pretty face.

Instead, he smiled. "Ah, Grace. A nice girl, yes. She also has a nice baby, a daughter, one year old. As Americans say, Esperanza wraps us all around her finger."

"Yes, Grace told me about her daughter, but she calls her Hope. I'm eager to meet her. I grew up in a big family and was sorry to leave them. When I came to Gold Mountain, I knew I was unlikely to find a wife and make a family here, but Grace makes me believe I can." Man Fai gave him a sly smile. "I didn't know Mexican women were so agreeable, *Daai Lou.*"

That had been the worst moment, when the insolent boy named him both *big brother and boss-man* in a single breath.

He now tossed the plate of half-burned shrimp onto the shelf, slapped the bell several times, then stepped outside to better hear the young lovers' chatter, maybe douse the heat between them with an icy stare. Man Fai either didn't see him in the olive tree's shade or pretended not to. He didn't catch everything the pair said, only enough to regret teaching Grace bits of Toisanese and Cantonese, and curse whoever taught the boy bits of English and Spanish. Their conversation blended it all, filled in with longing looks that required no translation.

"My father give me money for buying land," Man Fai told her. "When I get well, maybe you go with me."

"I always wanted to see the ocean," she said.

"California?"

"I hear they have land to farm."

Man Fai's head bobbed like a seesaw, neither a nod nor a shake. "Land costs much in California, and weather is bad for TB. I wish to buy land in Colorado."

Her body pivoted as if with indecision, twirling her skirt open and closed, open and closed. "Colorado means red in Spanish."

"Red is important in China. Mean joy, long life, good luck."

"I know those Chinese meanings for red," she said. "Yankee taught me."

The boy lowered his voice and muttered something about "brides."

"In America, brides wear white," she replied.

"If we have wedding, you wear what color you wish."

Wedding? Was he serious? An immigrant with TB? Someone must warn her father. Eduardo's hatred of Yankee would come in handy. Surely he'd never let another daughter marry a Chinese man.

She bowed her head, hair hiding her face. "I can't wear white. I'm not…complete."

Man Fai muttered, "For me, you complete. For me, you wear color from my country."

She giggled. "In America, if I wear red, everyone will know I'm a bad girl."

"No matter. Yankee tell me, 'To Americans, all Chinese are devil.' So, you and me: both bad." At this, they laughed until the boy turned his head to splutter and cough.

Yankee was about to swoop in and carry her away, to prevent her getting sprayed with disease. She beat him to it, jumping backward while the boy waved her away. Along the restaurant wall, the café's chickens flapped against the sides of their coop, clucking in alarm.

Two-year-old Rose burst from the house toward the coop, shrieking, "Chickies!"

Five-year-old Mary ran after her. "Leave the birdies alone!"

Candelaria emerged in the doorway, shouting, "Stay away from that shack!"

She saw Yankee and followed his gaze to Grace and the boy. Then her eyes locked with his: a declaration of war or solidarity? "Girls. Inside. Now." She pointed at the house and snapped her fingers. They tried to skirt past her as they ran in, but she swatted Mary's rear and scooped Rose over her shoulder. Then she strode inside and slammed the door.

Man Fai ceased coughing, but he stepped behind the star-door and shut it while Grace turned back to the cafe, catching Yankee's stare before he could avert it. Her expression said she knew he'd been watching. She wore a pitying smile, not for the sick boy but for him. He returned to the kitchen, face burning. Pity was for the weak.

A new order caught his eye from the pass-through. What kind of idiots ate lunch at two? He snatched the ticket: Peking duck and pork short ribs. Idiots with money, that's what kind. He focused on cooking. He couldn't afford to get distracted. Love was so much smoke, which could either make his eyes water or be dispersed with a wave of his hand. Money was solid, something he could hold and count. He turned up the flame under the wok, splashed in sesame oil, and watched the smoke rise.

Grace had a cough. Yankee blamed Man Fai for luring her. Blamed her parents for letting her work instead of keeping her home. Blamed her for flirting. It took days for him to admit, and then only to his wife in the privacy of their bed, that he blamed himself for giving Grace a job.

Candelaria didn't comfort or correct him. "You *should* feel guilty. It was you who made her lonely by stealing her innocence, you who weakened her health by making her pregnant, you who put her to work serving men with diseases."

"I told her to leave the plates outside." But he knew she was right.

She sighed. "I'm tired of arguing. Let's not make a world out of nothing. We don't know the test results yet. It's probably a normal cough. It's not as if she's coughing blood." She only babbled like this when she was afraid.

"Will you pray?" he asked.

"Why ask? You don't believe in it."

"But you do."

She rolled away from him with such force the bed bounced him up and down.

Two days later, Grace appeared outside the café at dawn and beckoned him. He stepped onto the sidewalk, and she raised one hand like a traffic cop.

"Don't get too close," she said. "It might be catching."

He stepped back in alarm, for himself *and* for her. "Then why did you come?"

"My cough's gone today, and I want to be the one to tell you: the test was bad. It's tuberculosis." She stared at him, into him, through him.

If she were waiting for him to speak, he had no idea what to say.

"I was going to suggest you hire a new waitress, but I see you're ahead of me." She pointed at the window, where a sign in the lower corner declared in both English and Spanish, *Help Wanted: Waitress.*

He looked away. "It was Sam's idea."

When his eyes returned to her it was hard not to stare, imagining her face pale with death. Yet her cheeks were rosier than ever. He wanted to comfort her, if only he could touch her. Even if he could, she didn't want *him* but handsome young Man Fai.

"If Man Fai doesn't die, I'll kill him," he said.

She shook her head. "It's not his fault. I brought him food and conversation, but we kept our distance. He was already getting better before I ever talked to him, thanks to the care you gave him. Many people in El Paso have consumption. I could've caught it anywhere." Before he could reply, she held up a halting hand again. "It's not your fault either."

"That's no comfort if you die."

"TB patients come to El Paso because dry air helps. Man Fai got well. Maybe I will too."

"Then you can live happily ever after."

"If so, you shouldn't be bitter but happy. Man Fai will take the baby and me away. Then we can all make a new start."

"But you'll never see the ocean."

"A small price to pay for my life, and for a man who'll take care of us."

"What if he finds out Hope is mine?"

"It won't matter. You saved his life. Anyway, he hasn't asked Papá yet. He's waiting till I'm well." Empty words. She was sweet and forgiving, not obedient or patient: she'd never wait for permission. She would die or she would elope. Either way, she'd be gone.

But if she could pretend otherwise, so could he. "Your job will be waiting for you when you get well. Except you're no longer allowed to carry food to the outhouse."

She gave a nod that said her mind had moved on. "I came for another reason."

"Yes?"

"If anything happens to me, promise you'll keep my daughter safe."
It wasn't a question.

He gave a single nod, not trusting himself with more.

She turned to leave.

"Grace?"

"Yes?"

"Should I tell your sister, or will you?"

"Tell her what?"

"What the doctor said."

She looked puzzled. "I already told her. You do know my sister and I share everything?"

He pondered her words as she walked away. Maybe her bad luck wasn't his fault. Maybe he never could've taken one sister without the other. He recalled a Mexican customer who called his own wife "mi media naranja," *my half orange*, what Americans called *my other half*. Though the phrase referred to spouses, it aptly described the two sisters who turned Yankee's life upside down. Despite the difference in their ages and personalities, they were two halves of a whole: back and forth, up and down, yin and yang. He'd sliced the orange in two. Could one exist without the other? He pulled out his flask and gulped its cool liquid till it washed the question away.

39. The Grandmother Clock
1925 – El Paso, Texas

Candelaria lay nose-to-nose with Hope in the narrow bed, inhaling the two-year-old's milky breath. She pushed a sweat-damp lock from her niece's forehead, hair blacker and straighter than hers or Grace's, and tried to forget why it looked that way.

Hope pushed her hand away with a fist. "Want Mommy!"

"Mommy's sleeping. You're stuck with me."

The tiny fist swung into her cheekbone.

"Ouch!" She uncurled Hope's fist and tucked it under the blanket, then swaddled her, binding her arms against her sides.

Instead of resisting, Hope grew still. "More, tía!"

Her own children had resisted swaddling by the time they were one, but Grace's child seemed to fear her wild limbs more than most. Candelaria wrapped her so tight she couldn't budge. Hope exhaled contentment.

"Want to hear your mommy's favorite song?" Candelaria asked.

Hope nodded, eyes expectant.

Candelaria patted the blanket-cocoon in time with the song, *"At the gate of heaven, little shoes they are selling..."* She smiled as Hope's eyes closed.

Only Benny and Celia remembered when Auntie Grace used to sing them that lullaby. Only they had an inkling of why their mother was keeping Grace and her child at home after sending her own children to Uncle Miguel's. The rest of her kids called her "Mean Mommy!" She replied, "All family is a never-paid obligation," and made no effort to explain away their confusion. They must never know the truth about their father and Grace and Hope, about what kind of man they came from. Children shouldn't have to fear the blood in their own veins.

She stopped singing to listen to Hope breathe, in impatient little puffs like Grace used to do. "A mean mommy maybe, but good at singing babies to sleep, no?" She ran her fingers over the useless white ruffles of Hope's pillow, such a Grace thing to buy. Candelaria would never be more than Hope's second mother—like Segundo Barrio, a second neighborhood, second home, second choice. It was the best she could do. "Dream with the little angels," she said as she left the room, cracking the door to let in a sliver of light because Hope was afraid of the dark.

In the kitchen, ten-year-old Celia stood over the stove, the only child she allowed home briefly each day to help. Celia intently stirred a wood spoon around a pot, where a thick plop-plop-plop of bubbling liquid released the mouth-watering smells of chocolate, corn masa, and cinnamon. Champurrado. Celia lifted the spoon, blew on it, and slurped.

Candelaria's eyes watered with memories. "Did I ever tell you your grandma made champurrado for us the day we left Mata Flores?"

Celia whirled around, jostling a towel into the burner. "¡Híjole, Mamá! You scared me to death."

"Watch that towel. It's catching fire."

Celia snatched the singed towel and tucked it at her waist. "Auntie Grace mentioned champurrado. I thought it might make her feel better."

She craved not only to hug her daughter, who was growing so tall, but to wrap herself around her like armor, to protect her from the beast that would soon swallow her whole: womanhood. It was more urgent to protect her children from TB, so instead of stepping closer she stepped away, retreated to the parlor, and perched on the sofa. From there, she could still watch through the archway to make sure Celia didn't burn down the house.

Celia stared at her, frowning. "Mamá, you look tired."

She pressed a coy hand to her chest. "Awww, you say the sweetest things."

Celia propped her hands on her hips, reminding Candelaria of her mother, of Grace, of herself, a funhouse mirror of Rivera women. "I'm not kidding. You need rest. You need help."

"You're a big help, my perfect daughter!" She blew her a kiss.

Celia snatched the kiss from the air, slapped it to her face, and pretended it knocked her backward. But it wasn't that easy to throw her off track anymore. "Mamá, Benny's worried…"

"*Benny's* worried? What's Benny worried about, mija?"

"That you'll get sick like Auntie Grace."

She worried too, not about dying so much as leaving her children behind. She resisted the urge to cross herself. "Don't worry. I'm strong and healthy, and Tía Grace only coughs into those Kleenex tissues your father bought."

"But Mamá—"

"Celia, give it a rest, or I'll regret asking you to help instead of Benny."

Celia pulled the towel from her waist and snapped it as if at an invisible adversary. "Boys are too much trouble. Always trying to help, only getting in the way!"

"Depends on the boy. Some boys can be trouble. Others can save your life."

She prayed her daughter would never know the first kind and never need the second.

Candelaria's hands circled like clockwork: swirled the cloth in the bowl of water and ice, wrung it out, lay it on her sister's blazing forehead. Swirl...wring...rest. Swirl...wring...rest.

Her sister's questions circled in rhythm with the cloth. "What time is it?"..."What was the last thing Lalo said to you?"..."Remember when Miguel wore your clothes?"..."Can you get the honey out of my hair?"..."What time is it?"

Her answers circled back. "Nine o'clock"..."Lalo said, 'I'll protect you.'"..."Miguel wore *Mamá's* clothes, not mine. He looked prettier than either of us!"..."I'll wash it out with lemon juice."..."Ten o'clock." Morning or night? Didn't matter. Grace was back in the desert, nearly fifteen years ago when she was three, the day they all got honey in their hair when Benito's wagon turned over.

Candelaria rose and paced to the tick-tock of the grandmother clock in the parlor, feet wearing a path in the wood, around the bed she used to share with Yankee, where her sister's eyes now followed her. She wanted to scream, *Stop looking at me, I can't take care of you anymore, go on without me!* But how could Grace leave her? Although Marcela knew things about Candelaria nobody else knew, only Grace was the same thing she was: a tumbleweed blown from no place to nowhere.

She started at the sudden creak and rattle of pipes followed by a burst of water. Marcela drawing her a bubble bath. She'd shown up the day Candelaria told Celia to stop coming. Probably Celia had fetched her. After all, Marcela and Celia were close. Or maybe her old friend had sensed her need without anyone telling her, as usual.

Marcela had taken over the house: shopping, cooking, cleaning, and watching Hope. Candelaria only took care of her sister, while Marcela took care of her and kept her company in the restless interludes between duty and sleep.

She entered the steaming bathroom, let Marcela remove her clothes, and sank into the tub with her neck against the rim. Marcela gently scrubbed her with a washcloth, hand pausing at the imperceptible bump of new life inside her. She'd told no one, not even Yankee, concerned he might return from Sam's apartment and order her away from Grace. Marcela said nothing of it.

Though her friend washed every part of her, Candelaria felt none of the desire she'd confessed long ago, only the comfort of her soothing touch after weeks alone on a mattress on the floor next to Grace's sickbed. Was the heat she'd once felt a trick of youth, or was every passion destined to cool?

Next morning, Marcela sent for Mamá to sit with Grace, to give Candelaria a more complete break. She tried making excuses not to leave the house: *only she knew Grace's routine, how to salve her parched lips, what foods she could swallow, the way scratching her head calmed her when she flailed in weak attempts to escape the bed. What if Mamá frightened Grace with unnecessary drama: weeping, praying, or pulling her own hair?*

Marcela shook her head. "You know your mother better than that." She was right, as usual.

The moment Mamá walked in the door, she thrust a pot of soup at Marcela. "Heat up this albondigas, not too hot, and fill a bowl." When Grace had no strength to chew the meatballs, Mamá calmly mashed them. When she couldn't swallow that, Mamá declared, "Just the broth then." Candelaria didn't question the wisdom of filling a dying girl's stomach. For Mamá, food equaled love. She poked the spoon into Grace's unyielding mouth, sip by sip, while Candelaria left to watch a matinee featuring *The Thief of Bagdad*.

For three hours, including intermission, she forgot her life as she watched the swashbuckling Douglas Fairbanks leap through dazzling Arabian nights to steal jewels, bread, and a magic rope—shirtless, every muscle shining with Hollywood lights. Grace would've been dazzled. Candelaria leaned forward in her seat, memorizing every moment so she could describe it to her sister: moonlight on the towers of Baghdad, tigers guarding a palace with intricately carved windows, the thief using his magic rope to scale the walls in search of treasure, only to find a princess asleep amid delicate veils. He forgot the treasure and brought back nothing but the princess' slipper.

How Grace would laugh at that.

Minutes after Candelaria came home, Mamá kissed Grace's forehead and promised her she'd return. But when she left, she carried Hope with her. On their way out, she took hold of Candelaria's arm, and said, "It's time." Marcela had already left.

Candelaria and her sister were alone.

She returned to Grace's bedside as if to a new country. The blankets looked heavy compared to the transparent veils hung round the bed of the Princess of Baghdad. She stood silent as a thief and watched Grace sleep, afraid to leave but also afraid to wake her. She sat in the rocker Mamá had dragged into the room, and rocked.

She wondered how Grace's daughter would survive the chaos where Mamá was taking her. For the moment, everyone else but Yankee lived at Miguel's new house: Candelaria's four children, Mamá, Papá, and their four youngest, all crammed in with Miguel, his wife Esther, and their baby. The Riveras adored Esther, so they all pretended either to have forgotten the date of her wedding to Miguel or to believe their little girl was three months premature.

Papá depended on Miguel now, rejecting Yankee's help ever since Grace almost died in childbirth: "I refuse to owe anything to that man who ruined our sweet Graciela." For two years the Riveras shuffled from tenement to tenement, evicted whenever Papá lost a job or Miguel landed in jail. After Esther came along, Miguel settled down, which meant steady money, which meant the whole clan settled down—as much as any chasing, wrestling, pranking horde could.

Esther was a live wire but a demanding wife, who kept Miguel in line with the sparks from her electric green eyes. Candelaria didn't understand why her macho brother had fallen for the endlessly scolding Esther, but she was glad. A woman with a firm hand might be the only thing to keep thirteen people in a three-bedroom house from killing each other.

Add Hope and that would make fourteen. Maybe she'd feel comforted by so many arms to hold her.

Come to think of it, Candelaria would rather follow her into that chaos than be left behind, here, in this quiet room. She had expected Grace's labored breathing to grow louder as she struggled. Instead, it grew fainter.

Grace's weak voice wafted into her thoughts. "Tell me the movie."

The demand put her at ease. This was the Grace she knew, never asking, always insisting. Candelaria smiled. She was at her best when lost in a story, till being lost felt like home. She rocked in the chair by the bed as she verbally replayed every reel of *The Thief of Bagdad*.

"Wait," Grace interrupted at one point. "Ahmed drugged her with a rose so he could kidnap her? What kind of hero *is* he?"

"No-no-no, he *planned* to drug her, but when he kissed her he realized he loved her, so he took the rose and left. He said, ''Twas wrong to come.' Then her father let her give her ring to the prince of her choice."

Grace smiled. "She chose Ahmed."

"Who's telling this story, apestosa?"

Her sister fell silent till she reached the end of the tale:

"The thief flung his magic dust, and it turned into one hundred thousand soldiers. The Mongols ran for their lives. Then the thief and the princess rode away on the magic carpet."

"And lived happily ever after?" Grace asked.

She pondered this, unsure. "The stars wrote in the sky: 'Happiness must be earned.'"

She expected a skeptical retort. Instead, Grace gave a contented sigh and closed her eyes. She closed hers too…and found herself standing before a crooked adobe house that looked like a squat man with a red mouth and straw hat. He had no eyes but opened his mouth to welcome her home, and his tongue became a bell, ringing, ringing…

She opened her eyes. The room was dark. The ringing continued. The parlor's grandmother clock chimed the quarter-hours: Ding-dong-ding-dong…Dong-ding-dong-ding…the silence between each chime longer than the last, as if time were slowing. Then the hours: Bong… Bong… Bong…ten times. Then her sister breathing, bubbles rising underwater.

"Candelita?"

"I'm here." She drew closer to Grace's face than she had since her sister was a baby. Her breath smelled not of decay but of flour tortillas. It smelled like home.

"I hate sleeping alone. There used to be four of us, remember?"

"I remember." Though the house was stuffy, she slid into bed with Grace and wrapped herself around her, the soft bump of her next child pressed against Grace's bony hip.

"Take care of Hope as if she were your own daughter," Grace said. "Promise me."

"I promise."

"Tell her the story of how I saved a man with only the sound of my voice. Promise me."

"Must you always be so bossy?"

"Tell me the story."

She sat up and gathered Grace in her arms. "Once upon a time, there was a girl named Graciela, who had the bossiest mouth in the Rivera family…" Grace's smile told her this was the right way to tell the story. The teasing was part of it, and the story would be incomplete without it. She told of two evil men who tried to set Benito Chung on fire until Grace found her family's voice and roared. "Graciela was a hero. She saved us all."

Grace's murmur startled her. "The time stopped. Listen."

It was true. The grandmother clock's pendulum had stopped swinging, no longer tick-tocking each second. She sighed. "I'll have to pull the chain to rewind it."

"I sleep better when I can hear it," Grace said.

She was scared to leave her alone. "Do *you* want to do it with me?"

Grace looked up at her, eyes filled with trust, for once letting her big sister decide.

She lifted her and stood, surprised at how easy it was. Grace weighed little more than the feather pillow that had supported her head. Her bones felt fragile under downy skin, arms akimbo as wings, cold toes curled like talons below the ruffle of her nightgown. Candelaria carried her to the parlor, then reached above the mantel to open the glass case of the polished walnut clock. She wrapped her hand around her sister's so that together they pulled the chain and gave the pendulum a gentle push. She didn't reset the hands. Had no idea what time it was.

She couldn't bring herself to set her sister down again. Instead, she circled the room cradling Grace in her arms. "You're the hero, and the hero should live. He deserves to die, not you."

"You'll be me," Grace said.

How could she be two people? Grace once dreamed of so much: to ride a train, become a movie star, fall in love, get married, live on a farm, have a family. She always believed she'd see the ocean someday. Yankee had found Man Fai a job in Denver, and the young man had promised to send for Grace when she got well. Then all her dreams shrank to one: saying she must get well so she could be a good mother to Hope. Such a small wish for a girl with such a big voice.

Grace said nothing more. She'd used the last of her energy to help her sister restart time. Candelaria rocked her to the pendulum's rhythm till she felt her slip upward to a place she couldn't follow—not flying so much as running barefoot into the first glint of sunrise that entered the house behind the International Café.

40. The Gardenias

1926 – El Paso, Texas

The gardenias woke Candelaria in the middle of the night, opening their white petals to sing into the dark, a humming chorus of longing. It was five months since her sister passed. Her guitar was gone now too. Five months ago, she carried it down to the river and let it float away. But music wasn't done with her. Every night the gardenias sang without words, yet she heard their lyrics just the same: another unfinished story.

Or maybe it was a warning. But of what?

She rolled over—on the mattress they'd bought to replace the one where Grace spent her final days—to find Yankee gone from the bed, his side still warm. Lately he often shuffled around the house, or sat on a stool in the courtyard staring into the dark, unable to sleep through the night. Did he hear the music too?

She rose, pressed her forehead against the coolness of the half-open window, and peered into the courtyard at the bush full of tiny white blooms unfurling in the moonlight, releasing thick layers of perfume. She inhaled until the aroma opened a hollow place inside her.

Marcela was the only one she thought might understand the gardenia's song. But she couldn't face her friend again, not yet.

The morning Grace died, Marcela returned to find Candelaria still rocking her, slumped in the rocking chair because she couldn't carry her anymore. She didn't remember what Marcela said, only that she wanted her to put Grace back in bed. They moved her together because death made her hard to carry. Tucked her in like a child, then held each other's hands and watched her for a time, neither speaking nor praying nor crying, their sorrow too deep for those things. Then they lay on the narrow mattress on the floor, where Candelaria had lain awake so many nights in case Grace needed anything. Now she needed nothing, so Candelaria slept. Marcela hung an arm across her, to prevent her from constantly jumping up out of habit.

After that, Marcela took over again, making most of the arrangements the Riveras couldn't cope with in their grief. Candelaria tried to feel grateful to her friend, but it was hard to feel anything at all.

In the coming days, Yankee returned to their bed with its new mattress. She still needed an arm lying heavy across her to keep her from jumping up in the night. He was in bed with her the night she dreamt she held Lalo in her arms on the bridge, blood pooling in her lap. She woke to terrible cramps. She hurried to the bathroom, hand between her thighs, trying to hold the blood inside. But the baby she was carrying had already let go.

Because too much had happened, she cleaned up and returned to bed as if nothing had happened. She'd been sure Yankee would notice the bloodstains come morning. If he did, he didn't say so.

Only Yankee and Marcela had known she was pregnant. Not that she'd told them, but they were the only living souls who'd touched the invisible curve of her belly. When the curve grew no bigger, they must have guessed why. Yet they gave her expectant looks, as if they wouldn't believe it until she spoke the hateful words. She told Yankee in bed, where they shared all their worst news—she sometimes questioned the wisdom of this, but where else? There were always too many people around.

His tenderness surprised her, as if they'd lost a child who'd been born and named like the others. He gathered himself around her without demand or expectation, quiet and still. After a time, he said, "It was too big a strain, taking care of Grace."

"Don't even think about blaming Grace."

"No, I know it wasn't her fault. She didn't deserve to die." His voice carried a note of regret.

Was that enough for her to forgive him?

A few days later, Marcela followed her around the courtyard as she watered her many potted flowers, using the watering can Yankee gave her in the wake of their private loss. He painted it himself: powder blue with bright blue birds and tiny dark blue flowers. Blue for boy. She was surprised how much it comforted her.

She scattered a small shower on her pink roses and told Marcela, "I lost my baby."

Marcela followed her to the geraniums in silence.

Candelaria probably would've said more, sooner or later. Marcela had a way of drawing her out. Not this time—because of what Marcela said next.

She knew her friend meant to give comfort with her words: "I'm so sorry for your loss, but maybe it was a blessing in disguise. Maybe your unborn baby returned to heaven because he knew your sister's baby would need you more."

"Maybe." Her habit of accepting Marcela's wisdom ran deep.

Candelaria fell into a daze, watching water pour from the spout, drowning her beloved gardenias, till the watering can ran empty and began to shake. She turned her back on Marcela, strode to the well, and furiously pumped the handle till the can overflowed, though she had already watered all the plants. She stared at the cheerful painted bluebirds on the side, but they only enraged her more. How could it be that Yankee understood better than Marcela?

She wanted to tell her friend that no blessing can remove the curse of losing a child. That she alone had seen how helpless her son was: no angel of light sacrificing himself to God, only a dark speck of flesh-and-blood so tiny she almost couldn't find him when he fell from his home inside her. She wanted to say, *Some things you carry forever no matter how deep you bury them.* But the words crowded her throat and stuck there.

"Are you all right?" Marcela asked, her hand over Candelaria's on the handle. "I'm sorry. Forgive me, I didn't mean—"

"I'm fine," she murmured. "Can we talk about something else?"

But conversation dried up, Marcela left in confusion, and Candelaria had avoided her since.

She'd always confessed her sins to Marcela, things she dared not tell a priest. But she couldn't seek her forgiveness this time because of something only the gardenias knew: that she was angriest not at Marcela but at herself. Hadn't she killed her unborn son the moment she put caring for her sister before her own children? Hadn't she lost him because she carried her sister even in death, forgetting the life she carried within.

Even if she forgave Marcela, she would never tell her the secret of the gardenias. She had buried the remains of her sixth pregnancy in the large wood flowerpot where the perfect white flowers grew. Even though Yankee was so understanding, she'd never tell him either. If he knew their tiny offspring fed the blossoms that sweetened the night air, he might insist she dig up the remains. She imagined the bush's roots going into shock, its petals turning brown with distress. No, this became her truest secret of all, the kind she kept only to herself.

The next time she heard their hum in the night, she was alone in bed again. She tiptoed toward the front door, intending to follow the

call of the gardenias to the grave they marked. Except, as she entered the parlor, the hum came from the opposite side of the house, through the half-open door of the girls' room. Hadn't she closed it after she read their bedtime story?

The flowers fell silent, the only sound the tick-tock of the grandmother clock.

She crept to the room where Hope slept in the narrow bed her mother used to share with Candelaria. She often slipped into the children's rooms to watch them sleep. It usually made her feel peaceful. But now she needed to overcome a feeling of dread to bring herself to peer around the half-closed door. At first, what she saw moved her. Yankee usually paid no attention to Hope, as if she were invisible. Now his silhouette hunched over her sleeping form in the dark. He didn't respond to Candelaria's approach, and she hesitated to startle him and wake the girls.

"They were both too weak to live," he whispered, "but you were strong enough to survive." His voice sounded tender, yet a spasm of panic seized her throat. His back was turned, muscles bunched, hands hidden. Was he holding her niece's pillow? Why? Her eyes darted to her three girls in the other bed, and she was relieved to see them sleeping soundly. Or were they squeezing their eyes shut to hide from the monster in their room?

Her own whisper filled the ticking silence, "Yankee!" After their initial courtship, through thirteen years of marriage, she'd rarely spoken his nickname. Usually, she called him nothing at all, or when she must: viejo, mi amor, Mr. Wong, Baba if they were with the children. She told herself these were endearments, never considered she might dislike saying his name.

He stiffened, but didn't turn, though his arms shifted. Was he hiding something? Hope whined. Candelaria felt tempted to scream. Then he turned and gave her a smile so serene it knocked the scream right out of her, though her heart still beat too fast. He put one finger to his lips, then pillowed both hands against his cheek to mimic sleep, indicating she should be quiet and not wake the girls. He beckoned her toward the bed.

She hesitated, roots reaching from the soles of her feet through the floor, twining into the earth, trying to gain a purchase. She swayed atop the cold wood boards, then told herself, He's no flesh-eating beast, he's just a man, maybe a weak man or a bad, but still your husband. She stepped forward, though terror rolled through her in waves. His arm went around her. She looked up at him, straining to see what she hoped to see: a father checking his children.

They both gazed at Hope. Her pink blanket twined between her arms and legs, knees scissoring as if she climbed it like a vine. Her eyes were shut. Yankee trapped one foot in his hand to stop her climbing, adjusted the blanket to tuck her in, then lifted her head and placed it atop her big pillow—she must've knocked it aside in her sleep. Unless he was holding it over her face when Candelaria came in? The tinier, ruffled pillow her mother gave her lay on the floor. She picked it up with a shaking hand and tucked it next to Hope, who hugged it to her cheek.

"We lost a son but gained a daughter," Yankee said. "In China some might consider this an unfair trade. But we're in America, and it's time to look forward." His chin puckered as if holding back emotion. "She looks like her, don't you think?"

Candelaria was speechless. In the months she'd mourned her sister, it hadn't occurred to her that her husband might be mourning someone he thought of as a lover, however perverse. And how did he feel about Hope? Did she blame her for killing both Grace and his son? What had he said a moment ago: "They were both too weak to live, but you were strong enough to survive." Was it blame or admiration? She dared not admit her suspicions, lest he confirm them.

She turned her attention to Celia, Mary, and Rose, crowded into the bed on the opposite wall. Celia said she couldn't share a bed with Hope because she thrashed in her sleep. Mary claimed the tiny girl pushed her out of bed. Candelaria always tucked Rose in with Hope, and they started every night with arms wrapped around each other in sisterly affection, but by morning Rose could usually be found crowded into the other bed with Celia and Mary.

Whatever the reason, Hope slept alone. Maybe her changed status in the family unsettled the others. Candelaria had never explained why their cousin came to live with them.

She had promised Grace she'd take care of her daughter. But how could she if she couldn't protect the girl from her own father? She still wasn't sure what she'd seen: her husband tucking Hope in, or about to smother her in her sleep? What brought him in here tonight? Affection? Revenge? The need to obliterate the living evidence of what he really was?

She refused to break her promise to her sister, but maybe there was a better way to keep it. Before Grace died, Miguel mentioned a friend from Los Angeles who told him things were booming on the coast, unlike here:

"El Paso's not what it was, hermanita." Miguel's eyes looked blood-shot as he slouched against his Model T, white t-shirt bright in the dark, loose pants held up by suspenders. He took a drag from his hand-rolled cigarette and turned to blow the smoke away from her. "Time for me to go back to L.A., where the living's easier."

"Didn't a guy there threaten to kill you?" His smoke drifted her way, and she choked back a cough—hated to give him an excuse to tease her.

He chuckled and waved the smoke away. "A *few* guys threatened to kill me, sister, but hell, Mamá threatens to kill me all the time. There's a difference between talking and doing."

"Then why'd you leave California?"

"I wasn't sure *they* knew the difference." He snorted. "Anyway, that was years ago. My friend says there's new guys out there who'd appreciate my skills at moving merchandise."

That night she had convinced him *not* to leave his family in a lurch, not with Grace sick. Now Grace was gone. Now their little brother Sal was old enough to get a part-time job. If Miguel and Sal both found work in L.A., maybe they could afford to take the whole Rivera family—including Hope. Maybe Sal could even get a legitimate job, instead of the questionable ones Miguel did for businessmen who sold more than they talked about in their shops, restaurants, or offices.

So long as it got her parents and siblings as far from Yankee's kingdom as possible, that was all she asked. As for her and her own kids, she'd do her best to distract the king while waiting for the chance to run away and join the others. She still had time. She was only twenty-eight.

The time had come, at least, to speak to Marcela again. So what if her friend didn't understand her as perfectly as she once thought? Marcela was family, and if the family she was born to must go away, she would surely need the family who chose her. Marcela chose her despite her flaws, what she didn't understand she accepted, and what was hard to accept she forgave. Could Candelaria fail to give her the same gift?

As for Yankee? With him, sometimes it was best to say as little as possible.

Still gazing at Hope, she leaned a head against his shoulder, rose on tiptoes, and murmured in his ear, "Come to bed. My body's healed and I'm ready to stop mourning."

His befuddled look was boyish for a man of thirty-six. "Are you sure?"

She nuzzled his neck and emptied her mind to let her body fill with desire. Pretended to believe he cared whether she was ready, that his love wasn't as false as the fortune cookies he gave customers: cookies invented in Japan, not China; futures foretold by California factory workers, not Chinese fortune tellers. The lies she told herself were worse. Because she still wanted him, craved to enfold herself in his power, which felt like security, even now.

He bounced her into their firm new mattress, and she gasped. She inhaled the scent of gardenias drifting through the window, the smell of the world's first garden. Then she exhaled, and her flowers resumed singing, praying for all the dead.

PART THREE

THE BEAST

41. Bitten

1931-1934 – El Paso, Texas

The lunatic chorus of the coyote pack woke Candelaria every night. It used to be that coyotes rarely ventured so far from the hillsides except to devour the occasional chicken, cat, or dog. Then the raids hit Segundo Barrio, led not by coyotes but Anglos, men on the hunt for Mexicans.

In America, everyone took a turn as the enemy. For years, the Chinese took the blame for stealing jobs. Now it was the Mexicans' turn. The rag-tag band of Mounted Guards who used to keep out the Chinese had grown into the hundreds of armed lawmen of the Border Patrol. At first, they focused on smugglers, but as the country fell into a depression, they banded with other federal agents, Texas lawmen, and ordinary men loaded with guns, alcohol, or rage, with one purpose in mind: to drag all Mexicans to Mexico.

America declared no new law, no act or proclamation, yet suddenly it was illegal to be of Mexican descent. El Paso was more than half Mexican, and more than half of those were born here, but that didn't stop angry white men from hauling her people away all the same. It felt like a war, except there was no way to fight back. The people of Segundo Barrio were poor, outnumbered, and outgunned. Some panicked and left before anyone came for them.

By 1931, most of her neighbors were arrested, deported, or chased across the border.

She wrote Miguel in L.A. to ask if it might be safer for her and the kids to come there and stay with her parents. She'd dreamed of doing just that long before the Depression.

Eight years ago, she stood at El Paso's Union Depot, where nine railroad tracks promised eighteen escapes, listening to Papá shout over the chugging smokestack of the Sunset Limited, biggest train she ever saw: "The journey isn't so long," he said. "We can visit each other all the time!" He didn't wink, though, her first clue it would never happen.

Each year, Mamá wrote to say it was too expensive to buy tickets for every Rivera and unfair to leave anyone behind. Each year, Yankee made her give the same excuse for the Wongs.

Until she turned twenty-eight, she never lived more than a few blocks from her parents. By age thirty-six, she struggled to picture them anymore—maybe because she'd buried her face in her mother's neck on the platform that last day, reluctant to let go. The only memory she saw clearly was the Sunset Limited, red caboose shrinking as the fastest train of all carried her family away, whistle blowing, wheels pumping, toward the ocean Grace had longed to see.

Finally, she was ready to follow. Until Miguel wrote back and warned her not to:

Querida Candelita,

Don't come, it's not safe!

In Los Angeles, thousands of Mexicanos have been rounded up like cattle, dragged from their homes, beaten at their jobs, stolen off the streets. Police herd them onto buses and trains in broad daylight. They've sold the empty houses of neighbors who were born here, to "pay for their transportation to Mexico." I heard they cart away sick Mexicans from the hospital. One guy with consumption was dumped on the street in Tijuana.

Best to stay home in El Paso and don't attract attention.

Un abrazo fuerte,
Miguel

She followed her big brother's advice: stayed home and hid as her neighborhood emptied around her. The City of El Paso demolished many an abandoned home and shop. A lot of the remaining tenements and shacks leaned this way and that, like drunks who forgot the way home.

No vacancy lasts forever. Hobos who rode the rails camped amid the barrio's skeletal remains, built fires from broken tables and chairs, and begged for bottles of booze. Weeds poked through floors, trees burst through ceilings, and rodents set up housekeeping. Coyotes went on the prowl, and each night their freakish howls drew closer to her family's door.

At the edge of a ghost town, the International Café limped its way to 1934. Two of their Mexican waitresses disappeared, so Candelaria pitched in. Her second daughter, Mary, helped after school. There wasn't much to do. Business slowed as their customers vanished too. Her tips were dismal, Mary's worse—most of their regulars were men, and fifteen-year-old Mary looked like a female Yankee, poor thing. Benny and Celia took over Yankee's Chinese Café downtown, which had more white customers and fared better.

Five-year-old Vivi and three-year-old Guy ran wild in the courtyard while the older kids went to school. With fewer customers, it was easy to keep an eye on them. After school, twelve-year-old Rose walked Tommy and Julia home, then babysat till closing.

In the twenty-two years since she first waited tables, customers had gotten cleaner, but many men still acted as if paying for a meal bought them the right to say and do as they pleased. A few Anglos had no qualms about loudly discussing their opinions of the so-called "Mexican Repatriation," right in front of her as if she weren't there.

"Can't blame wetbacks for wanting to live in the land of opportunity, but our own folks gotta come first. Charity begins at home." Jack was a gringo regular who worked at the smelter.

Carlos, a Mexican who worked with Jack, called from a nearby table, "You picked the wrong place to talk repatriation. Right, Yankee?"

"Carlos, you know I don't talk politics," he answered. He always said it didn't pay to choose sides among customers. Crossing the wrong one could cost their lives.

Jack assured Carlos, "I wasn't talking about you, buddy. All's I'm saying is when strangers overstay their welcome, the polite thing is to go home."

"How can we go home to a place we never lived?" Carlos said. "I was born in El Paso. So were a lot of my friends who got 'repatriated.' Maybe *you* should go back to Germany."

"I'm American."

"So am I."

Nobody asked what she thought. If they had, she might've blurted that she never swam the Río Grande, that when she held her brother's bleeding body on the footbridge it was her front that got wet, not her back. But she kept her mouth shut because, unlike Carlos, she wasn't born here. If Jack found out, he might report her. To whom? That was the problem. Nobody knew.

A week later she was taking Jack's order when he told her Carlos was missing. He shook his head. "Damn shame. He was a good Mexican."

She turned to hand her order book to Mary. "Will you take this table? I need a break."

She went to the courtyard and sat under the olive tree watching Vivi and Guy play. Guy threw olives at the chicken coop, despite Vivi's assurances this wouldn't make the hens fly.

Candelaria called out, "Hey, little Firecracker, leave those poor birds alone."

He grinned at her, turned around, and pelted olives at Vivi instead.

She didn't fight sleepless nights but embraced wakefulness, brewing coffee at all hours, alert and ready to defend her children should men storm the house. After several years of pacing between the girls' and boys' rooms, she'd worn a dull path through the house in the middle of the floorboards. She imagined that path as a border dividing her family into three countries: Candelaria in Mexico, Yankee in China, the children in America. She was determined not to let this happen. Being separated from her parents was bad enough. But to be separated from her children? She would die first.

They had three strikes against them: 1) Yankee had slid into this country on the lie that he was born in America, his birth record burned in a fire, 2) there was no record she'd been born anywhere, and 3) half their children were born at home. Yankee's U.S. Army documents now seemed like nothing but paper, which anyone could throw out at any time.

"Which country would they deport the kids to?" she asked him late one night. They spoke not in bed but in the dimmed café so the children couldn't hear. Her thumb rubbed nervous circles against a cup of green tea, which promised to keep her up just like coffee. "Do you think they'll send them with me to Mexico, or with you to China?"

"Mexico, I guess."

"But they were born here, and they don't look Mexican—not exactly."

"They don't look Chinese either."

"That's what scares me most. What if looking odd is what makes them targets?"

In the morning, she admonished the kids not to venture too deep into Segundo Barrio…or wander downtown…or talk to white strangers…or any strangers…not to stay out after dark…

Yankee said she was overreacting. The Great Depression was entering its fifth year, and he pointed out they could only keep eight children—two now adults—trapped within shouting distance for so long.

She hated it when he was right. They treated her rules to stay near home as if she'd dared them to do the opposite. And why oh why was it eight-year-old Tommy, the most bookish and timid of them all, who snuck away the most? It was the only way he took after his father. She felt more protective of him than the rest, her soft-hearted little turtle without a shell.

One night Tommy and seven-year-old Julia failed to return until after dark. She begged Yankee to interrogate them.

"Why me?" he said.

"Because they're more scared of you."

"But why? I've never laid a hand on them, and I've seen *you* spank their behinds."

He looked so earnest she couldn't help laughing.

He pouted. "I thought you hated me being stern with them."

"That was before. If it keeps them safe, then I'm a big fan of shouting and insults."

With that, he stood the pair in the middle of the courtyard and lined up their other six children against the wall as witnesses. The silent solidarity of their two most obedient offspring in the face of his inquisition was impressive. All the kids were terrified of Yankee, even twenty-one-year-old Benny and nineteen-year-old Celia.

He mostly shouted at Tommy. "Fai Chaai! ¡Inútil! Useless boy!... Why didn't you bring your sister home when the streetlights came on?... If I have to ask again, you're getting the belt."

They didn't budge. Maybe because he'd never hit any of them with the belt before.

Then he said, "Okay Tommy, then I'll make Julia stay in the tunnel till you answer."

He'd never done this either, but Tommy apparently found it easier to believe. He mumbled his answer so softly Candelaria didn't know what he said till Yankee responded:

"What do you mean, you didn't *see* the streetlights come on?"

Nothing.

He bent to Julia's level, voice softer but still menacing. "How is that possible, young lady?"

Julia looked down at her dirty bare feet, one set of toes curled over the other.

Tommy blurted, "There's no streetlights where we went." He put his hands behind his back and faced Yankee, though he looked through his father, not at him. "It's my fault. I wanted to explore the empty buildings. I told Julia not to follow, but none of the girls will play with her."

Yankee always told her Tommy was weak and blamed her for turning him into a "mama's boy," but now he gave his middle son's shoulder a hearty clap, as if he were proud.

Tommy flinched.

"Aren't those buildings dark inside? I thought you were scared of the dark."

Tommy shook his head rapidly.

"Okay. Just don't do it again."

That was when she snapped. He'd all but announced that facing Segundo Barrio's ghost town was a way to earn his respect. She leapt forward and shook Tommy, hard. "You want bad men to steal you?!

You want them to follow you here and arrest Mommy? To take us all away?"

Tommy remained stoic, but Julia wept.

She let go of him then, turned her back on them all, and swallowed her own urge to cry.

Guy charged forward on his stubby legs, babyface scrunched in purple rage, and threw fierce arms around his sister. "Don't be scary, Julia! I'll punch the bad men!"

Yankee guffawed and ruffled his hair till it stood on end. "I'm sure you will."

The tiny boy swatted his hand away. "I mean it!"

She stroked his hair flat. He swatted her hand too. She swatted it back, which had no effect on him. "Rose, give our little Firecracker a bath. God knows how he got filthier than any of you when he never left the courtyard."

Then again, she wasn't sure about that. Guy had a knack for disappearing only to reappear with a bang the moment anyone noticed his absence. It's why Celia nicknamed him "Firecracker," because he was "such a little noisemaker." Now he roared and led Rose on a chase round the courtyard, anything to avoid a bath. The other kids joined in, laughing and shouting.

She pulled Yankee aside. "How can we protect them?"

"We can't. It's a dog-eat-dog world. It's time they learned that, or they'll get eaten."

She didn't disagree. He should know. He was one of the dogs.

The café door banged open and set the bell clanging like a fire engine. Candelaria was eating lunch at a vacant table, and she looked up, hoping the bell signaled more customers—at the moment, they only had three. Instead, Tommy, Vivi, and Guy barged in. Guy was trying to wrestle free of Vivi's grip. Tommy was limping and sobbing. Bullies often beat him up after school, though he'd only admitted it once. She had insisted Yankee talk to the other boy's father.

He'd returned from that confrontation laughing. "You should see how little that kid is!"

"So is Tommy," she'd said.

Her son had run from the house, face deep red.

He hadn't mentioned bullies since, though he once hid blood-stained clothes at the bottom of her laundry basket. If Tommy was willing to come into the café crying, knowing his father would see, then something serious had happened.

She rose, caught sight of his pant leg, torn and bloody at the ankle, and ran to him.

Yankee, busy cooking in the kitchen, called out over the pass-through shelf, "Waa! Take that crying out of here, little girl! You'll ruin everyone's appetite."

Mary stood gaping at Tommy. So did her three customers: a young Anglo man at one table, an elderly Mexican couple at another.

"Mary, watch the customers!" Candelaria said.

She led Tommy behind the half-wall between the kitchen and dining room, then sat him on a crate. He clutched his bleeding ankle and rocked. He still cried, but silently, now that Yankee was working right behind him.

"Mijo, move your hand so I can see." She pried his fingers loose and rolled up his shredded pant leg, to reveal his ankle was also shredded. More like a bloody pork shank than a boy's leg. Not wanting to scare him, she slowly pressed his hands back over the wound with a matter-of-fact nod. "It's okay. Just hold it." Then she hollered, "Baba, I need a hand!"

"Wait-wait! I'm cooking an order." The wok sizzled louder to prove his point.

"¡Ay cabrón!" she muttered, then hollered, "Sam, get out here!"

Sam opened the door of the office, where he was figuring the books. "May I help you?"

"I need you. *Now.*"

He took one look at Tommy and his face fell. "Wo! That's bad."

Without asking what she needed, he rushed over, lifted Tommy, and carried him to a table. She cleared it off, and he laid the boy on top. Then Sam stripped off his own button-down shirt and the tee-shirt under that, balled them up, and put them under the leg to prop it up.

"Thank you, Sam," she said. "Now fill a basin with hot water, soap, and clean towels."

He ran to the kitchen.

The three customers gathered closer to watch.

"Wow. You should clean that wound with soap and water," the young white man said.

She shot him a look, then yanked wads of napkins from a dispenser to sop up the blood.

"Boy needs stitches," the old Mexican man said.

"Get him to the hospital," his wife said.

She recalled Miguel's letter: *I heard they cart away sick Mexicans from the hospital. One guy with consumption was dumped on the street in Tijuana.* No, no hospital, not if she could help it. The napkins quickly soaked through.

"Mary, don't just stand there, grab more napkins!" She took Tommy's hand. "Tell me what happened."

Guy leapt forward and crossed his arms over his chest. "I'm a brave boy, Mommy!" Which meant whatever happened was Guy's fault.

Tommy ran a sleeve across his leaky nose. "It bit me."

"What bit you?"

"Doggie," Guy said.

Vivi spoke up. "Not a doggie, dummy, a coy-o-te."

"Wanna save the doggie," Guy said.

Yankee finally came out—holding a beer. "What's that boy crying about this time?"

Tommy sat up taller to address his father: "A coyote was hopping down the street with his paw trapped in a milk bottle."

"The doggie's foot stucked," Guy said.

"Guy walked right up to him," Tommy said. "I jumped between them."

The bell rang again. A couple stepped inside, took one look, and hurried out.

Yankee smacked his forehead. "This is costing us business."

"Is that all you care about?" she said.

He looked taken aback. "If he needs a doctor, how do you think we'll pay?"

Guy admired Tommy's gaping wound. "Does it hurt?" He reached out a finger.

Tommy slapped it away. "Whaddaya think? Don't be a numbskull."

"I'm not a nusko!"

Sam hurried over with the sloshing basin.

She washed the wound, taking shallow breaths, trying not to inhale the smell of blood, like pennies. The coyote hadn't stopped at one bite. His leg looked chewed. She turned to Yankee, who sat on a chair with his head between his legs. Since when was he so squeamish?

Rose ran inside pulling Julia by the hand. "What's going on?" She saw the blood, screamed as if she were the one bitten, then swayed as if she'd faint—she did that sometimes. Candelaria cast her eyes heavenward. So dramatic, this one. She scanned the faces around her, waiting for her to decide what to do. The young man who'd suggested soap and water was gone, must've seen his chance to skip out on the bill. The elderly couple were the only customers left.

She nodded at them. "You were right. But he might not only need stitches. He might need a rabies shot. We're going to the hospital." She stood and shouted, "Sam, get your car. Yankee, carry Tommy. Rose, watch the kids. Julia, mop this bloody floor."

Everyone jumped to comply except Yankee. "I need to find the coyote."

"You need to go with us to the hospital. You need to think about your son."

"This *is* about my son. It's about all my children. What if the coyote comes here looking for food? What if Guy wanders off and it mauls him? He's so small and helpless."

She cast a skeptical glance at Guy, who chased Rose out the back door, threatening to wipe his bloody finger on her, which set her screaming again.

Yankee stuck to his guns. "Think about it. If the animal *isn't* rabid, Tommy won't need shots. But if it *is* rabid, then it's a danger to us all."

She nodded. "Okay, find the coyote. Sam and I will drive Tommy to the hospital."

First, Yankee hoisted Tommy over his shoulder, staggered outside, and laid him across the back seat of Sam's freshly waxed, royal blue Ford Lincoln. She climbed in after Tommy, cradled his head in her lap, and propped his bleeding leg on the towels Sam had thrown down.

Sam leaned over the back of the driver's seat. "Try not to get blood on the upholstery."

"Go-go-go!" she said.

He gunned the engine and they sped away.

Sam had no wife or kids of his own, but he was always kind to her children. She never fully trusted him though Yankee often said they could trust Sam with their lives because they were the only family he had. The idea made her uncomfortable—it wasn't as if they were close. But it also made her sad for Sam, who had nobody else, so she always tried to be nice to him. Today, at least, he proved himself a bigger help than Yankee.

42. The Coyote

1934 – El Paso, Texas

Yankee watched Sam's new Ford pull away and congratulated himself on his wisdom in befriending the loyal but awkward boy he met at Angel Island twenty-three years ago. He felt confident his worried wife and wounded son would be safe with his old friend at the wheel.

In the café, Mary cleaned blood off the table, Julia mopped blood off the floor, and the old couple chattered on about Tommy's bloody wound. Yankee strode to the register and opened the drawer below, revealing an old cigar box, and inside that: his little Browning .380. He carried the gun to the storeroom, found a length of rope, and returned to the dining area.

The old woman shrieked.

He followed her gaze to the rope and gun in his hands, and shrugged. "Never hunted a coyote before."

The old man stepped forward. "You need help?"

"No. The animal is in Segundo Barrio, the abandoned section. You're Mexican. Do you want to be found wandering there like a vagrant?"

The man's Adam's apple scaled up and down like a slide whistle. He stepped back. "Good luck, Yankee."

"Mary, you're in charge of the café while I'm gone."

"Yes, Baba." Her eyes gleamed at this sudden rise in power.

He didn't like leaving Mary in charge. She was hardworking, but not clever like Benny or Celia. He suspected she made up for that with deviousness. He felt certain she was why the register was often short, but he'd never caught her even though he periodically searched the girls' bedroom. It was one reason he sent Celia to work with Sam and Benny downtown, despite preferring her company to Mary's. There was more cash to worry about at the downtown café. Here, he could keep an eye on her. Usually. He sighed. He wouldn't be gone long.

How hard could it be to find a coyote with one milk-bottle leg?

Yankee trailed up and down empty roads until he forgot the gun in his pocket, the coiled rope in his hand, why he was there. He must've looked the part of the scary Chinese man some parents still warned children about: a *boogeyman*, a *cucuy*, a *mo gwaai* prowling for prey. No youngsters played in this derelict stretch of Chihuahuita, deserted except for one hobo peering through a boarded window. Yankee heard nothing but his own footfalls and uneven breath.

His busy life afforded little time away from chattering customers, annoying employees, and noisy children. He savored silence like a delicacy, like sucking salty dried fish till the salt was gone. The thought made him thirsty. He drank from his flask, which only made him thirstier.

Then he heard it, a faint, repeating musical note: *tink…tink…tink.* Mei Yin tapping on her gravestone, Bing Sam tapping on the hull of the SS *Siberia*, Grace tapping on his bedroom window—though Candelaria assured him that sound was merely a branch from the gardenia bush outside.

Tink…tink…tink. The sound of a milk bottle on the leg of a coyote.

The first two huts were empty. In the third, the door hung askew. He inched through the narrow opening, then waited for his eyes to adjust to the dark and his nose to accept the decay. Vague shapes re-solved into a pile of small bones, lumps of charcoaled wood, and a lone coyote with one front paw trapped in a clear glass bottle. A shaft of afternoon light penetrated the glass, wobbling like water, so the leg appeared broken where it entered the bottle's neck.

Yankee bent his knees and dropped his shoulders, ready to run. The coyote did the same, yet it didn't bare a single tooth or give the slightest growl. It smelled overpowering: a wild musk of fur, piss, and fear. He felt the gun in his pocket. If he missed, the report might startle it. Its only means of escape was behind him. The beast was nothing but fur and bones, but it could still bite. Doctors needed the head to diagnose rabies. If he failed to retrieve it, Tommy would need shots. He'd heard this was a painful, and expensive, procedure.

He backed up to the door, eyes fixed on the beast, squeezed himself outside, shut the door, and leaned against it. He studied the rope in his hand, reminded of the last time he saw his father-in-law, Eduardo, eight years ago.

They'd thrown the Riveras a going-away party at Yankee's house. As the party died, Eduardo, Yankee, and his eldest son Benny, only thirteen at the time, lingered in the courtyard. Eduardo was reminisc-ing about his cowboy days when Yankee asked him to demonstrate his skills with a lasso. Benny offered to caper like a calf while Eduardo taught Yankee how to rope and tie him. Yankee kept getting the rope hung up in the olive tree.

Candelaria leaned out the door and said, "So long as you don't lasso my gardenias, borrachos!" What was it with her and those damned flowers?

"Relax, mija," Eduardo said. "This might be my last rodeo in El Paso."

"Of course, Papá," she said, eyes brimming, then left them to their game.

The old cowboy demonstrated incredible skills, not just roping and tying his grandson but also performing tricks that sent the circle of rope overhead, around his feet, side-to-side. A small audience gathered under the tree, laughing and applauding as he danced and strode around the spinning rope. Its mesmerizing whirl called to mind Grace, who once twirled for Yankee to show off a new skirt. She still tied the family together, bound in mutual repentance.

That party marked the last time he saw Grace's daughter, when she was three. Hope was eleven now, no longer his to worry about. Candelaria's children were.

Now, leaning against the hut, Yankee slid his circle of rope back and forth through the knot, expanding and shrinking the loop until it seemed the right size. He filled his lungs with air, cracked the door again, and slipped back inside. The hut offered insufficient room to swing the lariat, but he didn't know what else to do. Didn't dare grab the creature, risking tooth and claw.

The coyote didn't dodge the rope when he threw it, merely cowered, wedging itself in a corner. This was cleverer than Yankee expected, given the stupid move of putting its paw in a bottle. By curling in a corner, the coyote made it impossible to lasso its neck.

The rope uselessly slapped the canine again and again till Yankee grew desperate. He flung the door wide, let in a blaze of sunset, and lunged at the animal with a full-throated roar. The coyote lurched out the door, paws scrambling: *skitter-hop-tink*. The bottle slowed the beast enough for him to stalk it outside with broad, restrained steps.

He gave the lasso a vast, crooked spin, hearing Eduardo's patient voice: "Put yourself in the animal's mind. Don't think about where he *is* but where he's *going*, and throw the lasso there." Surely the hobbled predator knew it couldn't outrun him and would therefore seek the nearest cover. So, Yankee tossed the lasso toward the open doorway of the next hut.

He missed. "*Argh!*"

The mangy pelt bolted through the door he predicted.

Consumed with frustration, he rushed in after it and kicked blindly in the dark until his foot connected with something that gave. The canine yelped. He kicked again, and it scurried to another corner, snarling. Heedless of the bared fangs, he kicked again, but instead of drawing his foot back, pressed the animal's ribs into a wall as he lowered the noose around its neck and drew tight. The coyote writhed, but he held firm, yanked it off its feet, and flung it onto its back.

He dragged his enemy outside, writhing, snapping, and growling, bottle-clad leg tapping, *thunkity-thunk-tink, snap-growl-tink, whine-slaver-tink*. It made for a long walk home, dragging the coyote through the dust in the dying sun. The animal tried every move to break free: struggled to its feet, fought the rope, dug in its paws, yanked its head sideways, dropped its haunches, bit the tether. He now saw why his youngest son felt a kinship with this beast.

With each pregnancy, Candelaria's birth pains had shortened and the babies had come faster. Benny was delivered by his grandmother. Celia, Mary, Rose, and Tommy by midwife. After Grace gave birth to her baby in a hospital, Yankee felt it his duty to do the same for his wife. That meant Julia and Vivi were also born in Hotel Dieu. They almost didn't make it there in time with Vivi. Guy, the most impatient of all, was born at home. Yankee delivered their youngest himself.

He panicked when he saw the umbilical cord wrapped around the infant's neck like a noose. "The baby's choking! We're going to lose him."

"No we won't." His wife spoke with the calm of someone who has chatted with death over many a cup of coffee. "Just treat it like any tangled rope. Unwind it the opposite direction."

He did just that. He could swear the baby rolled and turned in rhythm with him as if to aid his own escape. Once the boy was free, Yankee cut the cord, flinching in horror that this might hurt the child. He didn't worry about hurting his wife, who seemed invincible.

If anything, the near strangulation only strengthened Guy, who didn't cry but grunted like a wild pig satisfied to be free. He lifted the boy, nose-to-nose. Guy stared into his eyes, screwed up his face, and, instead of mewling like most newborns, howled in defiance of the giant before him.

Guy had been defiant ever since. They tied him into his highchair, but he slithered out. Caged him in a crib, but he climbed out. Locked him in the house, but no door could contain him. Spanking didn't stop him from slapping his parents, kicking his siblings, or throwing rocks at strangers. The word "no" didn't stop him from riding the neighbor's German shepherd like a pony. It was as if breaking free of his umbilical cord had taught their little Firecracker to ignore all future restraints.

How could Yankee let anything harm his own brazen little beast?

He dragged the coyote for blocks, both of them limping, skidding, and sliding over dirt and tar. His scant neighbors stepped outside to stare.

One man said, "Is he taking the damn thing for a walk?"

A woman replied, "Don't be silly. He's gonna kill it."

"Good," another woman said. "Damn pests keep killing my chickens."

He hadn't thought that far ahead. He had no idea what to do with the coyote. Take it to the hospital? To the police? How?

By instinct more than purpose, he made his determined way home, bypassed the café, and opened the side-gate. The courtyard was empty. "Candelaria," he croaked, throat dry as bone. He waited, panting, palms hot with rope burns, right hand numb from the rope double-wrapped round his wrist. The emaciated animal collapsed beside him, heaving. He knew how it felt.

Candelaria stepped out of the house and stared from man to beast without comment. He'd told her he planned to hunt the coyote, but her expression suggested she'd been waiting for this moment since they'd met. She didn't fold her arms like other wives, but stepped off the porch, fists loose at her sides as if ready for a boxing match.

"You're too late," she said. "The doctor couldn't risk Tommy getting rabies. He said when a wild animal bites, they can't be sure of finding the animal."

"What're you saying?"

"They already gave him the first vaccination. He needs to go back four more times."

"You act like it's my fault."

"Isn't it? You're the one who let the children run loose. Tommy screamed when they gave him the shot. He asked if that white doctor was punishing him for being Mexican. He asked, 'Will they report us and take us away?' He's terrified to go back to the doctor."

"Maybe he won't have to. Maybe this coyote has no rabies." He tugged the rope, but the coyote barely lifted its head. "The doctor can still check."

"How? What're you going to do? Drag that half-dead animal to the hospital? Call the police, so they can deport us? Prove to the children our stories about the bad men are true?" She tossed her head toward the gate. "Take that thing away."

It took a moment to register that Tommy stood in the house's doorway, while Mary, Rose, and Julia flanked their mother. They all looked blurry. He rubbed his eyes. "No, dammit!"

"No what?"

"I'm not dragging this goddamn coyote anywhere else! I'm done, you hear me?"

He hauled the coyote toward the covered porch. It gave up trying to flee and lunged for him, snapping. He jerked the slack rope to shorten it, until he dangled the scrawny monster off its front feet, swaying and snarling at arm's length. Then he continued lugging it toward the porch.

Tommy retreated into the house. Julia hid her face in her mother's side. Mary gaped.

"Mamá, make him stop!" Rose whined.

"Get back!" Candelaria hustled the three middle girls toward the restaurant doorway across the courtyard, where Celia, Vivi, and Guy emerged.

"Doggie!" Guy's grin was a lightning flash in the dusk. He waddled forward.

Vivi hauled him back. "No! The doggie will bite!"

The beast, perhaps sensing allies, strained toward the children, wheezing. With one great pull, Yankee flipped it onto its back, then threw the coiled remainder of rope over a porch rafter.

"Baba," Celia was matter of fact, "you can't kill it here."

"Who says I can't? Isn't this my house? My restaurant? My family?" He pulled the rope so taut the coyote rotated, its three paws and bottle grazing the porch, neck straining the noose, throat making a strangled sound. It couldn't hurt his children anymore. He was in control.

Guy howled, "Baba, nooooooo! Don't hurt him!" He twisted in Vivi's arms, kicked and bit, trying to break free.

"Help, I can't hold him," Vivi said.

Celia lifted Guy from her. He pummeled Celia too, but she didn't let go. The rest of the children huddled against the restaurant wall, sobbing. Rose fainted; this time it looked real.

Candelaria said in a choked voice, "Please, Yankee, the children."

"Who do you think I'm doing this for? The rest of you pay attention! Julia, wake Rosie. We're not victims in this family. If anyone or anything hurts us, we fight back. This beast bit my boy!" He pointed at the house. "Get out here, young man!"

Tommy reappeared in the doorway, sidled along the porch as far as possible from the dangling coyote, and limped across the courtyard to join his brothers and sisters.

"I won't always be here to protect you! Someday you'll have to take care of yourselves." Certain everyone was watching—except Benny, too bad he was at the other restaurant and not here to witness this lesson in manhood—he pulled with all his might, hoisted the coyote till it hung from the rafter by its neck, paddling its paws as if trying to swim.

"It looks like a piñata," Julia murmured.

"Shut up," Mary said.

Yankee pulled his Browning from his pocket and aimed. He didn't see Guy bite Celia's arm and writhe free, but Guy's liquid scream poured hot in his ear till the gun's report deafened him to all but his victory over the deadly beast. The first bullet pierced the coyote's chest and continued onward to shatter a corner of the parlor window, splattering the remaining glass with viscera. No longer having any use for the head, he shot that too, and sent the jaw winging into the gardenias.

He felt something wrap around his ankles, looked down to see Guy lying there, sobbing as never before, not kicking or biting, but limp and begging. The little Firecracker's voice must have been loud for Yankee to catch any of the boy's words over the ringing in his ears. "Baba, please save the doggie! Please!"

Yankee looked from the shrieking boy at his feet to the silent coyote swaying overhead. He let go the rope—hearing neither the thud nor the shatter as both the body and the milk bottle hit the boards, the trapped paw finally free—and reached for his baby boy.

Candelaria got there ahead of him and cradled Guy to her breast. Then she rose, still holding him, and led her weeping daughters inside. Tommy limped in last and shut the door, but not before giving him a look glassy with hate. His soft middle son still didn't understand.

He turned to see Sam standing in the café's back doorway, considering Yankee over a dwindling cigarette. Sam dropped the butt, reached out a toe, and ground it into the brick stoop. Then he stepped inside and shut not only the screen but also the inner door. No customers had come outside. El Pasoans knew to run away from gunshots, not toward them.

Yankee stared at the felled beast. If he had it to do over, he would've shot it amid the ruins of Chihuahuita and returned home alone. The fact remained it had to die. Surely everyone would see that.

He pulled out his flask, unscrewed the top, and tipped it in the coyote's direction. "You put up a valiant fight." Then he sat on the porch next to the body and nestled his fingers in the bloody fur ruff at its neck, which remained surprisingly soft. "I'm sorry, my friend, but what choice did I have?" He laid his face against its yielding neck and wept.

43. The Patriarch

1934 – El Paso, Texas

Two whole days of quiet made Yankee feel rabid. How could nine people conspire to create such a hush? He caught himself whispering to everyone, even to request more rice or tortillas, coffee or tea, as if such things were no longer his right as head of his household. Perhaps he didn't choose the best way to handle the coyote, but the choice was his, not theirs. He protected this family, and they behaved like ingrates.

What troubled him most was the way his little Firecracker, the one child whose insubordination he secretly enjoyed, turned mute. When Yankee so much as belched, Guy flinched. If he muttered a simple *please* or *thank you*, Guy trembled. Once, he tried to hug him goodnight, and Guy bolted from the room. What had he done to deserve such a cowering display? Had he ever struck the child? Any of them? Never!

He stood as a pillar of his community. Many El Paso Chinese owed him their lives, their jobs, their American Dreams. But in his own home, he was a pariah?

He'd spoiled his children too long, let them become too American. They failed to respect their elders, did as they pleased instead of obeying their father. This would never happen in China.

Worse, their mother encouraged them to grow soft, too tender-hearted to kill a beast that threatened them. They couldn't tell the difference between family and enemy. Bad enough that gangs of federal agents and vigilantes had the power to carry them off without warning or consequence, but one mad coyote? Ridiculous. What would they cower from in future? Defending their right to exist? Running their own lives, owning their own property, starting their own businesses?

He must turn his kids around before it was too late. So, he turned their weapon against them, used the isolation they built around him to hatch a plan to save them from themselves.

His quiet plotting so consumed him, it took a while to notice when the house returned to its former volume: rising from murmurs, to conversations, to laughter and chaos and fights. At first, they only spoke to each other. Then they started speaking to him again. Not much, mostly to offer him food or coffee or bless him when he sneezed.

Sometimes the kids tested him: brought home rescued rabbits, snakes, or frogs. He ignored these attempts at rebellion. What did he care how many pets they kept? He did *not hate* animals. The coyote was *rabid*. Why did they refuse to understand? Now and then he threw out a half-hearted, "Get that beast out of here while I'm eating!" but only to remind them he was in charge.

One evening at dinner, Candelaria was the one who insisted he put his foot down. "Baba, tell Julia she must apologize to Rose for scaring her."

"Your mother's right. What if your tarantula bit her?" he said. Then he leaned closer to their radio cabinet to listen to the faint strains of "Moonglow," as if a large poisonous spider were beneath his attention compared to Benny Goodman's clarinet.

In truth, Julia's new pet got him thinking: Back home, in Toisan, we have no tarantulas. Rabbits, snakes, and frogs are food. We have no coyotes. Sometimes dogs are pets, but usually they're family guards, or meals. And nobody complains.

It was the dream of every good Overseas Chinese father to buy a quality education for his sons, and if he had wealth to spare, his daughters too. He'd grown complacent, leaving this duty to America's public schools. What did he expect for free? His children came home as self-important as *gwai lou*, learning only the history, customs, and language of the *white ghosts* who wanted nothing to do with them. They learned nothing of China, or even Mexico.

No more.

Though Yankee wasn't wealthy by American standards, in China his humble income translated to riches. The money he sent home had helped his brother build a large home for their parents before they died. Tsi Chaum had moved home with his wife to look after them, but she'd died in a cholera epidemic without giving him sons. His brother now lived in the family mansion alone, a single grain of rice tumbling around a large wok. Since he had no children, why shouldn't he act as guardian to Yankee's brood? Tsi Chaum and the Wong elders would teach these youngsters filial duty. Yankee would hire tutors to improve their Chinese language skills, which were atrocious to nonexistent, and to teach them about China, a land civilized when the West was still wild. Benny could find a Chinese wife, all but impossible here.

His rambunctious brood might even enjoy a far-off adventure. In the end, they'd thank him for returning their pride. In China, nobody would call them brainless because their skin wasn't white. They would become his crowning achievement.

Candelaria would see the sense of it too as it eased their financial woes.

Yankee and Sam could manage both cafés without Benny's or Celia's help. Candelaria would have time to pitch in too, once all the children sailed overseas. Except Guy—the Firecracker was too small to leave his mother. Of course, she'd miss the others, but even she would admit this was an opportunity to promote their future.

In his dreams, he sat by Mei Yin's side at the edge of Bok Nan's village pond, in front of the mansion his money built, watching his children play. "Beloved," he said, "I went to Gold Mountain and became king of a dynasty."

"I'm glad you've come home," she said, then wiggled her fingers in the water, creating ripples of light that turned into fat gold koi.

When he woke, he kept his eyes closed, trying to recapture her face. But it was gone.

He opened his eyes and watched his wife sleep, soft cheek pillowed on her hands. His heart grew tranquil at the thought of being alone with her again—except for Guy, who would supply their days with laughter. Mei Yin was a dream, but Candelaria was real, queen of his American empire. She would become precious to him again after her small army was gone. Once China trained them to honor their father, he'd be happy to see the children return.

With the coyote attack a week behind them, it was time to share his plan with Candelaria.

He waited till sunrise coaxed open her eyes, sleepy but untroubled. No sign she still clung to her grudge over the coyote "lynching." That's what he'd overheard her call it that first night, when she'd whispered the story to Benny upon his return from work. Now he saw another story in her eyes, which shone in the early light like liquid gold. A reflected story. His story:

He loved her.

He had no idea when it happened. Maybe he'd loved her from the start. His mood softened by this wonder, he rubbed his nose against hers. His ban zau swelled, almost making him forget what he planned to say. No, best not give in to his urges. After lovemaking was when she always broke difficult news to him, when his defenses were down. That timing never worked the other way around. He needed his wits.

"Sweetheart"—he rarely called her by American pet names, but English felt like neutral territory—"I've come to a decision about our children."

She gave him a skeptical look. "What's that?"

He outlined his plan with enthusiasm. But his mood turned to dismay as the color drained from her face. The mattress beneath them vibrated with her tension. At least she didn't interrupt, at least she was a wife who listened even if she didn't like what she heard. Once he made his case, surely her motherly instincts would tell her this was best for her children. He ended with the comforting assurance that the kids could always come home to visit.

She rose from the bed looking dazed, as if still asleep though her eyes were open. She pulled off her nightgown, opened the wardrobe, reached out as if to select an outfit, but let her hand fall and turned to stare at him. Naked. Hers was a mother's body, yet it remained strong: thighs broad but not soft, belly round but not fat, breasts loose but not fallen. And her face, ancestors, her face! Its beauty blazed with rage. He once saw Guy roast an ant with a magnifying glass in the sun, and whatever the ant saw at the end must have looked much like this.

Yet she sounded calm as a lullaby, "You terrorize our children, then punish them for their fear—"

"Woman, don't exaggerate. I killed a wild beast that mauled our son—to protect our children, not terrorize them. How will they survive this world if you hide them from it?"

"So, to teach them survival, you'll banish them from their home and family?"

"Who said 'banish'? I'm entrusting them to their Chinese home, their Chinese family. They'll hardly be alone: seven brothers and sisters together."

"Don't you mean eight?"

"Guy is too young to go."

"You'll separate him from the others?!"

"I'll entrust him to his mother."

"While you punish his mother by taking away all her other children!" Though she refrained from shouting, her breath blew hot in his face. Not like Kei Lun, more like his mother, the only woman who ever scared him. Either way, he half-expected fire to consume him.

"I'll miss them too," he said. "But I want to give them a better life, a better education."

"A *Chinese* education you mean. What value is that in America?"

"Already Americans don't value them," he said. "They need to learn who they are."

"And who do you think they are?"

"They're not only Mexican. They're also Chinese."

"They're American," she said.

"This country will never let them be American."

"This country won't let you or me be American. Someday *they* can be, if *you* let them."

"I can't afford to give them here what I can give them there. What if this Depression continues ten more years? What if we lose the restaurants? We have ten mouths to feed."

"When I was a girl, we often had nothing except each other, yet my parents never broke up the family, not by choice. Don't pretend this is about money or education. You tortured that animal to prove how powerful you are. Now you want to torture me for the same reason."

"That's not why… But maybe if you had taught our children respect—"

"—You mean maybe if I was Chinese!"

"Why must you always fight me? Even Grace was more obedient."

"How dare you bring up Grace!" she hissed. "I've been faithful through all the womanizing, the drinking, the bootlegging. You preyed on my brother, ruined my sister, brought death to this house. Still I stood by you. And I know you tried to kill Hope…"

"I did no such thing!" He realized he was the only one shouting. He grew aware of the wakefulness of the house, his children listening. She was making him lose control, something he'd fought his whole life not to do. He turned away and took deep breaths till he was able to lower his voice. "If I had the courage, I *would* have killed her, to spare her the life of a bastard. But I couldn't. Don't talk about my daughter when *you're* the one who sent her away."

"To protect her from *you*! God, you don't even know what you are, do you?"

"What am I?"

"The devil."

He laughed. "Then you're the devil's bride!"

He strode up to her, hating her more than he would've thought possible moments ago, now that he felt the full force of her hatred. He panted loathing into her face, nose-to-nose, conscious of his morning breath, hoping to offend. She didn't flinch. He pinched one baby-chewed nipple between his fingers. Her eyes held his. He slapped the breast aside. "I've decided. The children go to China. But if you're so sure I'm the devil, so sure you're a saint among mothers, I won't stop you from going with them." He folded his arms. Let her argue with that.

Her face went blank. "To China? Me?"

"Yes, you." He couldn't lose. If she stayed, she must accept defeat. If she left, he'd be free of this ungrateful bitch.

She searched his face, and he saw realization sink in, that he was serious. She swayed, reached for the bed, and sat down hard. So, this was where Rose got her dramatics. She clasped her hands behind her head, set her elbows on her knees, and hunched over to inhale deep breaths.

He knelt before her, uncertain. "Candelita, are you okay?" Had he gone too far?

"I go where my children go. I choose China." She lifted her head but didn't look at him. Stared inward with a serene smile as if contemplating a pleasant dream. Then she went too far. She rose, pushed past him, and reached again for the wardrobe—as if she'd...forgotten him.

He stood, grabbed her shoulder, and threw her on the bed. She made no protest as he stood over her, ready to thrust inside her, to remind her that, whatever she thought had just happened, *he* made the decisions. She looked up at him, but her eyes told him that, no matter what he heaped inside her, of pain or pleasure, her tranquility would remain. Her smile wavered, but only as if she were underwater, a creature drifting far below him, under the house, under the desert, deep in a hidden aquifer where he couldn't reach.

He did not fall on top of her, but onto the bed next to her, turned his back, and pulled the covers to his chin. He pretended to fall asleep as he listened to her rise a final time, dress, and cross the house. Only opened his eyes again when he heard the soft click of the back door.

He'd wanted her to accept her place as his wife, not choose banishment. Yet she wasn't choosing banishment either, which only worked if the banished feared their fate. Her smile had looked more than calm. Expectant. Could it be she preferred to live thousands of miles away, across desert and ocean, in a place where she knew no one and didn't speak the language, rather than stay with him? Could it be she was eager to leave?

And if he remained alone in America, while every last member of his family lived in his homeland, then just who was he banishing?

44. The Leaving

1934 – El Paso, Texas

Her final weeks in El Paso, Candelaria woke the children the same way each Sunday, to ensure they'd never forget. To create this kitchen brujeria, she started her day early and alone: set her mother's clay pot on the stove, filled it with water, and lit the burner. She lowered a sweet mahogany cone of piloncillo into the water, then plucked two cinnamon sticks from a jar and floated them on top. It smelled like Christmas, which to her would always smell like Mata Flores, the first home she ever knew.

While she waited for the water to heat and the piloncillo's cane sugar crystals to dissolve, she ground the coffee, pushing the grinder's handle round and round to churn the dark roasted beans to dust. These were the last days of her Mexican life.

In China, they would drink tea. She loved teas, their bright but subtle tang that evaporated on her tongue like the past and set her brain tapping like the future. But she would miss the lingering bittersweetness of coffee, especially café de olla from Mamá's earthen pot, which anchored the body to the present and the soul to home.

She poured in the grounds and stirred, sending fingers of coffee, sugar, and cinnamon through the house to tickle her children awake. She then slid the pot off the burner, covered it, and turned to warm a saucepan of milk for the little ones.

Next came the bag of bolillos, which she tumbled into a towel-lined bowl, an El Paso addition to Mamá's tradition. She loved dipping the little rolls into her brew till the bread softened and soaked up coffee like a sponge. Sponges grew in the ocean. Would traveling across an ocean make her soft like a sponge, ready to absorb new things? Or would brittle pieces of her break off and sink, like a bolillo stirred too long in a cup of coffee?

A wiry arm grabbed her waist, plump lips loudly kissed her cheek, and a man's hand shot around her to grab a bolillo.

She slapped his hand before it captured his prize.

His laughter exploded in her ear. An echo of Yankee, except lighter, more open.

"Wait for the coffee, Benny!"

Her grown son gave her a sly grin as she handed him the cheese-cloth. He stretched it over her aluminum coffee pot, and she poured coffee from the Mexican clay pot into the American-made metal one, trapping the grounds in the cloth. She used to ladle coffee straight from the clay into the cups, which tasted better, but the little ones complained about the dregs. This way, she was the only one who complained—she never got used to the taste of the metal.

Celia appeared, kissed her mother's upturned cheek, then lifted the saucepan of warm milk from the stove while Benny lifted the metal coffee pot. She then followed her brother down the line of chipped clay mugs on the table, and in tandem they poured the café and leche: more leche for the youngest, more café for the middle kids, café nada más for the eldest.

"Will we have café de olla in China, Mamá?" Celia asked.

"I'm not sure we'll have coffee at all."

Tommy snuck up beside Candelaria and whispered, "Let's take some with us."

"I'm not sure that's legal," she whispered back.

"I could smuggle it in my luggage." He poked out his tongue.

"Don't use that word."

Tommy had changed since the coyote, still soft-spoken and studious but full of sly ideas, as if the creature's bite had imparted its trickster ways. Or as if he needed to prove something. Or maybe he'd been this way all along and she'd mistaken his quiet nature for a timidity he never possessed. He slid the bowl of rolls off the counter and set them on the table.

"Good morning, Mamá," Rose and Julia said in unison, then pecked her cheek and went to the icebox to fetch the eggs. Rose fussed at her little sister not to break the yolks, and Julia accepted her bossiness without complaint.

Celia set two mugs of milky coffee next to the stove for the two younger girls to sip while they fried the eggs. Then she handed a mug of darker brew to Candelaria, who had switched to chopping nopalitos. Celia laid a gentle hand over her mother's, stilling the blade, then eased it from her hand, which shook unaccountably. "Let us serve you today, Mamá."

Vivi took Candelaria's other hand and led her to the table, just in time for Guy to run in and hurl himself into her lap. "¡Mamá-Mamá-Mamá!"

"No need to shout. I'm right here. What do you want?"

"¡Da me un beso!" He pointed at his cheek, demanding a kiss, and she obeyed.

Tears blurred her vision. Why? She was going *with* her children, who were her life. Or were they? She was leaving a man she didn't love. Or did she? She was leaving a place that wasn't home. Or was it?

She soaked a bolillo in her coffee till it softened to the point of mush, handed it to Guy to suck on, and thought: *Mama,* that word, at least, would be the same in Chinese…except the accent would change to tones. She knew a few polite Chinese phrases: *Nei hou maa?* (How are you?), *Do ze* (Thank you), *Sik zo faan mei aa?* (Have you eaten?). But soon the only people she could have a real conversation with would be the ones in this kitchen.

Yankee had offered many times to teach her Chinese, but she never felt the need in El Paso, where most everyone spoke English, Spanish, or both. Maybe she should take him up on it. They still had a month before leaving. Then he would travel with them, which would give them another month. Plus the month he planned to help them settle in his hometown.

If only they could find a way to resume speaking to each other.

Maybe she should apologize. He was in the wrong, but what good did it do to insist on that? He'd never understand. Did the devil know he was bad? Probably not.

As if her thoughts called him, he flung open the front door, burst into the kitchen, and launched into rapid-fire Chinese. Mary followed but offered no translation and avoided everyone's eyes. Mary always opened the café; something must've happened. As Yankee's rant went on, Benny and Celia, the only two fluent in Chinese, jumped to their feet. Benny dropped his bolillo in his coffee with a splash.

Alarmed, she looked out the front door, which Mary had left wide open. The restaurant didn't appear to be on fire. She gave Guy a comforting bounce in her lap, but it was unnecessary. He chewed his coffee-soaked roll with lip-smacking pleasure, unaware the mood had changed.

Tommy and Vivi sat with rolls dangling above their mugs in suspense.

Rose and Julia, curious what the fuss was about, turned their backs on the frying pan till the butter started to burn. "Oh no-no-no!" Rose shrieked, uselessly flapping her arms till Julia rescued the spitting pan with a clatter.

Candelaria reached over to the stove and turned off the burner. "Enough! Someone tell me what's going on."

Benny swallowed. "Sam didn't show up this morning—at either restaurant."

Celia pulled out her father's chair at the other end of the table. He sank into it and stared at the lines on his palms.

"I don't understand," Candelaria said. "Is Sam sick?"

The ever-stoic Mary explained, "The safes are empty. There's no sign of a break-in. He took everything."

Her first hopeful thought spilled out before she could stop it, "So we won't go to China after all?" She covered her mouth.

Everyone turned to Yankee. Nobody breathed. He picked up the closest mug, gulped a mouthful of coffee, spit it back—he hated milk. Only then did he answer, "It's more important than ever that you go to China, all of you, because most of our money is gone. We can't afford for you to stay. As it is, I might have to sell one of the restaurants. Mamá, it's up to you to take the children to China without me."

This was more dire than she could've guessed. She often asked him, *Are you* sure *the money won't be safer in a bank?* Every time, he reminded her of what happened in '29 to all those "suckers" who trusted banks. He told her to leave money matters to him, so she did. No use crying over it now. All she said was, "You mean, you won't come and help us get settled? You'll send me alone? To a country where I've never been?"

"You won't be alone. Benny and Celia will be with you. They speak plenty of Chinese. Even Mary speaks a little. They took that one trip with me, remember? They'll be a big help until you get to Bok Nan, where my brother will take care of you till I can send money."

She was only thirty-six and he expected her to lean on her kids like an old lady? Benny and Celia stood tall and brave, but their eyes popped round and white, a startled cartoon cat and surprised cartoon mouse. They weren't ready to lead this family. She must rise to the occasion.

Yankee would easily recover without her. He was the unofficial mayor of El Paso's Chinatown, a man with connections. Meanwhile, free of his unpredictable demands, she would lead the children—into the unknown. Why not? She was a Rivera.

She lifted her chin. "I'm their mother. I don't go with *them*, they go with *me*. I'll hold this family together until you come for us."

She knew her words might give her children the impression she believed Yankee *would* come for them. She knew it might give Yankee the impression she would miss him. So be it. Sometimes family is a fiction, but that doesn't make it less true.

Benny and Celia walked to her end of the table, stood behind her chair facing Yankee, and each laid a hand on her shoulder.

Yankee rolled his neck like a prize fighter. "I made that fucker everything he is, and this is how he repays me?" His head jerked to a halt as if struck, and he doubled over laughing. "*I made him everything he is!*" he repeated as if it were a revelation. He looked her up and down, and smirked, "Now we'll see what I've made of you."

She smirked back. One thing she knew: whatever she became next, it would only be what she made of herself.

Candelaria loved the jingle bells above the door at the West Orient Grocery, the way they echoed the playfulness of the family who owned it. Raising four sons had pulled Marcela down from the sky and Estefan up from the earth, leaving the Wu family in a jolly place between. Despite the bells' inescapable good cheer, Estefan didn't look up and see her come in. He was too preoccupied with an anxious customer.

He was explaining to a wide-eyed young Mexican wife that soy sauce, rice wine, and sesame oil were key ingredients to transform Chinese dishes into domestic bliss. Now and then, Candelaria ran across other Mexican women married to Celestials, yet they were few and far between, so she considered introducing herself. Then she remembered she wasn't staying in El Paso long enough to make new friends. She doubted she'd meet any Mexicans at all where she was headed. But she was braver now than last time she moved far from home, and she dared hope she might make a new friend in China.

She drifted away from Estefan and his customer, down a narrow aisle, where she found distraction in a charming, blue-flowered tin of Oolong tea. She felt at home amid the shop's aromatic cloud of salty fish and sharp ginger. Life with Yankee made these smells as familiar as the cumin, chiles, and oregano of her mother's kitchen. But, to her, the shop smelled of Marcela. Unlike her, Marcela was *born* with a foot in two worlds and moved between them with more ease. She felt a forgotten yearning: her old wish to be more like her friend.

Marcela often visited China with her father and, with her eye for opportunity, she'd turned her travels into a business. That's what brought Candelaria here. Marcela continued to cultivate the trust of border patrol and customs agents, and those efforts helped her provide specialized travel services. The lion's share of her business consisted of booking passage for Chinese men, who lived in Mexico but sought to sail home via the convenient port of San Francisco. U.S. Customs required them to be bonded and escorted, to ensure they didn't disappear into America. Marcela provided those services too, often escorting them personally.

Candelaria hoped her friend's unique skills as a travel agent would come in handy for a Mexican woman trying to get to China with her half-Chinese children. Yet her guts twisted in knots as she prowled the aisles, anxious she might be asking too big a favor, that time had unraveled the invisible ties that once wove them together.

The West Orient Grocery wasn't far from the International Café, and the Wongs and Wus still saw each other often. As Candelaria had foreseen, she and Marcela easily forgave each other eight years ago— within days of their misunderstanding in the courtyard.

Marcela had apologized in her usual flowery language, the result of her continued love for books: "I was cruel to insist you see light in the darkness when what you needed was for me to sit with you in the dark. You needed a friend to hold your hand while you mourned your baby. Sometimes I'm a coward, as frightened of death as anyone. Please forgive me."

She'd apologized for her own failing as well. "I know you meant to comfort me. I got angrier than you deserved because I felt guilty for choosing my sister over my baby."

"You made the only choice: you did what you had to do. You're a good mother and a good sister. We're women, not saints."

Nonetheless, their old spontaneous intimacy didn't return. They no longer stole moments to walk together, sit together, or nap together, arm-in-arm as they once did—with or without coffee or tea, conversation or excuse, breathing each other's thoughts. This wasn't Marcela's fault, or hers. When the sky tears in two, it's hard to put it back together.

The Mexican customer scurried out of the shop, and Estefan wandered down the aisle. "Miss, can I help y—Candelaria! Why didn't you say hello?"

"Hello! Nei ho maa?"

"Hou hou!" He took her hands in his. "¿Cómo estás, mi amiga?"

"Bien, gracias," she lied because, in her experience, when a man asked how you were, he didn't really want to know. "I believe Marcela is expecting me?"

His sympathetic nod told her he knew how things really were with her. "Go ahead. She'll be happy to see you." He waved her into the back office just as the shop door jangled again, calling him down the aisle to greet his next customer, "Come-come-come!"

"Come-come-come!" Marcela echoed her husband, waving her into the office. Marcela rolled her chair back from a desk piled with papers and rose to enfold Candelaria in her arms.

She let her friend soothe her in a way she hadn't invited in years. Sorrow fell from her like a heavy stone she didn't know she'd been carrying.

Many heartbeats passed before Marcela stepped back to look at her. "I've missed you."

It was only a few days since they'd last seen each other, but she felt it too, the sense of something long-lost returning. "I'm sorry. I didn't know how to be myself with you."

"It's hard to be yourself with anyone when you live with someone who discourages it."

"If you say so, oh wise one." Their laughter flowed into her like a river in a desert.

"Now you'll go someplace new and discover who you can become."

"I don't know about that. I only know my children are leaving, and so am I. But it sounds like you already knew that?" She cocked an eyebrow.

"Nothing so surprising in that. Your husband told my husband he's sending his children to China for a 'proper education.' I know you well enough to know that where they go, you go."

She sagged with relief at not having to explain.

Marcela led her by the elbow to the wood chair facing the desk, wheeled her own squealing chair across from it until they sat knee-to-knee, and cupped Candelaria's face between her soft palms. She closed her eyes to savor the feeling. Her own hands had grown rough from the constant handling of children and their needs.

Marcela sat back and clapped once. "So, you want me to book your passage."

"They say you're the best, though I know family travel isn't your specialty."

"*Trust* is my specialty, and there's no greater trust than that between friends. If you need to go to China, I'll handle everything. Don't give it a—"

"—I expect to pay of course. I won't take advantage of our friendship."

"You'll take a friendship discount, because what good is a friend if you can't take a little advantage?" Marcela held up a finger to forestall protest. "I made up my mind before you came."

She leaned forward. "I have a confession."

Marcela leaned in too. "I'm no priest, but you can tell me anything."

Their eyes locked. "I'm terrified."

Marcela winked. "That's why I'm going with you."

She gripped her chair, so overwhelmed she felt lightheaded. "It's too much to ask."

"Don't be silly. I'm chaperoning two clients to Hong Kong anyway. We'll plan your trip at the same time. I've got to come home sometime, but I'll stay with you as long as you need."

They pressed their foreheads together, too fast, so that their skulls hit with a *clunk*. But it wasn't awkward, even when Marcela rubbed her forehead and said, "First, I'll get the aspirin."

She wondered if she and Juliana would ever have had a falling out if she'd spent her whole life in Mata Flores. Probably. To go through a lifelong friendship without learning a single ugly thing about your friend, or yourself? Unlikely. She felt grateful for the memory of that unscarred friendship, but even more grateful for the survival of the one with the scars.

45. The Peaceful Ocean
1934 – San Francisco, California

The day before they boarded the train in El Paso, Candelaria made a rare visit to the beauty parlor and left half her long dark hair on the floor. Her new bob barely brushed her shoulders, curled and flipped "like Dolores del Rio, the Mexican movie star," just like she told the hairdresser. She walked out with head high, hair swaying free, grinning to herself even as she ignored the stares of her male neighbors all the way home. Feeling bold, she went straight through the front door of the International Café.

The restaurant was empty until Yankee's head popped up behind the kitchen pass-through. No doubt he'd been searching the hidey hole in the wall behind the grinning Kitchen God's altar, thick with candle wax, in hopes of finding any money Sam might've missed. Thank God he never found the $500 she'd hidden under the floor in the girls' room, now sewn into the lining of three of her travel outfits.

He took one look at her half-naked head, and declared, "Oh, no-no-no! No wife of mine will go to China looking like a tramp, especially without her husband."

She refused to let this crush her. "What do you want? I can't grow it back overnight."

He convinced her to at least tame it behind her ears with a ribbon. She swept into the house and turned her scrap box upside down till she found a red one. Let him try to stop her.

She was trying it on in front of the bedroom vanity when he walked in. They exchanged wary looks in the mirror.

He nodded. "You look pretty in red." Then he walked out of the house, leaving her speechless.

It turned out that, after he left, he took the trolley downtown and bought her a fitted red hat. She had to admit it flattered her face. But why had he bought her more red? Then she remembered: to the Chinese, red wasn't a color of rebellion but of their most valued achievements: happiness, health, luck, good fortune. He was outfitting her as standard bearer for their family's worth.

Also: fire and beauty.

All right, then. Let red be the color of her new life.

The next day was a blur of nausea, thanks to the train's rocking. It was a rough day for Guy too. She rested her cheek atop his head where it lolled against her breast, but the Firecracker wanted none of that. He hollered himself into a frenzy, his endless "Noooooo!" as sorrowful as the train's whistle. His was the true voice of Candelaria's goodbye, a grief she dared not express—Yankee might use it as an excuse to make her stay.

Once Guy quieted, she looked over his head, past Julia's, past Yankee's, for a stolen peek out the window. She knew why her husband took the window seat, wedging their two youngest between them: he still wanted to spite her for calling his bluff and taking him up on the offer to leave him. She didn't complain. Going to China was a small price to pay for freedom. She remained on the aisle as he suggested,

"In case you need to attend to the kids." Surveying all eight of them spread across three rows, she thought: that's a lot of attending.

For now, she only attended to the window, fixated on Mexico and America, or rather, the hidden seam where the Río Grande separated El Paso from Juárez. Twenty-three years she'd lived on la frontera, and still couldn't tell where one country stopped and the other began. In a moment, both would become nothing but a memory. She didn't blink. The train picked up speed, downtown shrank, houses scattered, pecan groves spread pale green leaves, until it all gave way to desert, hills, and dashes of adobe blended with earth.

With that, her old life was gone.

Yet, in the molten gold of afternoon, as they passed through New Mexico and the swaying train lulled the rest of her family to sleep, she did see a wonder: broad, black, and still, in a patch of grass at the edge of a mesa: a bison. Its humped back rose like a traveler's pack, and its wooly head hung low like someone determined to get where they were going. Alone, with neither companions nor shelter, the beast must be vulnerable to predators. How had it ended up so far off course, well south of the Great Plains? Maybe it was a hallucination brought on by exhaustion. She squeezed her eyes shut, opened them again. The buffalo was still there. Far from home or herd, the last of her tribe perhaps, but real and stoic and still standing.

She reached across Julia to shake Yankee awake, then thought better of it and let her hand fall away without touching him. This piece of America she would keep for herself.

A week later, Candelaria stared up at the SS *Lincoln* and pitched backward, stunned by its immensity. She flailed for balance, and Yankee caught her. She wondered if it was a mistake to leave this man, always so strong. Then a breeze wrapped round her like a lover and freed some of her hair from its pert little red hat, forcing Yankee to let her go and spit out a mouthful of curls. They both laughed. A distant trolley bell rang.

She craned her neck and again tried to take in the steamship. At 14,000 tons, the Dollar Line passenger vessel dwarfed the surrounding boats in the Port of San Francisco—a far cry from the wagon she rode across the desert to America. At least a dozen of Benito's old wagons could fit on the top deck alone, with room to spare. The ship was navy blue, white, and red, like an American flag. The nostalgia those colors evoked surprised her. Why? For a country where she always felt like an outsider, clinging to its hem, hoping not to be kicked loose.

The bright, chilly spring day turned dark and warm, as a pair of familiar hands covered her eyes. She grinned and reached up to pat the slender fingers but didn't turn, reluctant to break the connection. The prankster smelled of sesame and tea, bubble bath and lavender. Marcela. She wheeled around to hug her so tightly anyone else would've complained. She stepped back, but their arms remained twined like vines that have grown together. They said nothing, for this friendship required no words to sustain it, neither sunlight nor rain. It grew of its own accord.

"What a surprise to see you." Yankee's tone remained flat, lips a straight line.

Marcela gave him a playful hug, laughing and shaking him, insisting he join their camaraderie.

He usually hated public affection, but Candelaria could tell by the way he straightened his bowtie that he only pretended annoyance and felt secretly pleased at the attention.

"One of my passengers *will* surprise you." Marcela tossed her a conspiratorial grin, leaving her as baffled as Yankee. "You didn't think I'd take my friend to China without a proper man for protection?" She turned to the quay's jostling crowd and beckoned someone. Candelaria couldn't see who. Marcela was supposed to escort two Chinese men. Did Yankee know them?

She spotted a familiar cowboy swagger busting a wide path through the international crowd. Joy stretched forgotten muscles in her face. "Benito!"

"If it isn't our Little Candle!" Benito Chung bellowed, his voice louder than Yankee's ever was but without the bullying tone. "Candelita, you light up this whole dock."

She threw herself at him in a way that suggested she'd let him carry her on his shoulders if only she were smaller. She looked around for her kids, eager to share this moment, to see Benito give Guy the piggyback ride she was too big to take. But his namesake, Benny, had taken them all for ice cream, despite Yankee's warning they'd throw it all up from seasickness.

She sighed, "Ohhh, I wanted you to meet my youngest… But wait… what…why…?"

"Didn't I tell you?" Marcela said. "My baba is one of the clients I'm taking to China."

"I'd like to see my homeland once more before I die," Benito laughed.

Candelaria punched his arm. "You'll never die."

"If you insist." He bowed.

Yes, red was her color now as emotion burned through her like fire. Her heart fluttered, threatening to run away from her. She pressed a hand to her chest. Was this happiness or a heart attack? Whatever it was, she was boarding that ship. She'd come too far to stop now.

Marcela prodded Yankee. "How do you like the elder I've chosen to escort your wife?"

Please, God, she thought, don't let him change his mind.

But he gave his magnanimous boss-man grin and pumped Benito's hand. "I've heard so much about you. Thank you for taking care of my girl." He snuck a trembling arm round her waist. Was he jealous, chilled, or something else? "And my darling brats too of course."

"They're in good hands." Benito nodded at his daughter, indicating she was in charge.

"I don't doubt it," Yankee said.

Candelaria exhaled relief. Then she looked around. "Is Isabel coming?"

A dark look crossed Benito's face. "She's sailing from Acapulco instead, with a couple of friends. They'll meet us in Hong Kong. She was scared to cross the border, what with the gringos kicking out so many Mexicans."

Mexico had in turn expelled many Chinese. Maybe he wasn't traveling, but fleeing. She didn't ask, reluctant to pry. A painful silence overcame the group till Marcela's other client joined them.

A studious-looking man in his thirties, he bowed to each of them, losing his fedora every time. Yankee kept catching it and handing it back, then pumped the man's hand with delight upon hearing his family name was Wong. Candelaria never understood why this excited him so; thousands of Wongs came from Toisan. *This* Mr. Wong lived in Chihuahua but was traveling home to his grass widow. He'd grown up in a village near Yankee's, and the two fluttered their hands like old gossips while jabbering in Toisanese. Except the words for *Chinese chess, lucky money,* and *pretty cousin,* she understood none of it.

When the children returned, they boarded. Yankee went along to see their cabins.

"Sorry it's so crowded," Marcela said when they reached the rooms.

But Candelaria gaped at the two luxurious staterooms she would share with the kids. Granted, they'd have to sleep two or three to a bed, yet it was more than she'd dared imagine—with an ocean view! Yankee often told stories of how he'd first sailed to America in steerage. He'd had better lodgings since, but his face told her the silk art-deco chairs and quilted bedspreads outdid *his* expectations as well.

She tugged his sleeve to whisper in his ear, "I had no idea second class was like this."

"It's not," he whispered back. "Marcela must've paid extra for first."

They both insisted she'd done too much, though Marcela maintained she had many contacts and often "pulled strings" without spending a dime. The room she and her father would share down the hall was equally splendid. (Mr. Wong would ride below, but in second class, not steerage.) She waved off their thanks and left them to their goodbyes.

Yankee clapped. "Okay, okay, okay. Everyone line up!"

The children obeyed, tallest to smallest, a line that spilled out of the room into the hall. One by one, he kissed the top of each head and handed them each a *lai si*: a small red envelope decorated with swans and flowers, with Chinese lucky money tucked inside. One by one, they said, "Thank you, Baba," then bowed and ran off in different directions.

The youngest children jumped on the beds like trampolines, the middle children turned the bathroom faucets on and off or chased each other up and down the halls, while Celia and Mary ran to the top deck to catch the view. Benny grabbed his camera, ready to do the same.

Yankee stopped him, "Wait, son, let us walk with you. Before we say goodbye, I'd like you to take a photo of me with my beautiful wife." He held out his arm to Candelaria.

She took it. She never could resist his little acts of chivalry.

On deck, he made quite a production of posing: hand on the railing, standing tall, one possessive arm heavy around her shoulder, face filled with the solemnity of farewell.

She would have many occasions to study that photo in time to come. Sometimes when she looked at it, Benny would peer over her shoulder and joke that his father was quite the actor, looking so grave when in real life he smiled often and laughed loudly, charming everyone he met. But Yankee's expression struck her as more than grave. He looked bereft.

She would spend more time studying her own image. She wore a stylish pleated skirt that showed off still-slender ankles, suede heels with smart buttons marching up the front, her coat's jaunty lapel open to the ocean breeze. She had put away her new red hat, worried it would blow away, and reverted to the red ribbon, which Yankee preferred anyway. He said it made her look young. Later, she'd gaze at the photo, search her eyes, and feel her heart pick up pace as it did that day, an urgent little beat that refused to tell her how she felt: scared of the journey ahead, or eager? Relieved to be free of the man next to her, or lonely?

The woman in the photo looked neither happy nor grave, only expectant. The fact that she carried her ninth child might have something to do with that. No, her tenth—she would never forget her unnamed son, sustaining the gardenias she left behind. This pregnancy was another secret she kept from Yankee for fear he'd stop her from leaving.

Yankee shook Benny's hand in both of his. "Take care of your mother."

"As if she needs it." Benny winked at her, then walked away.

Yankee cleared his throat. "I got you a surprise."

She cast a curious glance at his pockets.

"No, not lucky money," he chuckled. "I had your gift delivered to the boys' room." Without warning, her block-headed, middle-aged Chinese husband took her in his arms and kissed her like some swashbuckling Douglas Fairbanks, ignoring the snickers of nearby passengers. Then he was gone, though the dry, dusty taste of El Paso lingered on her tongue.

All she could think was: what sort of gift? She hurried to the boys' cabin for the answer.

Candelaria arrived at the boys' stateroom to find the gift sitting on the bed nearest the door, in a leather case curved like a woman. She opened the case with a soft smile, ran her fingers over the amber wood of the guitar within, and plucked a single string. Low E. It vibrated with an off-key hum. She took the guitar in her arms like a new lover, younger than her—who dared think such things?

She tuned it the way Papá had taught her, twisting the pegs and thumbing the strings till each one held a tune all its own. He'd shown her how to press her fingers on the frets with a relaxed arch, to pluck notes crisp and clear, never muddy. Would she ever see him again?

She began to play, then to sing. One by one, her children followed the sound of her voice into the cabin. They jostled, poked, and pinched each other as always, but in silence for once, as she poured her melody over them like a benediction.

El corazón está hecho de risa. Así es como aumenta.
El agua está hecha de deseo. Se queda en casa mientras se va.

The heart is made of laughter. This is the way it grows.
The water is made of longing. It stays home even as it goes.

"All ashore that's going ashore!" A voice boomed over hers like a command from God.

"The boat's leaving!" Vivi shouted.

"It's not a boat, it's a ship, tonta!" Tommy said.

"Don't call her a tonta! Call her a so zyu." Celia laughed. "We're going to China now."

"I'm scared," Rose said.

"You're always scared," Mary said.

"Let's go look," Julia said.

Guy darted out the door, and the rest of the kids tumbled after him.

Marcela squeezed against the flow of children to enter the room, belatedly applauding Candelaria's song. "You brought your guitar!"

"I didn't. After Grace died I, I took it to the river and…" She stopped, eyes brimming. "I haven't played since." She caressed the instrument's voluptuous dark curve. "It's a gift from Yankee."

Marcela sat beside her and touched the instrument. "May I?"

Candelaria slid the guitar to her, and they both heard it: something sliding inside. Marcela tipped it the other way. There it was again, a soft skitter. Marcela looked mystified as she turned it over and shook it, sound-hole down. A folded slip of paper slid out and got caught in the strings. Candelaria plucked it free and unfolded it, pausing to register surprise when Marcela strummed the guitar and unerringly discovered all its most discordant notes. Was her friend tone deaf?

She turned her attention to the paper's handwritten note:

I'm sorry, my one and only wife. I wish you were staying with me to build our life again. Come home soon. I love you, Yankee

She made a strangled noise and reached for her throat. Marcela stopped playing—one small thing to be grateful for—and waited. Candelaria didn't explain. She had to think, fast.

She wasn't leaving alone. She was going with Marcela, who knew her better than Yankee did, yet who could never enter her as he did, never feel the physical depths of her, never map the compass points of her flesh. And Marcela couldn't stay in China forever.

If Candelaria wanted, she could leave this ship right now. She'd married a devil, yes, but the devil loved her, a possibility she hadn't considered. In a house no longer crowded, they could start over. He'd said she and Guy should stay. It was up to her.

"I need air." She rushed out.

Marcela followed but held her peace. For both those things, Candelaria was grateful.

The gangway was still in place when she reached the deck. The bottleneck of disembarking visitors was shrinking but unrushed. She had time. She looked down at the dock, searched the crowd. Around her, hundreds of passengers waved. Streamers flew across her vision. Then she spotted him below, waving up at her, arms crisscrossing over his head. His face betrayed an emotion she didn't recognize. Hope? Grief? Both? Maybe those were her feelings, not his.

She turned to her friend. "I don't know what to do."

"Yes you do. It's all right to let go of the past. It's all right to embrace the future."

"Where's my future?"

"Wherever you want to go."

She pushed her mouth to one side—the way Tommy did when he struggled with homework. She sighed, not with resignation but recognition. "I want to go with my family."

She looked at Yankee. They had made a family, and what they'd created she must protect. Her children were leaving, so she must go. In China, her eldest son might be head of the family, but she was the mother, and she would lead them. More importantly, she'd lead herself. Without Yankee, she could do as she wished. What did she wish? This was her chance to find out.

She raised her arms overhead and waved wildly at her husband till she tired. His face looked small, featureless as a faded photograph, already far away. The gangway rose, the ship's horn blasted like a melancholy beast, and the vessel nudged free of the pier. She clutched the rail and watched Yankee shrink into a dot of confetti amid the teeming crowd. San Francisco's towers turned into a squiggly line like the long slanting signature on her passport. Soon most of the passengers dispersed till all she saw was ocean, an infinity of water daunting as a desert.

A hand rested on her shoulder. She looked up to see Marcela's father, Benito.

"At least there are no dust storms out here," he said.

They both collapsed into helpless giggles, like children.

Marcela shook her head at them as if they were crazy.

"Did I ever tell you the story of the sandstorm?" Benito asked Marcela.

"You both have, many times." She scrunched her face. "But maybe Candelaria's children would like to hear it…again. Let's go find them."

Candelaria let go of the rail, swaying with the subtle rise and fall of the waves below, arms out for balance. Marcela cupped her elbow to steady her, but she eased herself free. "I've got it." She smiled. "But it's good to know you're here, just in case."

Candelaria squinted over her shoulder, past the stern, where morning sun seared the ocean blinding white. Then she turned toward the blue of open sky and followed her friends to the bow. It struck her as odd that the ship must head west to reach the Far East. But it also made sense. If she kept going far enough, sooner or later she was bound to find her way home.

ACKNOWLEDGMENTS

It's tradition at our house that my husband's most peaceful moments of solitude end with me popping up in front of him, gripping my laptop, asking, "Can I share this with you?" So, my first thanks go to Dale Jolley, my most loving defense against me writing anything less than my most authentic story. Dale, thank you for your unwavering support on this crazy ride.

So many people who contributed to the creation of this novel have passed away that it would be too sad to note who among the following are still with us and who aren't. They all live in these pages. *Candlelight Bridge* wouldn't exist without Caroline Lee, the paternal grandma I called Mom, who throughout our time together on earth shared many personal and family stories that inspired this novel. Thank you, Mom, for sharing your "secrets," for believing in me, and for encouraging me to sit on your lap and read to you—how I loved that.

Thanks to Gerald Lee, my Grampa, who bought me my first books in droves, encouraged my every creative impulse, and never doubted my early years of babbling to myself were proof I had some weird gift worth sharing. Thank you, Grampa, for talking to me about my family history even when you didn't get why your thoughts meant so much to me, and for your lifelong support.

Thanks to my father, David Lopez-Lee, who offered personal insights into our family story and cultural insights into the experience of being a mixed-race Mexican American. Thanks, Dad, for always showing your pride in me, which is only matched by my pride in you.

Thanks to my sister, Miraya Lopez-Lee, who rounded out my mental picture of our grandma so I could better imagine her stories, and who is a devoted cheerleader for my work. Miraya, thank you for your endless capacity to listen to my endless words.

Thanks to Uncle Roy Mar for generously sharing memories of his beloved Mexican mother and of his life in El Paso and Hong Kong. Thanks to his loving wife, my Aunt Mona Mar, for supporting our visits and offering her own insights.

Thanks to Manuela "Meni" Mar, for sharing her fond long-ago memories of El Paso.

Many thanks to Leila Mar, who shared her home, her stories, and her delicious *mole*.

Thank you to my Aunt Virginia "Lon" Wilhelm, whose loving recordings of Spanish and Chinese songs for her children and grandchildren offered a window into the multicultural milieu of her mixed Mexican-and-Chinese heritage.

Thank you to Ma Man Wai, my distant cousin who taught me so much about what life was like long ago in Toisan, China, particularly life in his village, which is the same village where my ancestors were born. Thanks to his granddaughter, Ma Gam Fung, who translated his words with kindness and humor. Thanks to his entire family, who showed me such warm hospitality, I truly felt at home. Thank you, Ma cousins, for the honor of including me in Ma Man Wai's ninety-ninth and hundredth birthday celebrations.

Thanks to Ed and Martha Samario for your insights into the Mexican American lifestyles, customs, and traditions of El Paso and La Frontera, and for guiding me through my travels there. A special thank you to Ed for sharing your own colorful family history.

I'm overwhelmed by the kindness of those Mexican friends who served as my guides during my research throughout El Paso, Juárez, and the state of Chihuahua, Mexico. Out of respect for their privacy, I'm not naming them, only thanking them for opening their homes to me, helping me safely navigate La Frontera during a volatile time, and offering vital cultural feedback on *Candlelight Bridge.*

Thanks to Anna Fahy, one of the few historians who specializes in the small but significant historical role of the Chinese and Chinese Mexican cultural communities of El Paso. Thanks to El Paso historian David Dorado Romo, author of *Ringside Seat to a Revolution*, who specializes in the culture, history, and ephemera of El Paso and Juárez, especially the role of those border cities in the Mexican Revolution. He also helped me illuminate the role of El Paso's Segundo Barrio as an important corridor of Frontera culture.

Thanks to all those El Pasoans with Mexican and/or Chinese roots who shared their memories and their insights into the history, leaders, and cultures of the border. Special thanks to David Wellington Chew, former Chief Justice of the Texas Eighth Court of Appeals, for sharing his local knowlege, and to Carmen Stearns for sharing her family stories and giving me a walking tour through the El Paso of her youth.

Thanks to Ben and Susan Wong, who told me about the days of their youth in Toisan and their early married life in El Paso. They painted a vivid picture of Toisanese culture and strengthened my sense of how much more prevalent the Chinese once were in El Paso.

Thanks always to my dear friend and fellow author, Candace Kearns Read, whose gentle-but-tough counsel never fails. Candace, thank you for holding a lantern to my work and for your unwavering belief in me throughout my many years writing this book.

My profound gratitude to Luis Alberto Urrea, the mentor whose commitment to writing beautiful stories that make a difference inspires me every day. Thank you, Luis, for your wisdom and advice that guided me across the finish line.

A million thanks to Rebecca Berg for sharing with me the first tools that gave me hope I could write a novel, William Haywood Henderson for teaching me how to write this one, and Andre Dubus III for teaching me how to rewrite it.

Many thanks to Erika Krouse and Doug Kurtz for helping me understand structure and process. Thanks always to my trusted readers and advisors, Kimberly Drake Rebchook and Mark Graham. Thanks to author Seth Brady Tucker and filmmaker Alexandre O. Philippe for opening my eyes to the endless possibilities of what a story can be.

Thanks to Lisa Brackmann and Jennifer Silva Redmond, who knew exactly the editing notes I needed to transform my final manuscript in ways I didn't know were possible.

Thank you, Lighthouse Writers Workshop, the phenomenal writing community that lifted me up with immeasurable support and guidance. A special thanks to Michael Henry and Andrea Dupree for creating Lighthouse, a unique treasure in the writing world.

Thanks to my beloved Sunday writing group, for your patient listening and wise feedback. Special thanks to Alex Stein for his unflagging support and for helping me take the final steps of this project.

Thanks to the translators and language instructors who deepened my appreciation of the special bond a teacher-student relationship can offer. Special thanks to Fiona Zhu, for her Cantonese and Mandarin translations and cultural advice, and to Winnie Tse and Jingjing Li for their tutoring in Cantonese language and culture. Special thanks to my longtime Spanish instructor, Guillermo Salazar, who never gave up on me despite my painful grammar, and my more recent Spanish tutor, Ivonne Benitez, for believing in my quest to reclaim the language of my beloved grandma.

Thanks to all who helped me with a mountain of geographic and historical research, including: Casey Dexter-Lee, interpreter for California's Angel Island State Park, who educated me about the immigration hurdles Overseas Chinese faced upon arriving in San Francisco long ago; the El Paso County Historical Society; Former Superintendent of the Chamizal National Memorial, Fernando Gustavo (Gus) Sanchez Jr. and his rangers; and Prince McKenzie, Director of the Railroad and Transportation Museum of El Paso.

Many thanks to Colin Graham for having my back during book production, and to Carlos Fidel Espinoza for putting so much heart and soul into designing this book's beautiful cover.

One person I can never thank enough is my editor, Edward Vidaurre, for believing in *Candlelight Bridge*. Thank you, Edward, for the warm welcome into the *FlowerSong* community, and for your valiant commitment to the voices of marginalized people.

To all those who've ever taken an interest in talking about, listening to, or reading the pages of *Candlelight Bridge*: thank you for your faith in this story. I hope it gives you something in return.